"Where's Elminster gotten t—ah, there!"

Belkram looked up to the balcony where the Old Mage was unconcernedly puffing on his pipe. Elminster waved lazily.

The Harper shouted in horror. Behind Elminster, a bone-white face had appeared, a gleam in its dark eye sockets and a widening grin stretching its ghastly jaw. Long, skeletal arms reached for the Old Mage, and there was nothing—utterly nothing—that anyone could do.

Sharantyr threw back her head in despair, and screamed. "Mystra, aid us all!"

FANTASY ADVENTURE

Shadows of Doom

Book One

The Shadow of the Avatar Trilogy

Ed Greenwood

To Cathy, for Sharantyr's spirit.

To Paula, for Storm's gentleness.

Most of all, to Jenny, for Jhessail's love
and for always being there.

Vincit qui se vincit

SHADOWS OF DOOM

First Printing: March 1995
Printed in the United States of America.
Library of Congress Catalog Card Number: 94-61684

9 8 7 6 5 4 3 2 1

ISBN: 0-7869-0300-7

TSR, Inc.
201 Sheridan Springs Rd.
Lake Geneva, WI 53147
U.S.A.

TSR Ltd.
120 Church End, Cherry Hinton
Cambridge CB1 3LB
United Kingdom

It is the doom of men that they never know quite enough wisdom until it is too late.

Elminster of Shadowdale

Hearken now to a tale of the Realms, ye jaded lords, ladies, and gentles. Oh, it is a grand tale, to be sure. It has murder, and magic, and lovemaking—and, as usual, you'll misunderstand every word of it.

Be not angry, mind; the fault's not with you, or me. Life's like that, you see.

Lhaeo Rhindaun, Scribe to Elminster

***There is a slim, dark and dusty tome few have
ever read. . . .***

It lies hidden beneath a rune-graven flagstone under
the circular table in the innermost chamber of Candle-
keep. This tome is called The Book of Mysteries, and it
sets forth all that the writer—whose name, of course, has
been forgotten—knew of the nature and powers of Mystra,
the goddess of magic.

Chief among the book's secrets of Realmslore is the
matter of Mystra's essence or vitality. As mistress of
magic, her power is far greater than that of the other gods
of Toril. Yet, to mortals at least, it seems not so. Therein
lies the secret.

Throughout history, as long as there have been gods,
and people of Toril to worship them, the essential power of
Mystra has been held not only by the goddess herself, but
by a self-willed, loyal demigod—Azuth, who was the
greatest archmage of his day—and a handful of mortals.

These mortals cannot wield what they hold of Mystra's
power, but they can withhold it, even from the goddess
herself. This self-will, and the mortals' often widespread
travels, keep Mystra from ruling all of Realmspace and
prevent any other being from doing so through her.
Should Mystra ask to use the power that they hold, each
of the mortals can willingly let it pass into her, but they
cannot be coerced into doing so. At the moment when one
of these mortals dies, the power that he or she holds
passes into the greater essence of life in Toril, returning to
Mystra slowly but usable by none except her.

Down the ages, many beings have shared this mystery.
For their own protection, they have not heralded the

power they hold, yet it leaves its mark upon them. They cannot be located or affected by magic that spies upon the mind or tames the will. If not slain, they live many hundreds of years, resisting disease, poison, and the ravages of time. Their eyes tend toward blue, and their hair to silver. They attain something of the grace, wildness, and humor of Mystra herself. And, being mortal, they suffer far more—and learn more wisdom in the wielding of magic—than even Mystra herself. Some, tired or sick of their burden of power, have willingly sought death. Others find death unlooked for, at the end of a searching spell or a flashing blade.

One who always carries the burden of the mystery is the Magister, the mortal (and oft-changing) representative of Mystra, who holds that title by might-of-Art. Others who hold Mystra's power tend to be powerful archmages.

Elminster, the Old Mage of Shadowdale, is one who bears Mystra's burden. Two others are Khelben "Blackstaff" Arunsun, Lord Mage of Waterdeep, and Laeral, his consort and fellow archmage. Laeral's sisters also hold some of Mystra's power. One sister is the Witch-Queen of Aglarond, called the Simbul. Another sister is Alustriel, High Lady of Silverymoon.

Of the other sisters, one is a mystery little spoken of. Another, Syluné of Shadowdale, held Mystra's power but perished in dragonfire, breaking her staff to destroy her bane and protect the dale. The last two sisters still hold their shares of Mystra's power. They are the bard and Harper Storm Silverhand of Shadowdale, and Dove of the Knights of Myth Drannor.

A handful of people, plus one demigod, hold something of Mystra's power. The goddess herself holds as much power as all of their combined burden, or so is the usual ordering of things.

What, then, befalls when Mystra falls?

* * * * *

It was the eve of the Time of Troubles. Magic had not yet gone wild across the Realms. The gods had not yet been cast down in the Fall. The chaos of spilled blood, lawless strife, monsters unleashed, and avatars roaming Faerûn was yet to come.

Unbeknownst to mortals, the gods had been summoned together. Among them was Mystra, grown proud and willful over the passing aeons. With the others, she was about to be stripped of godhood.

Unlike most of the gods, however, Mystra's pride was born of wisdom, of being part of many bindings and most releases of power in Faerûn, down thousands upon thousands of years. In the beginning, Ao the Overgod arranged the division of Mystra's power so that she could not easily be overthrown or used as an almighty weapon against the other gods—and so she could never rule over all and would not be tempted to try.

The secret of her power gave Mystra an idea. She made certain preparations involving a pendant, and began to keep an eye on magelings and apprentice wizards of little power, looking always for one who would be right. Perhaps she knew she was choosing her successor.

Perhaps she hoped only to gain an advantage over other gods in the Realms. It is doubtful that even the Lady of Magic could have foreseen clearly enough, or acted swiftly enough, to shape the pendant and choose the youngling Midnight as its recipient in the very short time between Ao's denunciation of the gods and the Fall.

Mystra could not have acted as she did purely to cheat the Overgod. Those sages who have spoken with Divine Lord Azuth (who was present at the Fall) agree that such behavior is unlikely in the extreme. Some—Elminster among them—believe that Ao, the Unseen One, laid these plans in Mystra's mind, because the power of the goddess of magic had to survive the Time of Troubles to preserve the very fabric of magic-cloaked Toril.

It is certain that, in the few mortal breaths between the doom that Ao laid upon the gods and the Fall, Mystra acted on earlier preparations. She had no time to reach Midnight or the pendant but was already—as always—linked with those mortals who bore the burden of her power. She had only seconds to act.

To shift enough extra power to Faerûn in order to do what must be done later was no easy thing. A single mortal must hold much of Mystra's power, for she had no time to feed power into more than one. (If done too fast, it would surely destroy the recipient on the spot.) A lone mortal must carry the greater share of the god's divine energy without being destroyed or driven wild, until Mystra could reclaim her power.

It was the fate, or luck, of some mortal to do this—involuntarily and without any preparation. As luck or fate had it, this was the occasion of Elminster's Doom.

The Overgod spoke. Mystra acted. The Fall came upon all the gods, and a certain doom upon Elminster. Our tale begins then, before mortals know of the Fall, in a place unshaken by the great storms that swept much of the Realms during that time. Elminster and Midnight have not yet met in the Stonelands, and the world has not yet been changed forever.

As the Overgod Ao is reputed to have said, "Forever seems a shorter and shorter time, these days." Before the Change that everyone alive in Faerûn at the time remembers, when new stars appeared in the sky and new gods and goddesses rose up while others fell, a profound change came upon the fleeting forever of one man.

One man a little (he will not say how little) over a thousand years old.

This is the tale of Elminster's Doom—and of the heroes it created.

1
Mist, Stars, and Mages On Their Knees

Elminster was reading yet another book when it all began.

It was the day of Aumry's Feast, when the folk of Shadowdale gathered to toast their lord in the name of a much-beloved predecessor. In his leaning stone tower, well away from all the festivities, the Old Mage sat in the creaking chair by the hearth, his long pipe alight, sighing and muttering his way through a thoroughly hopeless grimoire of some long-ago necromancer of lost Netheril.

The writer had been a perfect crazed-wits, Elminster decided early on, and paranoid to boot. What little magic the Netherese mage had set down was twisted by the periodic ravings of a tenuous sanity and by the suspicion-driven cloaking of facts in a torturous maze of codes, obtuse jargon, deliberate misinformation, and mystical gibberish. The obvious intent was to conceal magical truths from unauthorized readers—all relatively sane wizards, for instance.

"A good one?" His scribe, Lhaeo, was rising from the hearth-cauldron with a long ladle in his hand and an amused look on his face. He'd seen Elminster's disgusted looks a time or two before.

"About five good breaths of blaze, on a hot fire," Elminster replied, hefting the old tome in his hands and looking meaningfully down at the flames under the cauldron. He glanced at the book again and shook his head.

"Sixty pages," he said with a sigh, "and only three real spells so far, one of them hopelessly skeltered at that. Yet he may have hidden a gem or two *somewhere* in all this nonsense. As ye know, I live in eternal hope."

Elminster snorted, rolled his eyes comically at Lhaeo, and turned another page. His pipe also snorted, puffing out a little burst of sparks.

Lhaeo chuckled and turned back to the herbs on his cutting board. Elminster watched him with a fond smile. When Lhaeo wasn't cooking, cleaning, or actually acting as a scribe, he was gathering herbs, gardening, gathering or shopping for food, or talking about recipes and culinary lore with every caravan cook who passed through the dale.

Elminster sometimes wondered why his scribe wasn't as wide as old Luth's fabled bull. If Lhaeo wasn't eating, he was cooking (and tasting). If he wasn't cooking, he was thinking about food, and if he wasn't doing any of those things, he was asleep and dreaming about food. Or so it usually seemed.

As the old illusionists' saying has it, however, seemings and truth are often as far apart as one's mind can put them. As smoothly as any warrior, Lhaeo suddenly spun back to face his master. He'd heard a sudden, queer sobbing noise—a sound he'd never heard Elminster make before.

And then the illusionist stood quite still, precious herbs dropping forgotten from his hands.

Power filled the room. Blue-white flames blazed along the Old Mage's gaunt limbs and flared in his eyes like two cold fires. Elminster looked at Lhaeo with those burning eyes and did not see him.

With a sudden crackling of energy, the book fell from Elminster's fingers. Had there been some trap waiting in it?

Lhaeo shrank back, reaching out behind him for one of the flasks on a certain shelf. Elminster had prepared a number of such flasks for emergencies. They held protective potions and antidotes for poisons. But even as his fingers felt along the row of cold, dusty stoppers, Lhaeo knew he hadn't an inkling of what to do. The fire under the cauldron had died to almost nothing, and it seemed as if a great weight were in the air, filling the kitchen.

And then both men heard it: a voice that was kind and yet proud, in pain but enthused. A mind-voice that rolled through Elminster's mind so loudly that Lhaeo heard it clearly across the room. A voice that crawled with echoing power.

The voice of a goddess at the height of her aroused power, and yet in need. The voice of Mystra.

"Elminster! I need thee!"

"Lady, I am here," Elminster whispered. Blue-white flames licked from his mouth as he spoke. He rose from his seat, staggering as if under a great burden.

Behind him, the chair suddenly roared into a column of fire that reached for the low roof-beams overhead and then was gone, dying in the instant the chair was utterly consumed. Elminster lurched and almost fell.

Lhaeo shivered in horror at the sudden release of power great enough to burn away a chair between two beats of one's heart, but started toward his master. Elminster frantically waved him back, struggling as if in a high wind, and that great voice spoke again.

"Old Mage, my time is done. I am going, and have no time to tell thee what has befallen, or thank thee for the years thou hast given me.

"You must bear the load, old friend. You must be the one. Hold my flame for the one who is to come." A hint of amusement echoed in the voice. "You'll like her. You always do fancy young maids." Then she was gone, with no farewell but a flicker of communicated pain—and something whispered after it.

Elminster stiffened. Abruptly, the roaring, blazing force of Mystra's magical power—her very essence— surged into him, filling him in relentless waves. It brought burning agony, daggerlike fingers tearing through his ancient body. He tried to roar but could not.

In Elminster's numbed mind, the force of Mystra's magic swept bindings, odd memories, and safeguards before it as a tidal wave tumbles wreckage along in its uncaring, destroying foam. His hands jerked and flailed about helplessly, and he fell.

It had been many long years since sheer intensity of Art had hurled the Old Mage to his knees. He could scarcely remember the last time he'd felt overmatched by sheer power of magic. A wry thought came unbidden then. He'd known this would happen, sooner or later. He shook his head and gradually became aware of a faint, raw, frantic screaming.

Where—? A protesting thought whirled into Elminster's mind. Why do the worst problems always come when one is ill prepared? He strove to focus on the direction of the sound, raising a hand in front of his face as if to wave away the blue-white mists before him. Slowly, slowly, he drifted closer to the agonized shrieking, saw Lhaeo's shocked face coming closer through the mists— and realized the sound was coming from his own lips.

Elminster of Shadowdale spread his hands apologetically, struggled up from his knees, and fell headlong into Lhaeo's reaching arms as another surge of Art carried him away, chilled and burned all at once.

In a place of drifting mists, Elminster of Shadowdale gathered his will to banish the pain. Ice took him by the heart and throat as he groped for his Art amid the roiling magic that filled him.

He found nothing. The Art that had served him for many hundred years was burned away. All his power had fled from him. His magic was gone.

* * * * *

From a place where only gods walk cometh the Fall to cast down all the gods. Among them is Mystra, the goddess whose thought shapes and controls the eternal fires men call magic all across the world of Toril. What befalls that world if all the bounds and enchantments of its magic should burst at once, to let the fire flash free?

The world perishes in flames, of course, and so this must not befall. Even in her destruction, a goddess can strive to do something noble, a last act of love for the world she's watched for so long.

No time remains for a considered and orderly passage of power. No mortal frame can hope to hold her essence without burning to nothingness. No mortal mind can carry what she knows, without being snuffed out in an instant.

Azuth must carry more. All of her Chosen must carry more. But one mortal must carry the chief load, lest all perish with Mystra's passing. One mortal must be chosen in an instant. One who can carry more than most. One who can resist the temptation to twist the power to his or her own ends, and by meddling doom all the Realms. One must suffer Mystra's Doom.

In pride, folly, and despair at the moment of her passing, Mystra knows the mortal who must be chosen. Only one can hope to survive. Only one may succeed—and perhaps, much later, forgive.

"Remember me," she whispers to the chosen one, with her last thought. There is not enough left of her to shed the tears that are the price of her long burden. "Remember me."

*   *   *   *   *

"Lady Mystra," Elminster whispered in urgent reply, as he lay on the stones of his kitchen floor. "I love thee! I will remember. Take my thanks!"

He could not tell if Mystra ever heard him, or if she was gone before his thoughts were formed. Elminster looked up at Lhaeo and felt tears wet on his cheeks.

"She's gone," he mumbled, rather unnecessarily. Lhaeo nodded, and bent over him.

"Aye," he said gravely, "but what has she done to you?"

Through fresh tears, Elminster met a gaze that was wary and the gray of cool steel. He noted Lhaeo's ready grip on a belt dagger and made no move with his own hands.

"I am still myself," he said quietly. "Or as much as I can be with no magic left to me."

Lhaeo stared at him in shocked silence for a long time. Then he whispered, "Old friend, I am sorry. Very sorry indeed." He knelt down and took Elminster's hand. "Gone for good?"

Elminster shrugged and then slowly nodded. "I fear so."

Lhaeo's look was grave. "There is no gentle way to ask

this," he said slowly. "You have lived beyond most men. Without Art, will you soon crumble away?"

Elminster grinned feebly. "Nay, Lhaeo. Ye're stuck with me awhile longer."

"Then I suppose," Lhaeo said solemnly, "you'll be wanting to get up off this floor. I haven't swept it yet today."

* * * * *

In a dark chamber far away, the silent, floating ring of beholders drew back as Manshoon, High Lord of Zhentil Keep, gasped and halted in his cold address to them. He stumbled, caught himself, and straightened to face them again, but on his bone-white face was a look of fear it had not worn for years.

The beholders waited watchfully, many dark and glistening eyes staring at the human archwizard, ready to rend him in an instant if it should be needful.

Manshoon looked around at all those eyes, took a deep breath, and licked suddenly dry lips. "Something has happened. Something terrible." He shook his head in disbelief. "Bindings have failed all across the Realms."

The largest beholder drifted a little nearer. The cold, hissing voice of Ithaqull sounded coldly amused as it rolled out around the archmage. "An event that has possibilities, does it not?"

* * * * *

As the sun went down over Shadowdale, Elminster sat, long pipe in hand, beside a placid little pool. Power still roiled within him, but there seemed less of it now than at first. Perhaps it was leaking away or leaving him by some means prepared beforehand by the Lady of Mysteries, or perhaps he was just getting used to it.

He raised a finger and tried to light his pipe with a little cantrip he'd learned long ago. Nothing happened. He tried again, holding up his finger and staring at it as he gathered his will.

The spell was still there. He'd had it in his mind before

Mystra had spoken, though he couldn't feel any enchantments hanging ready any longer. He could think clearly and remember all that he'd done, but Art simply would not come to his call. Feeling a little ashamed, he stuck his pipe, unlit, back in his mouth and stared out across the water.

Night came creeping across the sky like thieves' fingers, long, dark blue clouds coming in low from the west. Small croakings and singings sounded around the pool. Amid the stones at its eastern edge, Elminster sat as if he were stone himself, and made no sound at all.

Lhaeo came out to him with a steaming jack of hot spiced wine. Elminster only smiled a little as the scribe placed it in his hand, and looked up with eyes that did not see. Lhaeo put a hand on his shoulder in answer and went back in. Elminster did not speak, for he was very busy talking—in his mind, which was a crowded place just then.

The Divine Lord Azuth was there, and with him Nouméa, the Lady Magister. There was also Storm Silverhand and High Lady Alustriel and Nethreen. Most of all Nethreen: Witch-Queen of Aglarond, widely feared across the Realms as the fiery-tempered, awesomely strong archmage the Simbul. Elminster loved her very much.

They'd held each other and whispered their truenames in the wake of the coming to power of the spellfire-maiden, Shandril Shessair. Since then—in their own independent, far-traveling ways—they'd been lord and lady to each other.

In the flurry of mind-spoken questions, comfortings, and advice, the Simbul's quiet voice tore at Elminster's heart the most. As night came to Shadowdale, Elminster sat amid the ever-louder chorus of crickets and bullfrogs, and thanked his friends for their care and good wishes. Feeling sick at heart, he told them plainly that he didn't know what to do now. Concerned thoughts flew like flashing swords, but in their midst the Old Mage grew ever more tired and heartsick. He was beginning to feel that the power to link thoughts with others who carried the burden of Mystra's power was a curse, not the comfort and safety it was intended to be.

Yet the Old Mage cared for all who reached out to his mind this eve, and none of them were unfriendly or unperceptive. They knew he carried a terrible measure of power he did not know how to call on. Worse, they all knew his own Art, or at least his means of grasping magic, was gone. They knew, too, that he was very tired and wanted to be alone.

One by one they wished him well and withdrew. Soft soothings echoed and re-echoed in his mind. Elminster felt their own weariness, bewilderment, and fear for Mystra and for the fate of them all, and had no comfort to give. He saluted them as they parted, until at last—as he knew would happen—only one thought-voice remained, riding his mind with the easy familiarity of intimacy.

Nethreen. Lady most mine. Elminster let her feel his gratefulness. *I am right glad of thy company.*

I know, Lord, came the calm reply. *I know. I was ever lonely until I came to thee and found another I could trust.*

Elminster smiled in the darkness, and then hastily caught his pipe as it fell. *I love thee, Lady.*

And I thee, Lord. Stop all this formal fencing, El. We're alone now, and you're in perhaps the worst danger you've ever really faced. Have you decided what to do next?

Elminster's sigh slid into a rueful grin. *No. I've thought, but not decided. I was hoping—*

That between us all, we'd decide on a path for your feet? came the dry reply. *That is not laid on through life for any of us, Old Mage. You of all folk know that well.* The rebuke was lost in the same ruefulness that Elminster felt, shared for a moment before it faded. When the Simbul spoke again, her mind-voice was gentle. *Will you come to me? There is a hidden place deep in the Yuirwood, a refuge I've used before, as others of Aglarond did before me.*

Nay, Lady. Elminster's feelings were firm and certain about this, at least. *This danger is, as ye say, mine to face. Moreover, I menace any mage I am near. Even if I did not*

*love thee, Aglarond needs thee against the spite and greed
of Thay, whose meddling mages would be that much
closer to me in thy refuge than they are now.*

*Right now, all who learn of your misfortune and would
do you ill know exactly where to find you,* Nethreen reminded him sharply. *Don't misthink yourself into a grave,
my lord!* Her mental tone shifted into curiosity. *Why are
you a danger to any mage? Are you afraid the power in
you will tempt me, or another like me?*

Elminster's reply was subdued. *I know not if Mystra's
power will leak from me. Mayhap it will be unleashed in
some sort of magical blast. In either case, it may destroy
any mages near, or render them feeble witted or dead to
Art as I am now.*

*Moreover, I am sure to attract the overly ambitious, if
ever my fate becomes known. I would not want ye to face
hourly visits from the likes of Ghalaster of Thay; that Calishite, Murdrimm the Hierarchmage; or Manshoon,
backed by all his Zhentarim. One or a number of them,
working against thee or me, might taste too much of Tymora's good fortune. Those who would seize Mystra's
power will do anything, and more than anything, to get it.*

What must we do, then? The Simbul's voice seemed
close to tears.

If ye would help me, Elminster replied carefully, feeling
his way as he spoke to her, *watch over Mourngrym—and
Randal Morn in Daggerdale—as I have done, and help
the Harpers as best ye can. Storm will tell thee how. I
need thee to take on my tasks while I am unable to do
them—if ye deem the doing necessary and good, for I will
not tell thee how to judge, or that I have been right in
what I've done.*

There was a little silence, and then the reply came, soft
as a falling feather. *I will, Old Mage. Remember that I
love thee.* That was all, and she was gone.

Elminster sat alone again in the night, waiting for
moonrise.

He could not see the silent tears the lady in the tattered black gown shed then. Far away, in the highest
room in a night-cloaked tower in Aglarond, the Simbul

wept for her doomed lord. She hated to break their link together—now, when he needed her most—but she couldn't hide her pity any longer. That last pride she would not take from him, whatever befell. It was nearly all he had left.

* * * * *

Sitting alone in the soft darkness, Elminster watched the stars slowly wheel overhead.

"I wonder," he said at last, aloud, "if every mage who strives with Art to change the world were swept away tomorrow, if it would make one breath of difference to the Realms."

"I know not," came a quiet reply from out of the night, "but it's never stopped any of us from trying."

Elminster nearly jumped right into the air. Heart racing, beard bristling, he contented himself with jerking around toward the voice as he flung away pipe and wineglass.

Delicate eyebrows arched. "I know I haven't done anything to my hair since this morning," Jhessail Silvertree asked calmly, "but do I really look that bad?"

"Mystra's mercies, lass! Must ye creep up on an old, enfeebled man like that?" Elminster sputtered, peering at his onetime pupil. Instead of her customary man's tunic and breeches, the Knight of Myth Drannor wore a dark, splendid gown. Her long hair, unbound, curled about her shoulders. Her eyes were very dark.

The lady Knight leaned close enough in the dimness for him to see her smile. "It certainly seemed effective," she agreed. "How are you tonight, Old Mage?"

Elminster sat very still. Then he said simply, "Not good."

"I know," Jhessail said softly, sitting down and wrapping smooth, strong arms around him. "It's why I've come."

"Ye know?" Elminster asked dully. Realizing how very much he needed the friendly warmth of arms about him just now, he slowly relaxed in her embrace.

Jhessail nodded, her hair brushing his cheek. "Storm sent me. Worry not; no others in this dale know." She snuggled closer. "Storm has two guests—Harpers—this night and thought you needed someone to hold you."

"Well," Elminster said dryly, "there's always Lhaeo."

"He's busy," Jhessail said, "getting out all your old clothes and wands and traveling boots, and cooking up a storm just in case."

"In case, good lady, of what?" Elminster asked rather testily.

"He knows how restless you are," Jhessail said gently. "Even if you're so shaken right now that I could walk right past you to the tower and back again without your noticing."

"*Shaken?*" Elminster suddenly found himself shouting, trembling in a red fury. He drew back a hand and hit out hard. "Have a care, wench!" he snarled. "I've—"

When he realized what he'd done, ice clutched at his spine, and the anger was suddenly gone. He was alone in black despair, sinking, and without magic. "Oh, gods, lass," he whispered roughly. "I'm sorry."

There was silence. She did not move.

"J-Jhessail?" the Old Mage asked almost frantically, "Have I hurt thee? I—Smite me with Art, I deserve it! I am most sorry, but I cannot undo what I've done. I deserve to make amends."

There was a soft chuckle in the darkness, a chuckle with a catch in it. Then Jhessail's arms went around him again. Elminster couldn't help noticing what a shockingly firm and heaving bosom pressed against him as warm lips kissed his cheek.

"Just had to catch my breath. You've a mean right arm, for all your years, Old Mage," Jhessail said happily into his chest. "I'm glad, not angry. It seems you'll be all right, after all."

"No," Elminster said miserably, "that's just what I won't be, lass. Without magic, I won't be all right ever again."

Jhessail kissed him full on the mouth, stopping his bitter words. "Ever notice," she said, a long breath later, "how some wizards think the sun rises and sets on their shoulders, and their feet hold the Realms together as they walk on it?"

Elminster, still reeling from the kiss, asked roughly, "What d'ye—? Are ye implying—?"

"No," Jhessail replied sweetly, "I'm saying it straight out. And more. I'm telling you to get up, help me find the glass and pipe you threw my way a little while ago, and go in and have dinner. Lhaeo's worried about you. *I'm* worried about you. And when I get home and Merith sees this magnificent bruise on my ribs, *he's* going to be worried about you."

"I didn't—I'm sorry, lass!" Elminster protested wretchedly, but firm hands lifted him from his seat and propelled him into the night. He heard her chuckle again, and in anger and despair cried out, "Jhessail! My Art's gone, I tell thee!"

"Yes, yes," Jhessail said quickly, "and now the whole dale knows, too!" Her voice broke then, but she rushed on. "Gods, Old Mage, don't make this any harder for me than it is already. I'm scared sick at what might happen to you, and to this dale without your protection. I'm trying to cheer you up, but it's cursed hard work, and—and—" Tears came then, and she reached for him in the darkness and embraced him again.

"If you're quite finished with the first act of this little love play," Lhaeo's dry voice came out of the darkness a few breaths later, "a late feast—late indeed, by now—is laid ready in the kitchen. There's enough for three."

2
Mystery, Doom, and a Long Walk

Storm was laughing in a flying web of steel, her flashing blade holding off two others in a deadly dance. It was the bright height of the day of Lord Aumry's Feast, and no clouds marred the circle of blue sky above her as she ducked and pivoted. The two men she fought had no spare breath to do more than grunt and gasp.

The Bard of Shadowdale was training two Harpers at sword work, showing them how with skill she could force their blades and bodies continually nearer each other, driving them into each other's way as they circled about the moss-carpeted glade. More than once the two men in leathers had stumbled into each other, muttered apologies and oaths, and leapt hastily out of the way of the weaving blade that stung them, teased them, flirted with their own steel, and slid past their sword hilts to touch them again and again.

It was a rare chance to cross blades with Storm Silverhand. Among Harpers she was as famous as Mintiper or Sharanralee, veteran adventurers of whom many songs had been sung and tavern tales told. Semiretired now, she dwelt in the green fastness of Shadowdale and trained Harpers in the ways of music and battle. Many came, some skeptical that one woman could really be so special. They left amazed and changed, and spoke of their meetings with her in awe and with fondness.

Storm Silverhand was really that special. An impish humor danced in her eyes as she faced them now, long hair bound back out of her face, her leathers creaking with the strain as she twisted and leapt and danced as lightly as a child at play.

Belkram and Itharr, rangers and Harpers both, wore faces as delighted and eager as boys at a favorite sport.

They had come almost as much to see if the legends were true as to hone their sword skills. Both had seen many deaths and much battle, and thought few could teach them more than a trick or two with a blade.

Now they knew they faced a true master. Thrice, five times, a dozen more the lady bard could have slain them, had that been her goal. Her slim but very long silvery sword leapt again and again through their guards to kiss shoulder, breast, forearm, or flank. Yet so skilled was she that she pulled back ere steel tasted flesh, time and again, even when blades met so hard that winking sparks flew, and the fray moved so fast that the two men were scrambling and all three panted like winded dogs.

A rare chance, this, to face one skilled enough not to hurt you but to keep the sword work as hard and as fast as if it were to the death. Belkram and Itharr, parrying the blade that seemed to be everywhere, found themselves helplessly maneuvered again into each other. They bumped shoulders, sprang apart murmuring apologies, and exchanged glances. Their eyes met for only an instant—it was all they dared spare time for—but each saw admiration for their opponent in the other's eyes. This Storm was truly magnificent with a long sword in her hand.

Belkram shook sweat out of his eyes for perhaps the sixtieth time and sprang back a pace to avoid any lunge the bard might make while he was doing so. Had this fight been in earnest, the awe he now felt would have been stone-cold fear. Storm, as she had been doing since she discovered both her opponents were good bladesmen, was smiling as she fought. Smiling merrily and, between gasps for breath, humming a sprightly tune that Belkram had often heard harped in Everlund.

Anyone who could toy with him—and with Itharr, who was as good as himself or better—as this lady was doing, and spare thought and breath enough to hum a tune, could be the death of him whenever she desired. Belkram had seen many quick swords in the years since he'd joined the Harpers, but never the equal of Storm Silverhand. He was old enough to realize the gift she was giving them: A chance to strive against one much better with a blade and have time enough in the fray to try all they knew against her. To feel, face, and master their fear rather than being paralyzed with terror and, an instant later, sinking into eternal red-edged darkness.

Belkram matched Storm's smile as he remembered a crossing attack he'd seen in a sea fight long ago. He arched to his left, parrying Storm's blade with a series of short, binding, feathering strokes of his own blade. His own side was exposed now, but Itharr should be attacking from that side, protecting it.

Then, not for the first time in that clash of steel, Storm was gone. Ducking smoothly to one knee, dropping below Belkram's parries, she spun back to face Itharr, tossing her sword to her left hand and raising it to parry his descending blade. In the same motion, her now-empty right hand grabbed Belkram's ankle and jerked.

The ranger hopped, trying to twist his foot loose, and fell helplessly. Storm straightened and put her shoulders into two furious strokes that drove Itharr—a burly man a hand shorter but at least six trade-blocks heavier than she, with arms and wrists twice as thick—back across the clearing. With a twist of her blade she disarmed him, sending his blade singing off into the trees.

Belkram chuckled ruefully as he rolled to his feet and brought his own blade up barely in time to turn aside her sword point, inches away from his cheek. He dodged and twisted, his moves slowed and blunted by growing weariness. In an attempt to win past her blade, he tried a circular cut that extended into a lunge.

In the midst of the ring and skirl of their blades, Storm's face suddenly twisted. She stiffened as a blue-white glow surrounded her hair. Belkram didn't even have time to gape in astonishment as his blade slid into her breast.

It went into the leather-clad swell of her bosom just as easily as a hot knife into butter, as they say—a good three inches or more before he could stop. Beside him, Belkram heard Itharr gasp, but Storm made no sound. Her eyes had closed, and her mouth was parted in pain.

"Gods, you've killed her!" and "Oh, Lady! Forgive—" rang out together as Storm swayed, clutched the steel that stood out from her breast with both hands, and opened her eyes at last.

"My apologies, both of you," she said in a low voice. "Something . . . linked to me . . . took hold for a moment. No blame to you, Belkram."

Storm smiled at them, but the two Harpers were staring at her as if she had suddenly become a ghost or a dragon. Her eyes were two dancing flames of blue-white fire, and more flames crackled in her mouth as she spoke. Her hands moved down Belkram's blade, and in their wake blue-white fire danced along the steel. The ranger, who still held his sword, felt a tingling in his hand. The tingling grew to a painful burning. Without thought he let go of his blade.

Slowly Storm drew the steel out of herself, the blade blazing with cold, silent, blue-white fire from end to end. She laid a hand on her breast, and flames licked between her fingers. Then she smiled and glided forward to hand the blade hilt-first to Belkram. She did not move as if she were hurt.

In wonderment Itharr asked, "Are you all right, Lady?"

Storm nodded. "I am." The fire in her eyes was dying down, and she looked almost herself again.

Belkram felt the eerie tingling spread up his arm from the blade and said quietly, "Lady, I am sorry. It was as you said; I could not stop in time. But you have shown us both that you can halt your blade where you will, time and time again. I have never seen your like in battle, and hope never to do so. Tell me, if you will. Are you a mage also?"

Storm shook her head. "I am a bard and no more. This"—she spread out her hand and looked at the fading blue-white glow with interest—"is not of my doing. It was what . . . caught me and gave us all this scare." She raised eyes that were normal again, but somber, and added, "Let us bathe and then go in for wine and talk. I've no more stomach for fighting, this day."

"Aye," the men agreed together and put away their

swords. Belkram had slid his weapon half into its scabbard before he remembered Storm's blood and hastily pulled the blade out again. A sword must never be sheathed wet, lest it rust. This blade had traveled long and far with him. Yet to wipe it clean in front of the very lady one has just wounded with it . . .

Storm saw his look and laughed. "No need, Belkram. See?" She caught hold of his blade with two deft fingers and turned it. Light flashed along the sword's length. It was shiny-clean and glowed faintly blue as if freshly oiled. "It will never rust now," Storm said softly. Both men looked at her without speaking.

Storm looked back at them. "It has tasted Mystra's fire," she explained. When she undid her leather jacket and peeled it unconcernedly off, her naked skin beneath was unmarked. There was no sign of the bloody wound that should have been there, and that should have drained her life away.

The Harpers stared and then quickly looked away with muttered apologies. One does not stare at a lady so. They had gone another six steps toward the stream before they realized that no sweat had glistened on her skin. That, too, must have been burned away.

They were very quiet as they stripped to bathe in the stream with her, and kept a respectful distance. One does not speak loudly or appear overbold when walking with one who might be a goddess. Storm tried to put them at their ease with light talk but dared not tell the two men what had really happened to her in the clearing. And so another legend of Storm Silverhand was born.

* * * * *

In the clear and early dawn, Elminster swung a cloak about his shoulders, left the tower quietly, and went for a walk in the dew that cloaked Shadowdale.

He felt as if he were drifting this morn and not really alive or present at all. Hardly surprising, he reflected; he'd not slept a wink all night.

The moon had gone down before Merith Strongbow

had slipped into the tower looking for his wife. He'd found Jhessail asleep by the fire, wrapped in furs and snoring ever so faintly. Lhaeo provided slumbrous harmony from the stool in the corner, and Elminster sat sleepless, silent watch over them both, his pipe lit and his eyes as empty and dark as the night outside.

He and Merith had shared a silent toast to Jhessail's love and caring with chill green Calishite wine. Rather than wake her or Lhaeo, Merith had curled up in Elminster's last chair to sleep. Elminster had finished the bottle of wine by himself, and thought much.

Answers and clear paths seemed as elusive as ever, but after a time Elminster arose and opened the door. There he softly spoke a word and pointed into the night with one of the wands Lhaeo had found. His heart leapt as lightning crackled and spat into the darkness. This sort of magic, at least, he could still command.

He went to a certain railpost on the stairs, bent to a particular spot, and pushed just so. A curved section of the post swung open, and a dusty, long-forgotten bag fell out. The Old Mage selected two plain brass rings from the bag, put them on, and went down to the door again.

The rings worked, too. Much heartened, Elminster drew himself a cool tankard of beer. Then he frowned and got up again to close and bolt the door, locking it for the first time in years. He and Lhaeo usually left it open, for anyone who needed them at night to get in with a minimum of fuss. He'd have to remember to change such habits now.

As he had been changed, the wry thought rose unbidden. He pushed it away and went to find another tankard. He did not take the rings off.

So the night had gone, stealing slowly toward morning. Grieving for his lost magic, Elminster walked alone as morning came. He was drawn, as always, into the welcoming green reaches of the trees that cloaked Shadowdale. He walked among them in soft-shod silence for what seemed a very long time as the dale awoke behind him. Birds called, small things scampered in the underbrush, and rising breezes stirred the leaves.

Elminster smiled, breathed deep, and looked all around. It had been long indeed since he'd taken the time to really see this forest. From ahead on the path, Elminster heard the sudden clear call of a child.

"Well met!" the young treble voice called out.

Giggles answered, followed by another child's voice replying, "Are we so, base villain?"

The children of the dale awoke early for farm chores and were now playing. The Old Mage stepped aside from the path, pulling his cloak around him, and leaned against a tree to listen.

He was startled to hear, very loud and close at hand, a young but confident male voice declaim grandly, "I, Elminster the Great, smite thee with fires and lightnings that none can withstand!"

There was movement on the other side of the tree. Elminster cocked his head to look around the trunk and saw a smooth but rather crooked twig cutting the air, flourished in a young boy's hand.

Its bearer pointed the stick across a little open place at a rather dirty little girl, perhaps six summers old, who was standing on a stone to make herself taller.

She faced the twig-wand without fear and replied triumphantly, "Well, *I'm* the Simbul, and my power is even greater. Besides, Elminster loves me and does what I want!"

The Old Mage found himself smiling. With the smile, hot tears came unbidden, and his eyes swam.

He waited until he could see the trees clearly again and slipped quietly away.

* * * * *

Sweat glistened on bare, knot-muscled shoulders as Storm Silverhand greeted the morn. A bastard sword with a blade as broad as a man's hand glinted blue and deadly in the rising light as it spun and leapt in her hands.

Storm wore only boots, tattered and patched leather breeches, and huge metal war gauntlets. She grunted from time to time as she twisted, lunged, and danced, fencing with shadows. When she was breathing heavily, Storm paused, leaned on her blade, and called softly, "Vethril! Vethril! To battle, sister!"

In the round-windowed room under the eaves, her two Harper guests awoke as Storm's soft words floated in through the open window. Belkram and Itharr yawned, rubbed their eyes, stretched, and winced. Both were as sore as old saddle horses after being ridden hard. Their eyes met ruefully. Gods, did the woman never rest?

She'd talked late into the night, matching them flagon for flagon. They'd fallen asleep listening to her sing soft, sad sleep-songs of lost Myth Drannor as she swept and washed up. Now she was up and about in the dawn after a day of battle—and that wound—that would leave most men stiff and numb for half a day after.

Perhaps it was this beautiful house and the dale beyond. Harpers, who tend to be folk of the open road, can seldom relax and rarely sleep without a blade to hand. This place was a refuge, a rare opportunity to let go for two men who had a lot of sleep to catch up on.

Nonetheless, they were Harpers. At the first clash of steel they were up, naked but with swords ready in their hands, and rushing to the window. Their jaws dropped together.

Outside, the half-naked Bard of the Blade, silver hair swirling about her, was fighting a ghost. Her translucent, utterly silent opponent swung a very real black-bladed battle-axe. When it met the great bastard sword Storm wielded, sparks flew from the force of the blow.

The two men drank in the sight of Storm's magnificence for a breath and then stared hard at the opponent who hardly seemed to be there. They exchanged glances and whistled soundlessly. The fighting down there was fast. Like their combat in the glade yesterday, it was obviously a friendly battle; no one was striking to slay. But as those huge weapons flashed and spun, crashed together and bobbed about in the hands of their dodging, dancing wielders, the Harpers were struck by just how fast the two women were going at it. Perhaps their own work, yesterday, had looked like that. They'd been far too busy to watch.

Two women? Aye, for the ghost—if that was what it was—was a slim, long-haired woman in a gown. Shorter than Storm, she looked very like the Bard of Shadowdale in features, build, and movement.

The two men could see right through her, but from time to time as she moved, her features grew clearer and more solid. This seemed to happen when emotion rose, whenever the silent figure made an exultant grin, a delighted, soundless laugh, or a grimace of remorse at a missed chance or bad bit of weapon wielding. As the two men watched, Storm leapt high, slashing the axe aside with her own blade, and crashed down on her ghostly opponent with knees drawn up. There was an audible thump as they fell to the trodden turf together.

Itharr leaned out the window to see what had happened just as the axe leapt skyward again and there was a clanging flurry of blows. His naked sword grated for an instant on the window frame.

The silent figure stared up in terror and melted away in an instant, the axe falling. Storm batted it away with her blade, but not fast enough to avoid taking a long slice as the axe blade caught on one bare forearm and slid past.

She shook her head, smiling up at them ruefully, and said, "Fair morn, men. I can't seem to avoid getting cut open when you're around." Clapping a hand to the welling blood, she asked, "A little practice? Or dawnfry first?"

"Uh—food first, if that's your pleasure, Lady," Belkram managed, trying not to stare. "Err—who was that?"

Storm took up the axe in the crook of her arm and started for the door beneath them. "Come down and I'll tell," she called.

Hastily pulling on boots and breeches, the two Harpers went down. They brought their swords because they were, after all, Harpers. The kitchen was as cool and inviting as it had been yesterday.

"Well met." Storm grinned, muscling a cauldron of

soup off the hearth, an apron wrapped around her hands to ward off burns. Wordlessly, Itharr went to her and turned up her arm. A long white scar there was fading already. He raised his eyebrows.

Storm gestured with her chin at a shelf behind him, under the stairs they'd descended. "Healing potions there, if you need them."

Belkram cleared his throat. "Lady, at the risk of seeming a complete idiot, I'd like to ask you to tell us whatever you care to about what we just saw—and for that matter, about what happened yesterday."

Storm waved them to seats, whipping warm bread from a hearth pan, and said, "Of course. One of my customs is to limber up of mornings with the heaviest blade I can comfortably swing." She cast a fond glance at the great bastard sword. The two men looked at it leaning against the wall, and both raised their eyebrows at its length and evident weight. "From time to time I call on a sparring partner, whom you saw."

"A ghost?"

"If you like. A soul who dwells here with me and can materialize for short periods. The rest of the time she is my watchguard. If ever you have a message for me and can't find me here, speak it aloud and she'll usually make some sign that she's heard. Moving a chair, for instance. She's handy that way for scaring off thieves."

Itharr nodded slowly. "I can imagine." He looked all around. "She's here all the time?"

Storm nodded. "She doesn't like to show herself to any but me, and I don't like to reveal her to others. I came up to wake you two—with a kiss and a hot mug of bitterroot, as I did yestermorn—and you both slept right on. Well, it's never failed before." She grinned again, and Belkram rolled his eyes. "So I thought you were safely snoring for a bit, and called her."

Itharr nodded again and said, raising his voice only a little, "Ah—well met, Vethril! I'm sorry we broke into things; you swing a mean axe."

A little chill went down his spine as a feminine mouth and chin appeared in the air before him for a moment, over the table. The mouth smiled and was gone.

For a long moment, Belkram stared at where the apparition had been and said, "Yes. Well. Lady, will you tell us about yesterday?"

Storm nodded, not smiling now, and said, "Something happened. Something very important that wisdom forbids me to tell you about. Something, as you know, connected with Mystra. All I can say is beware magic for some time to come. It may go awry in strange ways. More than that; in the days ahead we must all be wary, ready for trouble. It's all too likely to come."

She sighed and broke off a large chunk of bread in her long, strong fingers. Itharr looked from them to the gauntlets and back again. Then his gaze drifted up her naked torso, to be caught and held by Storm's own eyes. She was not smiling, and her eyes held them both as if on two dark sword points. Her voice, when it came, was very soft.

"There is more. For the next little while, the most important being in the entire Realms is the archmage Elminster of Shadowdale. He must be aided and watched at all times by every Harper, so spread the word. He must be kept alive, and he might not be able to use his own magic. We must guard him as if he were a defenseless child. Nothing you do in your lives, gentlemen, is likely to be half so important as this, believe me."

Deep silence fell, and lasted five long breaths before Itharr shivered. They all stirred, and Storm smiled at them again.

"That reminds me," she said briskly, "that we'd best go see Elminster. So break bread, men, and let's be washed up and done."

"Ah," Belkram said, eyeing her, "can we get dressed first? You seem used to going about near unclad and all, but . . ."

They all chuckled, and Storm rose and took down the leathers she'd worn the day before, from a drying-rack in the beams low overhead.

Itharr looked up at her and said softly, "Vethril? Vethril, are you near?"

The empty chair beside him turned by itself. Itharr nodded and said, "That's your truename, isn't it?" Silence gave him reply. He drew a deep breath and said, "Well, I think it is. And you are a friend—no, a sister"—he heard a sharp intake of breath from nearby—"to a fellow Harper. Know, then, that my truename is Olanshin, and I would be pleased to know thee."

Belkram nodded at the formal words and added, "And mine, unseen lady, is Kelgarh. Well met."

Itharr was startled, then, to feel the touch of soft, cold lips upon his cheek, then wetness. But he was a strong man and a Harper, and did not flinch or bring his hands up but only smiled.

He did not wipe the tears from his cheek. Storm looked at him with an expression of thanks and pride that Itharr would remember to the end of his days. She said huskily, "And mine, friends, is not mine to give. If I could, know you that I would."

Belkram nodded. "We understand," he said, rising from the table with the dishes in his hands. "Mystra forbids."

Storm looked at the empty air. "Truly, sister," she said with a smile, "we've two good ones this time."

The reply, when it came, startled them all: a hissing, ghostly whisper. "You'll need them," was all that Vethril said.

* * * * *

When they were out on the dale road, walking toward the junction that would take them to Elminster's tower, Itharr turned to Storm and said quietly, "That's your sister Syluné, isn't it?"

Storm smiled and nodded, and Itharr saw that her eyes were suddenly bright with tears. "What's left of her," she said, very softly.

"We'll come back to visit you both, when we can," Belkram added. "She's tied to your house, isn't she?"

Storm nodded. "Would that Elminster were, too," she replied. "It would often make my tasks much easier."

* * * * *

One never pays all that much heed to what one has and what one has grown used to, Elminster reflected wryly, looking down at his left hand. Yestermorn these fingers could have hurled lightnings or raised walls of shimmering force with but a thought, but now they could call forth nothing. The same as the hands of most men, the Old Mage reminded himself. Few have been as fortunate to face life with the arms and armor of Art I've wielded. And, oh, Mystra, but I've grown used to it!

Lady, why me?

An instant later, Elminster raised his head defiantly and looked about. Why? he thought, then answered his own question. Because, look ye, I was the best she could turn to. The best. No less.

So I carry her power within me. It has unmanned me, aye, but my wits are still my own, my strength—forgive me, Jhessail!—has not failed me . . . yet. I may be old, but I carry wisdom and experience more than most. I've seen what one can and cannot do with a blade, and can show most young swagger-swords a thing or two!

Perhaps I should seek out Storm and practice some blade work. But no. She also carries Mystra's burden. What if one or both of us were hurt by some mischance, or by the attack of a Manshoon or Ghalaster? What then? We'd perish, aye, but what of Mystra's spilled power? Lost to the Realms forever, perhaps blasting Shadowdale to dust on the way? Or stolen by a tyrant-mage to use as a whip to bring the Realms to their knees before his rule? No, that's out. Even meeting with others who bear the burden would be ill judgment, with all the foes I've made.

Storm abides in Shadowdale. I am too close to her already. Besides, the longer I tarry here, the more likely someone calling on me for aid will discover what has befallen me. When the word gets out, Shadowdale first, and then what I hold dear in the Realms, will be doomed as I am doomed. Absent, I remain a threat—someone who might return in fury to smite down any invader.

I must go. Slip away, and lose myself—forever, if my magic does not return. Whither, then?

* * * * *

There was a sudden burst of laughter around his very feet. Bewildered, Elminster looked down. He'd walked one of the narrow trodden paths that twist and cross in Shadowdale's backwoods like the web of some giant forest spider. The children he'd seen before, joined by several other dale urchins, had dashed about by other ways. At length and by chance, they'd met with him. Surprise and delight lit their voices as they crowded around his robes, patting and tugging.

Elminster managed a smile and found his gaze caught —and pulled in, as a fisherman drags close his catch—by a pair of very brown, very beautiful eyes. They belonged to a little girl, the one who'd earlier pretended to be the Simbul. Her hands and frock were dirty—she'd evidently fallen down or been pushed—and she was barefoot, but she drew herself up under his gaze with unconscious dignity. Her eyes alight with wonder, she crossed her arms on her breast and bowed from the waist as they did at court in Suzail and on the Sword Coast when meeting royalty.

Elminster stared down at her, oddly touched, his mouth curling in a smile. The bow had been done out of respect, not in the obsequious or emptily formal way he'd seen so often in real courts. He gave her the low, hand-sweeping bow of gallant knights in return, solemnly and with none of the archness with which he bowed to, say, Torm of the Knights in jest.

The girl was silent for a moment and then, very slowly, she blushed. Wonder sparkled in her eyes. She turned suddenly and made as if to dash away but halted, like a bird snagged upon a thorn, as another young voice rang out in protest.

"Jhaleen, you promised! You said you'd ask him! Well, here he is, so . . ."

The girl, her eyes very large, looked back at the boy

who'd spoken and then at Elminster, like a trapped hare. Elminster smiled invitingly.

Jhaleen blurted out, "Lord Elminster! Old Mage! Make magic for us, please! Please!" A chorus of young voices joined her bold one, and she added excitedly, "A dragon flying. Only a little one, just for us!"

Elminster smiled, felt tears near again, and knelt down to embrace her. "Not this morn, little one," he said softly, his eyes very blue. "Magic must be saved up, like coins, and used only when other ways fail."

She blinked up at him, disappointed, and Elminster chuckled and rubbed her cheek with the back of one long, gentle finger. He remembered, then, where he'd seen this brown-eyed girl before. In one of his dreams.

"Nay, be not downcast, Jhaleen. I see some things, know ye, in my dreams. Things I know will come to pass, in summers still to come." He leaned close to her, and whispered for her ears alone, "I've seen thee—much taller than now, and stern—riding a dragon."

She looked into his eyes and saw truth, and her mouth dropped open in awe and trembled just a little in fear. It is one thing to dream of dragons, and quite another to know with cold certainty that someday you will be touching one. More than that; flying high above the ground on a dragon's scaly back, with empty air as high as castles beneath you, and a twisted death below should you fall.

Elminster chuckled, and clapped her on the shoulder. "Go on playing thy games," he said, "and watch close what the Queen of Aglarond says and does when she visits us. And perhaps ye will befriend and even come to command dragons." Then he rose and walked slowly away from them all.

* * * * *

White-faced and silent, Jhaleen watched the Old Mage as he moved away into the depths of the forest. She'd seen the glint of tears in the archmage's eyes and could only think he foresaw something terrible that would happen to her. She stood watching him go until the trees hid him from view, then turned and hurried toward the path that led out of the trees toward home.

"Jhaleen, where be you going, then? Don't you want to play at high magic, anymore?" the boy who'd pretended to be Elminster called.

Jhaleen wheeled around so suddenly that the smaller children, who'd followed her out of habit, jumped back in apprehension. With a fierceness that surprised even herself she hissed, "I'll never play games about magic again! Never. It's . . . not something to play at."

She turned about again and ran out of the woods as if the black-armored warriors of Zhentil Keep were chasing her, faster than she'd ever run before. Her lungs burned and tears swam before her eyes, but the black terror that ran after her was worse.

Her fleet bare feet pounded along the earthen paths, stumbling and hurrying, until she came out into the dapped sunlight at last. Panting like a winded horse, she tore her way through young branches and, with a little shriek of fear, almost ran into someone. A tall lady clad in leather armor stood in the meadow beyond, brown hair flowing down over her shoulders in a fall almost as long as the slim sword scabbarded at her hip.

Jhaleen twisted to avoid running right into that blade, and fell. In an instant, gently strong hands raised her again and steady gray-green eyes looked into her own.

It was the Lady Sharantyr of the Knights. "What's wrong, lass? What's to run from, so?"

A breath later, Jhaleen was sobbing out all the Lord Elminster had said and how he'd been crying and had walked away.

The lady ranger held Jhaleen close. Sharantyr comforted the girl, turned her back to face the trees, and told her firmly never to run from what frightened her but to back away from it calmly and carefully, to see what it did.

Jhaleen felt a little better and managed a smile. She nodded when Sharantyr told her to take a walk in the sunlight and think carefully about what Elminster had said, so as to remember it properly later.

* * * * *

Biting at her knuckle to hold back fresh tears, Jhaleen watched Sharantyr go on into the wood. The lady had looked so sad when Jhaleen had told her about the Old Mage, and now she was hurrying through the trees as if to catch him. Something was wrong, very wrong. And with the Lord Elminster at the heart of it, who could tell her what was right, and what should be done, and what the truth of it all was?

As Jhaleen backed carefully away from the dark trees into the warmth of the full sun, she looked around, but no one came with answers. She was all alone with the trees and the grass, and there was no one to guide her. She walked without a known way before her, unsure of what to do next. Like someone she'd just seen, she realized suddenly.

Just like the Old Mage, walking away into the trees.

* * * * *

Elminster walked on into the deepening forest, just walking ever onward, tree-cloaked hillsides rising and falling under his feet. He felt empty and weak, as useless as a rotted log, and at the same time restless with the power that fairly crackled within him. Power he could not use, could not touch, dare not try to unleash. "By Mystra's touch," wizards often swore. By Mystra's touch, indeed.

His wandering feet brought him to the edge of a little gully, and Elminster paused a moment, gazing about to choose his route onward. He heard the faintest of sounds in the underbrush far behind him and nodded. The fifth time . . . too often for all such noises to have been small, disturbed forest creatures.

Someone—or something—was following him. Someone intelligent and with deliberate purpose. Someone who took care to keep out of sight. Elminster sighed and turned to face back the way he had come. "Ye may as well walk with me," he announced to the woods, "though truth to tell ye I'd prefer silent company this day."

Silence greeted him, the listening, waiting silence of the forest. The old wizard joined its wait for a breath or two and then shrugged, turned about, and went on. Not a friend, then—or not overbold, at least.

His hand strayed to the hilt of the belt knife he'd almost forgotten and then fell away again. Perhaps the magic he wore would suffice—in rings and pipe and wand, and even in the dagger strapped inside his right boot, whose soft sole was already wearing thin—even if the Art of his head and hands had deserted him. Elminster feared he'd soon have to find out.

He shrugged, trotted down a little bank, and plowed through a hollow that was ankle deep in dry leaves. He climbed its far side steadily and walked deliberately on into the rising land beyond, but paused in a stand of massive shadowtops to listen.

After what seemed like a long time, he heard the sound he'd waited for. Now was as good a time as any to look at death, he supposed wryly. He turned and took one step around the dark trunk of a forest giant, laid a hand on his belt knife—and the world fell on him, gauntleted hands smashing brutally into his face and stabbing steely fingers at his throat.

3
Doomed Not to Walk Alone

Death came for them with cold fury. The four brigands, intent on robbing an old man in fine robes, the sort of person who might well have a gold coin or two stitched into belt or boot top, did not hear their doom coming down on them.

One looked up too late. Long brown hair swirled as a leather-clad figure raced through the trees, sword held high. The staring brigand raised his dagger too slowly. He spun to a blood-spattered fall, throat cut open, as the swordswoman stormed into their midst.

Then her silvery blade was leaping everywhere, like a many-headed striking snake. Storm Silverhand had taught her things with a sword, and she was almost as fast as the famous Bard of the Blade.

Balrik Daershun was also counted fast and able with a blade. He'd ridden in the forefront of Lashan's troops, not so long ago, when they'd cut down full-armored Sembian lancers on the road south of Essembra. He'd killed four that day, leaping from his mount to carry the last lancer out of his saddle, his dagger finding the visor-slit even before the antagonists struck the ground together. Men had spoken of Balrik's fighting with awe and praise, and he'd been toasted with much wine.

Toasts had been fewer since, but Balrik's blade still served him. In the final rout of Lashan's leaderless host, Balrik and a dozen comrades had carved their way through a well-armed Cormyrean horse patrol to escape.

Outlaws led a hard life. Since that battle, Balrik had learned to fear arrows and quarrels from afar. He had only three companions left now, but two of them were nearly as good with a blade as he was, and he feared no man who came at him with a sword.

After that first whirl and flurry of steel, Balrik began to think he'd not be given time enough to learn to fear *women* who swung swords.

Elminster twisted free of the tall, hook-nosed man who held him, and dove for the ground to avoid the sword slash he knew would come. The expected blade flashed past overhead, then the man was turning at the leader's shout to face the new threat.

Elminster's rings and the wand he wore at his belt had saved his life. The brigands been so intent on grabbing and breaking fingers and snatching away the smooth stick of wood to stay any magic he might hurl, that they'd not put a dagger in his throat.

He began crawling away from the trampled ground where they'd struggled, looking back all the while to avoid being taken from the rear. If he could get away—

Then he saw the newcomer and struggled to his feet. This was no rival brigand come to settle scores or win a share of the loot. This was Sharantyr of the Knights. As he straightened, she spared time to flash a smile at him through her dance of striking steel. The three brigands were all around her now, tripping and stumbling over the body of the fourth. Her blade slid in and out, not daring to lunge full out in a killing thrust and thereby give another foe an opening to buy her death.

These were experienced warriors, not mere hungry hackers and stabbers. They would not fall easily, for all that they still gaped at her in wonder.

A woman—and so pretty, too, though her eyes held cold death for them, and her blade hissed like a striking serpent in her hand. She wore good leathers, but save for a gorget, she bore no metal plate to turn sword tip aside. And already she was panting, winded. Aye, for all her blade flashed so, they could take this one.

Abruptly she gasped and bent double. Grinning, Gaerth Wolfarm stepped in, drawing back his blade for a killing thrust.

"No!" Balrik roared from behind him. " 'Tis a trick, Gaer—"

His words died in his throat, too late by far, as Sharantyr straightened with a smile that chilled his blood, slashed open Gaerth's throat with a sweep of her sword, and shoved his body backward into Balrik's.

Cursing, Balrik stumbled aside, blade flailing in a desperate defense. But she was not coming for him. She'd turned, that beautiful long hair swirling, to slay Albeir.

Albeir o' the Axe. Albeir the veteran of half a hundred mercenary skirmishes on the Westgate caravan roads and in the Vilhon. Albeir the steadfast, who abruptly turned, white-faced, and sprinted away. Sharantyr took two running steps in pursuit, saw how he held his sword and that he was running toward Elminster, and snatched a dagger from her hip.

Balrik saw the blade spin to catch Albeir's ear in a gout of blood. He saw Albeir stagger, catch himself, and bear down on the wizard. The brigand grabbed the old man by the throat, swinging him around with brutal haste to serve as a shield.

Sharantyr halted and cast a look back at Balrik. He came on toward her, beginning to grin. Then he saw Albeir's grim face suddenly twist in pain. The old warrior's eyes went wide and he took a half step toward something unseen. Still staring, he crashed to the ground. Elminster looked down with evident sadness at the bloody dagger he held.

Balrik knew cold fear. The lady in leathers was turning back to him, blade low and deadly. It had seemed so easy, four on one, and an old man, too. Tymora spits on us from time to time, that minstrel had said back in Scardale. And look, 'twas the cold truth.

Then that blade came leaping at him again, and Balrik had no time for thought. Steel rang on steel inches from his nose as he parried desperately in the last instant before death would have found him. Then he had to do it again, gasping for air. Gods, this woman was not human! Where in the name of Tempus had she learned to wield a bla—*there!* Balrik saw an opening. His thrust, delivered with all he could put behind it, ran down her arm and laid open the leathers in a smooth, sliding strike. Her sword arm.

The silvery blade flew free, as he'd known it would, but she did not scream or fall back. She stepped into him, hard, and smiled into his face. "Good fight, carrion," she said calmly, eyes not a hand length from his own, and Balrik felt a sudden cold wetness in his gut.

She shoved him away and ducked aside from his last desperate slash. Balrik's fingers found the dagger—gods, hilt deep!—and his lips found time for what he had to say before blood welled up to choke him. "I am . . . a dead man. Lady, I am Balrik Daershun. Who are you?"

"I am Sharantyr of the Knights of Myth Drannor," she answered as the man fell heavily to his knees. His eyes had gone dark before her words were all out, and she never knew if he'd heard them. The brigand toppled from his knees, falling on his side with a rattling groan, and lay silent.

Sharantyr looked down at the flapping tatters of her forearm leathers, watched the bright blood dripping from her elbow, and shook her head. She must be getting old.

Elminster stood up slowly and brushed leaves from the chest of his robes with hands that shook only a little. Then he looked at the lady in leathers, the beginning of a smile at the corners of his lips. In his hand was his purse, plucked up from where it had fallen when the brigands had cut it away. From it he'd taken a vial of clear liquid that he held out to her, nodding at her arm.

"I wondered, for a time, if life was still worth the living. It is, and I thank you for saving mine to run awhile longer." Elminster looked around at the trees and added quietly, "How much longer, I wonder?" He shrugged.

"Old Mage," Sharantyr asked, as he knew she would, "why did you not use your magic? I've seen you lay low Zhent soldiers by the armful. Zhentarim who hurled spells against you, even! What befell?"

Elminster looked away for a long moment. Then his eyes met hers calmly and he said levelly, "My magic is lost to me. All of it—gone."

Silence hung between them for a moment as they stood in the leaves looking at each other. Without taking her eyes off his, Sharantyr uncorked and drained the vial. Then she asked, "If you will tell me, what will you do now?"

Elminster looked far off for a moment. Then he sighed and said softly, "I've a lot of neglected reading to be about. Perhaps in the palace library in Silverymoon, and in the Heralds' Holdfast, to start with. And then . . . I used to harp, once."

"Long ago?" Sharantyr asked lightly, using the toe of her boot to roll over the body of one she'd slain and bending smoothly to salvage a dagger.

"Aye, under the skilled teaching of a fair lady," the Old Mage replied.

"Fairer than me?" Sharantyr teased, holding out the dagger to him.

It hung in the air between them for a long, silent breath as their eyes met. Elminster's hand slowly reached out. The Old Mage took the dagger as gingerly as one handles a bloody corpse when dressed in finery, and said slowly, "My memory says yes, but what are mind images beside living beauty? She's long dust, now."

Sharantyr took his elbow and led him firmly to where the brigands had tethered their horses. "Long ago? How long ago was this?"

"In Myth Drannor before it fell," Elminster replied in a voice that was almost a whisper, his eyes on something far away and long ago.

He felt Sharantyr's arms move gently around him, the warmth of her leather-clad body against his shoulders. "Oh, Old Mage," she said tenderly into his neck, "I wish you well. You deserve fairer than this."

"I'll be all right," Elminster said firmly. "Stop soaking my robes with tears, look ye! They cost me three silver pieces, they did, in—" He fell silent and then added, "Well, in a place gone now."

Then he snorted. "Which is where we'll be, if we stand about sobbing until winter finds us here." He grinned suddenly. "Aye, lass, I'll be all right."

* * * * *

There came a knock on the door—not the first time that had happened, nor yet the last. Lhaeo opened it without delay, his eyes anxious.

Storm stood on the doorstep with two men he'd not seen before, so Lhaeo spoke to her in simpering tones. "Well met, Lady Storm. How does this fair morn find thee?"

"Restless to speak with the Lord Elminster," Storm replied crisply, with a wink. "Is he within?"

Lhaeo's eyes warned her. "Nay, Lady," he said softly. "He is gone, alone, this dawn, walking and troubled. You know why. Look to the trees. I have no doubt you'll find him therein."

With a look, Storm collected the two silent men at her side and bowed. "Our thanks, Lhaeo. We go. Those who harp will look out for the Old Mage."

Lhaeo bowed in his turn and said, "My thanks for that, and farewell. I hope to see you all again, in happier meetings."

He went in and the door closed. Itharr and Belkram looked at Storm, than at each other, and spoke at once.

"Is *that* Elminster's scribe?"

"What now, Lady?"

Storm looked at them both. "Be not hasty in judgment of Elminster's true friend," she said calmly. "He is not as he appears, for good reasons, and he is very worried for the safety of Elminster. The task I set you both now, friends, is the guarding of the Old Mage wherever you find him. Go now and seek him out."

Itharr looked at her. "You will not be with us, Lady?"

A shadow passed across Storm's face for just a moment. She looked at them both, and suddenly it seemed as if she were about to cry. Then she shrugged. Her hand dropped to the hilt of her blade and clenched about it like a thing of iron.

"I cannot. I want to, very much, but this thing I must not do. Itharr, Belkram, please believe me. There is a good reason that I cannot be with you in this."

"The burden of Mystra?" Belkram asked, very quietly. The taller of the two Harpers, he had frozen into treelike immobility but for the flashing of his keen eyes.

Storm looked at him in silence, her face going slowly white.

"I read a lot," Belkram added, almost defiantly. "Always old books, the sort others have forgotten. You learn more that way."

Storm nodded very slowly. "Be very, very careful," she said to him in a voice that trembled a little, "Belkram of Everlund. The things you know could kill you very quickly if the wrong folk hear."

"Such as myself?" Itharr asked half in jest. The shorter, burly Harper spread his hands in a wry "gods, why me?" gesture.

Storm looked from one man to the other and then threw strong arms around them both and swept them into an embrace. Three chins touched. She bestowed two swift kisses, looked deep into both sets of eyes so close to hers—at least one owner blushed—and said briskly, "Go now. Take much care, and come back alive to tell me what has befallen. Hurry! For all his years, Elminster walks fast and can find trouble as well as men half his age. Or less," she added meaningfully. "Tymora smile upon thee. Which reminds me: Trust in no magic nor any god or goddess, for strangeness is afoot."

"As usual," Itharr answered solemnly as they drew blades and saluted her in a flash of steel. "Our thanks, Lady. I shall never forget crossing blades with thee."

"Nor I," Belkram added simply. "If you grow lonely, mind, and want a man about the place . . ."

Storm laughed and shooed them on their way. "Get you gone! Elminster waits for no man, nor woman!"

* * * * *

Sharantyr looked about. They had come to a land of wild ridges, trees, and winding, steep cart tracks linking overgrown farms. "Where are we? Northwest of Shadowdale, I know, but—"

"Dagger Wood," Elminster said briefly. "Daggerdale begins over that way." He waved to the northwest. "Not a place to be caught out in by night."

"Shall I find us a place to sleep?" The lady ranger looked about. "Or go hunting? I had no time to find food, and it looks as if you brought none."

"I never do," Elminster replied. "It's the work of but a thought and—" He fell silent, then whispered, "And a little magic."

Sharantyr's only reply was a firm, wordless clasp of his shoulder. Then she was gone, with the whispered words "Wait here" floating back to him. Elminster snorted, took a long stride after her, then stopped, shrugged, and felt for his pipe. Trust the lass to choose a place with no stump to sit on.

*   *   *   *   *

It was nearly dark before she returned. Two plump rabbits hung in one hand; the other held berries, mushrooms, and other things Elminster couldn't remember the names of. "My apologies for the length of our parting," Sharantyr said. "This land is wild indeed. Twice I've had to dodge orc arrows, and—But ne'er mind. Come, Old Mage. I've found us a camp."

Elminster rose, smiled at her, and extended a hand for the rabbits. "You may need a free arm to swing a sword," he said impatiently. Dangling the rabbits before his eyes, he asked, "Dare we have fire?"

Sharantyr shrugged. "There'll be others about, no doubt."

"The orcs ye met?"

"They'll bother no folk again," was the calm reply. Elminster looked at her slim, strong shoulders expressionlessly and followed her down into a wooded gully.

"Magic gone for a day, and already I'm being ordered about by women," he said gruffly. Sharantyr cast a look back over her shoulder, and he winked. Shaking her head, she hastened on through a thicket of small trees whose branches caught at them both.

Elminster grumbled and flailed along in her wake. Sharantyr's blade reached back from time to time to hold aside the worst of the barbed branches.

They came out into a little open space that faced the setting sun. Below them the land fell away into a smooth-sloped hollow. It had once been a farm—Elminster could see the line of a ruined fence—but youngish trees now grew in its fields. The gaping, vine-cloaked ruins of a timber-and-stone house and barn rose on a far slope. Sharantyr nodded at them with her chin and said, "Come on. Let's get off this height. We can be seen for miles."

"Can't an old man even enjoy the sunset?" Elminster grumbled, trotting obediently after her.

"That depends on whether or not you want to live to see another sunset after this one," Sharantyr replied in low, wry tones. Elminster remembered a gesture from very long ago and made it in her general direction.

Sharantyr only grinned and said fondly, "Now, you *know* I'm too young to know what that means," and led him down a twisting, overgrown trail that took them by stones across a little brook, and up again to the waiting, gloomy ruins ahead.

Sharantyr looked at him in the gathering darkness. "Best move and speak quietly from now on. Can you cook?"

"If ye light the fire," Elminster replied, glancing at the rabbits again.

Sharantyr said only, "Wood," in reply and was gone again.

* * * * *

In the twilight, two Harpers stood over four dead men. "Not long gone," Itharr said, "and this one died by a dagger."

"Lawless men," Belkram agreed, on his knees beside another body. "And not robbed of the few coins they carried, either." He frowned. "We've found no other trace of him, and Storm did say he collected trouble as roaming cats find fleas."

Itharr grunted. "By the looks of this—if it was him—we're being sent to guard a marauding tiger, not a feeble old man."

"What think you? Is this a false trail?"

Itharr shrugged. "It's all we've found. It must be his doing, or he and another. There was a lot of running about here, and he may have someone else with him."

Belkram shrugged. "In these woods, we'll lose any trail in the dark, unless he plans to mark his passage with brigands' bodies every hundred paces or so."

They chuckled together. "That'd take a lot of brigands," Itharr replied. "We'd best drag these a good way off, to keep wolves and such from the tracks we'll want to find tomorrow."

Belkram nodded, and they worked swiftly, dragging the bodies all in the same direction, toward and then around thick stands of trees, to a spot where it was unlikely any survivors of the fray had headed. When the bodies had been removed, the two Harpers retired to the dale again, camping near ruined Castle Grimstead, behind the new temples that had been raised west of the river.

"We could be under Storm's roof this night," Belkram said softly after a time. Itharr looked at him and said nothing but grinned very slowly. After a moment, Belkram matched the expression.

A good walk away, in the dark woods, wolves wore similar grins as they came warily to four sprawled bodies and began to feed.

*   *   *   *   *

The fire was long out. Sharantyr and Elminster lay shoulder to shoulder in the darkness, wrapped in their cloaks, awake but unspeaking. Around them, the small night noises of hunting animals rustled, hooted, and from time to time squeaked or snarled. They lay still, like two breathing stones, and hoped the night would pass them by.

Suddenly, close by to the north, there came into being a glowing radiance in the trees. One moment it was not there, and the next it was. Magic.

Wordlessly they struggled up and pulled on their

boots. Sharantyr drew her sword but held her cloak up in front of it to ward off any flashing reflections. Elminster stepped to one side and melted into the dark shadow of what was left of a wall.

The glowing had begun as pale amber in hue. It brightened now and swirled, at times more ruddy, at times almost green. Perhaps forty paces away, across rising ground, the glow hung in a little clearing amid the trees, forming an upright oval in the air.

A mage-gate, without doubt. A moment later, a hard-eyed, wary man in the black armor of Zhentil Keep stepped out of the gate, a loaded crossbow ready in his hands. Behind him, a black-bladed saber appeared in the light, followed by the one who held it: another Zhentilar soldier.

The two warriors stepped forward, twisting to look all around, weapons held ready. A moment later, another man emerged from the flickering oval. This one wore robes of rich purple, a cruel expression, and a short, pointed black beard. He carried a wand in one hand and was followed by a third armored soldier.

The mage and his bodyguard stepped forward together. In the center of a protective ring of bodies, the bearded mage held the wand loosely in his hands. It shifted almost lazily back and forth, then seemed to quiver in his hands and point directly at where Sharantyr stood, unmoving, cloaked in darkness. A moment later the wand turned a bit to indicate where Elminster hid.

The mage hissed something, and the guards closed ranks in front of him, weapons coming up, facing the ruined farmhouse. There was a half-seen gesture from behind them, and suddenly the night was lit as bright as day, and Elminster and Sharantyr were staring right into the eyes of the four men.

The looks directed back at them were not pleasant. In the sudden silence they all heard one of the guards ask, "Lord?"

The man in purple replied clearly, "Kill them, of course."

4
Doom Strolls In

There was an instant of tense silence as everyone drew breath together. Then battle began, a race toward death that rent the night with the clangor of drawn arms and the roaring of unleashed magic.

The bearded mage obviously thought he faced only two travelers who'd been unfortunate enough to choose a sleeping place where they could not help but witness the gate, and must therefore be eliminated. He was not expecting another wizard and did not care to expend any more magic than he'd used this night already.

So he did nothing but watch as two of the black-armored guards lumbered forward warily, the one with the crossbow a little in the lead, and the other, blade out, keeping watchfully to one side. They came for Sharantyr first, no doubt judging her older companion to be in hiding out of weakness or fear.

Drawn steel they knew the strength of, and they were two against one and larger. Besides, this woman seemed atremble with fear and barely knew how to hold her blade, much less use it. She bit her lip as they advanced, and took a slow, unwilling step back.

The guard with the crossbow grinned and stepped to one side, Elminster's side, to a spot where he could fell either one of them. His companion came on toward Sharantyr to greet her with his drawn sword and a cold grin. She was pretty. Perhaps she need not die quickly.

He caught his friend's eye and jerked his head toward the old man, indicating that a quarrel would make short work of him now, leaving just the wench. The old man shuffled sideways a little, looking helpless.

The guard with the crossbow nodded and raised his weapon to take aim. It was then he saw that the old man was smiling.

The sleeve fell away from Elminster's hand, and lightning cut the world in two.

In the flash and sharp crack of the striking bolt, the crossbow jerked. Its bolt shot high into the night and away. The man in black armor danced briefly as crackling death played over him, then slumped to his knees and from there toppled to one side, lifeless. Smoke rose from his blackened helm.

Sharantyr waited calmly for the other man to reach her. Her eyes flicked only briefly to the mage beyond, for she knew why Elminster had waited. His bolt had traveled on from the guard with the crossbow to crackle its deadly way around both the third guard and the bearded man in purple. No one was standing by the flickering gate now. Black armor twitched feebly on the ground.

Elminster walked toward the gate, ignoring the last guard. That man had stopped, looking all around. His gaze swung back to Sharantyr. She was moving steadily forward now, a faint smile on her lips, all trace of nervousness gone. His comrades lay fallen where they had stood. The old man was strolling past as though nothing had occurred, too close to avoid his blade.

The guard cast a last look at Sharantyr, judged he could slay the old man and have time to turn back and meet the wildest charge she might make. He spun about, and in two swift strides his blade was reaching for the old man.

The wand, firing crosswise under Elminster's arm, spoke again. Lightning struck the Zhentilar full in the chest, plucking him from his feet and hurling him backward. He fell heavily, arms and legs flopping. Smoke rose from where he lay.

Sharantyr shook her head. "There's nothing like giving the wolves a cooked feast," she observed.

Elminster turned his head. "Both of these two yet live. Slay the mage, lest he work the same tricks I did, and we'll discourse pleasantly together with the last one awhile."

Sharantyr did as she was bid. Her eyes were hard but

her voice trembled a little as she said, "Well, that was easy work. Too easy, perhaps. Should we not move a pace or two away from this magic?"

Elminster shrugged. "Move around behind it, perhaps. After we've disarmed and trammeled this one a bit to stop him moving, and taken what we can from the others."

"Yes," Sharantyr said. "Of course." Her voice was grim. Elminster reached out a long arm to touch her shoulder.

"Is killing hard for ye?" he asked quietly.

"No," Sharantyr replied as softly, her eyes meeting his. "Not anymore. That bothers me, sometimes."

Elminster nodded. "So long as it bothers ye, 'tis well. When it does not, the problems begin. I'll draw the fangs of the living one, if ye'll rob the dead ones. Age hath its privileges, and choosing the nobler task is one."

She raised a dark eyebrow. "What? Elminster of Shadowdale choosing the nobler task? Are my ears ensorcelled?"

Elminster sighed. "Mockery," he observed heavily, "seems the paramount privilege of youth."

"Youth?" Sharantyr dimpled, and raised a hand to her hair coquettishly. "Why, thank you."

Elminster snorted. "Get on with it, lass. I'd like to speak to this one while he yet lives. I think the mage recognized me before he died."

"Which means?"

"Old foes. The Zhentarim, almost certainly." The Old Mage heard his battle companion hiss, raised his eyebrows, and continued. "Others, too, perhaps. And with me not at my best."

Sharantyr laid a hand on his arm. "We make a good team, Old Mage. Worry not."

Elminster rolled his eyes and opened his mouth to reply. Then he stiffened and his face changed.

Sharantyr's blade rose. "Elminster? Wha—magic? Attacking you?"

The Old Mage waved his hands in a weak negative. His face was paler than it had been, and he sighed heavily.

"Glad I am, lass, that we were through with that"—he pointed at the bodies around—"ere this befell."

"What is it? Are you well?"

Elminster nodded a little wearily. Sharantyr saw that his forehead was wet with sweat.

"Some power has left me. Azuth or Mystra or her successor . . . calling on it. Not a hostile thing, but disconcerting all the same." He looked up. "Well? Have ye turned out the boots and purses of the departed yet?"

Sharantyr grimaced. "Old Mage," she added very quietly, "there are things I must know first."

Elminster rolled his eyes again. "There always are," he agreed pleasantly, and waited.

Sharantyr made another face. "Elminster," she said, pointing with her blade, "you were deadly enough with that wand just now. Tell me, if we're to walk together awhile, just what magic do you carry? What does it do and, if worst befalls, can I use any of it? If so, how?"

Elminster's hand rose with exaggerated feebleness. "Wait, wait," he protested in the effete tones of a Sembian dandy. "I never can keep track of more than two questions at a time. There ought to be a law, to keep wenches down to asking just two of each man until they're answered."

Sharantyr just looked at him.

Elminster grinned and said, "All right. Ye are right to ask, and should know. Of what I carry, ye can use only the wand in my right boot—it hurls magic missiles: one missile if ye think the word *alag* and two if ye think *baulgoss*; my belt flask, which contains an elixir of health—ye know, cures disease, poison, an' all that; and the rings I wear, which work without any guidance on thy part. One allows ye to land lightly after any fall, and the other turns away some spells. There's another ring in my purse; it heals wounds when worn. It works but slowly, mind ye, so don't go being heroic. Got all that?"

Sharantyr looked at him again. Then she looked up at the night sky overhead and told the stars, "There ought to be a law . . ."

Elminster chuckled. "I also have the wand of lightnings ye saw and my pipe, which holds a trick or two. Naught else."

Sharantyr raised an eyebrow. "No? You surprise me. How you can stagger along under the weight of all that and look at me long-faced to say you have no magic is beyond all belief."

Elminster chuckled. "Baubles, lass. At least, until thy life depends on them and all else is gone"—his smile died suddenly—"as it has gone." Then he thought of something more. "Another thing: All of these trinkets are old and may not work as others ye have seen."

"Old? How old?"

"Ah, well, Myth Drannan, most of them."

Sharantyr sighed. "I'll just go and see to robbing these corpses, shall I?"

Elminster got out his pipe. "Not a moment sooner than I thought ye would," he grunted, watching the flickering gate.

Sharantyr gestured rudely at him with her sword and went to the farthest body. Strangling was the most fitting fate for mages. No, shutting several of them up in a room together to drive each other mad with their testy, interminable drivel—ahem, eloquence. Yes. That would be best. She had to survive all this to get to Berdusk and suggest the process to a few Harpers. It would definitely be a service to civilized folk everywhere.

* * * * *

Among them, the dead men had carried no more than a handful of coins, assorted daggers, two skins of water, two metal flasks containing what Sharantyr suspected were magical healing potions, and—on the wizard of course—a plain brass ring and a belt purse holding only a rusted, hand-size iron sphere.

Elminster's eyes lit at the sight of the sphere. "Devised long ago by Azuth himself," he said with satisfaction. "Those who use his truename can command any of these spheres, even if they don't know the command word of the particular sphere."

"And you know Azuth's truename?"

Elminster looked hurt. "Of course."

Sharantyr sighed. Of course. "So who was this Bilarro whom such spheres are named for?"

"A later, lesser mage," Elminster sniffed. "He saw one such sphere, learned through diligence and much misadventure how to make his own, and retired fat and rich on the proceeds of a life of selling such baubles to every swordsman fearful of magic. I've heard that a treacherous apprentice used one on him in the end, and cast him into a nearby pond to see if he could swim. But that may be just a tavern tale."

Sharantyr sighed again. Did wizards spend all their lives scheming and keeping score? She looked around at the night-shrouded trees, the ruins, and the glowing, flickering oval of light. Nothing moved. Firm schooling took her on a careful walk around the edge of the area lit by the gate, looking into the night more carefully. She could see no life, no lurking menace, but her sword did not leave her hand.

"Old Mage," she said as she rejoined Elminster, "let us make haste. I do not think it wise to tarry here overlong."

"And ye are right," he agreed grandly. Sharantyr was raising an annoyed eyebrow and parting her lips to speak before he slowly winked.

"It's a wonder," the lady ranger murmured to the guard, as she bent over to take him by the armpits and drag him around behind the glowing gate, "why anyone puts up with archmages long enough to let them reach their advanced powers. You'd think a lot more of them would be drowned or strangled—or have their tongues torn out by the roots—before they'd been a year or two at their studies."

The guard, flopping limply and heavily in her grasp, did not reply.

* * * * *

Elminster seemed to take a very long time getting ready to question the last guard. Sharantyr had removed the man's gauntlets, helm, and belt, using the latter to tie his hands together. After examining the mage's body thoroughly for hidden weapons or items that might be magical, she dumped it atop the guard, pinning his arms and midsection under its weight. Elminster nodded approvingly but kept on examining their booty, muttering to himself and making faces.

At length he opened both vials, sniffed them with the air of a connoisseur, tasted what his fingertip found of both, and said, "These heal, and as far as I can tell do naught else. Ye carry them both, for ye may well have more need of them." He grinned reassuringly and said, "Carry the mage's ring, also, but do not put it on. Keep it hidden in thy belt, to show as a token from him should we need such a ruse. We dare not try to use it."

Sharantyr took the proffered items and laid a hand on the Old Mage's arm. Her eyes were dark and serious.

"Elminster," she asked, "should you be getting into this sort of struggle—with mages you do not know and gates that go you know not where—in your present, ah, vulnerable condition?"

Elminster glared at her for a moment and shrugged. "Ye're young yet, Shar. Ye can't know. 'Tis not pride that makes me poke my nose into all affairs of Art that I come across. 'Tis what I am and what I do. When ye live as long as I have and have seen thy friends, foes, and homes all swept away, one after another, with the endless passing years, all that is left is what ye believe in and strive for. I dare not stay in Shadowdale, to bring danger down on it, but I'll not run away to cower or hide, daring nothing."

He patted her hand where it rested on his arm, then gently pulled free to face her. "Crawl off into a hole and die before I'm dead? Nay, this is what I stand for, and what I'll do."

Sharantyr nodded. "I meant no offense. I'm sorry. I wanted to learn your will, ere we were swept away into battles again."

Elminster grinned suddenly. "And I've told thee, as usual. Thy ears must grow very weary of my voice."

Sharantyr smiled faintly. "Such words would never pass my lips," she said with affected dignity. Then she added slyly, "but I often think them. Love stays my tongue."

" 'Tis a rare love that does that," Elminster said feelingly. He chuckled and said, "Shall we slap this fellow awake and treat ye to more of my tongue?"

Sharantyr grinned. "We shall. I'm getting too old to need sleep at night."

Elminster winced. "I'll be as swift as I can be." He laid a warning finger on his lips to bid her be silent. Unclipping his belt flask, he held it upside down over the guard's head, loosening the stopper so that a thin stream splashed on the man's forehead and ran down into his eyes.

The warrior shuddered, wrinkled his eyes convulsively. He snorted and awoke, knuckling his eyes and moaning.

"Well met," Elminster said briskly. "Thy name?"

"Mulser," the man said, and groaned. "I—it burns inside!"

"Those who defy the lords of Zhentil Keep must pay the price," Elminster said sharply. "This gate ye came here by, where does it lead?"

"Zhentil—? You are of the Brotherhood?"

"Aye," Elminster said solemnly. "My name is both near and dear to Lord Manshoon. I speak with authority that bows only to his word."

"Gods," the man groaned, and drew a trembling breath. "I . . . hurt, Lord. I . . . I'll try to serve you, but I fear I can't"—he struggled for a moment and then fell back with a groan—"can't rise," he gasped, sweating.

Elminster laid a hand on his forehead. "Rest and lie still. Answer my questions; that is all ye need do."

When he brought his hand away again, Sharantyr saw that it glistened with the man's sweat. The Old Mage bent close to the man and asked, "This gate, Mulser. Where did ye come from?"

The man gasped for breath a moment and then said, "The—the High Dale. Lord, why do you not know this?"

"It appears," Elminster said in heavy, sinister tones, "that some among us have seen fit to act on their own, as it were. Word of these doings has only just reached my ears. I need you, Mulser, to tell me who of the Brotherhood is in the High Dale, and what exactly befalls there. Speak freely. I value honesty, not toadying words. Tell me, now, who is master in the dale?"

"H-Heladar Longspear, Lord."

"He is of us?"

"A Zhentilar like myself, Lord. He served in the taking of the Citadel, and in Daggerdale. He is hard, but a good blade."

"Which mages back him?"

"Angruin Stormcloak gives him his orders."

"Angruin Myrvult?" Elminster sounded surprised.

"Aye, Lord."

"He's come far. Where does he get *his* orders?"

"Zhentil Keep itself, Lord." The man's breathing grew labored again, and he coughed weakly. When his voice came again, it was fainter. "I don't know who he reports to . . . not my right to know."

"How many wizards and apprentices are under Angruin?"

"Ahh—I can't think, Lord. Pardon, if you will . . . There's Hcarla; he's a bad one. I don't think even his mother ever trusted him. Then there's Sabryn, who was with us here. Is he—?"

"I'll deal with him later," Elminster said coldly. "Go on. These are the mages of power?"

"Those, and a quiet one called Nordryn."

"Any others?"

"Four lesser. Two who rode to battle in Daggerdale: Mrinden and Kalassyn. They're all right, and can hurl fire or lightning if called on."

"The last two?"

"Apprentices, sneaks and noses-in-the-air. Haragh and Ildomyl. They mostly do gate-guard duty on the roads."

"And how many swords does Longspear command, loyal warriors like yourself?"

"I . . . know not, Lord. Forty, perhaps. Not many more. With perhaps a dozen hireswords, mainly crossbowmen . . . from Sembia." Mulser groaned again.

"Easy, Mulser," Elminster said, patting his shoulder gently. "Rest easy. Tell me, what does Longspear, as ruler of the High Dale, have you men do?"

"We . . . we take passage tolls, Lord. One copper a head, two coppers a horse or mule, and two silver falcons per wagon. No priests or wizards are allowed in. All who carry magic must yield it to us until they leave. All who enter must pay. We've already had to escort envoys from Sem—urrghh—Sembia and Cormyr, complaining about the tolls."

"Why don't merchants just go around you, using the road through Daerlun?"

"I've been told," Mulser said, cynical humor dryly audible through the rough pain in his voice, "that the brigands are particularly bad just now. They're . . . in the Vast Swamp, Lord, and hired by whoever in the Brotherhood has sponsored Stormcloak. The road is . . . too dangerous for passage without heavy escorts. No lone wagons get through."

Elminster chuckled coldly. "I see how the land rises and falls. How are the dalefolk taking your presence?"

"It's fairly quiet, Lord. They hold no love for us. They call us bladesmen the 'Wolves,' but they're mostly old men. Since Stormcloak made an example of the high constable, they've knuckled under." He coughed again and added weakly, "We had to kill the constables and their archers, of course, to take the place."

"And the wizards?" Elminster's voice was suddenly like a sword blade sheathed in ice.

"I—we found none, Lord, so far as I know. Only a couple of fat old priests. Longspear has them locked up in the High Castle."

"Your barracks is there?"

"N—no . . . aghhh . . . Sorry, Lord. my barracks is up north of the castle, near this gate . . . the other end of it I mean, Lord . . ."

"But most of the bladesmen are at the castle?"

"No, less than half. Most are in Eastkeep or Westkeep, and there's another four barracks like mine. All the others are at the castle, yes."

"Are there any priests of the Brotherhood with you?"

Mulser was silent a long time, frowning. Then he said slowly, "Now that's curious, Lord. Saragh was saying to me just yesterday that he'd seen none with us in the taking, and we've neither of us seen any since. If there are any Dread Brothers there now, they're keeping well hidden."

"I see. Is there anything else of importance to the Brotherhood, Mulser, that ye think ye should tell me?"

Mulser coughed again, weakly, and shook his head. "I . . . don't think so, Lord. If there's any secrets in the dale, I know them not."

"Ye've been most helpful, Mulser, a credit to the Brotherhood. It has been many long years since anyone in our ranks has been so honest with me. Ye've done well."

"Thank you, Lord." Mulser's breath came in gasps now. "I . . . I thought I'd nothing to lose, Lord. I know I'm done for, an' . . . and I'd rather talk to you, than . . . go alone."

"Ye're not alone, good Mulser," Elminster said gravely. "Have you any family? A lass? Anyone we should send word to?"

"N-no. I thought . . . so . . . once, but—" The laboring, wheezing voice suddenly caught. Mulser made a little bubbling, choking sound and fell silent. Elminster looked into the warrior's eyes until they stopped seeing anything, then got up stiffly and said, "Go to the gods in peace, Mulser."

Sharantyr's eyes were tender yet angry. "You were kind to him," she said. Elminster shrugged. "And yet," she added slowly, "he is a Zhentilar, one of the Black Blades that have spent years carving up the Dales and the dalefolk that live in them. One of those we must fight every season. Zhentilar chained me as a slave, once. I was running from their cruelties when the drow took me."

Elminster touched her arm. "I've seen ye strike down Zhentilar before, right eagerly. Does doing so heal any of those memories?"

Sharantyr's eyes were dark as she said coldly, "No. Not yet." She lifted the naked sword that lay across her knees and added, "But 'tis not for lack of trying."

The old wizard sighed. " 'Tis not my place to judge. All of us are driven by things. Even this poor soldier." He nudged Mulser's body with his foot. "One of my tasks is to strike down the evil folk who drove him on, those who command the Black Blades. Such foes make the Zhentarim truly dangerous."

"If you're going to keep on at that task, I'll fight beside you with a right good will," Sharantyr said fiercely.

They regarded each other in silence for a breath, then the Old Mage turned away.

"Come," he said shortly. "We must hide these dead men and go on." He strode away into the night almost angrily, and Sharantyr looked after him with concern.

Elminster went only a little way, growled, and came back looking fierce. "My pardon, please, lass," he said grimly. " 'Tis a churl's act to make thee do all the carrion heaving alone."

Sharantyr, puffing under Mulser's dead weight, said only, "Take his feet, then."

They spent a few uncomfortable breaths puffing and struggling in the darkness and then were done. The bodies lay in a corner of the ruins where two walls met, buried under all the rubble Sharantyr could shift: stones, old beams, tiles, and a few tangled creepers.

Elminster walked slowly back and looked at the oval of floating, glowing light. Sharantyr rolled her eyes, breast heaving with her efforts, and set the last large rock on the pile before going after him.

"Well," she panted, as she joined him, "what now?"

Elminster smiled at her mildly, gestured at the gate flickering silently before him, and then calmly strolled through it.

* * * * *

They were somewhere dark. Out of the night above and ahead of them came a hissing crossbow bolt. Elminster calmly shoved Sharantyr to one side and leapt the other way. The quarrel hissed past.

They were crouching on turf, with mountains rising at their backs and far ahead of them. Just ahead, the ground descended into the High Dale. From the trees there came another bolt, this one close enough to stir Elminster's thinning hair though he was well away from the gate's glow. The shaft must have been fired blind.

Then from the trees came the unmistakable booming sound of an alarm gong, the finest brass-and-drum sort sold in Sembia for a gold piece each.

"Oh, *dung*," Elminster said clearly into the night. From somewhere off to his left he heard a snort as Sharantyr stifled a giggle. Elminster rolled his eyes and trotted forward. The sentinel *would* have to be up a tree, now that the heroic archmage of Shadowdale was getting a bit too old for climbing trees in the dark. Oh, dung and double dung, indeed.

5

Alarms, and
Adventure Found

Sharantyr had expected trouble on the other side of
the gate. A temple or gloomy spell chamber, perhaps,
crowded with evil-looking men and weird, gibbering creatures who slunk, slithered, or prowled the lengths of
their chains—or worse, prowled unleashed.

She'd expected trouble, and Elminster had not failed
her. They'd found it.

Instead of a castle or cavern, they stood under the open
sky between two mountain ranges. By the stars, they
were south and a little west of Shadowdale, and she was
facing south. Here it was a fair, clear night with a cool
breeze blowing gently from the east. The grass under her
feet descended to trees, the source of their trouble: an
alarm gong and someone who had fired two ready crossbows dangerously well. Or more than one someone.

That thought kept Shar crouched low as she ran forward across the little dell, dodging but heading to the
left, trying to get as far as possible from the amber radiance of the gate behind her. The gong sounded again, a
faster, repeated ringing as if the sentinel were scared.
Wise of him.

Sharantyr's rapid progress brought her to the lip of the
dell. A track—grassy and rutted, wide enough for carts—
descended toward barnlike buildings, lamplight, and, in
the distance amid a torchlit cluster of buildings at the
bottom of the valley, the unmistakable walls of a small,
stout old castle.

A faint crackling of branches warned her of the guard's
descent and probable attack. Sharantyr turned to face
the sound and shrank farther to the left into the concealing shadow of bushes. What was Elminster doing?

More crackling. The guard was descending a wooden

ladder, snapping branches aside in his haste. Sharantyr tried to look like part of the night, her blade held low and ready in her own shadow, her head bowed to keep her eyes small and screened by her hair. Soon . . . soon . . . Now!

The guard was hurrying the last few steps. His haste would carry him right past her. His gaze could not help but fall on her, and he could stick her with anything long and sharp he might have before she could even land a blow. Gods spit on us all!

A familiar, testy voice came out of the night from the other side of the ladder, behind the descending guard. "I'm over here, by the gods! Who taught ye to shoot a crossbow, anyway, Manshoon himself?"

Sharantyr didn't blame the guard. She could not have heard that taunt and failed to turn and look. The shadowy man pivoted as he landed, blade sweeping around to confront the unseen speaker. Sharantyr rose out of the night from behind him like a hungry shadow. Her hand jerked his head back sharply, covering his mouth and robbing him of breath at the same time. Her blade flashed as she drew it sideways with cold precision, and she ducked low to keep most of the blood out of her hair.

"Done this before, have ye?" Elminster asked out of the darkness. Sharantyr sighed loudly and shook her head as the man died in her arms.

"Old Mage," she hissed in anger. "Must you?"

Elminster spread innocent hands. "I'm not sure what ye're on about, this time, but we have only breaths before whatever comrades this fellow has—er, had—respond to his gong. Flip him over and drag him by the feet, facedown, to the gate. I want a trail of blood even a blind Calishite couldn't miss. Where'd he drop his crossbow? Ah, I have it. Come!"

Sharantyr did as she was bid. In the flickering light of the gate, Elminster's face was intent as he crouched low. "Down, lass. Against the light ye make a most fetching target, I must say, but 'tis not the time. Got thy dagger handy? Good. Make ye the Harper marks for 'Trap Ahead' and 'Keep Low' on his breast."

"On flesh or his leathers?"

"Leathers, lass, leathers. Harpers have to read 'em, mind, and they're apt to be as blind as the next cow, in the dark."

Sharantyr swiftly cut the two diagonally crossed inverted **T** shapes that warned of a trap, and then the circle bisected by a horizontal line, with a parallel line atop it, that warned observing Harpers to keep their bodies low.

Elminster nodded critically, laid the crossbow across the man's legs, and asked, "Head or feet?"

Sharantyr swiftly said, "Feet for me. Your turn for the blood."

Elminster wrinkled his nose. Together they lifted the body, swung it twice, and tossed it faceup into the oval of light. It passed through soundlessly and was gone. Sharantyr had to grin when Elminster bent to peek under the oval to make sure that the body wasn't just lying on the ground behind it. The grass was bare.

The wizard rose in a smooth pivot that brought him around facing the guard tree again. "Quick, lass. Show me the ladder," he growled, trotting across the grass again.

"The name's Shar, old man," Sharantyr told him, amused. He merely grunted. She raced past him with smooth strides in the darkness and laid her hand on the ladder. "Here."

"Right. Now find me the first tree in that direction ye can climb," he ordered, pointing west along the edge of the dell. Sharantyr gave him a look that he saw most of as she passed, but he merely grinned and followed her, taking out the wand that spat lightnings and muttering something over it.

The lady ranger turned, hand on hip, only her face visible in the darkness. "Here. Is that someone coming?"

"Undoubtedly. Take this"—he handed her the wand, butt-first—"and this." Into the same hand he put a strangling-wire taken from inside his boot.

Sharantyr frowned. "Where'd you—no, strike that. I don't want to know."

"Wise of ye. Take the wand up the tree and affix it there, somewhere sturdy where its aim won't slip with wind or working loose. I want it pointing squarely at the gate, and ye back down here, in a breath or less."

"Oh, yes, Lord," she said in mocking, breathless tones. Elminster grinned and patted some unseen part of her as she climbed past, stepping swiftly back to avoid a kick that did not come.

He bent his head to listen and heard again the hurrying thud of boots and creaking of leather and metal armor that meant death was swiftly coming up the track for them.

He got his other wand into his hand, just to be wise and ready. There was a thump beside him, and Sharantyr was coming back to her feet after her leap, breathing heavily. He took her hand.

"Done? Good, come!"

Together, hand in hand, they ran east. Sharantyr was astonished to find the Old Mage's long, scrawny legs twinkling ahead of hers, as swift as any stag, tugging her along faster across the dell. Abruptly Elminster's hand jerked her to the left along the line of trees, to where the rocks of the mountain began to rise.

"Here! Quick and quiet, now," Elminster panted. "Let's get as far as we can without making any noise." Together, like two heavily breathing shadows, they slipped away along the line of tumbled rocks, creeping and crawling where they had to, cushioning each other to avoid noisy falls, and more than once ending up face-to-face, gasping the same air in the darkness. Behind them they could see the torches and flashing blades, and hear occasional shouted orders of the large group of men-at-arms who were searching the dell and the trees around it.

"What now?" Sharantyr whispered into Elminster's ear as the rocky tongue of a mountain hid the last glimmers of torchlight from their view.

"We go on, east, the length of the dale," the Old Mage whispered back and turned to continue. "If the castle was down that track, we started from about halfway along the dale."

Sharantyr squeezed his shoulder, bringing him to a halt. "It's not that I don't mind losing an entire night's sleep fighting and running about," she whispered, "but I would like some answers, please."

Elminster nodded. "Ye shall have them, after we put another twenty breaths or so of travel behind us. I want no blades following us."

Sharantyr whispered back simply, "Lead on," and he did.

* * * * *

They crossed a small stream and another, babbling rivulets snaking amid the stones and winking back starlight beneath their feet. Elminster stopped finally, in a shadowed spot where they could sit on rocks and look out over a moonlit expanse of rock and scrub below, before the dark wall of the trees began.

"Ask, then," he bid her simply, passing his belt flask over.

Sharantyr wet her lips with its water. "The wand?"

"Most Myth Drannan wands can be speech-set."

Sharantyr chuckled softly and waited.

So did he, of course. She rolled her eyes. "Explain," she ordered flatly.

Elminster grinned in the darkness and said, "Unlike wands made today, ye can cause that wand of mine to unleash its magic by itself, with no hand upon it and no word spoken. Ye're familiar with the spell called 'magic mouth' by most? Aye, like that. When the conditions ye speak are met, the wand fires. I recalled that I'd never set that one—ye can only do it once—so I set it to discharge when someone in robes, or carrying a staff or wand, comes through the gate into the dale."

"Into—Ah, that's why the 'keep low' warning for Harpers. A nasty trap." Her last words had an edge to them.

Elminster looked at her closely. "Are ye all right, lass?"

Sharantyr shook her head angrily. "I'm just—Slaying Zhents is one thing, but killing people I have no quarrel with, and whose faces I haven't even seen, just doesn't sit well with me, that's all."

Elminster put a hand on her shoulder. "I'm sorry I've dragged ye into all this," he said quietly.

After a long, silent moment she put strong fingers over his and said as softly, "Don't be."

They sat together, silent and unmoving, for a long time.

After awhile, Elminster looked up at the stars, chuckled, and asked, "Can I have my hand back now, Shar?"

Sharantyr patted it and let it go. "I've another question, Old Mage."

" 'Elminster,' please. 'El,' if ye prefer. Ask."

"Aren't you worried about all those mages the guard told us about? Will they not find you by magic?"

"Nay, they can't find me. Those who bear Mystra's burden can't be put to sleep, held immobile, or commanded by magic that strikes at the mind. To all magic that searches, spies, or tries to control, we are simply not there."

"I thought thy amulet—the greenstone amulet like Storm wears—did that."

Elminster grinned. "I wear it to conceal those powers of the burden. Besides, if I wear it, I have it to give to a traveling companion in need of it. If I'd been wise enough to be wearing it when I went walking, I'd give it ye now."

Sharantyr's eyes were dark again. "Without it, how can I avoid being found by these prying magics?"

"Ah, yes." Elminster grinned and put a bony arm around her shoulders. "Now that's why these stars find ye and I hurrying about in the dark." He rose and tugged at her hand. "Come on," he said briefly, and she got up and went with him into the night.

* * * * *

"Nothing, sir," the ranking swordsman said, torchlight gleaming on his black armor.

"Do you mean," Mrinden said in a voice thick with incredulous rage, "that someone came through the gate, slew the watchman, and disappeared, all in the time it took us to get up the hill from the barracks? How stupid d'you think I am?"

"There's no trace of them, sir," the senior Sword replied stolidly. "They're either deep in the woods or are past us into the open dale already. Or they went back through *that*." He inclined his head toward the flickering gate. "You've seen the blood, sir."

Mrinden turned to Kalassyn. "Well?"

Kalassyn drew his fellow wizard into a face-to-face huddle and spoke in low tones. "If they're past us, we'll never find them. It's either a personal affair—a man, maybe even one of ours, bent on killing whomever we left on watch, for his own reasons—or a lone meddler who will turn up in the dale tomorrow. There's been no time to bring in a large band and hide them all or get away without us hearing. Most likely they went back through the gate."

Mrinden frowned. "That trail is just a mite obvious, isn't it?"

"A trap?"

Mrinden nodded.

Kalassyn shrugged. "We've no choice but to go through, unless you want to explain to Stormcloak or Bellwind why we did not. Sabryn went through earlier this evening, on some secret affair I'm not supposed to know the slightest thing about. Perhaps he needs help and tried to get to us."

"And the attempt ended in slaughter? That means we'll be walking into alert and waiting death!"

Kalassyn shrugged again. "You sound like one of the younger priests. What mage doesn't walk toward death, where'er he goes? Eh?"

Mrinden jerked his head about angrily to glare at the silently waiting men-at-arms. "We're going through the gate!" he snarled at them. "Form up in an arrow. I want twelve to remain behind and watch for any strangers in the trees. If you cross blades with anyone, send a band down to rouse the rest of the barracks. The rest of you, load crossbows and point them at the sky. Move!"

In weary silence the black-armored Wolves formed up, the senior Sword choosing the dozen who would stand rear guard. The two Zhentarim walked into the midst of the wedge of armed men, almost invisible in their black robes, and gestured curtly for the arrow to close around them, protecting their backs.

Mrinden addressed the men. "This gate is perfectly safe. Simply walk into it as if it weren't there. You'll set foot next in a wooded area where armed and ready foes may be waiting. Don't stop to gawk. If something moves, shoot it and move on in haste to let the rest of us through." He looked around. Expressionless black helms looked back at him. He drew in a deep breath. "Right, then move!"

Without an answering word, the black-armored dealers of death marched forward into the oval of waiting light.

* * * * *

"They've come this way," Itharr said, examining a faint heel mark of damp earth on a rock. "I'm sure of it."

"Elminster, aye, but who's the other?" Belkram asked, blade out, peering into the night-shrouded trees around them.

Itharr shrugged. "We'll find out, no doubt," he said dryly. "Come on." Silently they stalked on, alert and dangerous.

The two Harpers had been restless, unable to settle down for the night after they'd found Elminster's trail.

They'd been lying on the turf, heads pillowed on their boots, discussing where the Old Mage was most likely heading—northwest, it seemed, straight into the heart of lawless Daggerdale—when they'd both felt a peculiar creeping, prickling sensation. There was a sudden tension in their heads, a rising surge of power that slowly died away. This was followed by another flicker of force, then nothing.

"What was that?" Itharr asked, eyes wide.

"Strong magic unleashed," Belkram said. "I've felt it

that strongly only once before, in a battle near the Grey-cloak Hills against Zhents out of Darkhold, when the spellsinger Andarra was dying. She spent her life-force in a song that made all magic go wild, so Zhent wizards would have to fight, dagger and sword, like all others. We all felt the effect of her sacrifice."

"Strong magic," Itharr said slowly, eyes narrowing. "El-minster!" He rolled to his feet, wincing at the cold, and reached for his boots. "Let's hence!"

Belkram grunted himself upright, breath curling around him like smoke in the night chill, and pulled on one boot. "Hence away," he agreed, feeling for his blade. So they did.

They were now entering the broken, wooded country of ridges and ravines that marked Dagger Wood, the south-east edge of Daggerdale. It would be easy to lose the trail, so the two Harpers slowed. Since Zhentil Keep's forces had hounded Randal Morn and his folk into hiding, the dale ahead had become lawless country, roamed by hor-rific beasts, brigands, and marauding Zhent-hired merce-nary bands, mainly orcs. Not country for two men without magic to wander about in at night.

They were both thinking this, swords held ready as they came up over a ridge, when they saw a light ahead, an upright amber oval of radiance hanging motionless in the trees.

They looked at each other, nodded, started forward—and came to a halt almost immediately. Armored men had suddenly appeared out of the light, scattering into the open space in front of it with swords drawn. The two Harpers saw robed men gesturing commandingly.

They traded glances again. Belkram laid a hand on Itharr's arm and murmured, "Let's stay low and just watch. I'd wager a large amount that Elminster is in-volved in this, but I don't see him anywhere."

Itharr had been watching the men intently. "Aye. They seem to be looking for him, or us, or anyone about."

They sank down to their elbows, looked behind them, and shifted apart to lie under the shelter of shrubs, blades ready beside them. Itharr scratched his nose.

"Those are Zhents, or I'm a Calishite."

Belkram peered at him through the darkness. "No," he said, "you haven't turned into a Calishite, and I can't say I've noticed you oiling your hide and perfuming your gold coins these last few summers."

Itharr sighed theatrically. "No? I try to be so subtle."

Belkram snorted and they fell silent, watching the Zhentarim searching the woods, closer and closer. The two Harpers waited intently, as still as stone, like two hawks on a perch watching for prey.

* * * * *

"Nothing," Mrinden said angrily.

"Nothing save this," Kalassyn pointed out, nudging the sentinel's body with his foot. Mrinden made a rude noise and waved his hands in exasperation.

"Either we've been raided and the raiders have got clean away—we'll never find anyone in these woods, in the dark, unless by pure chance we fall right over them— or they're in the dale right now, whoe'er they are, and past us. In either case we must return. Call the men back."

Kalassyn gave curt orders to the Sword, who nodded and hastened away.

Mrinden stared angrily at the stars above and the trees around until the Sword returned and spoke at his elbow. "Lord, we are here and await your orders."

Mrinden tossed his head like an angry stallion and glared at the man. "Choose seven of your best to remain behind. They are to let no one through the gate but a ranking mage of the Zhentarim and those with him. Their orders are to slay all others; let no one see this gate and live to tell of it. When light comes, they must search the area carefully. No intelligent creature must elude their search, or it will go ill with all of you later. Understood?"

"Aye, Lord." A cool night breeze slid past them. Mrinden shivered and turned abruptly toward the light.

"The rest of you follow me." He strode back into the

radiance. The Sword was already waving a gauntleted hand; the main body of warriors hastened to follow. Kalassyn joined their line near the back, looking around one last time at the dark trees and the stars overhead.

As he glanced up, a star fell, trailing a silent path across the cloak of night. Kalassyn looked down, quickly, and said nothing. He wanted no soldiers reading ill omens into signs none in Faerûn were wise enough to interpret. Even as he told himself that, his own heart sank, and it was with fear that Kalassyn returned to the High Dale.

Perhaps the star brought good fortune. Kalassyn was safely through the gate, and the last of the returning Wolves with him, when two Harpers rose out of the night behind the seven-man guard like two death-dealing temple pillars. The guards had not yet turned from watching the last black boot heel vanish into the silent light when steel took the throats of the first.

The third man to fall managed a strangled roar as he went down, and the remaining Zhentilar wheeled around in frantic haste. An instant later, blades flashed in the amber glow, steel rang, and men twisted, lunged, and scrambled. Overhead another star fell, but each man there was too busy to notice it.

* * * * *

When Kalassyn strode forward and in a footfall returned to the High Dale, it was like stepping into an inferno. The rumble and flash of fire was dying away all around him. Somewhere nearby a man was sobbing, and smoke was so thick in the air that he could see nothing of trees or lights or the men who had preceded him.

Then, without warning, fire came again.

Kalassyn staggered in helpless, sightless pain, struggling to stand amid the roiling winds of the bright, searing blast. Off to the left, a man screamed, and an instant later Kalassyn fell over a huddled, armored form.

He landed hard atop another guard, whose black armor was hot enough to burn. Kalassyn rolled off as hastily as he could, cursing weakly. Crawling pain told him his robes were ablaze. Tears blinded him as he tore away his garb in flaming strips, shrieking at the agony spreading from his frantic, trembling hands.

Somehow he staggered on and sank to his knees at last in grass that was not scorched or ablaze.

He must . . . now would be the time to . . .

Kalassyn of Zhentil Keep fought for and found an instant to wonder if he was dying, but it was snatched away again by flames that roared in to fill his mind.

6
Fire in the Night

"Lord? Lord, do ye live?"

Kalassyn struggled to reply and discovered he was lying on scorched grass, legs twisted awkwardly under him.

He raised his head and, through a blur of tears, made out a dark, helmed head bent anxiously over him. Behind the first man, another guard stood holding a torch. Kalassyn winced, turning his eyes away from the flickering light.

"Aye," he said at last, struggling to move stiff, blackened lips. They cracked, with little twinges of pain, but the rest of him hurt far worse. "What—what happened?"

"Fire out of the night, Lord. From a tree next to the guard tree. We've surrounded it, but there's been no sound or movement since the second strike felled ye."

Kalassyn struggled. Pain stabbed at him. "Help me up," he snarled.

"Aye, Lord." Hands like heavy stones fell upon his shoulders, and he whimpered despite himself as he was gently hauled to his feet. Reeling, he fell to one knee. The hands steadied him, raised him again, and stayed there. He clung to them without shame and looked around.

After what seemed a very long time, as breath whispered and hissed in and out of his tortured lungs, he could see again.

It was not an inspiring sight. He was naked, covered with matted grass and burned hair. Behind him, smoke still rose from a ring of grass in front of the calmly glowing, unchanged gate. Within the ring lay the blackened bodies of five . . . six . . . no, eight Wolves and, facedown at their forefront, Mrinden. Bones showed here and there in the ashy ruin of the wizard. Kalassyn doubted he'd ever hear that nasty voice snapping orders again.

He looked away and saw other men groaning and clutching themselves in agony, their armor blackened and burned, or torn off. Others stood as if dazed or walked with the stiff strides of strong men in pain but determined not to let it diminish them. Of the band that had hurried up from the barracks not so long ago, only a handful still stood.

Kalassyn swallowed, thinking of Stormcloak's face—or the visage of sneering, sarcastic Hcarla Bellwind—and closed his eyes. The scorched smell of overcooked flesh hung sickeningly in the air. Kalassyn knew it would be a very long time before he'd want to eat bacon again.

He opened his eyes and drew himself up. Men were looking at him. There was anger in some faces and anxiousness in others. Something remained to be done. Something they were waiting for.

He stepped forward, free of the helping hands. "Get me my robes," he said hoarsely, without looking at the guards behind him. "The burned ones, all the scraps you can find."

He waited in the cool night breeze until a black form moved in front of him. "Here, Lord."

He angrily waved a torch nearer and with eager fingers probed the sorry scraps held out to him. Ah, there! He plucked out the brass-and-horn purse by its chain. The purse was ruined, twisted and scarred with the heat, but perhaps within all was well. He snatched out a certain ball wrapped in waxed paper, stepped past the guard, and faced the tree.

"Tell those men to stand back," he snarled, fighting down the fit of coughing brought on by raising his voice. Without pause he plunged into the hissed words and quick gestures of a spell.

Men were still scrambling back when his fireball lit the night with fresh flames. With a crackle and roar the entire tree went up, blazing and black from end to end. Then, like a tired warrior who takes an arrow in the throat, it toppled slowly, still blazing, against the tree beside it. The guard tree.

"Oh, gods be cursed!" Kalassyn snarled weakly. He turned hastily back to the guard, fingers clawing through what was left of his components pouch. He found what he needed, and a sudden blast of ice struck the trees, the ground, and the air around with a hissing like the sound of a hundred wounded dragons. Smoke billowed up, tree limbs creaked, and branches broke off and fell to earth.

Kalassyn watched them for a moment and then matched their fall. The ground, when it rose up to hit him, was surprisingly gentle.

*　*　*　*　*

The Sword's moustache and beard were smoldering, stubby smudges. The man who spoke to him took care not to let his gaze rest on them for more than an instant.

"What now, sir?"

The Sword bared his teeth in helpless fury and said, "Take the other end of this wizard and help me carry his useless carcass down to the barracks. The others can follow us. I want the four in best shape to sit in benches across the track, facing up this way to guard against anyone mad enough to come through the gate and powerful enough to survive the attempt. Spread the word and we'll flee together."

In the space of four breaths the dell was empty of the living. Smoke curled and drifted for a time, and the burned tree shifted once and lost a few more branches. Through it all, the amber oval of light glowed and pulsed in patient silence.

*　*　*　*　*

"Your report is incomplete," Nordryn said coldly. "Foes deadly enough to slay a mage of Mrinden's power, hurl Kalassyn into the very jaws of death, and fell almost all of your command—and you turn tail from the field and flee back here, not bothering to even look for them? Tell me, Sword, however do you expect to live a single night through? If you were that lax in Zhentil Keep, you'd have the bed stolen from under you and wake up as you were falling to the floor, as someone put his blade in your throat to slit it!"

The Sword just looked at him, two eyes of cold, weary death staring hard out of a face blackened and burned beyond easy recognition. "I didn't see you there, spell-hurler," he said deliberately. "Lacking a conscious commander, I followed the last orders I was given, which wisely took me to you. I now submit myself to your orders."

The two men stared at each other in silence for a long breath. The one in fine robes moved first, shifting back a pace.

The Sword drew himself up in his scorched armor, put a hand on the hilt of his sword, and added with the same slow, cold deliberation, "I trust, Lord, that your orders will be wiser than those Mrinden gave. He took us all into death we could not fight or avoid."

Nordryn's hand went to his belt, closing over a wand that was sheathed there. "And if I did the same," he almost whispered, "your task would be to obey me, without question or pause. Remember that." Their eyes met, coldly and steadily, like blades crossed and locked by straining men who sought each other's death.

"Aye, Lord, we will." The Sword's voice was cold and expressionless. "We will."

Nordryn held his eyes a moment longer before turning away and raising his voice. "Hear my will, then. All still able to walk will wear and wield what they can, and assemble without delay in the road. I want each to carry two quarrel quivers and two crossbows, one loaded. We march to the gate. There we form a ring, under cover, and each man is to load his second bow and keep both ready. At my order, fire at any target I name. Expect an attack through the gate."

He walked two paces and turned back to the room of silent men. "I've sent one of the message boys to the castle. If Lord Longspear pleases, he'll send healing. I'm coming with you."

He turned away again and walked on.

Behind him, one of the men muttered, "Tymora willing, let him be more bloody use than the last mages we had with us."

"He could hardly be less," another voice agreed.

"It's as well," a third voice cut in from afar. "His life may depend on it."

"Enough," the Sword boomed, silently indicating the mage's back, reminding them that he could hear every word. Grim smiles answered him; they'd meant him to.

Unseen, Nordryn smiled at the wall ahead and went on his way. Warriors were like cattle. They died in head-high piles when you needed them to. They ate and drank too much but could be useful the rest of the time, if you knew how to treat them. Like dogs, they needed proper handling. He showed his teeth to the wall again and continued on into the darkness.

"Mages who walk in darkness," went the old saying, "cloak themselves in it and think themselves strong—until the day it swallows them, and they come not out again." Nordryn remembered the saying wryly until memory told him who'd first said it: the Great Enemy, Elminster of Shadowdale.

Shaking his head and feeling anger building inside him again—a warmth in his chest rising into his throat—Nordryn went in search of a door that locked and a chamber pot beyond it. All goals in life should be so simple.

* * * * *

"The gods alone know where they are by now," Storm said quietly. "I think Elminster went west, but he could have a dozen or more gates nearby he's never told anyone about."

"A cheery thought," Jhessail observed sardonically. "Shall I tell Mourngrym to revise our plans for defending the dale to include a dozen or more unknown, invisible backsides that invading armies may rush through?"

"Easy, wench," Lhaeo told her gruffly. "Have some more firequench." He pushed one of the pair of decanters of ruby-red liqueur across the table. Storm made a silent grab for the bottle as it moved away from her, and was rewarded with a raised eyebrow from Jhessail. She returned it, with interest.

"Ladies, ladies," Lhaeo sighed, shifting his feet down from atop the table. "Must you spit and snarl like rival kittens?"

Jhessail shrugged. "It's what we've always done before," she observed with impish serenity.

Storm chuckled. A breath later, the others joined her, but the mirth in Storm's kitchen broke off abruptly as a bat as large and black as a small night-cloak flapped heavily in through the open doorway. It circled low over the table and seemed to twist and writhe in the air in front of the fireplace.

An instant later, the bat had become a tall, gaunt woman in a tattered black gown. Her hair and eyes danced wildly, and a fierce pride leapt in her face as she glided toward them.

"Sister," Storm greeted her with a welcoming smile. "Will you take some firequench with us?"

The Simbul nodded, sighed, and shivered all over like a cat after a fright. "Perhaps later," she said, taking a seat at the table, "after I try to learn what we both want to know."

"What all of us want to know," Storm replied quietly. "I've sent two good men out after them. Two who harp." Across the room, the strings of her harp quivered by themselves for a moment, singing faintly.

The Simbul looked around, not smiling. She nodded to Jhessail and Lhaeo, then bent her head and began whispering words of Art.

A heavy tension grew in the room like dark green smoke, and all the candle flames shrank to steady, watching pinpoints. The Simbul sat at the center of her gathered power, dark and unmoving, and the tension rose to an almost audible roar.

Her shoulders shook, she gasped, and the candle flames leapt and flickered again. The room was somehow brighter. And yet, Lhaeo thought, looking at the Simbul's forlorn and ravaged face, it seemed no safer or warmer.

The Witch-Queen of Aglarond said simply, "I'll need your help, all of you. Join hands with me and I'll try again."

Without hesitation they leaned forward around the table, the decanters standing like frozen red flames between them. The Simbul closed her eyes, shuddered again, and began to gather her will. As before, the room seemed to grow dim. "Think," she muttered, "of Sharantyr. Picture her face, her voice, what she looks like when she moves. We must focus on her, for Elminster is cloaked to all seeking magic."

Obediently they thought of the lady Knight. Storm's eyes were closed, her face calm. Lhaeo and Jhessail both frowned, their faces creased in concentration. This time, linked to the Simbul, they could feel her drawing in her power, feeding on their thoughts, emotions, and yearnings.

Power swirled around the kitchen. Then the Simbul hurled her questing, searching thought out a long way. She fell, like a fisher's hook plunging into dark waters, somewhere into a void of seeking where those linked to her could not follow.

After a long, tense silence of tight breathing and gathering weariness, the Simbul suddenly shook herself like a dog coming up out of water and said brusquely, "We need more. The Art twisted wild. Syluné . . . please?"

Two pairs of wondering eyes saw Storm's fingers and the Simbul's separate where they had been linked. Out of empty, smoky air between them, two slim, faintly glowing hands seemed to grow, gaining substance in ghostly silence. Each of these hands clasped a living one. A gentle whisper said, "I am here. Try now, sister."

Lhaeo and Jhessail stared at the half-seen, ghostly figure between Storm and the Simbul. Then they exchanged one quick glance and, as one, closed their eyes and threw themselves again into seeking Sharantyr.

An eternity passed. The candles burned lower. They breathed as one, low and deep. Toril, with awesome slowness, rolled steadily beneath them.

Then someone whimpered, and the circle was broken.

Storm held only empty air, and the Simbul fell heavily facedown on the table, upsetting one of the decanters.

"Storm?" Lhaeo asked anxiously, half rising. "Is she—?"

"Exhausted," the Bard of Shadowdale said faintly, leaning back in her chair. "As am I. It's a magic few know —thankfully, or there'd be mindless mages across half of Faerûn in short order."

Jhessail rescued the fallen decanter and silently held it out to Storm. The bard stared at it dully for a breath or two, then deliberately grasped it, unstoppered it, and took a long pull. When she replaced the stopper and handed the bottle back, it was almost empty.

"Storm," Lhaeo asked quietly, his voice almost steady, "was that—?"

"Our sister Syluné," Storm answered as quietly. "Yes, and what we tried did more harm to her than to either of us." She turned dark eyes up to theirs and added, "So now you know. Take up the weight of another secret, for the good of the dale."

Two intent faces nodded silently.

Then the Simbul stirred and said into the table, "Is any of that firequench swill left?"

After the laughter had died away, Lhaeo dared to lay tender hands on perhaps the most powerful sorceress alive in Faerûn, raising her and wiping her sweat-soaked brow. The Simbul smiled silent thanks up at him and said, "Well, you know we failed. Know more; there's worse news."

Lhaeo and Jhessail both looked at her sharply. "Tell," Elminster's scribe bade her simply.

"All Art in the Realms is going rogue," the Simbul answered, "for all who wield it, everywhere. We can unleash it, but our control slips and fades, and most of the time is lacking entirely. Magic has gone wild, and we can do nothing, it seems, to stop that. El and Shar are truly beyond our reach and aid."

Dread came and went on her white face, and she reached thoughtfully for the decanter again. "Across

Faerûn," she added softly but firmly, "not a single mage, archmage, or hedge-wizard can rely on spells anymore."

Lhaeo and Jhessail exchanged looks and then spoke together, framing the same question as one. "In the name of all the gods, why?"

Storm answered softly, eyes on the flame of the nearest candle. "That's just why. All the gods have been cast down into the Realms to contend among us, struggling and striving as we do. With Mystra gone, there's none to control magic. It's why Elminster's gone away."

"Cast down?" Lhaeo almost whispered. "By whom? Who has such power?"

Storm spread her hands. "In the oldest writings he was called the Overgod. Nowadays, to those who know of him at all, he is the 'One Who Is Hidden.'" She smiled. "If you meet him, you might ask his truename and aims. There are a lot of souls, mortal and divine alike, who'd like to know."

Jhessail drew a deep, ragged breath and smiled. "I'll get straight to work on it," she jested, and shook her head in rueful disbelief. Her hands trembled as they reached for the second decanter. When she put it down, it held far less than when she had taken it up.

Storm shook her head. "Easy, lass," she murmured, "or we'll have to carry you back to the tower."

Jhessail crooked an eyebrow. "Who, wench," she said readily, "will be carrying whom?"

Lhaeo sighed and rose. "Come, Jhess," he said. "Elminster and Sharantyr are on their own, and we've done enough harm this night. Storm needs her sleep, even if we do not."

Storm thanked the scribe with her eyes. Jhessail read that look and blew them all a kiss before taking Lhaeo's arm and slipping swiftly out into the night.

A long time passed. As the candles died, one by one, the two sisters sat at the table unmoving, eyes far away.

At last Storm moved unwilling lips. "Did you see or feel anything when you reached for Shar? Anything at all?"

"No," the Simbul said shortly, staring down at her

empty hands. "Nothing. I was like the worst apprentice I've ever had—alone, wavering, helpless in the dark."

"I saw three things, sister," came the eerie voice they had feared not to hear again. "Fire and tears and stars, overhead it seemed, though they were all mixed together. Our stars."

Storm raised her head, and there were tears in her eyes. "Syluné," she said softly, "my thanks. They're not dead, then."

"Yet," came the voice of Syluné's ghost dryly. "Yet."

* * * * *

It was dark in Dagger Wood, save for an upright oval of amber light, an unsleeping eye staring into the night. Overhead, glittering stars watched what the eye's glow illuminated: two blades that glimmered, leapt, and sang as they dealt death.

The two men who held the blades said nothing as they danced and ducked. Both knew they must keep the seven black-armored guards—well, only three guards now— from fleeing through the oval radiance to raise the alarm.

The men in full armor were strong, hardened veterans, efficient experts at dealing death with cold steel by night or day, in alleys or high streets, in open battle or in crowds.

The two men in dusty leathers, however, were Harpers and men who'd just spent some goodly time crossing blades with Storm Silverhand. They knew who'd win this battle.

As frantic moments passed, their opponents came to know it too, with the cold, sinking certainty of death. The Harpers caught each other's eyes once, in the skirling dance of steel, and laughed together. A few panting breaths later it was over.

Belkram and Itharr faced each other across the black-clad fallen, looked all about with trained wariness, and nodded to each other, signaling that they were both un-harmed. Then they turned together in silence to look at the flickering, man-high oval of light. It glowed silently back at them, waiting.

Belkram's eyes descended to a corpse that lay in front of the gate. He bent forward. "What's this?"

"Harper signs?"

"Aye." He leaned closer get a better look at the slashes on the corpse's leather tunic. " 'Trap ahead,' it says. 'Keep low.' " Belkram hefted his bloodstained blade. "Well? Ready?"

Itharr chuckled, and stroked the wispy beginnings of a moustache in a gesture Belkram had seen before. "Remember, adventure is where you find it," he replied, waving with his own blade at the light to indicate that Belkram should go first.

"Why, thank you," Belkram replied in exaggerated, courtly tones, and stepped through, keeping low.

7
A Night of Murdered Peace, and After

Beyond the gate, all was dark and silent. Grass whispered underfoot, and there were trees ahead—and a strong smell of recent wood smoke. Belkram took a pace forward, then crouched and leapt warily aside, out of the light. Itharr came through, saw Belkram's move, and turned toward the other side of the gate to do the same.

Then both Harpers heard the unmistakable deep *tung* of a crossbow firing. Itharr whipped around to follow Belkram and dived frantically to the ground. The first bolt whistled past his head as he fell. Then the night was full of hissing death, biting at them as they rolled, leapt, and ran to the left toward the trees.

A bolt from right in front of them came leaping out of the night. Itharr twisted desperately aside. The missile drew a line of red fire across his chest and shoulder, and was gone. Itharr snarled out his pain as he raced on. More quarrels sought his life, whirring past like angry wasps. He heard them clattering on rocks off to his left, and shot a glance that way. A mountain rose up beside them, and then he was following Belkram along its base, sprinting into the concealing trees.

A short scream ahead told him Belkram had opened a way through at least one defender. Itharr ran faster. To think he'd once dreamed of glorious adventures as a Harper, dreams that involved (between parties with beauteous women) charging castles single-handed! Dreams where no arrows ever struck hi—

Itharr grunted as a crossbow bolt struck him in the shoulder, picking him off his feet and hurling him a pace or two toward the rocks with the force of its flight.

He landed hard on his good arm, sprang up—spit on the pain; his life depended on getting up!—and ran on, hoping he'd not drop his sword from the hand he could no longer feel.

* * * * *

"After them!" Nordryn snarled. At the Sword's dubious look he almost shrieked his next words, so great was his fury. *"Get them!* They can't use any magic. I've cloaked them with a spell of my own! Go on!"

Around him, Wolves drew blades, but they looked to the Sword for orders, not him. The Sword looked at him again, long and coldly, then nodded his head at the fleeing men.

With a shout and a breath of creaking leather and flashing steel, the Wolves boiled up out of the trees and were gone.

Nordryn looked at the Sword, eyes hot. "I'll remember this," he spat.

The veteran swordsman looked back at him steadily, his eyes the same hue as the raised tip of his drawn sword. "See that you do," he replied softly.

* * * * *

"Where are we, d'you think?" Itharr panted as they raced along.

Belkram turned at the sound of his friend's voice. "Are you hurt?" He reached out a hand, swinging his fellow Harper around sharply.

The bolt protruding from Itharr's shoulder struck a nearby branch; he made a choked sound and stumbled back. Belkram's searching hands caught him, located the bolt, and felt the shoulder it was buried in.

Itharr tried to cough and whimper at the same time, and failed. He settled for making another little choking noise and fell down.

Belkram sighed, laid down his blade, and tore out the bolt in one swift, hard jerk. Itharr shook once under his hands and lay still.

The taller Harper thought for a moment, then rose

from his wounded friend and ran lightly back the way they'd come, melting into the cloaking gloom of a tree as a warrior trotted cautiously forward, glancing around in the dim night.

The woods were full of armed Wolves cautiously advancing in the darkness. The lives of two very outnumbered Harpers now depended on stealth and silence, so Belkram reached out with a long arm, slapped the man across the mouth from behind, and jerked hard. The man's head twisted sharply, and Belkram put all his strength into pulling. There was a brief crunching noise . . . and the man became limp and very heavy.

Belkram staggered, lowering the warrior as quietly as possible. A sudden crackling disturbance and a triumphant yell erupted nearby. Steel rang, men cursed, and there was a groan of pain.

"You fool," someone said weakly. "Can't you tell—?" The words ended in a gasp, followed by the heavy crash of a man falling heavily and helplessly through deadwood and living tanglethorns.

Belkram slipped cautiously back toward Itharr, only to hear branches whip and crackle close behind. He spun, blade up, and was almost knocked over by someone blundering past.

The ranger thrust with his steel and felt it turn aside on armor. His onrushing target gave a surprised yell and turned. Belkram saw a momentary flash of teeth in the darkness, put his sword tip there, and drove his blade in hard. The man crumpled and fell without uttering another sound.

This time the landing was not quiet, and Belkram hastened away. This game of cat and mouse was all too apt to turn against them swiftly, if these warriors brought torches or mage-conjured light.

He couldn't answer Itharr's question; he had no idea where they were. Perhaps if he could get safely out from under the trees long enough to get a good look at the stars . . . Well, they were somewhere not too different in climate from Shadowdale. Somewhere with mountains. Somewhere with at least one Harper—and, he hoped,

Elminster—nearby.

In front of him, he saw the flash of steel rising from the ground. He danced to a halt and hissed, "Itharr?"

"The same," came the weak reply. "Did you have to be so—agghhh! I'm bleeding all over everything."

"I've been rather busy," Belkram whispered carefully. "Use your blade as a crutch or put it away and lean on me, and with Tymora's kiss we'll get out of here!"

Itharr opted for the latter, and they hurried on together as quietly as possible. Steel still rang around them from time to time. Here and there in the night-cloaked woods, men crashed through brush and fell into unseen holes and over the trunks of fallen trees.

"A fine night out they're having," Itharr gasped, after awhile. "Could we stop for a breath or two?"

"Aye," Belkram murmured into his ear. "How d'you feel?"

"Fresh and fine," Itharr said sarcastically. "The night is young, brave sir, and all that." He sat down heavily on a tree stump, which promptly collapsed in a damp ruin of fungus and punky wood, dumping him onto the ground. He sighed.

That mournful sound made a few sputters of mirth escape Belkram. The taller Harper shook for a few moments and then leaned near, still chuckling. "I'd like to try to get back to that clearing. We should be able to see the gate's light. We could go around it, staying in the trees, and look for paths and such. These guards must have a barracks somewhere, where we can get food and mayhap even healing quaffs, for your shoulder. I was in Luskan, once. The idiots there had a barracks with a flat, unguarded roof. We rested above them, all the while they turned the city inside out for us, and hid most of their gear while they were out tramping around."

"Very nice," Itharr said. "Now help me up."

They went into the night together. Belkram had to use his sword only twice before they saw the amber light again.

* * * * *

"Now what, sir?" The Sword might have been a chamber servant back in Zhentil Keep.

Nordryn shrugged. "Wait here. Our duty is still to guard the gate while the others seek out these intruders."

The Sword nodded. "As you command," he said expressionlessly. Nordryn looked at him and then all around and found, with sinking fear, that the two of them stood alone by the gate. Their men were all blundering about in the woods. A sudden outbreak of shouting came from the trees, followed by a scream that ended in a dying wail.

"Ah," Nordryn said with satisfaction. "They've got one, at least."

The Sword raised an eyebrow. "Someone died, aye. In the trees, Lord, it could be one of us killing another just as easily as those we're after. You can't tell . . . until it's too late."

Nordryn looked at him. "Oh, no?" he scoffed. "Are you telling me Zhentilar soldiers can fight only in the full light of day?"

The Sword looked back at him, and shrugged. "No," he said briefly. "At night, though, we seldom know whom we're killing."

Nordryn stepped back hastily, eyeing the gleaming sword between them.

"What happens if you slay one of . . . of our men?"

The Sword shrugged again. "As I said," he drawled mildly, "by then, it's too late."

Nordryn backed two paces farther from the blade.

* * * * *

"A wizard?" Itharr breathed, staring into the night.

Belkram nodded. "No doubt. We go wide to the left now, down slope a bit. I see lights, so there'll be a track we can follow."

Itharr grunted. "Good. I've lost more blood than I thought I had in me."

Belkram sighed. "Hold up a breath or two longer," he said. "It would have to be your sword arm."

Itharr growled agreement deep in his throat. "Thanks

to Storm," he said, "I can at least use a blade properly with my left hand. Next time, run to the right, will you?"

Belkram made a little bow. "As you wish, Lord."

Itharr decided it was his turn to sigh. Again.

* * * * *

Thalmond shifted his weight off the stool experimentally and winced. The burned leg shrieked at him. He unbuckled his sword and leaned on it, scabbard and all, hopping awkwardly across the guardroom. Aye, it would serve.

Someone groaned from one of the beds. Thalmond hesitated, then turned and went out. None of the others could walk unaided. If he hurried, he would not be seen.

He'd fought for Black Master Manshoon more years than most of these lads had been alive, and knew a thing or two about standing orders. What he sought had to be somewhere in the meeting room.

He hopped along as fast as he could and saw no one on the way. Shouldering the door open, he leaned against the wall for support and waved a seeking arm along it. Metal dangles clinked; he'd found the cord that ran up to the lamp. He lowered the lamp and felt at his belt for his flint.

With the skill of long practice, he struck the stone a glancing dagger blow that showered sparks where he needed them. Six careful breaths later he was easing the door closed and turning back to a room lit by the warm glow of the hanging oil lamp. The object he sought would be somewhere within reach of this lamp, where it could readily be found in the darkness by feel. Not under the chairs or tables, for every blade who grew bored was apt to run his fingers along the edges of his seat or rub itching hands or forearms on the underside of the table edge, and might discover what Thalmond now sought.

No, it was somewhere—here? He stared at the map on the wall and carefully pulled at its edge. Nothing. He pushed. No. He slid the map carefully to the right and it moved—three finger-widths, no more.

There! In the revealed niche, two metal vials hung one above the other by leather thongs. Thank Tymora for her good favor. Even priests of Bane used the warrior symbols for healing! He'd just have a little, enough to stop this Bane-blasted burning in his leg.

Thalmond plucked the sword-rag from his belt—if he never actually touched the vial, no clever magic could tell he'd been here—wrapped the cloth around his hand, and reached out.

A gentle voice, very close by his ear, said, "My thanks, and farewell. Greet Tempus for me, old warrior." The steel at his throat was very cold. Thalmond had only a little time to feel surprised, time to tell himself that at last he knew what death would feel like, time to grow just a little angry that he'd heard no one behind him . . . and then, no time at all.

* * * * *

"Did you have to set the place alight with them all inside?" Itharr whispered, face white in the darkness.

Men rushed past them, shouting. Belkram raised the loaded crossbow carefully on his knee and whispered back grimly, "I had to kill one old warrior to get these. He flung up his hand as he fell, and by Tymora's favor broke the lamp that hung just above. Flaming oil everywhere! I scarce got out in time. Have you finished that yet?"

"Aye," Itharr said in the sleepy voice of one who has fought pain for a long time, or pushed too far and done too much and now finds ease.

"Stay awake!" Belkram said sharply. "Is one going to be enough?"

But he'd spoken too sharply. One of the running figures turned its head and took two steps toward them, sword raised. The Harpers lay still.

The man came on, peering into the shadows. "Who's—? Hold!"

The crossbow kicked and death hissed into the Wolf's throat. He fell on his side, convulsed, and lay still, one hand raised in a claw that would never close.

"I'm getting a little weary of all this bloodshed," Itharr said quietly. His voice was stronger.

Belkram nodded. "I'm not overfond of it, either, but a guard down is one less sword to hunt us. You sound better."

"I feel better," Itharr said, putting the second vial carefully into his belt pouch. "We're too close," he added, watching the flames leap higher. "We'll be well lit, soon."

"Aye," Belkram agreed, and they scrambled back into the trees. The dell, with its gate, was just a little way beyond.

Itharr looked toward it and then back at Belkram questioningly.

His friend shrugged. "We've not found Elminster, and I know he came here. I can feel it."

Itharr nodded. "Aye," he agreed, "and these look like Zhent Blackhelms to me, from what little we've seen."

Belkram nodded. "Any work we can do against them is well done, whenever we get a chance."

"Whither, then?"

Belkram tossed the crossbow away and stared into the night for a moment. "Do you see mountains beyond?" he asked.

Itharr held up a hand to shield against the light of the leaping flames and said, "Aye. Not too far off, either."

Belkram nodded. "Come day, they'll be searching these woods for our our trail. The rocks this side are the natural place to hide, and for them to look. Why not take ourselves across to those, over there?"

"And spare ourselves much of the hunters' attention?" Itharr asked. "I like it. Let's use the road, and look for a stream to turn aside from it. Now, before the flames bring everyone out to watch."

Belkram nodded, and they hurried around the back of the blazing building, flitting like shadows from tree to tree. Below them, houses and shops—and beyond, a smallish stone castle—rose out of the night.

"Where are we, then?"

"A mountain pass?"

"Aye." Itharr nodded slowly. "If there's a cart road

through the lowest part, there, I'd say yes."

"But where?" Belkram obviously did not recognize their surroundings.

Itharr yawned. "I'll think about it," he promised, "when we're safely hidden."

The two Harpers drifted into the night, seeking their stream.

* * * * *

"Bane curse us all," Nordryn gasped, too astonished for anger. "The barracks!"

"Now do you see," the Sword said in a voice of cold steel, "why I ordered the men to fall back there to make their stand? This is your doing, softskull!"

Nordryn stared at him, eyes glittering. "You would speak to me so?"

"Aye. Be glad I do not cut you down where you stand, mage. I'd be doing High Lord Manshoon a favor, if this is any example of the glorious bungling you'll inflict on his plans in times to come." He barked short, mirthless laughter. "I'd be doing you a favor, come to that, saving you from Manshoon!"

Nordryn stepped back a pace, raising his hand. The officer's sword slid out to float menacingly just above it, preventing the wizard from gesturing to unleash a spell.

"Don't," the Sword suggested in soft, heavy tones of menace.

Nordryn stepped away again, a brittle smile visible on his face where the leaping flames lit it. "What if I told Stormcloak that the foray into the woods was your plan?"

The Sword's eyes were bleak. "You'd be digging your own grave, wizard. Even if all the men who heard you giving orders were dead, and their bodies ruined past what dark magic can recall or speak to, there's this." He shook the gauntlet off his free hand and raised his fingers until Nordryn could see the heavy ring that glinted upon the middle one. "Look well," the soldier suggested.

The wizard felt cold fear creeping down his spine. He knew all too well what that sigil meant: Manshoon. This cold-eyed soldier was one of the High Lord's personal agents. He swallowed and turned abruptly away to hide the fear he knew was showing on his face—fear, and something else. The man had to die before Manshoon heard of this or Nordryn Spellbinder's career would be short and painful . . . or long, cold, and frustrating, posted to all the worst places, with new magic forever denied to him, and under the constant, cruel eye of some watcher appointed by the High Lord.

"Don't think of arranging my death," came the Sword's cold voice from behind him. "Lord Manshoon always probes such things very carefully—by speaking to the deceased, if necessary. He knows my worth; you'd probably have to face me again. If Manshoon got tired of raising me, you'd pay the price, never doubt it. You'd make an adequate walking dead man, I suppose."

Nordryn turned and walked toward the flames, wondering which of the careers he'd just seen so bleakly would be worse. The flames roared and crackled, warming his face even from this distance, and he just couldn't decide.

* * * * *

Sharantyr came awake slowly, enfolded in unexpected warmth. She opened her eyes and looked around hurriedly, coming up to one elbow and feeling for her sword.

During the night, the Old Mage had somehow wrapped his bony arms around her without wakening her. That simply shouldn't have happened, but Sharantyr did not move away when that familiar, wild-bearded visage smiled at her, only inches away.

"Fair morn, Lady," Elminster said with courtly formality and leaned forward with smooth speed to kiss the end of her nose.

Sharantyr blinked. Some sorceresses would die, or kill, or whatever, to trade places with her, no doubt. His beard tickled like something between a scurrying centipede or an amorous cat. After a few breaths, she remembered to smile in reply.

Elminster chuckled. "Up, lass," he said. The mists were rolling away down through the trees as they rose and stretched to ease the stiffness that comes from sleeping in the open on rocky ground. "I fear I neglected to provide us breakfast, but I remain both open to suggestions and thy humble servant."

Sharantyr shook her head incredulously and pecked him on the cheek, more to shut him up than anything else. Ye gods, what had she gotten herself into now?

*   *   *   *   *

The day grew both warm and splendidly clear. The ranger and the wizard spent the morning sitting in the shrubbery at the trees' edge, watching black-armored gate guards working the road into the High Dale. Eastkeep rose small but grim at the warriors' backs, and they were most efficient.

Sharantyr didn't know the place and said so, but Elminster told her grandly that he knew it and would recognize it for her. Sharantyr rolled her eyes, not for the first time. Their stomachs chose that romantic moment to growl together.

The gate guards went steadily about their work, extracting passage tolls from all travelers coming into the dale from the east, inspecting their goods and gear, and turning back all wizards. Traffic leaving the dale from the west was given only a cursory search. These well-armed guards expected no trouble from that front.

There was a stir, once, as the guards suddenly swarmed over the wagon of a fat merchant. A shout brought six more guards with drawn swords out of the little shanty that served them as a duty shelter. The newcomers surrounded the merchant with a ring of sword tips at his throat while the search went on.

Shortly, two stout guards clambered triumphantly down from the wagon, each showing something to the officer in charge. He nodded and waved his head; the two men trotted away to the guard hut.

"Their commander—have I seen that harness before?"

Sharantyr asked.

Elminster nodded. "No doubt. That's a Sword, and these are Zhentilar warriors or I'll miss my breakfast."

Sharantyr grinned. "They're Zhents, then." As they watched, one of the guards returned with a scrap of parchment, which he handed to the red-faced merchant. The wagon and its occupant were brusquely ordered on with imperious waves of naked swords. The wagon rumbled away, the merchant shaking his head.

Sharantyr's eyes narrowed. "What's going on? They took something from him, aye, but what?"

Elminster assumed the pedantic air of the lofty scholar addressing a pupil too dense to be worth the time teaching takes. "Regard ye," he said in measured tones, "yon hut. 'Tis home to a mageling, I doubt me not. He has examined the items they took from the merchant and pronounced them magical. They hold these objects, returning to the unfortunate former owner a receipt. No doubt he has to inform them of the time and place of his leaving the dale, and they'll return his baubles to him—that is, if some wizard in authority here doesn't deem them too useful."

Sharantyr looked at him. "You're sure?"

Elminster affected to take mighty offense, blinking and clucking, drawing his nose high into the air, rolling his eyes fiercely, and saying, "Well!"

Sharantyr giggled.

"Come, lass," Elminster said with injured dignity, rising out of the bushes like a Calishite vizier making a stately palace entrance on a platform rising out of an underground room. "I want my breakfast."

Without pause or any attempt at concealment, he strode through the long grass, still wet with dew, toward the guards on the road.

Rolling her eyes, Sharantyr wondered again how she'd gotten herself into all this. It's what comes of feeling sorry for mages, she concluded. Lunacy if ever there were crazed thoughts. She drew her blade, held it low behind her to keep it hidden as much as possible, and followed.

8
Mysterious Attacks and Lawless Outrages

Death calls, it's said, on everyone. Some early, some later. Most find themselves not ready when the ghostly horn sounds—with much left to do and much more regretted. A lucky few die content, or unawares. A haunted handful of beings find death only long after they've desired its arrival. This includes most so-called "immortals." The bony arms of doom also enfold those who seek to cheat death by magical means, or have undeath or an undying curse thrust upon them.

The arms of death also extend to claim those who bear Mystra's burden. Of these Chosen Ones, some welcome death sooner than others. All render to the living attentive service, examples of life at its most splendid and active, and a certain silence, keeping secret the despair and weariness that long life brings.

And so it was that the late morning sun found Elminster, the archmage without any spells, eagerly eyeing the guards he'd been watching all morn. He'd made four long strides toward them, the unconcerned beginning of a direct attack, when the lady ranger who had come to keep him from harm caught up to him and put a firm hand on his shoulder.

He stopped and looked around questioningly.

Sharantyr looked back at him—at his white hair, thin limbs, and alert, intent face—and shook her head. "Elminster," she asked quietly, "when you do foolish, reckless things—like attacking yon sentinels, with a fortress at their backs and at least four things of magic we've seen them seize with our own eyes—aren't you ever afraid of death?"

Elminster looked at her for a long moment and said dryly, "Death has often come calling on me, but so far I've always been out, ye see."

And with those impish words he slipped from her grip and marched straight out of the trees toward the waiting Wolves. Sun glinted on black helms as they turned his way.

With a sinking heart, Sharantyr sighed, slowly raised her sword, and followed.

* * * * *

"Hold, old man!" The Oversword of the guard spoke impatiently, scarcely looking at the old man in robes. His attention was bent on a fat Sembian merchant who was sweating with fear. The many rings gleaming on his pudgy white fingers ran through the air like a starving fisherman combs the depths of an empty net. The merchant was almost gabbling as he assured the nine stone-faced guards that his wines were the best, oh, yes, only the best, why everyone said so, just ask at the Black Stag in Selg—or, well, perhaps not—nay, speak to the merchant Lissel, of nearby Daerlun, and he'd vouch for . . .

At about that time, the Oversword realized the gaunt old man with the overlong white beard had not halted and was proceeding with confident, unhurried steps toward the guard hut. He spun around, reaching for his sword.

"Old man," he barked, "hold!"

The gaunt figure in tattered robes continued on its way, beard flapping.

The Oversword caught up in three quick strides, ignoring grins that had begun to appear on the faces of his men, and jerked the old man roughly around.

Cool blue-gray eyes regarded him. "Yes?" a mild voice inquired, as if humoring a rude child.

The Oversword snarled and said fiercely, "Never ignore orders in the High Dale, old man, if you would live."

Slow eyebrows rose. "What orders?"

"I told you to hold, whitebeard, and I meant it! I'll see to you when I'm done here, and I care nothing for your haste or importance!"

"Oh. I see," Elminster said courteously. "I misunderstood ye."

The Oversword looked him up and down coldly. "My words were quite clear," he said slowly and dangerously. "What was your problem?"

"Ye kept saying 'old man,'" Elminster told him. "I assumed ye were speaking to someone else. I'm not old—not yet, by the sun, though if ye waste much more of my morning I may come to be." He turned and continued on his way.

The Oversword snarled again and gestured. Drawn swords rose to bar Elminster's way on all sides.

Elminster turned about. "Yes?" he asked mildly.

"Sirs!" Sharantyr's voice came urgently from behind them. "Please forgive my fa—"

"That will be enough, girl," Elminster told her sharply. "How can ye learn, if ye persist in speaking out of thy place? Be ashamed. And better, be silent."

He turned to face the Oversword. "My daughter," he explained apologetically. "She's not been out of Zhentil Keep before and is overexcited."

The Oversword's eyebrows drew together in a wary frown. "Zhentil Keep?"

"Aye. I was speaking with a friend there, Lord Manshoon, and as I was passing this way, he asked me to look in on a certain wizard for him. To—ah, forgive me—deliver a private message." He smiled. "While I appreciate your diligence, Oversword, I am in some haste. I was told that the one I sought would probably be here, either in yonder hut or in the keep beyond. May I?"

Politely he turned his back, pushed aside two blades with the backs of his open hands, and went on. Without turning, he called back, "Come, lass!"

Sharantyr bent her head and lowered her blade. "Yes, Father," she replied in tones of weary resignation. In wary silence the Wolves stood back to let them through.

The Oversword noted that none of his men would meet his eyes. Good. He turned savagely back to the fat Sembian and curtly ordered his men to slit open the seams of everything, including every stitch of clothing the man was wearing.

But somehow, he couldn't enjoy the fun that followed.

*   *   *   *   *

The fat man was making so much noise, wailing and cursing and calling on more gods than the Oversword had ever heard of, that it was a good while before they heard the disturbance from the guard hut: the sounds of shrieking and sobbing, and the frenzied cracks of a whip wielded with some strength. The guards did not react; they were clearly used to such sounds. One or two glanced casually back at the hut and saw the white-beard's daughter standing uncertainly near the curtain that hung across its open doorway. The guards shrugged and turned away.

That all changed two instants later. The white-bearded man strolled calmly back out into the sun, smiling at his daughter. He seemed as startled as the Wolves when an agonized cry rang out from inside the hut.

"Help! Cabalar! Dhondys! Aid, by Bane and Mystra both! Ohhh! She's killing me!"

The Oversword paled, jerked out his sword, and snapped, "Sabras! Mykhalar! Stay on the road! Everyone else come with me!" He swept his arm toward the hut and charged. Six black-armored men hastened at his heels, blades flashing.

The gaunt old man with the long white beard bent down and pulled something from his boot. As he rose, he threw off his tattered over-robes and charged to meet them.

The old fellow was scrawny. The Oversword could see his ribs as he ran toward them, beard streaming back over his shoulder. He wore only dusty leather breeches, gray with age and shiny at the knees, and his boots. A wand flashed in his hand, and from it blue-white death lashed out twice to strike one of the Wolves, leaving the soldier staggering and groaning in pain.

A wizard! And the crossbows were in the hut beyond him, by Bane's black heart! The Oversword looked over his shoulder and saw that Sabras and Mykhalar were already hastening to join him. He slowed, directing them with his blade, and watched his men race to meet the old man.

The girl, too, was running now, and she had her blade out again. A trained warrior, by her looks; all trace of uncertainty and awkwardness was gone now.

The old wizard must have some trickery ready. Why else charge alone against seven men in full armor?

Abruptly, fear rising cold and ugly in his chest, the Oversword came to a stop. "Spread out!" he roared. "'Ware a trap!"

As if heeding him, the whitebeard skidded to a halt. His hand ducked to his boot, replacing the wand there and coming up with a little brass scepter that ended in a spherical cluster of wrought hands.

The Oversword's heart sank. He'd confiscated that himself, early this morn, from a sharp-tongued, dark-eyed Sembian caravan guard-wizard. The scepter had fairly echoed with power in his hands. Inside the hut, Ildomyl had visibly paled and hastily set the thing aside.

What it was, exactly, the Oversword knew not, but he knew enough to fear it. For the first time the thought that he might have to flee for his life or die here on the road, as highsun stole nearer to end the morn, came to him suddenly and chillingly. The Oversword paled and looked about.

A surprising number of local folk had appeared up the road to watch. They stood silent, still as statues, gazing at the scene.

The old man held the brass scepter and spoke a certain word, clear and echoing and unfamiliar. There was a flash of golden, metallic light. The charging Wolves, who were almost upon him, staggered suddenly back. They scattered helplessly, arms and blades flailing, propelled away by magical hands that shoved and grasped and flung—hands as big as shields, each having three long fingers between two hooked thumbs.

The old man's hands were empty now as he dove nimbly forward to take the feet out from under a Wolf.

They crashed to the ground together, a magical hand spread out over the black-armored chest like some gigantic spider. The old man swarmed along the writhing warrior to snatch the sword from his hands.

The Oversword saw the stolen steel descend into the helpless throat of its former owner an instant before the constraining hand melted away into the air from whence it had come. All the other hands also quietly faded, pulsed, and vanished.

The old man stood calmly hefting the blade he'd seized. The Wolves recovered themselves, bellowed their fury, and came for him.

Heart in her throat, Sharantyr ran as she'd never run before, knowing she would not arrive in time, or do much good if she did. There was only one of her, and these warriors looked trained, strong, and fit. The one Elminster had hurt with magic missiles was still on his feet, moving with less pain than before. Six Wolves came on with murder in their eyes, the Oversword bringing up the rear with a sudden, snarling charge.

The armored forms closed in around the old man, and despite herself Sharantyr screamed. The sound brought a warrior around to face her. With desperate savagery, Sharantyr flailed away at him with her blade, hammering him so hard and fast that he had no time to do anything except fend her off.

Beyond, Wolves roared and swords clashed. Sharantyr murmured a prayer to Tempus to aid the Old Mage as her own sword slid in under the edge of her opponent's helm and came back dark and wet.

The man fell heavily, and Sharantyr sprang aside, peering desperately to try to learn Elminster's fate. Another Wolf was already running toward her. Despite that approaching danger, the lady ranger stood for an instant in amazement.

Elminster was still on his feet amid all those armored giants. Steel flashed in his hand, and he was laughing. She shook her head, struck aside the blade reaching for her, and stared again.

For a moment the image of the gaunt, sharp-tongued

old man in tattered robes seemed to fall away, and she saw the impish, snake-quick youth he had been many long years ago.

His eyes blazed. He dodged, lunged, and ducked under a reaching blade with the easy agility of youth. He laughed.

Sharantyr watched him in amazement, while almost without thought or effort her blade found the throat of the Wolf who had charged her. She no longer saw the Old Mage, but a man strong and supple, with the defiant pride of youth. A man of power delighting in the fray, the Laughing Hero of the North spoken of in legends, greatest of the carefree blades in the alleys of Waterdeep, slayer of fell things, prankster—and fearless fighter, even when alone against a host.

Elminster, half-naked and scrawny, whirled and leapt among the blades. Around him, the black-armored Wolves coughed or cried out and fell in their blood. Always there came that low laughter, except when Elminster rose up to bury his blade in the face of the Oversword of the guard and cried, "For the dale! Let there be freedom again for the High Dale!"

When the last man fell, there was no sound from the watching men and women. Most of the village folk seemed to have emptied out of the huts and shanties beyond the keep. A score or more had gathered to watch, and in a few hands Sharantyr saw axes, pitchforks, and clubs. She looked down at the huddled black hulks, shook her head again, and walked toward the Old Mage.

Elminster stood leaning on his blade, looking suddenly old again. He was panting, great shuddering breaths that shook his body, but none of the blood on him was his own. He looked at her with two eyes that were very blue, and managed a smile.

"M-my robes, Shar," he gasped. "Old bones feel the cold an' all." Sharantyr embraced him, rubbed his shoulders briskly, and hurried to snatch up his robes from where they lay.

The Old Mage dressed, throwing down the sword as if it were something diseased and foul. He shook his head.

"That draws deep," he said, eyes distant. "It gets . . . harder every time."

Sharantyr put an arm around his shoulders. "I'm still amazed," she said softly, "but shouldn't we be going? With all that noise, they must have been alerted at the keep."

The folk of Eastkeep stood watching them, not speaking. Sharantyr saw awe in their eyes, and leaping hope, and a little fear. Elminster did not seem to see them at all as he adjusted his belt and shrugged his shoulders several times to settle his robes comfortably.

In the stillness, they heard the faint sounds of weeping from the hut.

Sharantyr looked at Elminster. "The wizard," she asked. "Did you—?"

The Old Mage shook his head and silently motioned her to follow him. Together they went to the hut, and the Old Mage drew the door curtain aside.

Within was the stink of fear and sweat and death. A sobbing woman, cold gray manacles still about her wrists and ankles, swung a jewelled whip to rain blows down on a bloody, huddled form. The manacles and a wild look were all she wore. The chains that had held her dangled empty from a beam overhead.

She looked up, saw Elminster, and managed a savage smile of gratitude. Then, deliberately, she turned and brought the whip hissing down again with all the strength of a blood-spattered arm, though it was clear that the meat she struck could no longer feel it.

"Fly now, lady," Elminster bid her gently. "Flee before other wizards come to slay ye. Out, among the people, and throw both whip and keys into one of the streams as soon as ye can. Take nothing else or they'll know ye." Her dirty bare shoulders shrugged in reply, and he added, "Ye want to live, to see them all dead, don't ye?"

The woman listened to that, still panting out her fury in great sobbing breaths. She abruptly turned and snatched up a ring of keys from the mage's now-empty chair. Her eyes met Elminster's in fierce, silent gratitude, then she was gone into the morning.

Elminster turned eyes that had grown old again on Sharantyr. "I bade him good morning and snatched up that scepter you saw me use. He sprang up to stop me, so I tossed it where he'd try to catch it, tripped him as he bent, and emptied a bowl of his wash water over his head. I got his keys and freed her before he could be up and hurling spells." He smiled faintly. "She snatched up the whip before I'd even freed her ankles. I nearly lost a finger to it, plucking the wand out of his belt before he could."

Sharantyr looked at him and then at what was left of a man on the floor. She shivered for just a moment, then asked steadily, "The wand? What sort is this one?"

Elminster sighed. "Well, it can make things larger or smaller. If we had a tenday or two to spare searching this place, the keep, and any other haunts this mala-spell may have had, I suspect we'd find all manner of missing coins, gems, and other finery made very small. We might also find argumentative or very beautiful folk that the guard stopped, shrunk to the size of thy smallest finger."

Sharantyr stared at him, eyes large and round. "What a monster!" she hissed, looking around the hut as if every drawer and corner held coiled snakes waiting to leap out at her with hungry fangs.

Elminster shrugged. "Ever wonder why there are more evil mages than good ones?" he asked. As he turned to go, he added quietly, "It's because power like that makes it so hideously easy to rule all about ye. Remember always, there is no such thing as a mage that is not dangerous."

With a grunt of satisfaction, he took a handful of dusty, well-stoppered glass vials from an earthen jar by the door. "Healing quaffs," he said. "The only thing I dare spare the time to take. Let's be off, lass, before thy feared counterblow comes from the keep."

He stepped out through the curtain and paused.

"Ye might pick up all the food ye can find—and wine, for that matter." He looked out, seemed satisfied, and added, "Never forget the food. Coins, now, are hard on the digestion and don't seem to restore a man like simple bread and cheese do."

"Women," his companion told him dryly, "are no different. And my name's Sharantyr, 'lad.'" She met his eyes challengingly.

Elminster laughed and replied, "My apologies, Sharantyr. Now hurry, will ye? I'll be giving this wand to one of the folk here, to hide away and use to free shrunken friends later."

A few hurried breaths later, they vanished back into the woods, Sharantyr's belt heavier by eleven daggers she'd stripped from the fallen Wolves.

It seemed they'd left these trees very long ago, but up the road, the fat Sembian merchant in newly slit-into-rags clothing could still be seen, sweating pounds off his rotund frame as he fretted, clambered, and pleaded to get his wine-wagons safely away before more guards arrived looking for someone to blame for the fate of their comrades lying sprawled bloodily in the dust of the road. Sharantyr cast a last look around, found herself grinning, and followed the Old Mage into the concealing green depths of the woods.

* * * * *

Belaerus shook his head. "Who'd a' thought it?" he said, staring at the bodies sprawled all around. "Just one old man."

Durvin the cellarer slid the wand he'd just been given into his boot and looked at his friend sharply. "I saw only a young man, a man with a long beard, braver than we. Young enough and brave enough to fight an entire guard of Wolves for the dale. To win back our homes for us."

Belaerus nodded hastily. "Aye, brave enough."

"Brave enough," echoed another merchant, and there were nods and murmurs there on the road. Men straightened and set their jaws. Durvin remembered old words, long unsung, and began, his rough voice rumbling loud along the road.

Six breaths later, when mounted, full-armored Wolves swarmed out of the keep and thundered down the road like a black wind, they found men with fierce, hard eyes and no fear in their faces standing amid the black-armored bodies on the road, singing the old Shieldsong of the High Dale.

* * * * *

Men rode hard that day, galloping importantly here and there about the dale. Longspear's message riders, hard eyed and quick, spurred from castle to keep and from keep to posts and barracks. In their wake, the aroused Wolves gave the High Dale a waiting air of armed alertness.

Bands of soldiers rode the roads, peered into inn rooms and farm kitchens to check again what had been checked many times before, and plunged repeatedly into the dark cloak of trees that covered the northern slopes of the dale.

Longspear himself, stout and hook-nosed and massive in his worn and well-used armor, sat on an armor-plated war steed as big as some cottages in the dale and eased himself around the streets beneath the frowning walls of the High Castle. Commanding and stern he looked, eyes hard and jaw grim, as he waved and pointed with huge iron-gauntleted hands. Attentive message riders galloped in obedience to his every order. But for all his authority and their energy, the intruders who'd hurled spells enough to destroy half a handful of the lord's feared mages and sent twenty or more Wolves to their graves in blade-to-blade battle remained uncaught.

Heladar Longspear surveyed the mountains fearlessly. Unmoving, uncaring of the might he commanded, they walled in the High Dale to the north and south, at once protecting him and shielding his newfound, mysterious foes. Was Sembia behind this? Cormyr? Outlaws trying to seize a home? Or worse?

Deep inside, a chilling whisper repeated the thought he'd been pushing down since the first blood had spilled on the Daggerdale side of the supposedly secret gate that linked him with the Zhentarim. Was a rival priest, mage or faction within the Brotherhood seeking to bring him down, to work some dark and hostile plan?

It might be someone here in the dale. Angruin, perhaps, angry that he'd not been given open rule. Or one of the lesser mages, ambitious and impatient to better his standing in the Brotherhood. That would be bad. Danger close at hand, and skillful enough that he'd not seen it until twenty or more blade-brothers had fallen.

Perhaps the alternative was worse. Someone—it could be anyone—in the Brotherhood striking from the shadows, pursuing an unknown plan with unknown strength. A beholder, half-a-handcount of liches, a rebel cabal of priests . . . all such had happened before. It was even whispered that Manshoon cold-bloodedly worked behind such intrigues, keeping rivals down and everyone afraid of each other—and of him.

Heladar found himself sweating and forced his thoughts to more comfortable matters: affairs of war fought with swords, with no magic more than priestly healing and a few flash-and-bang spells cast by obedient magelings. Scouring the High Dale was his task right now, then a good evenfeast. After the meal, the council would gather. He'd called the moot, and he'd have to see past the masks of smooth words and stiff faces that each man there always wore. His own life might well depend upon it.

Not for the first time, Heladar found himself thinking of the high constable he'd deposed, and wondering if his own fall would come as swiftly as the one he'd arranged for Irreph Mulmar. He felt the weight of watching eyes on him: the dale folk, who hated him as much as they'd loved Mulmar. He kept his face hard and fearless as he looked slowly around at the patiently watching mountains. Then he directed his mount unhurriedly toward the castle. Though the sun was still high and the day fair, a cool breeze seemed to come out of nowhere, tuck cold fingers over the high collar of his armor, and wind its way slowly down his spine. Heladar Longspear rode into the High Castle and wondered how much longer it would be his.

9
Death to the Tyranny of All Mages

The great doors boomed shut, causing torches to flicker up and down the walls of the high-ceilinged great hall, reflected flames glimmering on the motionless helms and breastplates of the lord's honor guard. The Council of the High Dale was in session.

Lord Heladar Longspear looked glumly down the great table. The searchers had so far come back empty-handed. Their mysterious enemies had slid away from seeking blades as a breeze loses itself in the woods. An old man and a girl, if the report just in from Eastkeep was to be believed. Only two, with swords and some magic, against all his warriors and the mages of the Brotherhood.

Yet there were almost thirty fresh graves up behind the barracks. Worse, the arch-backed chairs halfway down the table where the lesser mages sat were empty. Mrinden, Kalassyn, and Sabryn were not here. Of the three, only Kalassyn still lived—and he lay abed, still too near death to walk about or sit in a chair half the evening. No one looked at the empty seats.

Silence fell over the murmuring councillors as Heladar's gaze ranged over them all. Twelve pairs of eyes looked back at him. Longspear did not bother to rise, smile, or utter empty words of welcome. They all knew why he'd called them here.

"Councillors," he said heavily, his eyes on the few faces he did not know as fellow agents of the Brotherhood, "I thank you for your swiftness in answering my call. Haste is of importance in dealing with any violence, unless one wants open war to erupt. We must deal speedily with the mysterious attacks and lawless outrages that have occurred in our fair dale this day and the night just past."

He left a little silence then. As usual, the most stupid

of the local merchants rushed in to fill it. Fat Jatham, they called the wheezing, heavy-lidded, pudding-bellied weaver. He wore a splendid tunic, his own work no doubt.

"Hem—ah, Lord," Jatham breathed, "we've all heard wild rumors of battle, and spells, and many of y—our brave warriors slain. But I daresay most of us—as I, myself—were abed, asleep, for most of what went on. Will you tell us what befell?"

Longspear stared at him, not letting anything show on his face. Was the little man's slip about the sword brothers deliberate or merely slow wits? Everyone in this room and the dale around knew with cold certainty that the men-at-arms—his Wolves, the people called them—obeyed only Longspear and the mages. It was not polite, however, to say so. If open defiance started, it would spread like a wind-driven fire in dry grass. And if stamping it out meant a weaver's body swinging on the newly built gibbets on the castle walls, what of that?

He raised his hand to indicate Angruin. The cold-eyed mage brought him orders from Zhentil Keep, often making it clear he thought swordsmen like Longspear were just barely intelligent enough to obey them. He made it clear that Heladar was to take orders from him, in private, or suffer the wrath of Manshoon—after the pain of whatever dark magic Angruin Myrvult cared to inflict on him.

Well, then, let Angruin obey Lord Heladar in public, and do it well. Called himself Stormcloak and thought himself a big man because he could work a few nasty spells on folk, did he? Let him do some work.

A long-ago memory came to mind: an old Zhent warrior drinking himself to death, telling Heladar, "Priests and mages both are deadly to ye, boy. Deadly to us all. Mind ye keep 'em busy, for they're most apt to get into trouble and do ye ill with underhanded work when they've time to plot and scheme and skulk. Keep 'em too busy to dig ye a grave."

Angruin dragged his cold eyes only slowly from Longspear's face and said to the weaver, "Unknown persons—at least two and probably many more—have somehow entered our dale. They used magic against our loyal troops, so we suspect magic allowed them to sneak in among us. Our patrols first met with them in the practice field above the barracks, just north of here"—he nodded toward the window, but not a single head in the room bothered to turn and look—"last night, and there was a battle."

He paused for effect, looking around the table. "Magical fire was hurled against our forces. For safety, we advise that no one approach that place. Spread the word among the people: Avoid the upper field. There's nothing to see there, in any case, and the magic that still lurks there can twist the unwary into the forms of snakes, newts, or worse. Our soldiers have set a guard to discourage the curious."

"Is that," the urbane, poker-faced Sembian merchant asked calmly, "what happened to the mages who are not here with us today?" Xanther Srildar sat in his usual seat, right across from the empty chairs. Not for the first time, Longspear wondered if he was more than he appeared to be.

Angruin obviously felt the same. "Yes," he said flatly. "We lost some of our swordsmen but repulsed the intruders."

"How many?" The blunt question came from dark-eyed, dark-browed Blakkal Mord, a local leather worker. This one was no friend to any newcomers to the dale—including, of course, all men of the Brotherhood.

Angruin's eyes narrowed. Certain councillors were always trying to find out just how many soldiers the lord commanded in the dale. Were they truly simple enough to believe they'd ever be given a truthful answer?

"A score and three," Angruin said promptly. "At the field, when we chased these enemies through the woods, and this morning, when they attacked the road guard at Eastkeep."

There was a stir up and down the table. Not all here had heard of this before. Not surprisingly, Xanther and the other Sembian merchant, the wine dealer Saddusk, spoke together. "What befell there?"

Angruin looked meaningfully to the Lord of the Dale. Longspear motioned him to continue and picked up his flagon. It was good wine. He gave a silent nod of thanks to Thammar Saddusk, who returned it gravely. Then he turned back to the wizard. It had been happy fortune that the wine merchant had decided to move to the dale, in semiretirement from the bustle and high prices of Sembia's crowded cities, just after Longspear had taken it. The wine at the High Castle, by all accounts, was better than what one could get in Zhentil Keep itself, unless one was both noble and too rich to care what was charged for it.

Angruin began with a shrug. "Two people—an old man and a young woman, the watchers on the keep wall say—came out of the woods and fought with the guard on the road. They prevailed, entered the guard hut, and then fled."

"Prevailed?" Gulkin Hammarlin asked, his tone none too friendly. "Were all the guards slain?" The burly former hiresword was no friend to Zhent newcomers, either, and apt to be difficult. He was the best carpenter, glazier, and roofer in the dale, though; too useful to silence.

"Yes." Angruin's mouth shut like a trap, leaving only the single word hanging in the air over the table.

"Nine armed men?" Saddusk's dry voice asked. "What of the guard-wizard? What's his name—Dommil, or whatever?"

Stormcloak gave Longspear another inquiring look. Heladar took great satisfaction in raising his own eyebrows in mock surprise and motioning him to continue again.

"Ildomyl," Angruin said flatly. "Dead."

The mages Nordryn and Hcarla, Stormcloak's sneering lurkers-at-shoulders, both looked at him sharply. Nordryn and Ildomyl had been friends, and Nordryn looked shaken.

Hcarla just looked irritated, no doubt because Angruin hadn't told him of this before the meeting. Hcarla always wanted to know everything that was going on. On two late-night occasions when Longspear had shown certain traveling ladies the private chambers of the Lord of the High Dale, Heladar had caught sight of Hcarla's familiar—a small, ugly, bat-winged cat. On the second occasion, Heladar had taken great delight in cutting the spying creature out of the air with his blade and watching it plummet into the moat. Hcarla had been weak and white-faced for days.

But enough ancient history. No doubt everyone in the dale knew by now that the mercenary band that had seized the High Dale by deposing High Constable Mulmar and slaughtering the constables he commanded had come from Zhentil Keep. Anyone with wits at all knew that no independent band would include more than a handcount of wizards. The dalefolk knew that Heladar Longspear was here at the pleasure of the Zhentarim, even if no whisper of that had ever passed the lips of any Brotherhood agent.

Yet would that connection, even proven, spur a neighboring realm, nearby merchant, or hard-luck mercenary or outlaw band to challenge the rule of the self-proclaimed Lord Longspear? Nay. 'Twas more likely to discourage any open attack.

So, did these magical attacks, first launched through the Zhentarim-created Daggerdale supply gate, come from rivals in the Brotherhood, or were they mounted as some sort of devious test? Heladar studied the faces of the men who sat at his council table, wondering (not for the first time, nor yet, he feared, the last) which ones might be spies or waiting challengers—and who, or what, stood behind each.

With half the wizards gone, twelve sat before him at the table. Stormcloak, Hcarla Bellwind, and Nordryn—the Zhentarim mages, openly menacing, sure of their power. Everyone at the table knew they ruled in the High Dale as much as he did.

Heladar kept his face impassive—it was second nature by now—and looked to the others. Three were Zhent agents, their loyalties known to himself and the mages but not, he hoped, to others in the dale or to watching outsiders.

There was the local blacksmith, Kromm Kadar, staring back at him impassively. A recent addition to the council and a Zhentilar warrior of bannerlord rank, Kromm was a silent, strong man who saw all and missed nothing. His predecessor, in both council seat and smithy, had been a Sembian spy, the first man Angruin had killed openly in the dale.

There was Alazs Ironwood, local horse breeder and trader, a sarcastic Zhentilar veteran, a Sword with much experience in battle.

Next to him sat the balding, birdlike alchemist who served as physic, pharmacist, and tanner to the dalefolk. He was also their only priest—a finger of the Black Hand, of course—and Heladar trusted him not a whit. He probably reported back to Fzoul Chembryl every time a mouse drew breath in the dale. Cheth Moonviper was his name, and as befitting a blood member of one of the oldest Zhent noble families, he was haughty, fussy, prissy, and far too perfumed and giggling for Heladar to want to approach him closely.

Those, Heladar reflected with dark humor, were his allies.

The other six men at the table could, in secret, serve half the Realms. Unless they were very foolish or unlucky, neither he nor any of these strutting spell-hurlers would ever know their treachery for sure until, of course, it was too late.

Heladar eyed them sourly, suppressing a sigh. He was tired of veiled menace, intrigue, and honeyed words. Swinging a sword was more his style. Did every ruler, even of such petty places as this, have to contend with such dung and serpents? It was a wonder more kings didn't hold daily executions!

He could think of a few that would do the High Dale, himself, and probably their wives and as-yet-unborn offspring a service by quickly and quietly swallowing a sword blade in some alley near the castle. Heading the list would be the fat weaver, Jatham Villore. The man was a loudmouthed pest and, Heladar suspected, far wiser than he pretended to be. But if the weaver was a spy, whom did he report to?

The leather worker, Blakkal Mord, seemed altogether more sinister. A warrior, before all the gods, and not out of practice, either. He'd lived in the dale a long time, but that didn't mean he wasn't the eyes for a local power. Sembia? Cormyr? By the beard of Tempus, he could even serve the Pirates of the Isles! Heladar sighed. Hopeless, this guessing, until the man let slip his true banner. Like all the rest.

The smooth-tongued, saturnine Xanther Srildar was almost too obviously a spy. The Sembian "rarities and collectibles" merchant could be the eyes for Sembia or any merchant cabal one might think of. He might even serve the Cult of the Dragon, the Harpers, or Gondegal the Lost King for that matter. He moved his hands like a wizard. Heladar frowned at those hands, not for the first time.

Then there was the surly, barrel-chested carpenter, Gulkin Hammarlin, one of an old naval family from Daerlun. Gulkin had lived in the High Dale for over twenty winters after a short, hard mercenary career, and fiercely resented Longspear's rule. His hatred for the mages was even stronger, suggesting it was Zhentil Keep he stood against and not Longspear the usurper. What was more, he didn't bother to hide his leanings.

Rundeth Hobyltar was another one. The local tailor and dyer was brighter than Gulkin, almost as much the snake as Xanther. Laconic and cynical, he took pains to appear easygoing. Heladar's informants said that, in the days before Zhentarim mages had first come to the High Dale, Rundeth had been a shrewd warrior, often hired by Sembian interests to ferret out and destroy outlaws in the mountains, and even thieves in the big port cities of the Land of Silver. Perhaps he was in the pay of someone in Sembia even now.

And last, Thammar. The wine merchant was the only witty, friendly, serenely apolitical councillor, interested only in getting good wine into the dale for all and in lining his pockets liberally along the way. Hmmm . . . retired from Sembia. Gods spit! Saddusk could be a

Sembian spy, or worse. With his contacts, he could be an agent for fabled Kara-Tur or someplace even farther afield. Often it's the friendliest one, the one you least suspect, who has the dagger waiting . . . and Thammar did wear a sword rather too casually for a soft, nearly retired Sembian merchant.

Oh, to the grave with all this pondering! Any one of them, or all of them, could well be behind this. Or it might be simply the work of a wizard gone off his head, with his daughter, apprentice, or pleasure-maid keeping him company.

Heladar realized with a sudden chill that, in the end, it didn't really matter. If Longspear was to rule in the High Dale more than a winter longer, he must assume all of them were in league against him and waiting for a chance to bring him down. If he didn't—well, one of them at least would try.

And if he was able or lucky enough to survive that attempt, the idea would be in their heads. One of the others would decide that the title of Lord of the High Dale sounded grand enough and—situated on the trade road between Cormyr and Sembia, while Zhent-backed brigands kept the Daerlun road dangerous and expensive— profitable enough to make a grab for it.

Even the best blade can grow dull, if it has to lop off too many reaching fingers.

* * * * *

Heladar's continuing silence had led Stormcloak on to bolder speech. Warmed by the heat of his own wagging tongue, the wizard had even begun to speak as if the High Dale's men-at-arms obeyed him and—the traditional failing of mages—as if the council would agree to his every whim because no intelligent being could help but see things as he did. Heladar just smiled and went on being silent.

Angruin was in the midst of exhorting his fellow councillors to stir their children, their neighbors, their neighbor's children, and any cats and dogs within reach to take up arms and scour every inch of the dale for these intruders, to slay them, capture them, or drive them out. The dale must be cleansed!

Ye gods, he sounds like one of the priests. Heladar turned his gaze again around the table. Of course the mages want every blade out and every child alert. The more who fight, the more they can hide behind, hurling spells from a safe distance.

This could be a real challenge, to the Zhentarim as well as to the lordship of Heladar Longspear. Cormyr could be lurking behind the attacks, or Sembia, or even powerful loners like the fabled Gondegal, Elminster of Shadowdale, or the willful, wandering Witch-Queen of Aglarond who flew endlessly about Faerûn in the shape of a black falcon, meddling. The only thing to do was to muster the entire armed might of the dale to track down the intruders, backed by all the magic the wizards could mount. Manshoon would order that if Heladar didn't.

There was something else, though. Even before these attacks, the wizards had been tense and troubled. Had this entire episode been prearranged by someone in Zhentil Keep, part of some deep plan to cast aside Longspear and change the rule of the High Dale again?

Nay. That would not worry the mages so collectively and deeply. They'd looked like lost men, especially the lesser ones. At the time, he'd assumed that Zhentil Keep had given them harsh and unsettling orders not for his ears. Now, though . . . Nordryn had been upset by the news about his friend, but now his face showed not so much shock and grief as it did fear for his own skin, and a sort of helplessness. He stared down at his open hands for a moment as if not believing that they could ever cast a spell again.

Heladar's eyes narrowed. Was that it? Ildomyl had seized a goodly amount of magic, by all accounts, and certainly the man had a wand or two. He shouldn't have fallen so easily. Had his magic failed him?

He smiled. Watching the mages would take long—perhaps too long. Better to charge in, swinging a blade, and force things his way. He smiled and said quietly, "Angruin is right, of course. We must rouse the dale."

Stormcloak's head turned in surprise. He had almost forgotten Heladar was there at all. Longspear met his eyes and added softly, "Yet there is something I must speak to him about in private. Something about . . . spells." He raised his eyebrows, awaiting Angruin's agreement.

That was it! There was something amiss with their magic. The mages were all looking at him as though he'd grown six hissing serpent heads, and all of them breathing fire, too!

Heladar smiled evenly at them all, looking mysterious and enjoying it. Let them think he had his own sources rather than dismissing him as a stone-headed, sword-swinging puppet who'd dance eagerly to whatever tune they told him Zhentil Keep played. This was more the way things should be. He drummed his fingertips in satisfaction on the hilt of his sword, below the edge of the table, and leaned forward.

The other councillors were agreeing, of course. They could hardly appear loyal, or even prudent in matters touching the safety of their homes, if they did not. If they were all spies, though, the coming turmoil could only give them chances to kill off Zhent mages and warriors, weakening the invisible but heavy hand in which Zhentil Keep held the High Dale.

"Have we agreement, then?" he asked softly, surprising them all this time. He gathered them in with his eyes, one by one around the table. All met his gaze. All, even the wizards, nodded to his authority.

Heladar Longspear rose to his feet and looked down that long table. "As we are all agreed," he began formally, "I have no hesitation in giving the orders: We loose all our hounds and go to war."

* * * * *

It was cold, churning along up to their knees in the swampy backwaters, and the smell was incredible. "See the far reaches of the Realms," Sharantyr muttered.

"Walk where no mortal has trod. . . . Is this what those mercenaries mean when they go spinning tales in the taverns?"

"To lure idle young bravos? Aye." Elminster chuckled. "This is exactly what they mean, though they sing a different song." He strode along in the muddy water unconcerned, his long robes drawn up through his belt into a ridiculous bundle. Seeing her look, he laid a hand suggestively on his hip, batted his eyelashes at her, and winked. Sharantyr saw that he'd tied the long end of his white beard into a club knot.

It was too much. She shouted with laughter, doubled up over the fetid water, then stopped suddenly, clapping a dripping hand over her mouth.

"Tymora bless me!" she hissed. "I'm sorry, Old Mage! The guards—"

Elminster chuckled. "Don't worry," he assured her. "That last cliff back there, the one like the ship's prow, marks the western end of the dale, or used to. We've slipped clean past Westkeep and into what they call the Hullack Stairs—or used to."

Sharantyr chuckled at that. "I'll be hearing you say 'or used to' in my sleep."

Elminster's eyebrows rose. "Oh?" he asked with dignity. "I was aware that I'd given thee leave to accompany me, young lady, and that ye'd behaved thyself—more or less—impeccably, given our physical proximity and, ah, dire straits. But I assure thee I do not recall giving thee any intimation that ye'd be welcome to listen to me while ye pretend to slumber!"

Sharantyr sighed, and shook her head. "All right, Old Mage, all right," she shushed him. "What now?"

"Now we look for the marker stone that should be right about . . . here." Elminster trotted around a clump of shrubs, over a fallen tree, and paused dramatically, pointing at a weathered pillar of stone.

"You knew where to find this?"

Elminster shrugged. "Unless someone took it into his head to move it since I placed it here, some three hundred winters ago."

Sharantyr rolled her eyes. "And having found your marker?" she asked the sky.

The Old Mage did not reply. He was leaning forward, staring at the stone. On the side closest to the High Dale, someone had written with the ashen end of a burned stick: "Death To The Tyranny Of All Mages." Elminster frowned at it for a long breath or two, then slowly grinned.

He turned. "Eh? Oh, aye. We sleep hereabouts, then turn back and enter the dale openly on the morrow. That's when our fun begins."

"You mean we attack these Zhents openly? But, your magic—"

Elminster spread open hands. "I have my baubles, and thee, to keep me safe."

Sharantyr sighed, then smiled and said formally, "We ride well together, Old Mage." Her eyes flashed.

Elminster bowed, gave her a sad, slow smile in return, and answered, "Ye're not the first lass that's said that to me, but I thank thee for saying it." And he leaned over and kissed her cheek tenderly.

Sharantyr looked at him, somewhat surprised. The Old Mage smiled back at her for a moment. Then he suddenly stiffened, turned white, and abruptly sat down on some ferns.

"Elminster!" She sprang forward and bent over him anxiously. "What befalls?"

The wizard shook his head and waved a hand at her before reaching up to unknot his beard. "Much power was suddenly drawn out of me. It was—upsetting."

He brightened, then frowned. "Perhaps Lady Mystra is with us again and had need of it. Or—perhaps another being has found a way to steal what I carry, and the Realms are doomed." He shrugged, and brushed aside a few branches to stretch out more comfortably.

"Ah, well," he said. "Stretch out here beside me, las— Shar, sorry. No doubt we'll find out which has befallen tomorrow."

10
Wizards' Woe

The sun rose and awakened them.

Sharantyr felt it warm her face. She came awake, alert in an instant. The ranger lay still, feeling the hard ground beneath her, the reassuring hardness of her sword hilt under her fingers, and a familiar warmth—and sound—beside her: the unconcernedly snoring form of Elminster of Shadowdale.

She smiled, shook her head, and eased away from him to stretch her stiff legs and aching back. The sounds promptly ceased, and a familiar, irascible voice said, "Ready to save the High Dale, then? I was wondering when you'd bother to stir your shanks."

Sharantyr paused. "You snore loudly when you're wondering about things," she told him, amused.

Elminster regarded her with dignity. "Simply giving the insides of my skull some fresh air," he replied. "As ye seem to do often, yawning the way ye do whenever we talk about anything."

Sharantyr waved a dismissive hand. "Simply straining not to miss a single inference or nuance of your fair speech," she told him serenely and walked away.

The lady ranger turned after a few steps. "I shall return in a breath or two," she announced. "While I'm gone, see what you can do about dawnfry. I'm starving, and my belly seems ever hungrier than that."

Elminster sighed. "I can certainly take thy mind off it, lass," he said gruffly, "and have thee running about in such a whirlwind of seeking spells and eager blades and shouting Black Helms that thy stomach'll soon have the heaves. But if it's real food ye want to feel sliding down thy gullet and warming thy insides, we'll have to buy that in the High Dale, as any wayfarers would. So the sooner we set off, the sooner we both eat."

"Fair fortune to that," Sharantyr agreed from behind a tree. "Can we leave off conquering the dale until after I eat?"

* * * * *

"Ready to save the dale, then?" Belkram asked cheerfully.

Itharr just looked at him. "Is there anything to eat?" A rolling growl from his stomach echoed the query.

"No," Belkram said just as cheerfully. "I saw a few berries yestereve, two ridges back, but there weren't more than a handful."

"Ummm." Itharr looked glum. "All this running about, hacking mages and Zhentilar strongnecks, seems a lot more enticing on a full stomach."

"One stride before the next," Belkram said reassuringly. "If we knock over enough mages, we're sure to find one with some food. If we have to take the lord's throne of this place to do it, we can throw a victory feast, and you can stuff yourself for free."

"Ummm," Itharr said again, stretching—and wincing at the stiff tenderness of his wound. "*After* we defeat all the evil ones? I'm not even certain this *is* the High Dale. What if we're somewhere east of Impiltur or in the fabled Far Isles?"

"Then we'll have a long walk back," Belkram said, not unkindly. "Let's look for an inn, or at least a tavern. There must be one. We've seen a castle and a lot of homes outside its walls. We'll ask folk there if anyone's seen Elminster of Shadowdale wandering about."

"Aye," Itharr grunted, reaching out of long habit for his blade. "And then we'll leap to our feet and try to carve a way out of the place, through seven handcounts or so of black-armored hireswords all howling for our blood."

Belkram shrugged. "Right, so we'll buy some dawnfry first and ask questions later."

Itharr nodded. "If I'm to be fighting for my life," he said, hefting his blade experimentally, "I'd prefer to do it knowing that I've at least had one last good meal."

Belkram looked at him and scratched the stubble on his chin. "A real brightheart, aren't you?"

Itharr grinned. "Let's put on our best Harper smiles as we rush to certain death, hewing and slaying with the best of them!" he chirped brightly and mockingly, and skipped down out of the rocky hollow where they'd slept, whistling a merry tune.

Belkram sighed. "Why is it always my lot to share trail with the lunatics?" he asked the gods above as he followed. As usual, the gods did not bother to answer.

* * * * *

Heladar Longspear stood on the castle walls and looked around at his dale. He strode slowly, gazing for a long time east down the tunnel-like valley and looking almost as long into the west. The sentinels on the walls saluted him in respectful silence and kept out of his way. Heladar was silently grateful for that.

He'd grown to love this harsh, stone-locked, backward place—a dale of history and importance balanced on a sword's edge between proud Cormyr and rich Sembia, a place that had bowed to him, however unwillingly, for over a moon now. A place he'd felt was strong and secure in his grip despite the ongoing schemes of the mages, and the rest of the council for that matter. Secure for long enough to relax and enjoy the place.

His High Dale. His until the night before last, at least. Now some unknown foe was lurking out there, perhaps even under his gaze right now, looking back at him from hiding, waiting to bring about his fall.

He wheeled, cloak swirling, to stride toward the stairs leading down. He'd ordered his best armor freshly oiled and laid ready this morn, and he'd feel better once he was in it.

He'd learned a thing or two in enough years of battle and guardianship, waiting and scouting, standing guard and snatching sleep whenever possible. He'd learned the ways of war, to trust his hunches, to smell danger, and to feel when something was wrong or when violence was coming.

Today, for instance. Strife would come here, to the heart of the High Dale, this day. Heladar could feel it, and an old soldier's bones never lied.

Who, he wondered for the twentieth time since dawn, was at large, swords out, in his dale? Who sought the downfall of Lord Longspear?

He was just swinging his boot forward to descend the first step when up out of the darkness came two dark eyes he knew and disliked. The eyes looked back at him, cold and knowing, not bothering to hide their own feelings.

Angruin. The mage who called himself Stormcloak and thought himself the true ruler of the High Dale.

Longspear came to a silent halt on the top step, hand on hip where it could rest by his weapons, and waited.

This whole affair could just be a clash of private plots and feuds among these mages. There need be no outside, lurking enemy, merely the creatures and servants of this ambitious, strutting Zhentarim or any of the lesser wizards beneath him.

Longspear did not allow himself to sigh. He kept his eyes bleak as Stormcloak swept up the last steps.

"Fair morn, Lord," the mage greeted him coldly and smoothly. "Are you well? Is there something dark on your mind?"

Longspear eyed him back just as coldly. "The safety of my dale," he said shortly. "As usual. Will you be ready, mage, to see to the safety of the High Dale, should we be attacked?"

"Attacked?" Stormcloak crooked one long, arched eyebrow. "Do you expect something as swiftly as all that?"

"Sooner," Longspear growled. "Sooner." He looked out again at the peaceful trees and fields of the dale below, then up to the frowning gray walls of the mountains beyond on both sides.

Then he brought his gaze down, hawklike, directly to meet the wizard's.

Stormcloak's eyes were steady upon him. He waited.

Silence. Heladar sighed inwardly and asked, "Well?"

"My lord?" The mage added the slightest mocking twist to the title.

"I asked you a question, mage." Heladar kept his voice cold, level, and patient. "Have you an answer for me?"

Stormcloak was silent. Heladar propped an elbow on the nearest stone crenellation as if he had all the time in the Realms, leaned against it, and waited.

The mage waited a moment more, testing Longspear's gaze, then said softly, "My spells are ready to defend the High Dale, for the greater glory of the Zhentarim."

For the Zhentarim—not for Heladar Longspear.

The Lord of the High Dale gave him a wintry smile to show that his verbal jab had not been missed and said, "What is it I hear from Zhentil Keep, then, of magic going wild and mages falling mad?"

Angruin took a step closer, frowning. "Wild magic? Who has told you of this?"

Longspear smiled a long, slow smile. "One," he said carefully, "whom it is better not to name. I assure you that you know him. He inhabits a lofty tower."

Angruin kept his face mildly interested, no more. Manshoon. Longspear's words could mean only one man: he who dwelt in the Tower High. Lord Manshoon, leader of the Zhentarim. This Heladar Longspear must enjoy more favor than he'd thought.

Longspear, who'd just launched his greatest bluff so far in his dealings with this haughty wizard, smiled and hoped he'd get away with it. "Well?" he asked again. "The day does draw on, Angruin. I can't order the men to best effect unless I know how much I can rely on your magic, and that of the lesser mages. What say you?"

Angruin Myrvult accepted the extended hand of peace somewhat reluctantly. "Our Art—the magic of all men, from what I hear and suspect—has become somewhat . . . unsettled. Yet we stand with you as always, Lord Longspear. Moreover," he added, lifting his hands to reveal the wand at his belt that his fingers had been tightening around as they spoke, "we are never without at least one . . . aid."

"Good," Heladar told him. Before Stormcloak could add

the inevitable threat, he spoke it for him. "I'll remember that."

The Lord of the High Dale went down the stairs, feeling cold eyes on his back all the way down. He kept his shoulders broad and square, taking satisfaction in his daring at turning his back on Angruin for so long. No one else in all the dale dared to.

* * * * *

Jatham Villore looked out of his shop, up at the frowning bulk of the High Castle looming above the trees. "Yet the eating of bad bread may make a haunt of the dreams of even a lord," he echoed the quotation. No, the word had been "kings," hadn't it? No matter.

Heladar and his bullying mages were upset indeed, for the first time since they'd come here. Perhaps their rule could be weakened or even broken altogether.

That would please his masters very much.

Jatham went quietly into his shop and bolted the door. This wouldn't take long. Just a simple spell or two to confuse and befog magical attempts to locate things and folk such as the mysterious enemies who'd twice been so bold as to strike out at the lord's Wolves and mages.

Or even more times, if Longspear and Angruin had not told all. Jatham grinned as he bolted an inner door behind him. These cloaking spells had saved his own skin more than once. Back in Thay, he'd learned their ins and outs very thoroughly, for wise masters had told him that his success as an agent—his very survival—depended on such knowledge. They'd been right, of course.

Jatham laid hands on what he'd need, closed his eyes briefly to gather his will, and began the whispered chant. At long last, it was time to act.

* * * * *

They had almost reached the hard-eyed guards when Elminster snapped his fingers and laid a firm hand on the inside of Sharantyr's elbow, dragging her to a halt.

"I must be getting old," he muttered. "I almost forgot." He gestured toward the bushes. "Go in there to relieve yourself," he directed.

Sharantyr raised an eyebrow. "I don't need to at the moment, thank you very much, Old M—"

As she spoke, Elminster smoothly produced the two wands he was carrying and slid them up the sleeve of the arm he was clasping.

"All I need ye to do is slide these under thy—'hem—chest, Shar," he murmured. "Beneath them, mind, where no searching guard will feel them. Hurry, now."

Sharantyr gave him a look and did as she was bid. She came out into the road fumbling with the lacings at her belt and saw two of the guards exchange amused looks. The wands felt cold and hard next to her skin.

He grinned at her. "I'll reclaim them as soon as I can, lass," he promised.

"I'll just wager you will," she replied in warning tones.

"One more thing," Elminster added hurriedly. "If I signal you—so—by scratching my ear, think hard of Sembian trade, merchant contacts, and making money there. Keep thinking of those things until I scratch there again."

"You mean someone might pry at our thoughts?" Sharantyr asked warily.

Elminster nodded and added loudly, "I've told ye, gel, if ye drink so much before setting out, o' course the walking'll see thee in the bushes all too soon!"

The guards smiled at his words, waving them to one side of the road and staring hard at them both.

"A copper each for passage into the High Dale," said the larger one shortly, holding out his hand.

Elminster meekly took two coppers out of his purse—two coppers he'd picked up in the guard hut at the other end of the dale, not so long ago—and paid them over.

"Stretch out arms afore ye," said another guard, blade drawn. "We have orders to search all who enter the dale. Resist us, or reach for any weapon, and you'll see nothing else in this life but your own blood, all of it leaving you."

*   *   *   *   *

Haragh Mnistlyn leaned forward in his chair. A warrior woman traveling with an old man was certainly odd. Best give these two the full scrutiny.

He stood up, making a certain sign. The guard who was watching for it drew his blade and motioned to another of his fellows. They took up positions near the two who were being searched, near enough to disrupt the casting of a spell with a quick lunge.

Haragh stood under his awning, watching the faces of the two narrowly, as hard-eyed as the guards, and began the casting of a spell to read minds.

*   *   *   *   *

Elminster scratched one ear and Sharantyr frowned slightly. Hard, probing hands wandered over them both. They waited, unmoving.

Until they heard a gasp.

Everyone turned. The mage who'd sat in the chair under the canopy, back from the road, was standing horrified in the midst of well-trodden grass. In front of him, as they watched, little white flowers were appearing, first singly, then in clusters of three and more. Swiftly, silently, the flowers appeared out of nothingness, without any fuss or spell-smoke.

The mage stared down at them, stunned.

Sharantyr glanced quickly at Elminster. His eyes had widened just a trifle, but now he was nodding, slowly, as if he understood.

He stepped forward, ignoring the blades held ready near him, and clapped his hands. "Beautiful!" he said enthusiastically. "I've seen no better in the tavern spell-contests of Waterdeep itself! My thanks, mage. Has the High Dale become a place where magic is embraced and its beauty appreciated?"

Haragh's mouth opened and shut, but no words came out. He stared down at his hands, then sat down suddenly in his chair, shaking his head.

Elminster's face fell. "Oh, dear," he said to the nearest guard. "Did he intend to cast something else? My apologies, if I've offended . . ."

The guard looked at him. "You a wizard?"

"Nay, nay," Elminster said with a regretful sigh. "Fascinated by the stuff. See as much of it as I can, and trade in it when Lady Luck has it so, but I can't call up even a spark, even when lowly apprentices take too many gold pieces from me for showing me how to. It's just not something the gods meant for me, it seems."

The warrior chuckled. "Aye, you and me both, old man." He jerked his head. "Go on, then," he told them. "We'd better see to Lord High-and-Mighty." He stared over at the chair with long-suffering good humor, and Elminster chuckled in the easy fellowship of one downtrodden jack to another.

"My thanks, goodsir," the Old Mage told him and trudged eastward into the High Dale, with Sharantyr in tow.

*   *   *   *   *

Elminster waited until they were safely screened from any curious eyes on Westkeep's battlements, then stopped and extended a hand.

Sharantyr calmly loosened the lacings of her leathers, looked swiftly about, and slid his wands out and returned them to him, somewhat warmer.

Elminster stowed them away as smoothly and said, "My thanks, Shar. We do work well together."

Sharantyr smiled at him. "Well, Mysterious One? What happened back there?"

The Old Mage shrugged. "Magic is going awry all over the Realms. We've just been treated to more evidence of that." He looked at her rather sadly.

"I must warn ye: Rely not overmuch on the magic we're carrying, either."

Sharantyr nodded slowly and took his arm. They walked on.

"Tell me," she said in low tones as they went over a

little rise and houses began to appear before them, "why you had no fear of being found out, if that mage could read minds? Did you know his spell would fail?"

Elminster shook his head. "If I could predict its working, 'twouldn't be 'wild magic,' now, would it?"

Sharantyr nodded. "Mystra's burden, again?" she asked softly.

"Aye," Elminster said briefly, his gaze leaping here and there ahead of them as alertly as any battle scout.

"That sounds very useful to a Harper—or a courtier, I suppose," Sharantyr said almost wistfully. "No enemy can read your thoughts or twist your will. Why do they call it Mystra's burden?"

"Think, if ye will," he replied, "of the loneliness ye would feel were ye to outlive all thy friends except fellow bearers of the burden. Ye'd see kingdoms fall, not once but again and again, and favorite places changed or swept away in the passing years. Think on this and ask me again why we call it Mystra's burden."

Sharantyr was silent beside him as they walked a long way. Then she asked almost timidly, "What, then, will we do now, Old Mage?"

Elminster looked at her in surprise. "Why, go and defeat this Longspear, of course."

* * * * *

Jatham almost fled out of his dark room, breathing heavily. The spells had worked, aye, but he'd never before had Art curl away from his control with almost contemptuous ease. Ye gods, what was happening to him?

He paused out in the shop to wipe cold sweat from his brow and restore his usual lazy smile before he threw back the bolt. The smile took a lot more effort than usual.

Rogue magic! What could have caused it? Was Stormcloak an even greater danger than he'd thought?

Or was it the mysterious enemies? What Art did they wield?

What dark creatures were they?

*   *   *   *   *

Belkram looked around at rolling fields, trees clustered along little streams that babbled down from the ever-present watching gray walls of stone above, and drew a deep breath.

"Ready?" he asked, loosening his blade in its sheath.

Itharr nodded. "As ever," he replied, adding a wry smile. "Harpers rush in"—he quoted an odd saying Elminster of Shadowdale had uttered just last summer, but which was already well known across the North—"where even fools fear to tread."

"Aye," Belkram agreed dryly. "So let it begin." He pushed open the door and they went in. Above their heads, the worn signboard told all passersby that they were looking at "A Good Inn: The Shepherds' Rest." The sign creaked slightly in a gathering breeze, but there wasn't anyone looking at it any longer, so it soon fell quiet again.

At about the same time, tumult wild and royal broke out with a roar inside the inn.

11
The Running of the Wolves

" 'A Good Inn,' eh?" Itharr murmured as they shouldered their way through dark, heavy windcurtains—old hides, by the look of them—into smoky, lamplit dimness beyond. "Well, mayhap it was, once."

"Long ago," Belkram agreed and made for a small table against a wall. The sizzling of bacon and the smell of buttered frybread was strong in the crowded, low-beamed common room.

A few old men and withered goodwives were huddled in silence at the smaller tables. Most of the room held hard-eyed, arrogant fighting men in a variety of ragged leathers. All sported black armbands, some edged in purple. Off-duty Wolves, no doubt.

The serving man was old, grizzled, and weary. He shuffled over to the two Harpers with a simple, "Dawnfry? Drink? Right, what'll it be?"

"Reddarn wine" Itharr replied with an eager smile. The hot spiced drink was brought quickly. It was saltier and thicker than in better houses but went well down their thirsty throats. Dawnfry was even better, and the two Harpers fell on platter after platter like starving men.

Or, one might say, like Wolves. One of the armsmen strode to their table. His armband had a purple border denoting rank; he was probably a Sword. Belkram looked unconcernedly up at him over a handful of hot, crumbling frybread.

The burly man's thumbs were hooked under the guards of a dagger at his belt. He met Belkram's eyes with a gaze as cold and as hard as a stone wall, and stood over them silently, waiting for Itharr to notice him.

Itharr finished his reddarn and said, "More, please,"

without looking up. Belkram kept his face straight.

Itharr winked with the eye nearest the wall, so only Belkram could see, as he waved his flagon. "More reddarn," he explained, "when you can. I'm enjoying this excellent bacon."

"I'm not," the man said flatly, "a servant."

Itharr turned his head, raised his eyes lazily from the man's belt to his face, and said, "Aye, I can see that. You a hiresword?"

The man frowned. "I'll ask questions and you'll answer, see?"

Belkram emptied his own flagon. "Get us more reddarn while you're asking, will you?"

A few chuckles came from the nearest tables of Wolves as the man turned cold eyes on him. "I serve the Lord of the High Dale," he said heavily, "and I don't recall any armed adventurers being allowed into the dale this last seven days or so. How long've you two been here?"

"Not long," Belkram told him. "We're wandering minstrels, come to pay a call on friends."

"You have friends in the dale?"

"Many—or at least, on our last visit there were many folk here we count our friends," Itharr said smoothly. "We haven't seen them this time around. Could something have happened in the High Dale these last two winters?"

Silence fell. The armsman scowled at Itharr, leaned a little closer, and asked loudly, "What brings you here *this* time?"

"We're trying to find a friend who might have come here," Belkram told him truthfully.

"Elminster of Shadowdale," Itharr added helpfully. "Have you seen him?"

The Sword stiffened and swiftly drew back. The room fell so silent that faint sizzlings could be heard from the adjoining kitchen. The two Harpers looked calmly around to see hands on sword hilts all over the room. These men seemed to know Elminster's name.

"And what are *your* names?" their interrogator asked from a safe distance away. He stood now beside his seat, and his sheathed sword lay on it near his hand.

"Gondegal. The Older," Belkram replied merrily, using the name of the legendary Lost King of Cormyr, a vanished usurper. Itharr added brightly, "Gondegal the Younger."

The man showed his teeth. "Smart tongues and ragged clothes usually mean Harpers," he said, and turned to address the tables of armed men. "Take them!"

There was a general rush. Itharr snatched up the last of the frybread and Belkram snatched up the table. He flung it easily, as a child lobs a stone, and took down one Wolf. His chair took down another.

Amid the general tumult, Itharr swept up his own chair and held it as a shield. "Brawling in an inn? What knavery's this?" he cried loudly. "Does justice rule no longer in the High Dale?"

Belkram nodded. "Aye! We demand to speak to Irreph Mulmar. A man should not have to fight to have a little dawnfry in this dale!"

One of the men chuckled, advancing. "Mulmar rules here no longer."

"What have you done with Irreph?" Belkram asked, his voice slow and quiet. "I knew him, long ago."

Itharr, who knew Belkram well, shivered a little despite himself when he heard his friend's voice.

The Sword laughed, not pleasantly. "He works full days at the mill now," he said, "docile as a well-whipped ox since Lord Angruin's magic bent his will."

"What?" said Itharr and Belkram together as their blades hissed out.

"Take them!" the order rang out again, and the room erupted into steely war.

* * * * *

The crack of the whip and the cold shock of the slop that was his morning meal being dumped on his sleeping body always awakened him. In the cold, misty grayness before full dawn, the dull-eyed thing that had once been a man always licked the slop from his flesh and the smooth stone he walked on.

They watched him. The moment he was done, the stinging crack of the whip came again, and his chains pulled him forward. It happened again about the middle of each day.

He was shackled to a massive wooden lever that ran to a central spindle. He walked on a great circle of stone in the darkness, around and around that spindle all day, pushing the lever. Above him, grinding stones rumbled and grain spilled endlessly down with a dry rushing sound. Thick dust rose and water always dripped somewhere, unseen in the echoing dark.

His hands had stopped bleeding an age ago. Shackles of stout metal encircled his throat and wrists. From each shackle, a chain as long as he was tall led to rings on the great lever.

When his body grew too foul for the overseers—he never saw them, just whips lashing down out of darkness —pipes were opened above and icy-cold water washed away the filth. The whips and water had taken his clothes long ago; he wore only a few tattered wisps of cloth around one ankle. His arms, shoulders, and thighs had grown huge and hard, covered with a latticework of white whip scars. His hair had grown long, jaw and chest covered with matted, furlike tangles. His eyes were always dull, no fire alight behind them.

Until this morn. The millstones rumbled overhead as usual, dust swirled, and the lever, as always, was smooth and very, very heavy. He pushed against it, driving forward a weight that seemed more than three or four dead horses. Endlessly forward. He had to shove and heave and snarl until he got it rolling, then he bent into a smooth, steady push that ate up the endless breaths of the day, around and around and around.

A thought came to him then, as he trudged, the first unbidden thought in a great while. His working day was really not so different from that of a lot of free men.

He chuckled at that as he pushed. It was a sound he had not made in a long, long time.

* * * * *

Belkram chuckled coldly as his steel found the throat of another Wolf. The Shepherds' Rest was awash with blood and smashed furniture draped with bodies. The warriors who'd been so loudly arrogant when the fray began were now silent forever or backed into a corner, fear in their white faces.

A few deaths back, several of the Wolves had tried to break past the two Harpers and escape. Out of a side passage to bar their way came the grizzled old serving man, smiling grimly, an ancient and rusting battle-axe in his hands.

One Wolf contemptuously tried to run him through. The old man slid aside from his lunge, punched his assailant hard in the throat, and trampled the fallen Wolf as he swung his axe at the next. When the Wolves fell back from that old axe, it descended to meet the head of the man on the floor, rising again before they could advance.

Itharr had reached the rear of those Wolves. Steel leapt and bit, men grunted, swung, and screamed . . . and a little silence befell. Itharr and the old serving man used it to share a ferocious smile across the bloody fallen.

Belkram stalked forward to confront the last few Wolves. "We've important business at the castle," he told them almost sadly, "so we haven't time to take prisoners."

Itharr sighed. "So sad," he murmured, and lunged. A Wolf shrieked and struck the Harper's blade aside at the last instant. His eyes were still on it when the dagger in Itharr's other hand came up into them.

As the man fell, two Wolves charged in desperation, swinging their blades wildly. Itharr ducked under the falling body and rolled aside, lifting a boot to trip one Wolf. Belkram's blade took the rearmost in the neck.

The serving man stood in the door, axe raised. "Who's first?" he rumbled, eyes cold. "Who'll die first?"

The Wolves hesitated for an instant, and that was long enough for Belkram to slay the one who'd fallen and for Itharr to rise again. The last two Wolves plunged forward desperately.

The old man's axe bore the first to one side, and Itharr

thrust him through from behind. The second leapt for the door and fell through the opening with Belkram on his back, stabbing with cold ruthlessness.

Silence fell again. Then the two Harpers rose, dusted themselves off, retrieved their weapons, and smiled at the old man. Belkram handed him six gold pieces. "For the furniture . . . and the floor show."

"Aye," Itharr agreed. "Our thanks. We must be off now."

A light was dancing in the old man's eyes. "Whither, lads? Come you to bring down this Longspear who lords it over us?"

The two Harpers nodded slowly.

"We came to find a friend of ours," Belkram said quietly. "But it seems the High Dale needs more attention than he does just now. If he were here, he'd been doing what we aim to. We're off to the castle, to rouse the dale against these Wolves and their wizards." He frowned then as a thought struck him. "Does the high constable yet live?"

"Aye," the old innkeeper said grimly. "After a fashion. As that carrion said, he's in chains, working the mill as if he were an ox."

Belkram looked at Itharr. "That ends first." His fellow Harper nodded, the grim expression matching his own.

"I'm coming with you," the old man said without another glance at the sprawled bodies in his taproom. The axe lifted a little. "I fought off outlaws aplenty, in my day." He handed back the gold. "And I won't take coins from men who do our work for us. No, take 'em! I haven't felt so good in many a year."

He stepped out to look up and down the street, then squinted thoughtfully at the frowning walls of the castle rising above the rooftops nearby. "Who's this friend you came seeking?"

Belkram saw faces peering at them from nearby doors and windows. "One Elminster, a wizard. Have you heard of him?"

The old man's eyes widened a little. "*The* Elminster?" he asked. "The Old Mage? That wasn't just talk, what you told the Wolves?"

"No," Itharr said. "We mean to find him. We promised a lady we would. Not to do him ill, either."

The old man nodded. "I saw him beat six wizards once in a battle of spells. East of here, in Sembia it was. They were slavers, going about using spells to make folks follow 'em willingly by chaining their wits. He got proper hot, I tell you."

He shook his head, a slow grin broadening his face at the memories. "It was something to see, that. He smashed 'em with lightning, hurled back the balls of fire they threw at him, opened a hole in the sky to swallow up a—a great tentacled thing they conjured up and sent after him, and crushed one of 'em under a huge rock. Snatched it off a mountain, in the midst of all, and sent it flying like a bird across most of Sembia to drop from above." He shook his head again, smiling. "I don't suppose he's here now, is he?"

Itharr spread his hands. Belkram squinted up into the sky.

"No," he said slowly. "No flying rocks."

The old man sighed. "I guess not. Ah, well. I'd hoped to see just one more good spellfight, to tell folks about, before I die." His eyes suddenly narrowed as he looked at one Harper and then at the other. "You don't know any magic, do you?"

The two Harpers sighed, looked at each other, half grinned, and sighed again.

"If we did," Belkram said ruefully, raising his still-bloody blade, "we wouldn't have to get this close to those who would kill us."

The old man looked at them both for a while, shaking his head slowly. "Well," he said at last, "without magic, how in the name of all the gods do you expect to stay alive long enough to reach the castle, let alone muster the dale against Longspear? He's got six wizards or more to back him up, Zhent Blackcloaks if I can still tell anything at all about folk I meet!"

"Well," Belkram said slowly. "We usually try to set things going—like we did here—then just get our swords out and run with what befalls."

"You wouldn't be Harpers, would you?" the old man asked quietly. He watched them exchange glances and said, "I thought so. That explains it, then. Some like to roll dice for coins, or trade goods, or even horses. Harpers and adventurers are the only folk who like to do it with their own lives."

Belkram chuckled as he wiped his steel on the sleeve of a fallen Wolf. The sound was meant to sound unconcerned and casual, but came out a trifle rueful.

* * * * *

Daera sighed and sucked her bleeding finger for perhaps the three hundredth time. Sewing flour sacks was something the gods just hadn't meant her to do.

She looked out the gap between two old, silvery wooden boards at the frowning mountain wall not so far away. It was probably about the three hundredth time she'd done that, too. Bright sunlight dazzled her; it was always dark in the mill.

Somewhere far below, Father was pushing a lever endlessly around and around, driving the grindstones. It was sheer cruelty. There was water enough—and mules or oxen, too—to do the task. No, Father was there as a reminder to the folk of the dale, as she was, set to work here as a drudge, cooking, cleaning, and sewing these bloody sacks.

Literally bloody, she thought grimly, pinching her smarting hands between her knees as she knelt on the coarse sacking. The dark spots of her spilled blood had traveled out of the dale on many a sack already. They'd seen a lot more of the Realms than ever she had, or was likely to.

Every morning, the jailers in their magical mantles of darkness came for her. They tied her hands behind her and crammed dirty cloth into her mouth, binding it there to keep her silent. Then they led her, helpless in their cloaking darkness, down the creaking stairs and uneven floors of the mill, down to the wheel where her father howled or gibbered in his chains.

That was her reminder. They untied her hands and led her outside in her soiled rags to load heavy flour sacks onto waiting carts, gasping and panting through her gag as hard-faced men in black armor stood guard around a group of silent folk of the dale—folk who had obviously been dragged from their doings and brought here to watch. If any tried to help or comfort her, they were clubbed senseless. It had been a long time since any of them had tried.

She was *their* reminder.

"Ylyndaera Mulmar," she told herself formally, "stop feeling sorry for yourself and get to work." On days when she didn't do what the jailers or mill maids thought was enough, her meal—leftovers from the evenfeast platters of the others at the mill, always cold—was smaller. Once, when she'd been too weak from sickness to work, she'd been given nothing at all to eat.

Daera sighed and picked up the needle again. She was alone here in the drafty mill loft—and cold, and bleeding all over her work again—but her father had it much worse, chained like a bull in the cellar below.

Time and again she'd prayed to the unheeding gods to deliver him, if not from his chains and the backbreaking work then at least from whatever magic they'd laid on his mind. His eyes were always cloudy. Even when she'd been able to make some noise—she always paid for that with brief but savage blows and whippings—and he'd looked up, he never saw her . . . or anything else. His moods swung between stupid placidity and snarling rages. They'd turned him into a lame-witted, crazed beast.

Daera finished a line of running stitch and bit off the thread. She was too young and weak to fight the Wolves herself. A maid had called her "a young colt—all long, gangly limbs and knobbly wrists and ankles." She must think of some way of getting aid, of calling on King Azoun or someone to rescue her father.

Most of all, Ylyndaera dreamed of the day when Irreph Mulmar would be himself again and rise to drive "Lord" Longspear and his Wolves from the dale, to reclaim his title of high constable. She was seeing that day now in her mind as she settled herself with another sack. Then the crashing and screaming began below.

She was cautious at first, fearing a beating if she wandered. Then she saw shrieking mill maids scurrying along the hall below her loft. She had to see whatever could make them run so frantically. There'd been no war trumpets or clash of arms—her first leaping hope, that the dale was under attack from Cormyr or Sembia, had died already—but something was amiss down below.

Where Father was.

* * * * *

"This is the place?" Itharr asked, squinting up at the mill. The old man nodded.

"Our thanks," Belkram said. As he turned, the tip of his sword lifted a little as if it were eager for battle. "Wait here," he added over his shoulder and stepped toward the stout, closed wooden doors before them. Itharr moved with him.

"Oh, no," the old man said emphatically. "I'm done with waiting and doing nothing. I'm going with you."

Itharr turned and flashed him a smile. "Be welcome, then," he said, "but follow our lead." He nodded at Belkram, who was courteously knocking on the door.

It opened, and a man with a ratlike face looked out, squinting in the bright light of day. "Yes?" he asked, though it was more of a challenge than a question.

Belkram flashed his brightest smile. "Good day, sirrah! We're with the Zhentil Keep Grain Inspectors Guild and have come at the express request of High Lord Manshoon to see what a fine establishment you're running here." He'd been pressing forward as he spoke. His audience stepped back, gulped, and taking the word "running" as a cue, sprinted off into the dimness as if a band of horse lancers were galloping after him.

"Thank you," Belkram told his retreating back. He turned to his companions, indicating the mill interior. "Shall we?"

"Indubitably," Itharr agreed, stepping past him with a half bow, blade raised.

The old man gave them both looks and snorted. "Young jack-fools," he growled, stumping after them.

Inside, the mill was a dim forest of stout pillars, stacked crates, spilled flour, sturdy barrels, and piles of sacks. The two Harpers strolled unconcernedly down a cluttered aisle that opened into a large threshing floor. There, darkness awaited them.

Four pillars of darkness, in fact, with the man they'd spoken to at the door busy beyond, struggling to get a crossbow ready.

"We're here," Belkram said briskly, "to see the former high constable." As he strode forward, he made a gesture only Itharr saw. The shorter Harper obeyed it, moving to one side.

The pillars of darkness were already advancing. Itharr casually tossed a dagger at the nearest. It struck something within the magical gloom and clattered to the floor. There was no play of lightnings, and the pillar shifted slightly; men walked within the darkness. The two Harpers sprang forward, converging on one dark column.

It stepped aside, drawing close to another darkness-shrouded guard so as not to be outflanked. Behind the two Harpers, the old man sighed and flung his axe. It flashed end over end across the room and caught the doorman in the shoulder. He shrieked, dropped his half-wound bow and windlass, and collapsed to the floor, moaning. Then the old innkeeper grabbed at the nearest barrel, toppled it, and with a few practiced heaves sent it rolling at the gathered columns of darkness. They scrambled to get clear and the Harpers darted in, blades flashing. There were grunts, curses, and heavy thuds as bodies bounced on the floorboards, followed by another deep rumbling as the innkeeper sent a second barrel into the fray. "Well done!" Belkram called back as the barrel crashed into a pillar, pinning a column of flickering darkness there for a dazed moment. Belkram's blade slashed into it, thrice, and it toppled, leaving only one column of darkness, which promptly fled, racing down a back passage.

"After him!" Itharr yelled excitedly. The old man shook his head as the two Harpers rushed off, muttering, "I'm young enough to fight but too old for a lot of charging about," as he retrieved his axe. Going from one darkness-shrouded form to another, he let his axe fall where their heads must be. Then he walked up to the writhing man with the crossbow, shook him, and growled, "How many guards are there here?"

"I—I daren't tell—" the wounded man began. The innkeeper punched his injured shoulder firmly, and when he repeated the question, the shrieking Zhentilar found sudden courage to dare an answer.

"Ondarr! Ondarr! We're being attacked!" the fleeing jailer shouted as he pounded down the passage. Belkram and Itharr sprinted after him in the dimness, bouncing painfully off the corners of stacked crates and the projecting ends of barrow handles. "Ondarr!"

They were running into the heart of the mill, where rumbling wheels ground endlessly. Passing through a succession of crowded chambers, they abruptly came out into a lamplit room where a sleepy-looking Wolf in chain mail was rising from a couch as darkness frantically tugged at his arm.

The Wolf's eyes widened as he saw the two Harpers bearing down on him. "Ondarr, I presume?" Belkram asked pleasantly. The Wolf got his blade out just in time to parry Belkram's thrust, leaving his left arm raised and underarm exposed to Itharr's blade.

Itharr of Athkatla ended his charge in a leap that brought him onto the bed, feet up. His blade burst through the Wolf's shoulder an instant before his feet slammed the man against the back of the couch, which broke off with a splintering crash, twisting the unfortunate Zhentilar onto the floor with Itharr atop him. The Harper's dagger made short work of the guard, and Itharr looked up to see Belkram slamming the last darkness-shrouded jailer against a pillar. The man collapsed, and Belkram thrust his hands into the blackness, groping.

"Lost something?" Itharr asked lightly. "Or is this some new thrill?"

Belkram made a face at him. "I'm looking for keys, Great One. If the high constable's here, he must be in some sort of cell—"

"Or right there," Itharr said, pointing. Belkram looked up and stared. The great wheels had ground to a halt because the man chained to the lever that drove them had stopped walking and was standing glaring at them with eyes that shone in the dimness like two flames.

"Irreph Mulmar?" Itharr asked.

"Aye," the man snarled, bunching his chains with a menacing rattle. "Who are you?"

"Harpers," Itharr said simply. "Itharr, once of Athkatla, and this is my blade-brother Belkram, from Baldur's Gate. We mean to drive the Zhents from your dale."

"But first," Belkram said, rising from the unseen body, "we have to find the keys to your shackles."

"Don't bother," the naked man in the chains said in a deep voice. "Just thrust yon spike into the spindle stop over there."

Itharr did as the man directed, and with a rattle of chains the man shoved at the lever. It shuddered but did not move. The man nodded in satisfaction, ducked under the lever—a wooden bar as thick as his arm, worn smooth by the hours his hands had grasped it—and braced himself against it, shoving in the opposite direction from the way he'd been pushing it for so long.

The lever groaned, and the man pitted against it snarled, veins standing out like ropes on his neck. His body quivering like a bent bow, he took a slow, deliberate step forward—and the great lever groaned and shivered and . . . broke.

And Irreph Mulmar, former high constable of the High Dale, stood tall amid the wreckage, tearing his shackles loose from the splintered wood, and said in a voice of iron, "No more."

"Well met," Belkram said calmly. Irreph gave him a terrible smile and gathered his chains into a bunch in his right hand. "My thanks, both of you. I've a mage to slay— and I must learn what has befallen my daughter—as soon as I'm free of this stinking mill cellar."

Suddenly, out of the darkness above, the pointed, rusting fang of a halberd stabbed down at him. Irreph twisted aside, flung a loop of chain over the weapon as it bobbed and reached again, and hauled hard.

Cursing darkness came helplessly down atop him. Irreph lashed it with his chains until its groans and shrieks had died into silence. Then he swarmed up the spindle in angry haste. Belkram and Itharr exchanged looks and followed.

Darkness fled from him along a gallery. Irreph followed, bounding along on legs stiff from not stretching for so long. Chained to the wood, there'd been nowhere to run. He laughed exultantly as he caught up with the darkness—just another man wearing a ring that cloaked him in concealing magic—and flung a loop of chain around the unseen throat from behind. A dagger clattered to the floor. Limbs flailed against him frantically and gasping sounds began . . . and then died away in slow agony.

Irreph strode on to the stairs. Somewhere ahead was the sun, and the men who'd stolen his wits and dale from him. They must die, all of them. Soon.

* * * * *

Ylyndaera hurried down the stairs like a ragged wraith, clinging to railings from time to time to peer ahead. Doors slammed here and there, men shouted and ran, their booted feet thundering on the old, uneven wooden boards, and from below came dull crashings, thumps, and an occasional short scream. What was happening?

Daera reached the ground floor of the mill, a huge room always piled high with full sacks—or, in winter, drifting snow—where stairs went up and down in all directions. Sunlight spilled in through the open door, and there were men running and fighting everywhere. She saw Yoster, the old innkeeper, hacking with a huge old axe at a Wolf as if he were chopping at a tree that wouldn't fall. There was blood all over the axe.

Beyond the two struggling men she could see others, more Wolves slashing and hacking at two men she'd never seen before. Where was Father?

There was no rumbling. The wheels had stopped! Was he dead? Free? Daera swallowed and had to duck aside as a man reeled out of the darkness, cursing, and almost fell over her. He charged on into the fray, clutching at his shoulder, trailing dark drops as he went.

This was no place for her. Carefully, Ylyndaera peered around a pile of sacks toward the light, just in time to see one of the guards fleeing her way.

She didn't have time to do anything but crouch in fear. He struck her with a crash, one very hard shin smashing into her side with bruising force. With a fearful curse he pitched over her and crashed to the floorboards, sword bouncing away. Winded, Daera rolled helplessly over against a pile of sacks. She did not even have breath left to moan.

A dark form strode past, not even seeing her. It savagely swung something long and heavy and metal—chains!—at the scrambling guard. Metal thudded down with a horrible, heavy, wet sound. Daera heard a sob, a groan, cracking noises, and more thudding. Then silence.

She lay still, struggling for breath. Booted feet rushed past her, and she saw the flash of a sword. It clashed and slid against chain, and Daera saw the black-armored swordsman flung back against a pile of sacks only to regain his balance and charge again.

The terrible chains swung again, and Daera heard the man's helm crumple. The sword spun from his hand, and he crashed heavily to the floor.

Father stalked toward her, gathering bloody chains in one hand as he came. Except for long matted hair, he was naked. Ylyndaera could not even speak as he strode past, not seeing her. But—gods be praised!—his eyes weren't the dull, unseeing things that had wandered over her as he howled in the darkness, but the sharp, clear eyes of the ranger of old, the aroused and angry high constable of the High Dale.

He was gone, out into the sun. The two strangers

rushed out after him, swords in their hands, and old Yoster with his axe followed, stumbling in weariness or perhaps because he'd been hurt. On her knees, fighting for breath, she could not tell.

Daera gasped for air, wishing she was at her father's side this instant to watch him smite down soldier after soldier of the tyrants. To see these black-armored Wolves fall . . .

Gods watch over us—their bows! He'll be slain, sure!

A terrified Daera, still doubled over in pain, staggered out into the light. She saw much blood, and men in black armor lying still in the midst of it, hands raised vainly to clutch at life now fled.

Dalefolk had gathered, eyes wide and excited. Down the road she saw her father's broad shoulders amid the small knot of hurrying men moving steadily on toward the castle.

Daera stared at her neighbors as they watched him go and screamed, "Aid me! In the name of the High Dale, aid! He'll be killed!"

They knew her as she shuddered, whooped breath back into her bruised chest, and staggered upright again. Pity was in some eyes, and rising anger in others. But at her cry, men looked away or shook their heads sadly, and women backed away.

"They've magic, lass."

"Aye, strong magic. We dare not . . ."

Tears were rolling down her cheeks now, but Daera wiped them away impatiently and ran grimly back to one of the bodies to snatch up a fallen sword and pluck a dagger from a belt.

She shook hair out of her eyes with a despairing snarl and rose to look around, hefting the sword. It was much too heavy; it was all she could do to hold the tip higher than her hands. She thrust the dagger through the bunched cloth at her hip, not caring what happened to the rags she wore, and used both hands to raise the blade, laying it back on her shoulder.

When she looked down the road again, her father's striding figure was much smaller. Would she be able to catch up with him in time?

In time to see him die? Daera shuddered, furiously blinking away fresh tears, and then saw men near her. She looked around wildly.

Old eyes met her own. She saw pride, and anger that matched hers, and shining hope in them.

Four—no, five—old men of the dale, graybeards she'd known as long as she could remember, leaning on fences to talk and smoke pipes, and shuffling into the inn for a tankard. Except on their chins, their hair was sparse, and they wore clothes as ragged as her own.

But in their hands shone old, lovingly cared for weapons, swords worn thin with years of sharpening, gleaming now, and axes with long curving blades. One carried a halberd in spiked gauntlets so old and worn that she could see his bony fingers through rents in the leather.

"We're with ye," one said simply.

"Aye," another spoke through a moustache that almost hid his missing teeth. "Like in the old days. We'll follow a Mulmar to the death, for the High Dale."

"My thanks," Ylyndaera said thickly, fresh tears streaming. Then she added hurriedly, almost sobbing, "Come, then, before it's too late!"

She hurried down the road. The graybeards trotted and shuffled and kept up with her. Some even had the breath to call out as they passed cottages.

"To arms!"

"For the dale!"

"Out, lads! To arms!"

One man looked out his door, amazed, and yelled, "Ho, Baerus! Where be ye off to?"

The old man just behind Daera grinned ferociously and waved his sword. "The high constable's free! An' we're following the maid, here—Irreph's lass—to the castle, to see to the running of these Wolves!"

There were roars of approval, and Daera saw men with pitchforks and axes running to catch up.

"For the dale!" another of the graybeards bellowed. The answering roar drowned out the fit of coughing that shook him a moment later.

"For the running of the Wolves!" a younger voice roared. Daera looked around. She was leading a band now.

"Death," she cried, "to all Wolves!"

"Death!" they roared back at her in excitement and anger, and swept down toward the castle.

12
Blood in the Marketplace

The sun shone down brightly. Eyes drawn into slits against its unaccustomed brightness, Irreph looked around his dale like a hungry hawk seeking dinner. In quick, sharp glances he noted changes without slowing. The chain grew warmer in his hands. Out in the sun, away from the damp, he stretched and stood taller, and felt better than he had in a long, long time.

Which was just too bad for the two Wolves who happened to cross his path.

The first drew steel and tried to charge in and gut him. Irreph swung his chains, danced aside, and swung them again. The man grunted, dropped his blade from numbed, broken fingers, and never had time to pick it up again.

The second drew sword, too, then turned and ran, crying the alarm. He got about three houses away before a goodwife hobbled hurriedly down her steps, fell in front of him, and reached out carefully to trip him with her cane as he ran past. Irreph did not give him time to get up.

"Irreph," she said eagerly, as he helped her to her feet. "Lord, are you come to lead us to war?"

Mulmar looked down and smiled through his mask of dust, sweat, and blood. "My thanks, Ireavyn. I am. Tell all, if you will, to bring arms as soon as they are able. I march on the castle."

"Alone?"

"Aye," he said grimly. Her face fell.

"And, Ireavyn, I'm your high constable, not your lord. No lord rules in the High Dale."

She nodded almost sadly and looked around. No Wolf was watching, but over Mulmar's shoulder her face lit.

"Look! Folk have risen, Irreph! They come! They come!"

She stared harder and her jaw dropped open. "Is that your Daera with them?"

Irreph whirled, almost felling the goodwife with an errant swinging shackle.

"Gods!" he cursed as he saw Ylyndaera's white face amid all the old men. Their eyes met, and the high constable suddenly discovered something wet was blurring his eyes.

The sun. Aye, the sun. He ran to meet his daughter, love and pride rising almost to choke him as he went.

*   *   *   *   *

The high constable of the High Dale walked slowly toward the castle, his chains in his hand. A crowd gathered in his wake, and those who bore weapons grew steadily in numbers. Beside him was his daughter, Ylyndaera, and behind them walked many old men of the dale, gray of beard and snow-white or thin of hair, with wrinkled old faces and stiff old limbs. They clutched weapons green or rust-red or worn thin with age, but carried themselves like old lions looking for a fight. Pride, joy, and a certain reckless defiance showed in their faces, and their eyes glinted when they looked ahead to where death awaited. At long last they were going to strike back.

A tyrant's banner still floated from the battlements ahead. An outlander still called himself lord of their dale, took tax coins from deep in their pockets, slew them at his pleasure, and told them what to do. Enough—as some forgotten warrior had said ages ago and half the Realms away—was enough. At long last they were going to war.

The road under their marching feet grew wider and cobbled. For this time of day, the way was strangely empty.

Word had spread, and the dalefolk hid and watched, or found what arms they could and came out to join Irreph. The Wolves must have gone to the castle for orders—the marchers could see the glint and gleam of helmed heads on the walls, looking down—for none showed themselves as the ragged but growing band of dalefolk approached the dark bulk of the High Castle.

The castle rose like a tall stone ship out of the houses in the center of the dale. A steep-sided earthen ditch surrounded the rocky ridge on which the fortress stood. A cobbled road descended steeply from its forekeep gate down to a large open space, the dale's marketplace. Since the arrival of Longspear, a dark, gaunt double gibbet had arisen in the center of this space. The great open well, once freely used by all, had been covered, its locked pumps used for the Wolves and their horses only.

Angry murmurs rose from the crowd as the dalefolk came out into the marketplace and saw these hated reminders of unwanted rule. The murmurs became a roar as they saw what awaited beyond.

Where the cobbled road to the castle rose out of the beaten earth, a line of Wolves stood in full coat-of-plate battle armor gleaming silver and deep blue in the sun. Swords and daggers were at their sides, and in their hands they held the long black-shafted lances they were wont to use from horseback. They barred the way grimly, the lances coming down like a forest of leveled, waiting teeth as Irreph strode steadily toward them.

Cold eyes met angry ones. The crowd came to a slow, milling halt just beyond the sharp, steady-held lance points. The sun beat down on them all.

The leader of the Wolves with the lances was Kalam Bloodsword, a veteran of Zhentil Keep's armies. He looked coldly at the angry dalefolk and kept all fear from his flat, commanding voice.

"Mulmar, go back to your work at the mill or perish, in the name of Longspear, lord in this place. Go back now, and take these old men with you, or we shall slay you all before highsun."

Silence was his answer. No one moved.

Kalam glared at them all, looking slowly from left to right, at old men with fire in their eyes, a young maid— Mulmar's brat?—and the man in chains, who looked back at the Wolf with death in his eyes.

Kalam cleared his throat. "You'll all miss your meals, and your loved ones will wait for you in vain—forever. Think on this and go back to your homes."

Still, no one moved. Kalam blazed a silent curse at this Mulmar for somehow getting free of the wizards' spells, and added another at the mages. For all their arrogance, wizards were flighty, careless fools one could never rely on save to send one speedily to the grave.

"Go now, all of you," he said, keeping his voice level. "Or we shall put Irreph Mulmar to the death, here and now. The stain of his blood will be on all of your hearts."

"Stand with me," Irreph said almost gently. "Stand fast, folk of the dale."

They stood. Long moments dragged past. Kalam made another silent curse, added a prayer to Tempus, and motioned his line of men forward.

They pushed forward to take Mulmar. Practiced old hands struck aside lance points and ducked under the long shafts. Mulmar raised his chains to his shoulder, ready to flail. The Wolves, trained not to let foes who might have knives get in under wielded polearms, halted and stepped back.

"*Stand back!*" Kalam roared. "Any who bar our way will hang as outlaws! Back!"

He drew his sword and strode forward. Old men with eyes and faces like cold stone stepped into his path, weapons raised. Kalam whipped his blade back and forth like a man threshing grain. It clanged against old axes and short swords and pitchforks until sparks flew and the numbed hands of their wielders wavered. Some fell back.

Kalam, too, stepped back and glared across the small open space he'd created. "Get back, and go to your homes!" he ordered sternly. "I want no blood shed this day. What gain will you see, if you lie dead here in the marketplace before highsun?" He looked around at cold and silent faces. "Go back!"

No one moved. Deliberately Kalam sheathed his sword, stepped back into the line, and took up a lance.

"Lances down!" he ordered, and the line of sharp points was leveled again. Glittering death took a step forward. And then another.

A stone fell by Kalam's feet as if from the empty sky. The leader of the Wolves glared at the mob angrily. "Who threw that?"

Another stone sprang past his eyes and rattled down a shield behind him. Kalam Bloodsword aimed his lance in the direction from which the stone had come and charged forward with a yell. The line of Wolves followed.

The lance tore through a shoulder, forced a second man to leap aside, and stuck solidly into a wooden shield that was as gray with age as the bearded man who held it. The old man staggered under the impact but gathered his feet under him defiantly and set himself against Kalam's shoving.

Kalam snarled and gained a step. Then another. A man with red hair joined the graybeard, then, and the lance went no farther.

"Make way!" Kalam spat. The red-haired man met his eyes steadily and shoved . . . and it was the leader of the Wolves who was forced back. A low, murmuring roar of approval rose around him. For the first time since he'd come to this place between the mountains, Kalam was truly afraid.

Another stone came winging right toward him. He lowered his head hastily and the rock struck his helm a solid, ringing blow. Kalam snarled and jerked the lance up and down roughly, trying to tear it free.

Folk were moving now, looking over their shoulders and scattering to the right and left. Good! Reinforcements had arrived, no doubt, and not a moment too soon.

Pushing forward into view from the rear of the crowd were two men in worn, nondescript, bloodstained leathers whom he'd never seen before, with naked swords in their hands. An old man with an older war axe in his hands followed them, grinning from ear to ear. The first two men fixed eyes on the leader of the Wolves. As he met their gazes, Kalam's blood ran cold. They meant his death.

The leader of the Wolves let go the lance and snatched at his sword. He got it out in time to strike aside the first reaching blade, but the man danced past, moving with Kalam's parry, and struck at him from behind.

Kalam ducked and dodged, and grunted with the sudden pain brought by the second blade, running up under the edge of his breastplate. He reeled away, doubled up against the burning, stabbing pain, and found himself face-to-face with the graybearded veteran who'd stopped his lance. His blade swept up as he snarled, "Death!"

"Aye," came the calm reply. "Yours."

The short sword that stopped his own blade as if it had been driven against a stone wall leapt suddenly into his face, and Kalam of the Wolves had time for only a gurgle or two before he fell and was trampled in the general surge forward. The last, fading thing he heard was a voice far behind him yelling, "Freedom for the dale! Death to the Zhent Wolves!"

* * * * *

Shoulder to shoulder, Heladar Longspear and Angruin Myrvult Stormcloak stood on the battlements, looking down as the mob below surged forward and the lancers were overwhelmed.

As their roar of victory rose and the ragged band surged triumphantly up the cobbled road, Longspear ordered curtly, "Now. Break their charge."

Guards around him hastened to the wall, loaded heavy crossbows in their hands. Their bolts fell like rain on the road below, and villagers fell back—or fell transfixed, to lie crumpled on the ground like crows slain around a guarded granary.

"And now?" Lord Longspear said, looking old. "Those are my people we're killing."

The mage who called himself Stormcloak turned cold eyes on Heladar. "What of it?"

"I'd rather not rule an open graveyard," Longspear replied coldly. "Who knows where it'll end, now that the bloodletting's begun? There's not a one left we can trust, and if we slay them all, what do I rule then?"

"A strategic pass that we can hold with twice our strength in two days, by means of the gate," Stormcloak told him. "If it's rabble you want to rule over, are there no prisons in Zhentil Keep? Are there no outlaws in these mountains? Manshoon's orders will bring all he wants to let out or be rid of, and if we spread the word in Cormyr and Sembia that there are hill farms for the taking, we'll soon have the dale as crowded as you like, Lord Longspear."

He turned away from Longspear and gave an order to the Overswords who stood behind them. "I want twenty full-armored men—lances and blades, all of them—mounted and ready in the courtyard as fast you can get them there."

The Overswords looked at him, and at the magnificently armored back of Lord Longspear. The back did not turn, and Stormcloak snarled, "Move at my orders, you thickheaded orc-sons! When I signal, send them out. They're to ride down the mob at full gallop, slaying any who resist. Longspear, you lead them."

The lord of the dale did not move or reply. The mage snarled and advanced on the Overswords, cursing them and raising threatening hands in gestures of spellcasting, until they wheeled and ran down the stairs. Men on the walls around them reloaded their crossbows and carefully looked away. Stormcloak gestured at Heladar's back.

The Lord of the High Dale straightened rather stiffly and turned about. His eyes were clouded and distant, his expression set. Stormcloak looked at him in satisfaction and said, "Go down and lead your men, Lord. Ride to victory."

The charmed lord tramped across to the stair in his gleaming armor. As he passed, Stormcloak considerately thrust the visor of his helm down, covering his set face.

Then the mage glared at the men all around him and ordered, "Loose your bolts, then leave your bows here and go down to the courtyard to await my orders."

The Sword who commanded those on the battlements

said hesitantly, "Leave our bows? What—"

The mage wheeled on him. "Address me as Lord Angruin, if you would live!"

All around them, bows were grounded, and silent Wolves hastened to the stairs.

* * * * *

"Back!" Belkram and Itharr shouted together, waving their swords. "Back! What good do you for the dale, by going forward and dying?"

Crossbow bolts, fired straight out from the castle walls to carry as far as possible, hissed down around the shouting Harpers. Dalefolk groaned and staggered as they were struck. Here and there men fell, pitching onto their faces to lie still or writhing weakly in the mud.

Men were running, now, back across the marketplace, leaving the dead behind, revealing the bloody, trampled bodies of Wolves as they receded.

"No!" Irreph roared as the two Harpers came up to him. "What have you done, you fools? Once we've scattered, they'll ride us down one by one!"

"High Constable," Belkram said, meeting Ylyndaera's frightened gaze, "we must fall back now and rally the people in the shops and alleys around the edge of this open space, or we'll all go down under whatever magic those wizards can hurl!"

Even as he spoke, there was a flash of amber light, and smoke curled up from the foot of the castle road. In a spot that had been empty a moment before, Angruin Stormcloak stood grandly in his dark robes. He laughed, his cold mirth ringing out loudly across the corpse-littered marketplace, and raised his hands.

Stones flung at him fell short. Mulmar cursed and swung around to shield his daughter, picking her up at a lumbering run with the two Harpers, back into an alley mouth. "We haven't a bow among us," the high constable said bitterly. "They took them all, and most who could wield them were maimed, cut down, or hanged here in the square."

"You had a lot of bowmen?" Itharr asked as they crouched together against a wall.

Irreph looked at him. "All my armsmen," he said quietly, cold death in his eyes again. He looked across the square at the wizard and whispered harshly, "All of them."

The air crackled lightning then, and men screamed as the blue-white bolt spat and snapped down the street they stood in, dancing them with its fury until it passed and they fell burned and lifeless to the ground. As the lightning faded, men of the dale showed themselves at doors and alley mouths, waving weapons angrily.

Stormcloak laughed again and raised his hands with nonchalant, almost clinical grace. This time a ball of fire roared down another street. As the screams died away, the strong smell of cooked flesh was borne across the marketplace by a rising breeze.

Men began to flee, running down the streets and alleys in blind flight. The two Harpers looked at each other helplessly, then at Mulmar.

"I will not retreat," Irreph said slowly. "They will not take me this time."

"We'll stand with you," Belkram told him.

"No, you will not," Irreph Mulmar said in a voice of steel. "As I am high constable, hear and obey me. You will take my daughter, both of you. Guard and keep her safe, and get her away to safety—to Azoun's court or to a lady called Mineira, a healer, in Saerb. She can get word, via the Harpers, to the mage Elminster of Shadowdale. Ylyndaera must live to rule the dale in years to come, when these serpents have fallen and been swept away."

"We are Harpers, sir," Itharr said, "and we came here seeking Elminster, who has left Shadowdale. We think he has come here."

"Here?" Mulmar said, rising. "Then we may be saved yet."

As he spoke, two bolts of force, white teardrops with wavering trails of light, raced across the marketplace like tiny falling stars to strike Stormcloak. The mage roared in surprise and pain, and staggered back.

Another pair of missiles sought him. This time the watching Mulmars and Harpers saw their source: an old man in tattered, dirty robes, crouching amid the brine barrels in front of the fishmonger's stall. Beside him was a woman in leathers, a sword in her hand.

"That's one of the Knights of Myth Drannor," Itharr said excitedly. "Sharantyr!"

"Then that," Belkram said slowly, indicating the man with the wand, "must be Elminster."

Ylyndaera burst into sudden tears. "I knew there were gods," she said. "I knew they'd hear me!"

13
When Wizards War

Angruin Stormcloak snarled in anger. They had a
mage! So this was no simple uprising, but the work of a
powerful enemy—perhaps meddling mages from Sembia
or Cormyr, but more likely from within the Brotherhood.
This fool attacking him would doubtless be some apprentice given a wand and told to prove himself, but still . . .

Stormcloak cast fire again. This time, the air in front
of him turned golden, there came a melodious chiming as
of many bells, and the scent of fresh-baked bread wafted
past—but no flaming death blasted those who stood
against him. His magic had gone wild. Again.

He stood alone, facing enemies across an open place,
armed only with spells he could not rely on. Not a prudent situation.

Angruin turned and beckoned to those waiting in the
castle with both his arm and his will. The thread of magic
held. He reached silently down it and forced Lord Longspear, mounted at their head, to roar the charge and urge
his mount forward. Then the Zhentarim wizard scrambled
down off the road, to the side of the marketplace where
the fewest dalefolk waited to storm back at him.

A moment later, he heard the angry thunder of many
plunging hooves, and the Wolves swept down from the
castle into the marketplace, scattering to level their
lances and spur into the mouths of streets and alleys.
For a breath or two the world was all snorting horses,
creaking leather, and jangling harnesses. Then the
black-armored Wolves were in among the buildings, and
the ringing of steel—and the shrieking—began. Satisfied, Stormcloak stood watching as screaming men fled
and fell. The folk of the dale would pay in blood for their
defiance.

War came to a certain lane on charging hooves. The lances of two Wolves flashed down as they made for the mouth of the street, bellowing laughter and claiming specific targets as their kills.

The two Harpers there, crouched against a wall in front of Irreph and Ylyndaera Mulmar, rose smoothly, blades flashing. Belkram set his teeth and struck the lance of the first Wolf skyward.

As the lance flew up, Itharr leapt under it to tumble the Wolf off his horse with a kick. The second Wolf rode over him without slowing, leaning out to drive his lance through the naked high constable. As the glittering point swept down, Irreph put Daera behind him with one strong hand and raised his chains with the other.

Belkram's blade came down hard on the butt of that lance. The lance's tip leapt up and over Irreph's shoulder to skirl along the stone wall behind him in a shower of sparks.

Then the Wolf was past, hooves thundering down the lane, and Itharr was rising out of the dust with his dagger dark with blood, letting fall the visor of the first Wolf.

"Now!" Belkram bellowed, stepping out into the marketplace and waving his blade. "Strike them down in the narrow places! For Mulmar, and freedom!" Roars and waved weapons answered him; dalefolk were still up and fighting.

Across the open space, the Zhentarim wizard snarled and raised his hand. Belkram ducked hastily back into the lane.

An instant later, the old man on his knees among the barrels smote Stormcloak again with a pair of magic missiles, spoiling his spellcasting. The wizard's scream of rage could be heard clearly over the shouting and the thunder of hooves.

Then a mounted Wolf waving a long, dark mace was thundering across the marketplace toward the lane.

"Is that Elminster?" Itharr yelled as the two Harpers snatched up a lance and swung it together, like a great broom, to sweep this third Wolf out of his saddle.

"I think so," Belkram called back as the man crashed

helplessly to earth, boot heels bouncing. Itharr raced in to leap atop him, and their roll together was brief and brutal.

Long training made Belkram look back at where the second Wolf had gone, just in time to see him spurring back, lance first. Irreph was turning to face him, chains flying. Daera hadn't fled and now could only stare helplessly at the lance leaping at her throat—and scream.

Belkram shouted and ran, knowing he'd not be in time.

Itharr threw his sword, then his dagger after it. They flashed end over end through the air.

Irreph shoved his daughter hard and she fell. He stepped forward to swing his chains and smash the lance tip aside, but it was already dipping and turning to follow Ylyndaera's plunge.

A shuttered window on the other side of the lane flew open, and a red-cheeked goodwife shrieked defiance and hurled a chamber pot out at the galloping Wolf. It struck the side of his face squarely, whipping his head around as it shattered and breaking his helm, skull, and neck all in one dull crash. The falling body stopped both of Itharr's weapons on its way to the ground.

The goodwife raised horrified hands to her mouth and screamed. Her eyes rolled back in her head, and she fell back out of view.

The two Harpers ran to Ylyndaera, who was picking herself up gingerly, spitting road dirt and holding her scraped hands painfully curled.

"Go hide, girl!" the high constable roared, shaking her. Then he looked up at the two men in leathers and snapped, "Take her somewhere safe!"

"There is no such place," Itharr told him quietly.

"I will not run from this," Daera told her father in a trembling voice. "What good is life to me if you are killed after I turn my back and run away? I'm staying!" She went to the nearest fallen Wolf and tugged a belt dagger from its sheath. It glinted in her hand as she scowled at the galloping Wolves out in the marketplace.

Then she turned to her father, face white and hands trembling. "Let's kill us some Wolves," she managed to say before she turned away and was very sick.

"Our swords are needed!" Belkram bellowed as Itharr tore his weapons from the fallen Wolf. "If the gods will it so, we'll meet again after the bloodletting's done!"

The high constable nodded, holding his sobbing daughter tenderly with hands that still trailed chains. The two Harpers clapped Irreph's shoulder and ran out into the marketplace.

Bodies lay everywhere, and not a few of them wore the armor of the Wolves. Their surviving comrades were milling about the streets and yards around the market, hacking and howling. After the initial easy butchery done by their lances and the plunging hooves of their horses, they'd found themselves surrounded, often isolated, and lacking room to readily turn their mounts. Wolves were now losing as many struggles as they won in the alleys. Old men and young boys alike leapt on them from windows and balconies above, or toppled barrels under their horses. If a Wolf fell, there was a general roar and rush, and he seldom had the time to get up again.

Stormcloak saw that the only route he could hurl spells down without slaying Wolves as well as dalefolk was the lane that had emptied when Irreph Mulmar snatched up someone smaller and dove headlong through a window.

He also saw two men in leathers coming for him, blades out, and knew he dare not trust in his spells to bring them down. He set his will and called Longspear back from a bloody fray far down a side street.

The Lord of the High Dale, his armor spattered and dented, spurred his snorting, wild-eyed mount back into the marketplace, turned it with ruthless strength, and rode hard at the two men, pulling the curved horn from his belt as he came.

The call to "retreat and rally" rang out. To a Zhentilar, ignoring a signal horn meant death; to a man they turned and fought or galloped their way back toward the open market. At their heels ran or limped the folk of the dale, closing in again around the edges of the trampled, corpse-strewn marketplace.

They were in time to see Longspear lean out of his saddle and swing mightily with his great gore-bathed warhammer at a man on foot who wore dusty leathers and a grim expression. The man dove and rolled aside as nimbly as any acrobat and came up circling, sword flashing.

Another Wolf lancer charged at the man in leathers from behind, but two white stars whistled from a shop front to strike the soldier down. The horse was riderless when it thundered past the man with the sword.

Another man in leathers was running in at the lord's other side. Longspear jerked his reins about savagely, but the man's sword was already leaping for his throat. With a shriek of straining metal, the warhammer met the striking steel just in front of the lord's impassive helm and turned it aside, but the man dropped it and dove in, hurling himself at the lord's ribs and upper leg.

The horse bucked. Armored arms flailed for balance, and Lord Longspear crashed to earth. The first man he'd struck at was waiting. His dagger went in under the lord's helm with the speed of a striking snake.

A great, savage roar went up from the watching folk, and they were pouring out into the marketplace, running amid the still-gathering Wolves. The dalefolk leapt and swung weapons as if driven by the gods themselves. The Zhent warriors fought to stay in the saddles of bucking mounts and laid about themselves desperately with their own blades. The red, shouting chaos of Tempus, god of war, reigned over the marketplace.

"I'm missing something!" Irreph Mulmar snarled in frustration, hearing the tumult outside the shuttered shop he'd plunged into. He thrust his struggling daughter into the arms of the fat woman who sold rope, cord, and thread there. "Ulraea, watch her for me, will you? And keep her here!"

"Aye, sir," Ulraea began doubtfully, but Ylyndaera twisted out of her grasp like swirling wind and leapt across the room toward the window her father had brought her in by.

"By all the gods, girl, forgive me," he said, chains rattling, and clipped her on the jaw as she ducked past.

Ylyndaera Mulmar continued gracefully, face first, to the floor and lay there unmoving. Irreph snatched her up by the shoulders; her head hung limply. Without pause he swung her into Ulraea's arms and said, "Just hold her here, will you? She'll be right again, all too soon. I must be out there!"

He whirled, shackles gleaming, and plunged back out through the window. One of its shutters broke off as he burst out into the battle, to hang dangling in his wake.

* * * * *

Stormcloak swayed amid the milling horses. He clutched his head and his gut, feeling wretchedly sick and wincing at the splitting pain in his head, all at the same time. Gods! So that was what it was like to be linked to the mind of a man when he's killed. Ohhh, gods above!

* * * * *

When Irreph charged out into the marketplace, a slim figure ran with him: a long-haired, beautiful woman in tattered leather armor, the one who'd earlier been with the wizard with the wand. A long sword gleamed in her hand. Irreph frowned. What had the Harpers called her?

One of the Knights of Myth Drannor, they'd said. Irreph shot another look at her; she winked back. He'd heard of that band of adventurers—who in the Dales hadn't?—and she certainly looked as if she knew how to handle a blade. He glanced back. There was no sign of the old man with the wand now. Elminster or not, he'd vanished.

Irreph began to think, for the first time that day, that the High Dale could be his again. He just might live to see the last of these accursed Zhents gone. He bounded forward and swung his chains with a savage grin, smashing the nearest Wolf from his saddle.

The man fell on the other side of his horse. He staggered up and got out his sword before Irreph could reach him. The Wolf's broad blade swung up, and the high constable had to leap back. His chains were too slow and heavy to stop the flashing steel of a good bladesman in time.

Then a slim sword came past his shoulder to his rescue, taking the Wolf's blade aside. Its wielder fenced with the Wolf in a dazzling exchange of cuts and parries before sliding her blade in with silken ease through one eyehole of the Wolf's helm. The lady Knight! Sharantyr, that was her name!

Irreph turned to her. "My thanks, Sharantyr of Myth Drannor," he said formally, as if he wore court robes and not merely hair and dirt. "Welcome to the High Dale."

"The honor is mine, High Constable," she replied calmly, saluting him with her bloodied blade. "Shall we stand together awhile?"

Irreph smiled and indicated the fray before them with an offering hand. She laughed and ran forward.

The next Wolf was already beset by four dalefolk wielding pitchforks and clubs. Sharantyr ran her sword point into the back of his knee, and he fell from his saddle in pain. His attackers did not give him time to moan very long.

They ran on, Irreph bearing to the left around the main press of horses and struggling men. "The castle!" he yelled. "We must get at the wizards. Without them, these Blackhelms are just so many swordsmen."

Sharantyr nodded, and they ran at another Wolf in their way. Irreph's chains smashed the man from his saddle without pause. Beyond, they saw the Zhentarim wizard who'd hurled fire and lightning standing at the end of the castle road, in obvious pain.

Sharantyr plucked a dagger from her boot and threw it, all in one smooth motion.

Had they been closer, she might have struck the man down. As it was, he saw death flashing through the air toward him and stepped aside. They both saw him shake his head, look around, and back away. His hands moved and he was gone, vanished as if he had never been there.

"The castle!" Irreph snarled again, and Sharantyr nodded. To their right, the two Harpers were hacking and thrusting like men possessed, leading the men of the dale against the Wolves. Pitchforks and daggers held by grim and trembling dale farmers were sending horses down in rolling agony or goading them to bolt, dumping their riders as they fled.

Irreph determinedly smote another Wolf from his saddle with a sweep of his heavy chains. The high constable grabbed the reins of the terrified horse, hauled himself into the saddle by brute strength, and forced the animal's head around toward the castle.

The horse snorted and bucked, plunging and twisting. Irreph hung on, his chains flailing the air. Sharantyr used her blade and voice to turn another horse aside. She ran along beside Irreph as the high constable's borrowed horse suddenly burst into a gallop toward the castle gates.

There were Wolves in the way, those who'd fallen back to hold their line of retreat. Only one was mounted, and his horse reared and gave way. Irreph drove through the gap, flailing with his chains at the Wolves around him. On his right, Sharantyr's glittering blade leapt and cut like a shuttle on the loom of some mad weaver.

A last shouting Wolf fell under the wild hooves of Irreph's borrowed horse, and they were through. By main strength the high constable kept his mount aimed up the road to the castle. Sharantyr sprinted along behind him and to his right, sword out.

Quarrels hissed around them, falling like rain, as they drew nearer to the towering stone walls. Ahead, the gates stood open for the Wolves' return. Irreph leaned low over the neck of the horse and spurred it on.

His mount stiffened under him. A crossbow bolt had struck its flank. It started to rear and spasmed again as another quarrel struck its neck just in front of Irreph's face. The world reared and rocked, then the high constable felt himself dragged from the saddle, back and to the right. He fell heavily on the cobbles in a rattling of chains, beside Sharantyr.

She was clutching the chain she'd hauled him down by, and breathing hard. "Come!" she gasped, as a fresh shower of quarrels sought their lives hungrily.

The twisting, rolling horse was struck again, but its agonized bulk shielded them from a bolt or two. Sharantyr led their charge up to the gates. Grim-faced Wolves were waiting for them, blades and shields raised.

*   *   *   *   *

As Stormcloak cast his spell, he could see the naked, wild-eyed high constable and that woman heading directly for him. All around, men were yelling or screaming or dying. In an instant they were gone as the teleport whirled him away.

Stormcloak was suddenly somewhere quieter. The castle, yes, but—gods! He was falling, only empty air under his boots! Where—?

He didn't have time for any more thought before he slammed hard into something that collapsed under him with a human shriek and a crumpling, metallic sound.

Stormcloak lay still, fighting for air. Under him, an unfortunate guard lay unmoving. His magic had gone awry, dropping him from at least three man-heights in the air. He shook his head and struggled grimly to his feet. Another spell gone wrong, and this day was not over, not for a long time yet.

Wolves watched openmouthed as Angruin Stormcloak rose stiffly from atop the crumpled body of the guard. His brow glistened with sweat and his face was white. He did not look back at the man who'd been beneath him.

A simple light spell had gone crazily wrong this morn. Then a fireball had failed in the marketplace, and now this. What was happening?

Angruin Myrvult strode toward his nearest spellbook. Seeing his face, Wolves scrambled aside to keep out of his way.

*   *   *   *   *

An old serving man with a battle-axe in his hands stood leaning against a wall and panting. He was covered with blood, some of it his own, and his leg hurt abominably where some Wolf had slashed it before dying. His head hurt, and his chest tightened in stabbing agony from time to time.

He'd never before felt such pain in his life as this rending hurt within him, but he leaned on the wall, holding the comfortable heaviness of the axe in his hands, and was very happy.

Out in the open space in front of him, Wolves were dying; many lay dead already. His friends were driving the Zhentilar warriors out! A few old men and two handfuls of untutored goodwives, lads, and farmhands were beating Zhent Blackhelms! Even in his proud days, he and his brothers-in-arms had fled from Zhents, or kept civil and quiet and as far away as possible in taverns and inns. And now he was beating them, he and his friends! The axe in his hands had bitten short the lives of eight Wolves already today, and if the wizards stayed away, the men of the dale would win the day yet.

His eyes were suddenly wet, and he set his lips and looked around the marketplace in pride, seeing old friends and others he knew groaning on the ground or sprawled still and silent. The blood price had been high and the day was not won yet, but by Tempus, the folk of the High Dale had stood proud this day!

He growled as the pain took him again, then turned the sound into a shout. "For the Dale!" he roared, as he had heard those two brave Harper lads cry earlier. "For freedom!"

He swung the axe around his head and started to run, lurching and staggering as he wrestled with the hammering pain in his chest. There were Wolves still standing in his sight, still work to be done. "For the dale!" he cried again, wildly, as his running feet brought him to the Zhents. He took a sword blow on his raised axe and blundered on into the Wolf who'd swung at him, knocking the armsman down. A farmer who'd been fencing with that Wolf, scythe against blade, grinned at him for an instant and stabbed down with the scythe. The Wolf's scream turned wet and bubbly before it died away.

The old man raised his axe, roared again, and went on to the next Wolf. The men of the High Dale were earning a victory, blow by bloody blow, and he meant to see that they got it.

* * * * *

"Not too old yet for such games, are ye?" Elminster asked himself as he sprang out of alley shadows to the empty saddle of a wandering, riderless horse.

The beast snorted and neighed in alarm, bucking and twisting its head around. Elminster hauled himself up into the saddle with grim, iron-hard fingers and answered himself, "Nay . . . see? Look ye!"

The horse bugled. Elminster let it dance under him as battle raged in the marketplace ahead. Few horses were left now. From the castle came the sound of horns blowing the same call he'd heard earlier: the retreat and rally.

He'd have to move quickly or they'd all be in his way. Elminster crouched low in the saddle, grinned at the thought of how long it had been since he'd last done this, and set the horse into a gallop.

It hurled itself forward, putting all its fear into flight, and burst through the running, milling mob with only a few shouts and a near miss or two. Then he was charging up the road to the castle gates, beard streaming behind him, a few crossbow bolts whistling past.

* * * * *

In the fray, Itharr thrust a Wolf through the throat and turned to Belkram, ignoring the spray of blood that drenched him. "That *is* Elminster, isn't it?"

Belkram nodded, teeth shining in a sudden smile. "Definitely."

Itharr wrenched a shield from the Wolf he'd just unhorsed and slain. "Let's go, then. After him!"

Belkram looked about. They'd cleared a little space

around them, Wolves falling back warily before the blades of the two madmen in leather. He smiled at them and advanced.

Uneasily they gave way, and he moved to stand shoulder to shoulder with Itharr, who'd taken up the shield. Crouched together behind its angled protection, the Harpers hastened up the road to the castle.

Bolts thudded into the shield. Some snarled across the curving metal and were turned aside. Others stuck fast, dealing numbing blows to the arms beneath the shield. One pierced through, but its gleaming tip stopped a handwidth short of the two sweating Harpers. They traded rueful glances and hurried on.

Belkram kept a wary eye behind, blade ready, but the Wolves were too busy staying alive, as they fell back toward the castle, to chase two men already halfway up the road to the gates.

"Storm did promise us adventure," Itharr said dryly. A quarrel struck the shield sharply, jarring them both, and glanced away.

"I didn't think just catching up with a hundreds-of-years-old wizard would be this exciting," Belkram replied, "whether he was a trouble-gatherer or no. Well, I've been wrong before."

They were laughing together at that like crazed men as they came to the gates and found the high constable of the dale flailing away with blood-smeared chains manacled to his wrists, holding three battered Wolves at bay as the lady ranger Sharantyr fenced with them. A trail of blood and trampled, moaning guardsmen led from the gates to the courtyard beyond, where a riderless horse was rearing and screaming, lashing out with its hooves at the Wolves who tried to calm it. Elminster was, as usual, nowhere to be seen.

14
Doom Comes to the High Castle

Elminster of Shadowdale, once an archmage of Myth Drannor and now and forever one of Mystra's Chosen, clung to the reins as the horse moved powerfully under him, its neck strong and warm in front of his nose, its mane whipping at his face. He had time to wonder what in Mystra's name he was doing here, with quarrels whipping and humming like angry wasps through the air all around him. He also found time to shrug and grin; this was not a new thought.

A breath later, as the horse carried him away from the clash of steel and the cries of men, he found time to answer himself. He was here simply because he was who he was. This was the way he took life, making of it what best pleased him: a tapestry as rich and deep and colorful as he could manage, much longer than most ever have the chance to weave. *His* tapestry, whose great weight of years all too often hung by a single thread. Because he dared it so and would not have it otherwise.

As it hung right now. Elminster crouched low as a quarrel flashed by very close on his right, and saw the set, grim faces of angry guards growing rapidly larger ahead. Thinking on his recent conclusions about life, he told himself aloud, "My, aren't we high and mighty today, hmmm?"

Another quarrel hummed past close by his ear, and Elminster realized suddenly that he very much wanted to go on living, even if all magic was lost to him forever.

There was so much still to see, to read, to write, to do . . . and what a great way he was going about trying to cling to life, plunging himself into the thick of a battle between Zhentarim and desperate dalefolk—and, without his spells, advancing alone on a castle held against him!

He laughed so hard at that thought, he lost his grip on one rein and had to grab almost blindly for the horse's mane. Just then the hooves of his galloping mount struck a pocket of loose stones and slid, just a little. The horse bobbed and leapt on, straight at the guards, and the old man in tattered robes on its back made a hurried, ungraceful journey to the trodden turf beside the road.

The landing drove the breath from Elminster's lungs. He had only enough strength left to turn the violence of his fall into a roll, forward and to the right, down slope. He kept on rolling, hoping no sword would come seeking him before he could stand.

As the world turned over and over, Elminster felt for the wand that hurled magic missiles. From somewhere above, he heard the ringing protest of a horse, heavy hooves striking metal. After a short, broken-off cry, the dull thudding became the beat of hooves at speed, moving onward into the castle.

Well, at least his *horse* had attacked the castle.

Elminster came to his feet slowly, gulping air and holding the wand ready. The gates were still open—he could see the raised log portcullis from where he stood—and his horse had vanished within.

Guards still stood there, aye, but fewer than before. To his left as he'd ridden up, they'd been facing Sharantyr and the naked giant with the chains, engaged but keeping them at bay, standing as a human wall across the open entrance to the High Castle. These experienced, trained Zhentilar, cold-eyed and wary, were surprised at seeing war brought to them and ragtag dalefolk doing well against their sword brothers, but they weren't in any panic, or hurt or weary. In their own minds, the Zhentilar were easily a match for a woman with a sword and a naked man swinging his slave chains.

Now two Wolves at least were down, and the survivors were fighting in earnest to hold the gate. As Elminster climbed back up through the grass as fast as he could, a Wolf slowly went down, flailing chains beating a bell-like chorus on his battered helm. An arm hung useless—broken, no doubt—and blood made a sightless mask of the face as it turned, aware of nothing but darkening pain.

Elminster spoke gently over his wand. The sinking Wolf jerked rapidly and collapsed. One of his fellows turned, saw Elminster, and raised his blade with a yell, only to stiffen as Sharantyr's blade flashed like a striking snake into his neck from the side.

It swung on to parry another blow, before the incredulous Wolf spat blood at the climbing mage and started to fall.

Elminster watched him topple and wondered briefly why it is that men find it necessary to spill each other's blood so often and for so many reasons. More than a thousand years after he'd first asked himself that question, he asked it now and found no new answer.

An old conclusion still seemed the only answer he could see: It was, and is, the nature of the beast.

He glanced back at the marketplace, with its turmoil of jostling men, swinging weapons, and sprawled bodies, and then at the castle, where men in armor were hurrying to positions, scrambling to bring more horse-lances to serve as a bristling wall against attack. Aye, the nature of the beast. He shivered for a moment, sickened by all the butchery. Then he shrugged, looked around again, and tried to grin. Oh, well. Once committed, one must see it all through to the end.

Or, to quote an even older saying that was undoubtedly closer to the truth, he told himself as he darted over bodies of fallen gate guards into the High Castle, "Once a fool, always a fool."

He grinned ruefully at that, even as his feet (beginning to ache, now; was he finally becoming too old for this? A fine time to realize that) carried him across smooth-worn flagstones puddled with old rainwater, into a forecourt. Ahead, at the other end of this open space, a line of Wolves was beginning to form across the archway that led into the main courtyard of the castle. They were battling his rearing, terrified mount in a confused, shouting mass of men, but there were plenty of weapons out and no safe way through them for one old man with a little magic.

To his left and right, railless flights of stone steps climbed the inside of the castle's outer wall, leading to battlements above. The Old Mage looked around, saw no ready crossbows, and without hesitation mounted the stair on his right.

He strode up as if he belonged in this place, calm and even arrogant of tread, only his tattered robes making him look any different from a hundred other haughty wizards in the Realms. No doubt a few such Zhentarim magelings held sway here. He'd face spellwork of real power before the day was out.

Elminster had almost reached the battlements, where men were looking anxiously down into the marketplace and cranking their windlasses with whirring speed to reload the heavy crossbows propped or cradled in arms everywhere, when a great commotion arose from below.

Everyone ran or craned necks to look, in time to see Irreph Mulmar fell the last staggering gate guard with a brutal, crushing sweep of his chains.

Wolves shouted and ran to aim their crossbows down into the forecourt. The heavy weapons had to be supported on the stone parapet to fire steadily, and when so placed could not be tilted down steeply enough to menace the high constable below. One overenthusiastic Wolf lost his weapon trying to aim straight down the wall. The crossbow slid off the stone, eluding his grab, and pitched to the courtyard below, its shattering a crashing chord amid the shouting and running feet.

A moment later some Wolves reached the stairs. Cradling their bows on their knees, standing bent over, they fired. Bows jerked and quarrels shot wildly down. Sharantyr sprinted in through their fire and spun hard to the right, to race up the same stairs Elminster had taken. She found herself looking up into the eyes of two Wolves hurriedly reloading their bows at the top of the stair.

Elminster had gained the battlements moments before Irreph's dramatic entry and stood haughtily among Wolves who from long practice did not look directly at a wizard; the Zhentarim were quick indeed to take offense. He glided up behind the guards at the head of the stair, waited until they were in the frantic midst of reloading, then kicked hard at the backs of their knees.

They fell in a clatter of armor and a riot of startled curses. Sharantyr boiled up the last few steps, and her blade found their throats before they could rise.

Men on the battlements all around them shouted in astonished fury. Elminster turned to face them, wand in hand, wondering just whom to strike at first in the forest of angry Wolves. Many of the more distant warriors hadn't seen or heard the struggle on the stairs at all and were still leaning down into the forecourt, crossbows ready now, as Irreph mounted the stairs on the far side of the entry gate.

Bows thrummed and spat. A rain of quarrels found the high constable before he'd taken four bounding strides. One ran through his upper arm and came out across his chest. Another pierced deep into his thigh, where it stood quivering. Irreph struggled on for two strides more, shuddering in pain, then fell onto the stairs, cursing.

Elminster cast a glance over the walls and saw perhaps seven Wolves, no more, fleeing up the road to the gates, hotly pursued by a bleeding, pitchfork-waving rabble—all that was left of the folk of the dale.

"Shar!" the Old Mage cried, as the lady ranger reached him and coolly ran her blade through the body of the nearest Wolf. The Zhentilar was still cursing, juggling a loaded bow and trying to draw steel, as he went down. "Clear this height if ye can. Throw their bows away, or stamp on them, or kick them down! They'll be the death of us if we don't!"

Suiting action to his words, Elminster snatched up a nearby crossbow, triggered it—the quarrel ran into the flagstones a handspan in front of an onrushing Wolf, causing him to stumble and fall heavily with a startled oath—and tipped it over the battlements to be lost below.

Sharantyr overwhelmed the Wolf beside her with three quick slashes. The man reeled against the crenellations, clutching at his cut face and arm. Sharantyr snatched up his bow and fired it along the battlements into the chest of a guard who was just raising his own weapon. That crossbow in turn went off into the back of another Wolf, who screamed, staggered against the parapet, and was gone an instant later, leaving only a fading scream behind. The lady ranger flung her bow out over the parapet without looking and caught up her blade again to leap at the next Wolf.

"Use your dagger, Old Mage!" she snarled over her shoulder. Elminster looked at her and then down at the dagger at his belt. Drawing it forth with some distaste, he buried it in the still-writhing warrior Sharantyr had slashed. The Wolf stiffened, groaned, and went on moaning and clutching his wounds. Hmmm. Not so good.

Elminster looked behind him. There were few Wolves on this side of the gate. Below the walls, the ground fell away steeply in a tumble of rocks and scrub trees where no ragged band of farmers and merchants would mount an attack. Only two guards were running along the battlements toward him.

Elminster used his wand again on the foremost one, then turned back to the still-writhing Wolf. As he struggled to heave the blindly flailing man over the parapet, the Wolf's scabbarded sword bobbed and waved under his nose.

Elminster looked at the weapon, shrugged, and drew it out. He turned. The first rushing Wolf had slowed to a stagger, but the second was shouldering past the first to charge. Elminster fired the wand of magic missiles into the man's face. As the Zhent cried out and clutched at his eyes, Elminster leapt toward him and drove the point of his blade into the man's throat.

It slid in with such hideous ease. He'd forgotten that. Elminster looked down in disgust at the blade he held, feeling ill. He remembered to look up, though, in time to meet the other Wolf's charge.

Steel met steel. The man was strong, and in a fury of pain, and very good. Elminster managed two frantic parries before firing the wand into the man's open, snarling mouth.

Blood spattered the Old Mage's hair and beard. Sickened, he turned away from what was left of the Wolf, a headless body still jerking its blade about in a grotesque dance, and strode back to the one he'd taken the sword from. The man was twitching more feebly now. Elminster sighed, caught hold of his legs, and tipped him up and over the battlements.

Then he looked along the wall anxiously. Sharantyr was only one lass in leather armor, and he'd left her to fight alone for far too long.

His jaw dropped. Dead Wolves lay sprawled everywhere, heaped on the parapet walk. More were draped along the parapets themselves. Far around the curve of the ramparts, Sharantyr was fencing with two frightened-looking Wolves. Behind them, another pair of Zhents were hastily working their windlasses to ready quarrels for her death.

Elminster used his wand on them from afar, cast a look to his right—there were no bowmen atop the inner wall or anywhere else that he could see, and judging by the sounds from below, the dalefolk had reached the forecourt—and started running along the wall, swinging his sword to gain speed.

Sharantyr twisted aside too slowly and took a cut across the back of her raised left arm above the elbow. Elminster heard her sob and then snarl, and fired his wand at the man attacking Shar.

Sharantyr was tiring and in pain. Her long hair spun wildly about her as she panted and danced, the heavy ringing of steel loud in her ears as she traded blows with a Wolf who would not fall. They had no shields. Each blow and counterblow was taken on their blades with leaden, numbing force. Sharantyr reeled back, fighting for breath, and her opponent pressed forward, daring to grin for the first time.

Elminster's wand spat magic again, stars leaping to strike two Wolves. The man fighting Shar staggered, and behind him, one of the Wolves with bows fell heavily onto his face and lay still.

Sharantyr lunged wearily in to slash the face of the staggering Wolf, then shoved him aside. He fell into the forecourt with a strangled cry of protest, waving his blade as if it could catch hold of something and save him. It could not.

The lady ranger reached the last bowman. Desperately he brought up his heavy, half-winched weapon to block a thrust at his throat, then dropped it and ran.

Sharantyr took two running steps after him, then shook her head and collapsed against a crenellation, gasping for breath. Elminster watched the man cast a look back to see that he was not pursued. The Wolf went to a nook in the wall where another stair descended. The Old Mage's eyes narrowed. He was doing something in there . . . loading another crossbow?

Elminster fished under the body of the bowman he'd felled with his wand, dragged out the loaded, ready bow, and struggled to raise it. He was still puffing and staggering when Sharantyr's hand touched his shoulder.

"El," she panted, "what are you—oh." She dragged the bow out of his hands, staggered for a moment under its weight, and fired at the nook just as the Wolf cast an anxious look back at them.

Blood blossomed in the man's face. His head grew larger for an instant, then disappeared from sight. Sharantyr went to an embrasure in the parapet and shoved the bow out into space.

She turned back to Elminster, breast heaving, covered with blood and sweat, and said, "Next time . . . if you live . . . to pull a next time on me . . . choose someplace to go for a walk . . . that doesn't . . . have any gates . . . hey?"

Elminster chuckled and kissed her cheek tenderly. Then, his arm around her, he wiped the sweat from her brow with his sleeve and fumbled under his robes.

Sharantyr raised an eyebrow. Elminster pushed at her shoulder impatiently. "Sit ye down a moment," he ordered.

The ranger shook her head. "No," she panted. "Do that, and I'm finished. My arms . . . tighten up, everything'll hurt . . . I must . . ."

Her words died away as she saw him heft the sphere of iron bands in his hand. "Ye *will* sit down," he said, smiling crookedly, "one way or another."

Sharantyr rolled her eyes at him, sighed heavily, and with a lopsided grin sat down against the parapet. Elminster knelt beside her and triumphantly drew out a ring, which he slipped onto her finger. It was still warm from the heat of his body.

"Lie still," he ordered, "for a time, while I look below and see what befalls. There's been a strange scarcity of Zhent wizards since that one fled from the market. It worries me."

Sharantyr started to laugh weakly, staring around at the heaped bodies. "Worried? Now why should you be worried? Not so long ago, you were attacking this castle alone!"

"Alone? I had a horse," Elminster reminded her dryly. Her helpless laughter grew and grew until it became a bit wild.

Elminster laid a comforting hand on her shoulder as he looked around—along the battlements and at all of the High Castle's turrets, down into the forecourt and at what he could see of the main courtyard beyond without leaving Sharantyr. Then he glanced over the battlements at the shops and cottages below.

Of the Wolves who'd galloped forth into the market-place, not one remained alive except the handful who'd managed to get back inside the walls—unless, perhaps, one or two of the sprawled bodies yet held a grim grip on life, or a Wolf or two had fled down the streets or found somewhere to hide.

Outside the walls, the folk of the dale ruled, though they'd paid a heavy price in blood for their victory. On the battlements not a living Wolf stood. The Sage of Shadowdale and the lady Knight of Myth Drannor were alone with the dead.

In the forecourt below, weary men and women hacked and staggered. The dalefolk had determined not to let a Wolf live, and the Zhentilar were as adamant that they'd hold the castle and rally to crush this uprising later.

Or rather, most of them were adamant. As Elminster stood looking, Sharantyr's shoulder rising and falling under his hand with her still-heavy breathing, a door opened in the nearest turret.

It was a little way along the rampart, past several nooks. Elminster began to lower himself into a crouch and then shrugged. It was too late. He and a tired-looking Zhentilar in scratched and muddy armor were staring into each other's eyes across an easy bow-flight of empty air.

The man stepped forward but made no charge or threatening gesture. Behind him, other men pushed through the door: half a dozen or more Wolves, two carrying large and heavy coils of rope. The others had—Elminster's heart sank—heavy crossbows and large armory boxes of quarrels.

Elminster watched them as they all in turn looked his way. They got to work with windlasses to ready and load their bows. The pair with the rope spent some time fashioning a long, heavy knot to join the two coils, then threw the first coil out over the battlements to plummet down, pulling most of the rope behind it.

The sounds of battle grew louder below. More Zhents had emerged to defend the forecourt, or more dalefolk had found the courage to ascend the road into the castle. Elminster did not move to find out which.

The Wolves were looking down the rope, now, and tossing handlengths more of it over the wall. They planned an escape, their bows ready to shoot down any who saw them and moved to imperil their descent.

Elminster uttered a silent curse at the loss of his Art as he raised his wand. A Wolf who'd been watching him all this while was steadying a loaded crossbow on a crenellation, turning it Elminster's way.

Elminster unleashed the wand's powers with his will and the more powerful of the item's two words. Blue smoke curled up from its tip, and three pink flowers appeared in the air flying in a line heading toward the Wolves, grew rapidly in size and splendor. Then they were gone in little bursts of rosy light.

Mystra smile upon us all. Elminster watched the crossbow swivel around as he sank down against the wall beside Sharantyr.

She regarded him calmly. "What befalls?"

Elminster shrugged. "This failed," he said, waving the wand. "Unfortunately, I don't feel up to defeating the six or seven Zhentilar warriors who are up here with us." Sharantyr made as if to rise, but he held her down with a surprisingly strong hand. "They have loaded crossbows," he added nonchalantly.

Sharantyr looked at him and sighed. "Well," she asked quietly, "shall we crawl back along the wall as fast as we can, then?"

"It might be prudent," Elminster agreed. "Yet it claws at my craw to do so. They'll be over the wall, on a rope, and be gone, probably to raise the rest of the Zhents in the dale at our backs."

"I did not charge the gates of this place alongside a naked man in chains," Sharantyr told him with a smile that touched her lips for the briefest of moments, "to start being prudent now."

Elminster spread his hands in silent acknowledgement. An instant later they both heard the scrape of a boot on stone very close by. Elminster's hand plunged into his robes and came out with the iron sphere. Sharantyr was out from under his other hand like a striking serpent, crouching with her blade ready and a dagger poised to throw. She waited against one side of their nook.

The Wolves had decided to mount a sudden rush, the heavy crossbows cradled in their hands. There were two of them, and at such close range they could hardly miss.

Sharantyr flung a dagger into the face of the first as his bolt plunged into Elminster's ribs, and followed it with her sword, driven by all her strength.

As she struck, she shoved against the Wolf's bow, swinging his body between her and the second Wolf's weapon. It went off too late, the quarrel whistling past her and out into air beyond the wall.

The other Wolves were watching along the rampart. Sharantyr did not entertain them for long. She put a hand on the shoulder of the first Wolf, who was falling with a disbelieving look, his throat cut open, and vaulted over him to crash down atop the second. She hammered him brutally with elbows and knees, then used her blade before his hastily snatched dagger could find her.

Then she spun about, keeping low, to race back to Elminster. Sharantyr only hoped she'd be in time.

15
A Short Search for Death

Elminster of Shadowdale sat against the parapet, staring down disgustedly at the quarrel in his chest. A dark, spreading stain had already reached his lap. With trembling fingers, Sharantyr snatched the healing ring off her own finger and jammed it onto one of his.

He chuckled weakly and patted her shoulder. "Here," he said, pressing the wand into her hand. "Ye try." He nodded his head to indicate the parapet walk behind her, and Sharantyr turned angrily to see another four Wolves coming toward them.

She drew back her lip in a low-throated snarl, locked eyes with the nearest Wolf, who was raising his bow clumsily, and spat out the word she'd heard Elminster use: *"Baulgoss."*

The smooth, unadorned stick of wood in her hand pulsed with force, and two white bolts, trailing tails as if they were tiny falling stars, leapt from it. They struck the man before he could do more than open his mouth to cry out.

He groaned, shuddered, and dropped his heavy weapon, its bolt smacking against the parapet and glancing off over the forecourt.

Sharantyr crouched low as the other Wolves stopped and hastily raised their bows. Then she dropped the wand into Elminster's lap and dragged him bodily along the walk and around the corner, shielding him with her own body. One quarrel flashed just over her shoulder, tearing her leathers and leaving blood and burning pain in its wake, and another cracked hard off the parapet to the right. They were safely around the corner when the third quarrel struck stone somewhere.

Elminster was shaking in pain, teeth clenched. Sharantyr had time only to pat him on the shoulder before she sprang up and ran, bent double, along the parapet walk to the nearest fallen Wolves. There had been one or two with shields . . . ah!

She tore a shield from an unfeeling, limp arm, donned it, and hurried back to the fallen Sage of Shadowdale. Snatching up the wand, she held the shield ready and ran back around the corner.

She heard a shout, and the shield shuddered under a heavy blow. The head of a quarrel appeared beside her arm. Had she not been holding the shield well in front of her, it might have pierced her breast. Sharantyr snarled and dodged against the parapet, risking a lowered shield for an instant, to look.

At least one other crossbow was ready, but she'd have no time to worry about it. The three Wolves whose quarrels had just missed her had crouched down to winch their bows into readiness again. Interrupted, they were rising with drawn blades, perhaps two paces away. Sharantyr snarled and hissed the wand's command word again, staring at one Wolf under the edge of her shield.

This time the wand brought her pulsing, purplish light and an intense feeling of icy cold. No missiles of force appeared, and her opponents did not slow or seem to feel anything. Sharantyr slipped the wand into her shield hand and backed hastily away, snatching out her own sword.

They came at her in a rush. Sharantyr waited until they were between her and the ready bow she'd seen, then went to one knee, pretending to wobble and groaning in pain. The Wolves almost got in each other's way trying to be the first to carve her.

Sharantyr took the first blow on her shield and leapt up, moving forward against the body of its wielder. Hip to hip, she turned the Wolf to one side, driving him off-balance into one of his fellows while she parried the thrust of the other Wolf.

Then she spun away and was behind them all, tying up the blade she'd parried with her own. She forced it down and drove the edge of the shield into the Wolf's face as hard as she could. He fell, spitting blood, as she ducked low.

As she'd expected, a quarrel thrummed past her, low and well aimed, thirsty for her blood. Instead, it found the knee of the Wolf turning beyond her. He screamed and fell. Sharantyr fired the wand at the one who was left.

This time it launched a shower of sparks, but out of them a single magic missile coalesced, wavered, and streaked to its target.

The Zhentilar snarled in pain and came at her, thrusting viciously with his sword. The lady ranger struck his blade aside with her own, drove her hip hard into his armor-clad middle, and shoved him back against the parapet. Another crossbow bolt hissed past, close by. The Wolf struggled, hurling her back, and charged.

Sharantyr went suddenly to her knees again, bringing her shield up. It took his blade with a thunderous crash. She drove the shield up and kicked out under it as she rolled onto her shoulders.

The Wolf went over her, cursing helplessly. He had time for one throat-stripping shriek as he plunged headfirst into the forecourt below. Sharantyr let go her shield and rolled over. The Wolf who'd taken a bolt through the knee was crawling her way, face dark with pain, sword ready in his hand. She scrambled toward him, keeping low as she held off his lashing blade with her own, and reached his feet.

The wounded foot trailed uselessly; he kicked at her with the other. Sharantyr grimly laid hold of the trailing boot, twisted it, and set her teeth against his scream of agony. When the Wolf went limp, she dragged him up and pitched him over the battlements, looking wearily for the three surviving Wolves as she did so.

One was watching her, a loaded crossbow ready on a crenellation. Another had just started to climb down the rope. The third was holding the rope steady where it went over the wall.

The lady ranger fired the wand again. The man with

the bow staggered back, clutching his shoulder, and cried out.

Sharantyr charged, sobbing, fear and anger slowly rising to choke her. Had these black-helmed bastards slain the man she'd gone through so much to protect, the one man Shadowdale needed in the face of Zhentarim evil? The legendary mage half the Realms feared and the rest whispered glad tales about?

"Mother Mystra," she prayed aloud, "aid him now, for I cannot!" Then she flung herself aside desperately as the injured man, face twisted with hatred and pain, aimed his bow and triggered it.

The bolt slammed into her left shoulder and hurled her back along the wall. Sharantyr screamed as the trip along the rough stones twisted the quarrel, its point grating along her bones. She should have worn the shield again. She should have—oh, gods, the pain!

Using her sword as a prop, Sharantyr dragged herself up. Her left arm burned and felt dripping wet all at once, and the world seemed to be slowly turning around her. She found her feet, somehow, and ran dizzily toward the man with the bow.

His face was grim and white, but he drew his blade and came to meet the woman in bloodstained leathers. Her eyes met his like two daggers, but she swayed, and her left arm hung limp, his quarrel standing out of her shoulder.

"Just what," he snarled, "brings you here, maid?" His blade leapt at her throat. Long hair parted at its passing.

"Death," she said softly, parrying. Their blades met fingerwidths away from her throat. Steel snarled on steel, but her blade held and his was forced away. "Yours."

She triggered the wand still clutched in her nerveless left hand, whispering the word that awakened its greater power.

There was a burst of white light, and the warrior screamed. Sharantyr saw him reel back. A startled Wolf's face gaped at them both from outside the wall, at the head of the rope. She leapt forward with the last of her strength and brought her blade down on that tight-stretched cord.

Strands parted and flew, and frantic scramblings came from just below her. Then the rope was gone, and two throats were crying vainly to the passing air. Their songs of fear ended very suddenly in thudding sounds.

Sharantyr sank to her knees there by the turret door and looked about with dull eyes, fighting waves of pain. The Wolf she'd struck with the wand lay fallen beside her. She made sure of his death with her blade, then her gaze fell on his belt.

A metal vial shone there amid the blood. With sudden urgency she tugged it free, snarling. On hands and knees, she set off on the long crawl back along the battlements.

The vial bore a rune she knew. The magical drink it held would heal, if it could be trusted with magic going wild. Gods, but she needed it!

The old man needed it more, the man whose life was more important than any other in the Realms, the man she'd come here to protect.

Sharantyr crawled grimly back along the battlements, using her blade where life yet lurked amid her fallen foes, and tearing free six more vials as she went.

She was half blind from helpless tears of pain when she turned the corner, crawling feebly to where Elminster sat in his blood. "Tymora," she sobbed aloud, "let me be in time."

Then Tymora, or someone else listening with dark humor, rolled darkness over her like a great black cloak, and she sank into it and was gone.

*   *   *   *   *

"We've the gods to thank that they aren't still raining quarrels down on us!" an exhausted Itharr said, leaning wearily against a heap of corpses, notched and battered blade in hand.

"More likely we've Elminster to thank," Belkram replied, looking back across the forecourt. Quarrels stood up from fallen, silent men, wooden doors and framing, and cracks in the flagstones like a thicket of leaning weeds. "They left off rather suddenly, and there's been no rush from above."

Itharr squinted up at what he could see of the battlements—not much from here. Then he shot another long look at the slit windows around the courtyard, expecting quarrels to leap out of them at any moment.

The two winded Harpers lay resting with half a dozen men of the dale, all who could still stand and swing a sword after the bloodbath desperate Wolves had made of the forecourt. Many dalefolk had crawled or been dragged away out of the keep. Those still able to fight had no good idea of how many Wolves were left in the castle. They agreed that no members of Longspear's council had been seen elsewhere in the dale. Most or all were probably within these walls.

There was also at least one mage of power, Hcarla Bellwind, as well as the hated Angruin Stormcloak, who'd hurled death in the marketplace and then fled. The dalefolk couldn't think of any place but here, his seat of power, that he could have gone when his magic took him away.

Unless Wolves were roaming the battlements above, none remained alive outside the stone walls of the High Castle. Itharr and Belkram had led the men of the dale doggedly through a hail of death to hack down the line of Wolves defending the courtyard. None of them still stood, but the castle servants had loosed the war-horses, milk cows, and goats to mill about the courtyards, making charging or even staying together impossible.

The two Harpers and the men they led were too weary to do more than watch the roaming animals for a while. They lay, moving only their eyes, amid the bodies of those they'd slain. Their roving gazes kept watch for any emerging foes, but also searched out water, good weapons, and—

"Hey!" Belkram leaned forward. "Over there." He slid down the flank of the still-warm dead horse he'd been propped against, rolled onto his knees, and clambered over bodies until he reached a certain belt. He tugged, worked at leather thongs for a moment, and came back to them with a metal vial in his hand.

"Healing quaff?" Itharr asked.

Belkram nodded and held it out to Gedaern, the most badly hurt daleman. "Just a swallow, now," he cautioned.

The white-faced, sweating man drank carefully, holding the vial in both hands. Then he closed his eyes and let his hands fall slowly into his lap as the liquid worked its way down.

When the old shopkeeper opened his eyes a deep breath later, he looked at Belkram. "Let's be at them again," he said with a wolfish grin. "I want to see all of them dead or driven out by nightfall."

He passed the vial on as similar bloodthirsty smiles answered him.

"Well," Itharr said, looking around, "what's the best way to get in without getting ourselves quickly killed? They'll be waiting."

The oldest man laughed suddenly, a short bark hoarse from long disuse. "I know the best place! Aye—the bolt hole!"

"Bolt hole?"

"Aye," the old man said. "I helped old Lhassar fill it in with stones, when I was a lad. It's where the jakes all drained out before they dug the deep cesspool."

Belkram rolled his eyes. "I might have known we'd end up climbing through dung before this was over." He waited until hearty, rather wild laughter had risen and died, and then asked, "So where is this?"

The old man pointed at an inner corner of the courtyard. "Over there."

Itharr raised his eyebrows. "The jakes drained into the—ne'er mind. I'm just right glad I didn't dwell here then." He rose, amid answering laughter, and swung his arms about to loosen his stiffening shoulders. "Let's to war again, then," he said quietly.

Belkram got up. "Aye. For the dale, men, and freedom!"

"For the dale, and freedom!" they roared back, and plunged grandly in amid the cows.

Itharr rolled his eyes. "I hope Storm has no magic to be watching us now," he murmured as he and Belkram dodged and trotted amid anxious, milling animals.

"Why not?" Belkram replied. "This is going to look splendid, in a breath or two, when we chase all these horses out of here so the Wolves can't flee on them!"

In reply, Itharr rolled his eyes again.

* * * * *

Ylyndaera Mulmar turned, eyes flashing. "Well, watch over me, then! You'll have to do it on the run, though, because I'm going after my father! He needs me. I know it. I . . . I can feel it."

She looked toward the castle, unseen through a solid wall of Ulraea's shop, and spun fiercely back to face the shop mistress, eyes flaming, hair whirling about her shoulders. "Are you with me, Ulraea?" The dagger gleamed in her hand as she mounted to the window, where the shutters still hung in ruins from Irreph's handling.

Ulraea spread her hands helplessly and sighed. She went to a nearby table, took up a new, gleaming cleaver, and tugged the price tag from it with sudden impatience. She slashed the air with it a few times, her ample bosom shaking, and sighed again.

"At least, child," she said reprovingly, beckoning with the gleaming steel in her hand, "if you must die a hero, let us leave by the door, hey, and not my window."

Daera's sudden smile was dazzling.

* * * * *

"What? Where?" The words were out of Sharantyr's mouth before she knew she was saying them. Gentle hands were cradling her head and stroking her hair.

She lay on something hard but warmer than stone. She ached, here and there, and her shoulder throbbed, but the rending, blinding pain was gone. Wondering, she fought her eyes open and looked around.

Elminster's anxious face looked down at her. A soft breeze was blowing his beard caressingly across her forehead. "Shar?" he asked, voice rough. "Are ye all right?"

Sharantyr put a hand down and rolled to her side. "I . . . I think so." She looked around. She was lying on Elminster's robe, on the parapet walk. Dead Wolves littered the battlements around them. A few crows had found the bodies and were fluttering about and pecking experimentally.

The Old Mage was sitting unconcernedly in his clout and boots, the ring of regeneration gleaming on his finger. Sharantyr's gaze leapt to where the quarrel had struck him.

All she saw was a dark, angry-looking patch. Elminster smiled and held up the quarrel, dark with his own blood.

Sharantyr shuddered, and then dared a glance at her own shoulder. It had been clumsily bandaged with what looked like strips torn from Elminster's clout: cotton now stiff with dried blood. Her shoulder, unseen beneath— she wriggled it experimentally—felt whole. She raised questioning eyes to Elminster.

"The healing potions ye brought back," Elminster said. "Ye had all of them." He scratched at his beard and poked at her bandaged shoulder. "How d'ye feel?"

Sharantyr sat up, feeling light-headed. Under her torn leathers she was sticky and ached, her stiff and bruised muscles complaining, but her probing fingers encountered none of the fresh blood and deep wounds she had feared to find.

"Weak as a weaned kitten, Old Mage," she said with a smile, "but I'll live. Give me a few breaths more and I'll be up and swinging a sword again."

Elminster looked at the carnage around them. "I'll stand clear of thy way when ye do," he told her dryly.

Sharantyr answered his smile, briefly, but her eyes grew somber when she saw the dead. "I like this killing little," she whispered with sudden urgency, turning to him. "Believe me, won't you?"

Elminster put a swift, lean arm around her. "I do,

Shar. I know ye well enough, now." He looked around them and added, "Mind, we need ye to try thy hand at it a little time longer." He held up the magic missile wand. "Ye seem far more effective than this, I must say."

* * * * *

Daera came out into the street like a silent shadow. There was at least one man outside, in armor. A Wolf!

The man was grinning, one armored hand clutching a twisted handful of long hair. The woman he held grimaced in pain but dared not even whimper; the long curve of his sword was hard against her throat. Another woman watched from a nearby door, mouth agape, frozen in fear.

"A good horse your man has," the Wolf said, almost conversationally. "I've seen it." His hand yanked her back into the hard embrace of his armor, then came around to her breast.

Deliberately, he tore the worn cloth of her bodice away. "Almost as good as his taste in women," the Wolf said, caressing her with cruel, bruising fingers. The sword brushed up and down her throat, reminding her not to scream.

"You're going to take me to that good horse," the Wolf said grimly as he forced her steadily along the street. "Silence! You, too," he added to the watching woman in the doorway, "or I'll slit both your throats and forego the pleasure of your company."

The awkward procession continued down the street, the captive woman feebly pointing at an alleyway. With a face dark as a hailstorm, Daera waved Ulraea to silence and went after them on silent feet, dagger ready.

She knew he'd look around before entering the alley, and hurried. She had to get his sword away, but how?

The armored back was very close in front of her, the smell of sweat and oiled metal strong. Ylyndaera Mulmar looked at it, knowing she had only a breath more to act, and inspiration came.

She stepped to his blind side as the Wolf's head started

to turn, and slipped her dagger delicately up into the armpit of his sword arm, where armor plate ended and old, sweat-weakened leather began.

The man stiffened, roared in pain, and nearly dropped his blade. He whirled, snatching at it with his other hand, as three women screamed.

Ylyndaera snarled amid the shrieks and stabbed at the man's eyes from behind.

He shrieked, too, as blood fountained up from the wound in his armpit, and broke into an agonized, stumbling run. She watched him go, goaded by pain, as his bright blood ran down the dagger in her hand, and felt her gorge rise. No. She could not slay him that way, by finding an eye from behind, and feeling the blade go in . . . ohhh . . .

As her spew splattered on the stones in front of her, a thought came. She reached for a stone she knew was loose, from long-gone days when she'd played up this alley and down others.

The stone was large, flat, and very heavy. She caught up to the staggering Wolf, roughly tore off his helm from behind, and with both hands brought the stone down hard on his head.

He shuddered, started to curse, and fell. She did it again. Again. And again before something gave. His body jerked under her knees before it fell still.

As she rose, she looked into the great, dark eyes of the horse owner's wife, who stood watching, the marks of cruel fingers dark on her flesh. Daera managed a smile as she took up the man's sword, hefted it, and said, "Come with me, Jharina. I'm for the castle. We're going to kill us some Wolves."

From behind her, Daera heard a shocked gasp. Without turning she said, "Ulraea? Bring along Tanshlee, too. She'll catch a chill, standing gawping in that doorway all day."

Her eyes looked deep into Jharina's. The older, prouder lady looked back at the gangling girl with the sword and the bloody dagger, and drew in a deep, shuddering breath.

"Well?" Ylyndaera asked softly. "Are you with me?"

Jharina smiled. "Yes," she said, her voice almost steady. "Yes, I am." She stepped forward and embraced the high constable's daughter, treading on the fallen Wolf uncaringly.

"Lead us, lass," she said, "as your father does. Lead us."

Daera kissed her cheek, handed her the dagger, and started back out of the alley. "Hurry, then," she said. "The men may need us. All's gone quiet up there, and when magic's about, that means ill."

The bloodstained and mud-smeared Wolf who came stumbling out of an alley just then, to make a run for the castle, was unlucky indeed. The angry howls and screams of the women warned him before they reached him, but not in time for him to outrun them on a wounded leg. He swung his blade twice, jarring Ylyndaera with two hard parries, before his leg gave way and they had him. He did not scream long.

They paused for a moment to let Tanshlee be sick all over the body, then hastened up the road to the open castle gates. Men were hurrying about inside, halberds and swords gleaming in their hands. Wolves.

"Tymora," Daera breathed, "let us not be too late."

The words had scarcely left her lips when there was a great flash and booming sound from within the walls. A man's head, still wearing a helm and a shocked expression, flew past them amid a shower of stones, dirt, and other things best not examined too closely.

"Oh, gods," Daera cursed, and broke into a run. "Come on!"

They were almost at the gate before they heard the growing thunder of hooves clattering and pounding toward them. Frantically they flung themselves aside, diving to the turf, as the world exploded in racing horses.

"Daera," Ulraea quavered as they hugged the ground together amid rolling dust, "could you stop praying, d'you think? Every time you call on a divine one, something happens!"

"Oh," Daera replied, clutching her sword. "All right."

16
Stormcloak's Humor

Elminster coughed. "If ye feel up to standing," he said, "I'd best be putting my robe back on now. Thy reputation, ye know. Besides, 'tis cold when one is old and thin and not used to drafty battlements."

Sharantyr chuckled and rolled to her feet. She felt a little weak at the knees and caught hold of the rampart for support, but when she moved there was no great pain, and everything turned and flexed as it should. She found her sword and took it up. Its familiar weight made her feel all was well again.

Elminster held up his robe and ostentatiously brushed it clean. After an undignified moment of struggling as he put it on over his head, he smoothed his beard and hefted his much-used wand. "I fear more bloodshed awaits us," he said, almost eagerly. "Now, if someone will show us where the battle's gotten to . . ."

As if in reply, someone not far away laughed exultantly. They tensed, staring in the direction the sound had come from, and seeing only empty walks and stairs, lifeless turrets. The sound came again, from the far side of one of the turrets. A door or a window must be hidden from their view. In unspoken accord they hurried along the battlements as silently as they could.

"Fools," a voice that matched the laughter called, "you have come here, your hard and desperate way, only to find your own deaths!"

The taunt was not directed at them; it was hurled down into the inner courtyard, where men with weapons —pitchforks, old felling axes, and a few swords and daggers—stood warily in a corner, livestock milling all around them.

Elminster and Sharantyr exchanged glances and hurried on. They still could not see the speaker. In front of them was the turret the Wolves with the rope had emerged from. The voice must be coming from its other side.

"Rush in by that door," Elminster whispered to the lady ranger, "only after ye hear me shout. Move as fast as ye can. Only a Zhent wizard would be foolish and arrogant enough to gloat over foes instead of striking, but he won't go on forever. Don't give him a chance to use magic on thee." He clapped her shoulder affectionately and darted around the curving side of the turret. Sharantyr held her blade high as she came up to the door.

The storm shutters had been thrown wide on an arched window that commanded a view of the courtyard and the parapet walk most of the way around the inside of the castle. Leaning out of the window, resplendent in rich robes, a cruel-looking man wearing earrings and a triumphant sneer was fairly spitting his words down at the trapped men below.

"Thought yourselves victorious, did you? Country idiots! Longspear ruled only as far as we let him. Now that you've swept him away and most of his stupid swordswingers with him, what have you accomplished?"

The man raised his hand. Elminster saw that he held a handful of winking, glowing glass spheres that spun lazily around each other, and his heart sank. Zhent blastglobes!

"All you've done, worms, is thrown away your lives—and those of your wives and daughters and mothers—by hewing down all among us who might have shown you any mercy. Now you face wizards of power, dullards, and you'll discover just how we deal with defiance!"

The globes swept up, pulsing with sudden fire as he drew back his hand to throw them. "Know, worms, that it is I, Haragh Mnistlyn, who destroys you!"

Elminster leaned close then and conversationally said, "Boo."

The Zhentarim turned a startled face to the Old Mage, who smiled sweetly at him and bellowed, "Now, Shar!"

Elminster raised his wand with a confident smile and

tensed to fling himself back around the curve of the wall.

The Zhent wizard didn't disappoint him. Snarling in surprised fury, he flung the blast-globes straight at Elminster.

If they struck anything, they would explode.

The Old Mage hurled himself back as energetically as he'd ever done anything in his long, long life.

There was a frozen moment when the only thing he heard was his own heartbeat booming between his ears like the muffled, deep call of a far-off marching drum. His shoulder struck stone with bruising force, and he skidded on. Lights winked and flashed past his nose.

It seemed his life might stretch a little longer, after all. A loud crash came from within the turret, accompanied by a startled curse, as the blazing globes spun past Elminster, whirled over the inner parapet wall with a handwidth or so to spare, and plunged down into the forecourt. Safely around the curve of the turret wall, the Old Mage craned to watch the end of their flight and saw folk coming toward the gate from outside the castle.

Folk without armor. Folk of the dale—Women! He had no time even for a prayer to Mystra but brought up his wand and hissed desperately, "Alag!"

The wand gave forth—ah, praise be!—a glowing teardrop of force, firing it out over empty air with a soft *phut*. It curved gracefully down and then seemed to leap through the air to meet the descending globes just before they could reach the open gate.

Elminster stared hard at the gate—had he been in time?—and barely heard the thin scream, abruptly cut off, from behind him. On its heels came the fury of the blast, smiting his ears like spell-thunder.

Below, a door had just opened in a tower wall. Armored Wolves were hurrying out into the forecourt, halberds and blades ready. Well, he couldn't stop the luck of Tempus falling on them.

The women had seen the Wolves and hesitated. Yes, that would save them! Elminster laughed aloud.

Gods, if he only had his magic, none of this would be necessary. But still, they'd done well this day. He turned.

"Shar?"

A grim, blood-streaked face looked out of the door at him. "I live. That's more than can be said for this spell-hurler. He was quick, I'll give him that."

The lady ranger came out into the light again. Her face was white, and she was shaking with rage.

"What, lass?" Elminster asked, reaching out to her. Sharantyr turned blazing eyes on him.

"Those snakes are laying wagers on who will kill the most with their magic," she said, seething. "He screamed just after that blast, and someone called up the stairs to see if anything had gone wrong, shouting to ask if he still expected to outdo Stormcloak's body count and claim the victor's share."

Elminster looked at her. "So what will ye do?" he asked quietly.

Sharantyr brushed errant hair out of her eyes and raised the bloody tip of her blade. "I'm going down those stairs," she said fiercely. "Guard my back, Old Mage."

Elminster nodded. "I will, as best I can."

They gazed around the battlements—long years of experience made Elminster search the sky for dragons, but he found none—and slipped into the turret, pulling the door nearly closed.

The turret room was awash with blood. The arrogant Zhentarim was draped over the back of a chair, arms flung wide, staring forever at something unseen near the ceiling.

Elminster's stomach turned over. Sharantyr set her teeth and hurried to the steps.

A light glimmered below. They descended quietly, drifting to a stop when they saw men moving in the room at the foot of the stair. It was some sort of meeting room, where men were draining and refilling ornate goblets steadily as they sat at the table or strode restlessly around it.

"Oh, we're safe enough," one cold voice was saying as Sharantyr came within hearing range. "Stormcloak sent an extra guard patrol to the roof. Ten men, I believe, and the strutting 'prentice. What's his name? Ragh, or something of the sort? The dandy who always wears court robes. It'd take old Elminster himself to break in on us here."

In the darkness on the stairs, two sets of teeth flashed in mirthless smiles.

The voice that spoke next was deeper and shorter. "The question is: Now that we don't have Longspear to hold on to his reins, what will Stormcloak do? We need forty bowmen at least to hold the dale. They're all roused out there now. Even if we slay every man who's raised sword against us today, we'll have to take the dale all over again."

"A harder thing to do now, with Cormyr and Sembia both looking our way and beginning to suspect who our mages are."

"Aye," came the deep voice again, "but will Stormcloak call for the aid we need, or will his first concern be impressing Lord Manshoon and other Zhentarim of power with his own strength and battle cunning? He may well try to win the day alone for greater glory. He cares nothing for this place. All can see that much."

"Hush, will you. Hear? He comes. That must be his guard, for there's not another large band of sword brothers left."

Elminster laid a silent hand on Sharantyr's sword arm to check her. Silently she laid her own free hand over his and patted it reassuringly. No. The time was not now.

There came the sound of many booted feet, a door opening, and a single, measured tread approaching the table.

"Councillors," came a cold, confident voice, "we hold the castle. Only a few of those who attacked us yet live. I'm told that women and young girls are all who remain to storm our gates. We've not found the mage or the two warriors who led the rabble. I suspect Cormyr is backing them, but I'll find out soon enough. As you know, the real tragedy today is the loss of our lord, slain by those two warriors." He paused, but no voice broke the silence.

"With his fall, rule over this dale passes into my hands," the voice continued flatly, challengingly. The words fell into another silence.

Then a deep voice said, "By what right do you claim lordship here, Stormcloak? Your magic, aye, but have you any less . . . ah, brutish claim? It is customary for the council to choose who shall rule over the High Dale." A general stirring accompanied these words, a shifting, rising tension that died into heavy, anticipatory silence.

Stormcloak's reply was as cold as a glacier wind. "You must know, Councillor, where Lord Longspear came from and what men he led in battle. That place is where I and my fellow mages came from. You are not a fool; you tell me."

"Zhentil Keep," the deep voice replied slowly, waiting.

"Aye," Stormcloak agreed dryly. "Whose orders I have followed, and passed on to Longspear and others, since the day we came here. I held authority over Longspear from the first, whether he acknowledged it or not. As to the vote of this council, consider a simple sum. To be lord I need only a majority of votes, and all the Zhentarim will vote with me."

"There are fewer of you," the deep voice reminded him, just as dryly, "than there once were."

"Well then, good Councillor Gulkin, perhaps it is time that the real strength of the Brotherhood was made known to you—to all of you. Call it a necessity of war, if you will, and if any tongues here today should slip about it later, be warned that their silencing will also be . . . a necessity of war."

A wine goblet was set down deliberately. Men stirred and shifted again.

Stormcloak's voice came again. "Kromm Kadar is the most recent addition to this table. Our blacksmith serves Zhentil Keep. His predecessor was a Sembian spy, whom we killed. Kromm serves the same master I do; his vote will be with mine."

Tense silence was the only reply. Stormcloak's triumphant, almost taunting voice came again. "There is also Alazs. Am I not right?"

"Yes, Lord," came a new, thin voice.

"Alazs breeds good horses and has sold many to Lord

Longspear. I'm sure he'll continue to put good mounts under our men. He has orders to, from the same source as I get my directives. Alazs has swung a sword for the Brotherhood in the Moonsea North for many a year. Perhaps you've heard of Alazs Ironwood, the Sword of Melvaunt?"

Silence was the only reply. Stormcloak was moving about the room; his voice receded slightly. "Are you counting, Gulkin? Have I the votes yet? Not quite. Ah, but there's another. Our physic, Cheth, is more than a man of potions, drugs, and herbs. He, too, serves the Brotherhood—and his healing seems most successful when applied to those we want healed."

"Is this wise," a rasping voice came, "revealing us all, when you could have just voted this stump-head down?"

"I believe so, Master Moonviper," Stormcloak replied. "I think it's important that we drop the pretenses with which Longspear wasted so much of our time."

The listeners on the stairs heard the glass stopper of a heavy decanter set down, liquid gurgling, and the thud of the decanter returning to the tabletop.

"Sword, would you—?" The stopper was replaced and the decanter shifted again.

"Thank you." Stormcloak sipped, swallowed, and came closer. His voice was loud, very close under them, when he continued. "I have long had my suspicions, Councillor Gulkin, that some among us may well serve other masters, unknown to me. Perhaps you know something of this and can enlighten me? No? Well, feel free to unburden yourselves, any of you, should you learn of such misplaced loyalties among us. There have always been those who meddle—worshipers of dead dragons, the Harpers, and the Red Wizards, to name just three. I'll be very surprised if at least one man here doesn't know more of one such concern than he wants us to realize. Of course, we must always look to Cormyr on the one hand and Sembia on the other to take an interest in us, lying between them, the lightly patrolled backlands of both within our reach."

They heard him walking about almost lazily in the

deep silence that followed.

"That, Cheth," Stormcloak added lightly, "is why I'd like everyone here to know just how matters stand. Besides, this will give traitors among us something to do— trying to report back to those who hold their secret loyalty, and not be discovered by us while doing so."

"Yes, Lord Stormcloak," Cheth agreed.

"Ah, but let us have the vote," Stormcloak's voice came again, almost purring now. "Or rather, to save time and thirsty throats, councillors, let us hear who would vote against me. Simply speak out and name the one you would have rule the dale in my stead." He chuckled and added, "In view of the situation at present, please ensure that you choose someone you know to be still alive."

Elminster leaned over and murmured, his lips against Sharantyr's ear, "I'd not seen this humor in the man before. It's much worse than his cold, snarling side."

Sharantyr turned her head until her soft lips were at the Old Mage's ear. "I take it, then, that you're voting against him?"

Elminster chuckled silently. It made his beard dance against her cheek.

"I believe you're right, Cheth," Stormcloak's voice came up to them. "It seems I am lord in the High Dale, after all. We'll have to set a feast over this. Tonight, in the Great Hall. Give the orders, won't you, Councillor Gulkin?"

"Aye, Lord," the deep voice muttered. "Is this meeting at an end?"

"If the council agrees," Stormcloak said silkily. There was a gruff, uneven answering chorus of assent, the sound of chairs scraping back, and the noise of booted feet moving about. The sounds receded until they died away entirely.

"Follow the wine merchant," Stormcloak's voice came again. "He's been entirely too quiet and agreeable these six rides past."

"Aye, Lord," someone replied, and left.

Stormcloak's tread came closer until it was right beneath them. His hard, carefree voice said, "All right, Haragh, you can come down now. You've been crouching up there listening to all of it, haven't you?"

Sharantyr twisted out from under Elminster's hand and launched herself down the stairs like a vengeful arrow. Her sword flashed as she came out into the light in a leap that brought her down on top of the startled wizard.

Only the goblet in the Zhentarim's hand saved him. Her landing drove his outstretched arms up, and the goblet with them in front of his throat. Her sword cut it to twisted ruin, but Stormcloak's flesh beneath escaped, leaving him alive and able to shriek.

Sharantyr's training made her look up as they struck the floor together. Three fully armored, capable warriors were moving toward her, weapons grating out.

Veterans, and not alone. Two swordsmen had been going out the door after the departing councillors. They were already turning startled faces to her.

If she carved up this Zhent wizard, she'd have no time to hold back all the swords coming for her. And who would protect Elminster then?

Sharantyr sprang up, too busy to curse, and leapt to meet the first warrior. From behind her, a magic missile streaked into one of the faces at the door, quelling the shout it was widening to utter. The other missile must have struck the new lord of the dale. Behind her she heard him gasp, curse, and roll frantically away.

Then she was fighting for her life and had no time to watch Angruin Stormcloak frantically teleport away.

Harpies curse the woman, whoever she was, were his parting thoughts. He'd snatched the time to take that spell back into his mind as battle raged at the very gates of the castle. Now it was used and gone, with dangerous fools still lurking about.

Red butterflies suddenly swirled all around Sharantyr, and with them came a drift of snow.

She heard Elminster sigh and murmur, "Wands!" in exasperation. Then the first warrior slipped on something and fell heavily at her feet, nearly taking her with him. She caught the second blade reaching for her life at the last possible instant.

The first man was struggling and heaving beneath her, reaching for a dagger or trying for room enough to get his sword into her, no doubt. The second man was snarling and using all his strength to force into her face the broadsword she'd parried a finger or so in front of her nose. Sharantyr set her teeth and resisted, knowing he was stronger and that the struggles beneath her were forcing her up into the waiting blade.

"Lady, aid me," Sharantyr cried, calling on Mielikki, the goddess of the forest. "Tymora and Tempus, attend," she added for good measure, seeing death very close to her and reaching dark fingers her way.

Then the man above her grunted and was spitting blood and teeth as a tattered, dirty, and familiar boot took him in the face. Elminster had joined the fight. He stepped on her with a muttered, "Sorry, lass," as he bent to drive his dagger into the neck of the man beneath her.

Then he sprang up, robes swirling, to stamp on the sword hand of the man he'd kicked. There was a cracking sound and a roar of pain, and Elminster had the sword in his own hands and was bringing it up to parry the rushing attack of the third man.

"Shar," the Old Mage suggested calmly as a flurry of ringing blows drove him back across her toward the stair, "cut the legs out from under this fellow for me, will ye?"

Sharantyr grinned savagely. "I'll do better," she replied, and snaked an arm out from under the tangle of limbs to drive her sword up into the breeches under his armor skirt.

The man screamed, gave an awkward hop, and fell to the floor, writhing in agony. Elminster dropped the sword and went to the table.

Men were thundering back up into the room, hastily donning helms and drawing swords. Elminster picked up the heaviest chair he could find, and with a sudden rippling of muscles threw it across the room to crash into the foremost man.

The startled Wolf went down, and the man behind him tripped and went sprawling. Elminster hurled the iron sphere he was carrying at the next man and charged forward, snatching out his dagger again.

He used it twice with brutal haste before he reached the pinioned man. With a bleak smile he struck the sword out of the man's hand and shoved the man hard with his shoulder.

The man was wrapped in metal bands, like a cage that has tightened around its prisoner until the bars press into the skin all around and movement is impossible. Elminster drove the helpless man backward into the door frame, where he lodged amid cracking noises of wood and bone, and a scream of pain.

"Noisy, these Zhents," he commented as the man screamed again. Men behind him in the corridor outside the room began to curse, trying and failing to push the pinioned Wolf out of their way. "How do ye, Shar?"

Sharantyr came to join him, blade wiped clean. "I'm still alive," she replied grimly, eyeing the man, "but I like little the thought of hacking my way through that lot. What say we go back up again and seek another way down?"

Elminster frowned for a breath or two as unseen men shoved and cursed, doing something that made the caged man scream again. Then he nodded. "I don't like to leave magic behind, with things as they are," he said, eyeing the iron bands, "but there's no easy way to get that back without fighting all of them. I suppose I should thank Mystra and Tymora both for it merely working when I needed it."

Sharantyr nodded and took his arm. "Come, El. Let's be out of here before someone else finds magic that works and fills this room with fire—or worse."

Elminster looked again at the now-unconscious man, head bouncing and lolling from the force of blows he was taking from behind as impatient warriors tried to force their way into the room. He sighed, drew up his robes in both hands for faster climbing, and made for the stairs. Sharantyr glided just behind him, sword ready, watching their rear as they ascended. It was turning into a very long day.

17
Beware Ladies with Steel in Their Hands

"Is the high constable still alive?" Sharantyr asked as they came cautiously out of the turret and looked around. A quiet had fallen over the High Castle as the afternoon sun lit up its every nook and crevice. In the courtyard below, a few dalefolk could be seen cautiously probing bodies and piles of rubble and tumbled gear. Doors were closed, and turret windows shuttered. Save for a thin wisp of smoke rising from the castle kitchens, the fortress seemed deserted, as if no one lurked within, plotting victory and gathering swords and magic.

Elminster spread empty hands. "Mulmar? I barely recognized him, ye know, with the chains an' all. He headed for the battlements by one stair while we ascended by the other. I lost sight of him after that. I seem to recall hearing him cry out when they were firing all those quarrels at us." He winced. "If he fell there, in the forecourt, I may have sent him to the gods myself a little later when I hit the Zhent's globes."

At the memory, he drew the wand from his belt, looked at it quizzically, and sighed. "I can't remember what Art is left in this. It's gone wild so many times now, who can tell?" He shrugged. "Let us seek Irreph, whate'er befalls now. Thy thought is a good one."

Sharantyr smiled at him. "Of course. They always are." She handed her sword to him. "Here, hold this."

"The eternal saying of a woman to a man," Elminster observed wryly. "But why to me, and now?"

Sharantyr grunted under the dead, dangling weight of the corpse she'd picked up. "Because I need both hands . . . for this." She staggered back along the walk, the dead man on her shoulders, and dumped the carrion through the turret window.

"Drag a few over here, will you?" she called. "Before we look for the high constable, we'd best guard our rear."

Elminster dragged obediently. The lady ranger tossed the bodies down the stairs, Haragh first.

"They'll carve or crush their way past the one you trapped down there soon enough," Sharantyr said. "If they have to get past all of these to come after us—well, at least they'll be slowed down. Or if they use magic to shift them, we'll be warned." She puffed, heaved, and sweated until cold, heavy bodies choked the stair and covered the turret room floor. Then she squinted at Elminster, pulling hair out of her eyes, and said, "I'll be glad when this day's done, Old Mage. I'm beginning to feel old."

Elminster raised an eyebrow. "A thousand and more years old am I, and d'ye hear me groaning and limping and feebly protesting my age? Surely ye can manage the weight of a mere twenty-odd winters, lass!"

He grinned at her expression and added innocently, "Or is it thirty-odd?"

The Old Mage of Shadowdale then demonstrated the light weight of his years for all the Realms to see by running off as fast and nimbly as any naughty child at play. Sharantyr aided him by amply demonstrating his immediate need to do so.

* * * * *

"He lives," Elminster said tersely, kneeling by the sprawled, blackened body on the stair. Quarrels stood out from it like needles in a chatelaine's pincushion. The high constable lay in his blood amid a litter of chains, fallen Wolves, and odd weapons. "He'll want healing, even to see the moon this night."

"Then give it to him," said Sharantyr in a voice that trembled with fresh rage. "While I do what he was trying to."

Elminster turned. "And that is?" he asked mildly.

Sharantyr's face was bleak. "Destroy every Zhent still in this dale." Zhents had done this to a brave man who still wore their chains, just as Zhents had chained her, too, and . . . She thrust away those memories with a shudder, letting her rage build into the fire she'd need to slay as ruthlessly as she'd need to. As ruthlessly as *they* always did.

She found she was trembling, and that Elminster had noticed it and had begun to frown, so she drew in a deep breath and tried to assume a nonchalant manner. Hefting her long sword, she surveyed the notches and scrapes in its steel critically and added, "One of them owes me a new sword, too."

"Still feeling old and worn out?" Elminster asked her pointedly, slipping the ring of regeneration onto one of Irreph Mulmar's fingers and closing the limp, hairy hand of the high constable over it.

Sharantyr laughed harshly. "No. Not anymore." She turned away, whipped her sword through the air thrice, stretched like a great cat, and turned back to him. "Wish me luck, Old Mage," she said in a voice like silk falling onto waiting steel. "I've Wolves to hunt."

Elminster smiled. "All of Tymora's luck upon thee, and more. Take with thee all that Mystra and I have no need for." He rose hastily, smile fading, and reached out his hand to her. Wondering, Sharantyr laid her hand in his.

The Old Mage gently drew her to him. His lips were soft on her cheek.

"Take care, lass," he said roughly, "for I find more and more that I do not want to lose thee."

Sharantyr stared at him for a moment, openmouthed, then whirled about and raced away across the forecourt.

Elminster watched her go, shook his head slightly, and sat down on the step above Irreph, wand in hand, to guard the high constable of the High Dale. There are less steady jobs.

* * * * *

Sharantyr ran past the astonished women of the dale, who were clutching a variety of weapons and looking nervously at shuttered windows high above them, dark arrow-slit windows uncomfortably nearer, and closed doors. She gave them one hawklike, searching glance and ran on without breaking stride, drawn sword gleaming.

Ylyndaera stared after her and said urgently, "All of you, follow her! Come!"

Sharantyr ran hard, hair streaming, across the muddy courtyard toward a shadow in a back corner where the men had been earlier . . . men who were not there now. They must have found a way in. She would find it too.

Behind straw heaped up for the horses, Sharantyr found a pile of fresh stones. Then she saw the hole their removal had opened in the wall. Here the others had gone in. Here, guarded or not, she would follow.

She halted, breathing heavily from her run, and looked all around warily. Seeing no foe, she crouched to peer into the gloom, extended her blade, and followed it into darkness.

Her throat was suddenly very dry. She'd climbed into unknown dark places a time or six, aye, but always in the company of others—usually the merry, mighty Knights of Myth Drannor. With them, as they hewed down dragons and wizards alike while trading jests and insults, it was all too easy to feel invulnerable. But now . . . She crept onward, hoping no enemy archer or mage waited at the other end of this tunnel.

The strong smell of deep, damp earth rose around her with a faint, clinging odor of decay. Thankfully, there were no charnel or beast smells. This was no lair or bone pit, and the way ahead was short.

The tunnel opened out into a small, round room. Smooth-sided chutes—smaller, tubelike tunnels—opened into it on all sides and from above. The higher they went, the narrower they became. This was familiar, somehow. It resembled something she'd—of course! This was a privy pit, and the tunnels above—disused, by the lack of strong smell or dung underfoot—led to garderobes or cruder jakes in the castle above. But where had those dalesmen gone?

Two tunnels looked large enough to comfortably crawl in. The one to the left must lead toward the turret and the room they'd heard Stormcloak elect himself lord in. The one to the right went to the kitchens, great hall, guest rooms, and audience chambers.

Near the great hall, there'd probably be too many people about, and it would be too large to furnish easy cover against a crossbow. Moreover, there were—or at least recently had been—Wolves in the other direction. Lots of them. She peered down both tunnels but could find nothing distinctive about either, and no marks to show which way the men had gone.

She shrugged. Left, then. Sharantyr climbed into the tunnel, slid along uncomfortably on her knuckles for a time, thought about what a target her backside must make for anyone shooting a crossbow down this tunnel, and carefully sheathed her sword. Empty-handed, she could travel at twice the speed and found it far easier to be quiet. She went on, groping in deepening darkness, as the tunnel rose, met with smaller side tubes, and grew a little smaller.

Well, she was in the castle, but how to get out of this dark, close tunnel? Something small and four-footed scampered momentarily across her way. A rat, no doubt. Sharantyr started to wish she could see.

What if she met with something larger and hungrier, or a trap of some sort? She wouldn't even see it in the darkness.

She forced that thought down, concentrating instead on the sure knowledge that the chute carried waste down from somewhere, and so she must inevitably reach that origin.

Sharantyr hoped someone's backside wouldn't be covering it when she did. She could almost hear the sly voice of the thief Torm, her sometime tormentor in the Knights, making that snide observation. She smiled to herself and climbed on.

Then, very suddenly, her hands found a hard stone wall. She felt upward and discovered that her tunnel had ended in a shaft a little taller than she was, with some sort of grating as its ceiling. She drew her sword and probed carefully, searching for a trap. Her sword point pierced something yielding—cloth—and a stream of tiny pellets hissed down in a trickle past her face. She held out her hand to catch some of the grains and brought it to her nose. Rice! She had cut into a bag of rice.

Sharantyr probed carefully, tracing the outlines of the grating. Then she sheathed her blade, took a deep breath, crouched, and sprang up high, hands outstretched.

One hand smashed into a sack, scrabbled, and found a grip around a bar. The other smashed hard and painfully into metal. She gritted her teeth and hung by one hand for what seemed a long time, nursing throbbing fingers and shaking them in hopes nothing was broken.

Then she reached up, got a grip on the grating with her hurt hand, and started tugging and bouncing up and down. Her hand throbbed with every move, but the grating shifted slightly, lifting with her movements. She continued, as hard as she could, but the rice bags above held the grating down, and at last she had to admit defeat.

Sharantyr dropped again, drew her blade, and attacked the rice above her, stabbing again and again as hissing rice ran down into her hair, her bodice, and even through sliced and torn spots in her leathers.

She went on stabbing and jabbing until she could feel no weight on the grating above, then carefully worked the empty bags aside with her sword through the grate.

It was dark and cool in the chamber above. Very faint light filtered down to her. Sharantyr leapt up again.

This time the grating shifted as she struck it. She let go, dropped, and instantly sprang up again, striking the grating on an angle. As it lifted, she kicked the air hard and arched her body. The grating slid sideways with her clinging to it. The lady ranger twisted and arched her body again, and before the bars could fall back into place, she got the toe of one boot up through the opening.

The grating came down hard on her boot. Sharantyr grunted, heaved, twisted, and rolled all at once. She found herself sprawled atop more sacks of rice, still entangled with the grating, in what seemed to be a large and dark storage cellar.

Shar laid the grating carefully back in place, found the sacks she'd emptied, and covered it with them. Then she climbed over a great many sacks—some, by the sound, held dried beans—into a narrow trail among the sacks, crates, and barrels that crammed the room.

If this place was barred or locked from the outside, she was not going to be pleased. Sharantyr drew her blade again, held it carefully upright close to her breast, and went cautiously eastward, for the trail seemed to widen in that direction, and the faint light grew slightly stronger.

Her way ended in an old, stout wooden door. She pushed at it and then pulled, but it had no handle on this side. She felt around the door, found its edges, and carefully slipped her dagger up one of them.

As she expected, the blade struck a catch or hasp. If it was locked or pegged down, she was in trouble. But if it could be lifted by driving the blade upward—Yes! The door swung open, and Sharantyr reached for the hasp with racing fingers to quell any noise of its falling.

Done. The room beyond was also unlit, but light reached long fingers into it from a torch in a wall bracket beyond a door or wooden gate that was more gaps and knotholes than wood. Sharantyr drifted up to it, put away her dagger, reached nimble fingers through to lift the peg that held it shut, and peeked out into the corridor.

Two bored-looking men were seated not six paces away, sorting potatoes on a long table covered with what looked like a very old tapestry. They worked in silence, and when one of them suddenly spoke, his voice seemed very loud.

"If you'd just kept your jaw still when he asked about the wenches instead of tryin' sly stuff, he wouldna found us out, an'—" The voice held the exasperation of a renewed grievance.

"Shut up," the other man said in a tired voice. "Be glad ye're down here carving dirt-balls instead of up there, sweating in your armor and being carved up by the idiot merchants and farmhands that some crazed-wits has stirred up. They're still attacking the castle!"

He tossed a potato lazily over his shoulder. Sharantyr swallowed, reached up—There!—and snatched it silently out of the air. She set it down very carefully at her feet and took another silent step forward.

"Ye should have heard His Awfulness," the man went on, "when I went up to the kitchens. Fairly frothing, he was. He'd just finished telling the council that he was lord now—so there!—cool as ye please, when some wench in leathers comes tumbling down the stairs and nearly runs him through with a sword. He was screaming and scrabbling on the floor, they say, and had to 'port away, to escape. As it was, this gal carved up his entire bodyguard and some of us, too!"

"What?," the other man gasped. "All by herself? She took out Dannath?"

"And Uthren, and Balagh. Oh, aye, this must have been some play-pretty, in truth! I'd like to see her, let me tell ye! In the dark, and her alone, if ye catch my warmest thought . . ."

"May the gods," said Sharantyr conversationally into his ear, "grant thy every wish."

As he spun around to face her, she drove her knee up hard. The man could not find breath to scream. He simply bent double, eyes staring at her in disbelief as he collapsed. Sharantyr was already stepping past him to drive her sword into the other man's throat.

He gurgled and went down. She spun back to the first, caught his throat in a strangling grip to quell any outcry, and said softly, "Now that you've seen me, Zhent butcher, I'm afraid I'm going to have to turn down your 'warmest thought.' Here, have a potato." She plucked a smallish potato from the table, rammed it into his mouth, and held it there as her blade went into his stomach.

The body bucked under her, and Sharantyr felt sick. If he cried out she might die, so she held him down, vomited all over him violently, and then picked up her sword again. She held her aching ribs for a moment and leaned against the wall to clear her head before moving on.

The corridor ended in steps leading up into a passage heavy with the smell of stew. Her stomach lurched again.

Sharantyr shook her head and stepped boldly into the hall. She strode down it, past open doors and people chopping wood and bustling about stoking cookfires. One sad-faced, gray-haired woman caught sight of her, but Sharantyr raised a finger to her lips and went on. No alarm was raised behind her.

The passage ran east and upward. Sharantyr went up with it and was almost relieved to enter a room full of sprawled Wolves, half out of their armor, with a gaming board on a table in their midst and bloodied weapons leaning against the walls.

She tore into them, slashing and stabbing like a maniac. Startled men cursed, scrambled to reach weapons, writhed in agony—and died. Covered in their blood, Sharantyr went on. Gods grant that after this day she would never have to kill again.

But it is the nature of men, she thought savagely, remembering Elminster's dry voice at a campfire long ago, *to forget promises, to break agreements—and to kill.*

"Gods curse and damn all Zhent Wolves!" she roared, close to tears. Her outcry brought running, booted feet and their Zhentilar owners with them, many blades raised against her.

With a wild cry, Sharantyr charged in among them, whirling and leaping, her blade dancing and singing around her. She was no equal to Storm, or even Florin or Dove of the Knights, but they were not here and she was, and there were evil men to be struck down so that a dale might live again, and Elminster find a peaceful refuge for a day or three, and— It suddenly seemed to Sharantyr that she'd been fighting for a very long time, perhaps years, without a break, and that the blood spattering her now would never wash off. She began to cry as she fought.

They say in Zhentil Keep that women who weep with swords in their hands are widows of the slain. If a Zhentilar rides into a place where the hand of Zhentil Keep's armies has been felt before, and women weep and run for swords at the sight of the black-helmed warriors, he will take special care to slay those women, for they will not rest, it is said, until they have avenged their husbands or died trying, to join them in the Realm of the Fallen.

Wolves drew back from her in horror as old tales they'd heard as boys, scoffed at as youths, and forgotten as men came alive before their eyes. They stumbled back, faces white, as the woman in slashed and tattered leathers leapt and darted among them, dealing swift, endless darkness with a battered blade.

"Die, damn you!" she wept, and gave them death.

"How did she get in?" one man raged, parrying with all his might.

"What boots it?" another yelled back. "Run! Run, if you would live! Ru—uuughh!" Sharantyr's long blade found his throat from behind, and his run ended there in a dying plunge to the stone floor.

In the end they all broke and ran, those who could move at all, leaving her panting and blood-drenched, alone with the dead. Sharantyr cried and cried, kneeling among death, until she could cry no more.

She rose, white-faced in the torchlight, and thought of Stormcloak. He was the real foe, he and his mages. He must die.

18
Cheerless Obedience to Mages

As Sharantyr's sobs died away, Lord Angruin Storm-cloak, striding importantly from his chambers to the great hall, heard their last echoes and frowned. What was a woman doing in this part of the castle? Had one of the men—? He sighed and had drawn breath to curse their waywardness when his eyes fell on men running toward him, terrified, blades drawn.

"Hold!" he roared, reaching for a wand. Was this some sort of treachery? "Stand, all of you! Answer me. Why are you running?"

They came to a clattering halt before his fury. Men shifted and would not look at him.

"L-Lord," one armsman said, fear full in his voice, "there's a woman—a dragon she is, with a sword! I saw her kill ten of us or more, and—"

"And so you fled, all of you," Stormcloak said with contempt. He looked coldly around at them all, eyeing men now clearing throats and exchanging glances and looking very uneasy indeed. "Are you warriors?"

Silence answered him. "Are you men?"

Nods, and more silence.

Stormcloak took a step forward. "Are you *Zhentilar*?"

"Aye, Lord."

"Yes, Lord."

Stormcloak nodded wolfishly. "Good," he said with deep sarcasm. "I had begun to wonder about that." Then his voice changed again. "And what do Zhentilar warriors do?"

"Obey, Lord."

" 'Obey when told to slay,' isn't that how the song goes?" Stormcloak corrected.

Nods answered him again. Stormcloak looked around

at them all.

"Obey whom?"

A man swallowed. "Z-Zhentarim mages, Lord."

Stormcloak gave him a brittle smile. "And why do you obey mages, all of you?" He looked around at them all again. In the end, to break the heavy silence, he answered his own question. "You obey mages—myself, for instance—because if you don't, we'll unleash magic on you more terrible than any blade, more painful than any wound!"

He looked at them as the passage rang with those last shouted words, and let the echoes die away before continuing.

"Warriors who run one way can face one woman—with a sword," he added with a sneer. "Warriors who run the other way will face me," he said, raising his wand with slow menace and a silky smile.

In silence, the men called Wolves by the folk of the High Dale turned sullenly, raised their swords, and went back down the passage. Slowly.

* * * * *

Sharantyr stalked forward on silent feet, like a hunting cat. Many had fled down this passage. If she knew Zhents, they'd soon be back this way, a mage in their midst ready to use a spell or a wand to smite her down and impress all the warriors who watched.

So another way would be better. Were there no side passages in this place? She glanced this way and that as she went, and in the end chose a stair going up. If she could not go around, she must go over. She had only one life to lose and could not afford to fight fairly, or to face large groups of thirsty swords or a mage in a large open space.

"Well, then, Stormcloak," she said aloud, "let us see if one Knight with a sword can bring you down. It's been done to Zhentarim before."

"Who's that? Maerelee?" a voice asked from the head of the stair.

"No," Sharantyr replied truthfully, coming steadily on up the stairs. "It's me."

Then she was level with the man: a Wolf in armor, frowning warily, sword out. The weapon swept up as he saw her. "Who are you?" he challenged. "I've not seen you before, here or in the dale."

"I am your bane," she said calmly, walking toward him. Her expressionless face did not change as he tried to bat the sword out of her hand with his own. Nor did it change when, at her sudden lunge, he found himself two fingers away from death. Nor after, as he parried frantically, countered and found himself forced to parry even faster. He turned to run and she sprang after him, landing hard on his running legs.

He fell heavily, and her blade stabbed down as she landed atop him.

When she rolled back up to her feet, he lay still on the stones, facedown. Sharantyr looked down at him for a moment, sighed, and went on. Just how many Zhents were crawling about this castle?

"It only takes one to kill thee," she heard Elminster's long-ago voice tell her, and smiled wryly. Thanks, Old Mage. Well said. On with it, then.

She found the next one just inside the first room her passage entered, heading east. He was sharpening his sword and reacted with commendable speed, grinning as he whipped his blade at her stomach.

This Wolf obviously considered himself a matchless swordsman. Sharantyr parried two lightning-fast thrusts, leaned close to spit into his eyes, stamped on his toes, ducked her blade under his parry—he was good at attacking but not so good at holding off attacks—and ran him through.

She left him twisting in agony and snarling curses at her, waving his blade weakly and ineffectually at her from the floor. Mielikki forgive me for what I've had to become, she prayed silently. I've made myself a worse butcher than any Zhentilar soldier!

Shuddering, she opened the door at the end of the short passage she was traversing, found herself in a bunk room with four startled Zhents, sighed, and started slaying again. Just how long had she been killing? There were some days of her life that she'd very much like to forget forever, and couldn't in her darkest dreams. This was definitely turning into one of those days.

* * * * *

"This is fast becoming one of those days," Itharr said wearily as the Harpers battered their way through another door, stolen shields held high to ward off crossbow bolts or thrown spears from the Wolves waiting beyond. None came, so they flung the shields down and charged.

"You're not getting bored, are you?" Belkram asked in mock concern.

At his shoulder, Gedaern grinned and cocked his head to survey both the Harpers.

"Are the two of ye always like this?"

"Worse," Belkram replied mildly as three Wolves in full plate armor shouldered aside an anxious servant with a halberd and lumbered forward to meet them. " 'Ware, brothers!"

The two Harpers stepped forward to meet the charge. The Wolves came at them swinging heavy battle-axes in great roundhouse swings the lightly armored men could not hope to stop except with their bodies.

"Back!" Belkram called, waving a hand at the older dalesmen. He ran back to where they'd thrown down the shields, snatched one, and threw it to Itharr. Itharr ducked under a swing, dropped the shield, and had to scramble away to avoid being beheaded. The Wolves came on, grinning through the bars of their full helms.

"Itharr, you do the sticking!" Belkram called, and laid hands on the body of a Wolf he'd killed breaths before.

One Wolf charged him. Belkram heaved the corpse up into a cradled position across his own chest, puffing under the weight, and dumped it into the Wolf's swing, dragging axe and arm to the floor. The corpse's arms flopped loosely. Belkram sprang over them to land with both feet on the man's axe-wielding arm. The man roared hollowly inside his helm as Itharr arrived, daggers in both hands, to drive them into the sallet's eye slits. The roaring stopped abruptly.

The two Harpers sprang away just in time, leaping and rolling to avoid the wild, chopping blows of the other two axes.

There came a shuffling sound from behind them, and the dalesmen trotted past, carrying a heavy wooden table like a ram. They flung it into one of the Wolves, knocking him over, then snatched out their blades to attack the other Wolf together.

The Wolf drove one to the floor with his first blow. His second hacking swing struck sparks from their weapons with its fury. A dalesman screamed as his wrist snapped under the impact and his old sword flew from it to clang along the flagstones. Then Belkram leapt in from one side, tackling the Wolf waist-high.

They went to the floor together, but frantic axe work forced the Harper to break free and roll away without delivering any real blow.

Itharr was getting up off the table, daggers dripping. The Wolf under it would never rise again.

There was a shout from the room beyond, and more Wolves rushed into the room. They were lightly armored, but there were six of them.

Itharr rushed to meet them, trying to keep them entangled in the doorway. "To me, men of the dale!" he called over his shoulder as he sheathed one dagger in his boot and drew his sword again. "To me!"

His blades met those of the foremost Wolves, hurling them back for an instant. Then he ducked low and lunged in a move Storm had used on him—ages ago, it seemed. A Wolf made a strangling sound as the blade burst up between his arms to slip into his throat.

Itharr let go of the blade in an instant, spinning to one side, and avoided the angry counterstrikes of the other Wolves. Then Gedaern of the dale was there, his old broadsword in hand, taking one Wolf's blade on his and darting out an old, hairy hand to clasp the man's other wrist and arrest the streaking dagger it held.

Itharr spun two Wolves around with a series of lashing blows, forcing them to parry, and then lunged at one. That Wolf crashed backward into the one Gedaern was facing. Both staggered, giving Gedaern an instant to slide his blade free of the Wolf's steel and slash the man across the face. The armsman screamed as blood began to flow, and dropped his sword to clutch at his head.

Itharr drove another Zhent back with a flurry of lunges, using weight and fury to drive the Wolf who'd run into Gedaern's foe back into him again. This time Itharr's Wolf fell. A breath later, Gedaern took down the man he'd blinded.

Behind them, Belkram was still circling the armored Wolf with the axe. The man's swings were slower and shrewder now. He was tiring and knew the speed of the man he faced. The Harper wore an eager half-smile as they danced and spun, remembering Storm, sweat glistening on her bare shoulders, as she'd fought her way coolly through Itharr's best blade work, and his own. There was a trick she'd used . . .

Belkram feinted a lunge. The great axe swept up to block it, then drew back a little for a return blow. Belkram flung himself forward in a jump, turned his blade sideways, and thrust it into the back of the man's arms, driving them and the axe upward.

Then the Harper dropped to the floor, kicking against the flagstones and surging forward into a roll against the Wolf's booted ankles.

The man toppled, hitting the floor with a metallic crash. An old dalesman sprang forward, almost weeping in rage, and chopped at the man's helm until it rang like a bell.

The blade glanced off again and again as Belkram found his feet and was forced to deal with a Wolf charging down almost on top of him.

When he could turn back again, the Harper saw the old dalesman clutching a broken sword—it had snapped against the helm—and cautiously lifting the Wolf's head. It lolled loosely; the helm had held, but the neck must have given way. The old man knelt beside the man he'd killed and started to cry, gnarled old hands trembling.

Belkram wheeled and charged back into the fray. From the room beyond, someone called, "Aid! They're in the castle! They've broken in!"

Another voice called back, "Keep them from the great hall, or the lord'll have our soft bits!"

"What lord?" the first voice roared back.

"Stormcloak," was the terse reply.

The first voice snorted. "If it's him," it said, "let him use his magic to deal with these. Our swords don't seem enough."

"He'll find you, after, if you shirk your duty."

"Let him," the first voice responded bitterly, "if he lives. You haven't seen these idiots fight!"

Belkram grinned savagely, stepped around a dalesman who was falling with a groan, two swords through his body, and drove his sword point into the mouth of another Wolf. "Friend," he called out, "which way is this great hall?"

After a startled moment, the first voice said laconically, " 'Twould be the most foolish treason to tell you that it's through here, turn right, and behind the double doors at the end of the straight passage—so I won't tell you that."

The voice started to say something more but suddenly rose into a scream and abruptly fell silent.

"So die all traitors," rumbled a new voice.

"Hey!" Belkram called, hewing down another Wolf. "I liked that man!"

"Who speaks?"

"I do," Belkram yelled. "Who are you to ask?" The last Wolf fell, and he hurried to join Itharr's rush forward to the room beyond.

There stood a hulking armored form as wide as them both but of their own height. It lowered its war helm, and they had a brief glimpse of blond hair, scarred cheeks, and cold, calculating eyes. "I am Gathen Srund," the rumbling voice came hollowly to them. "I was Left Axe to Lord Longspear. I will avenge him, rebel traitors."

The armored man lumbered forward, hefting a huge

warhammer. There were other Wolves behind him, but they stayed well back to watch.

The two Harpers looked at each other and darted a glance behind. All the Wolves were down, and three dalesmen were with them. A fourth dalesman sat against a wall, clutching his broken wrist and cursing softly.

"Have you noticed," Itharr remarked, "how pompous these Zhent bully blades always are? They occupy some place, usurping rightful rule and law, and then squeak of 'rebels' and 'traitors.' It's odd . . . "

"I have noticed that, yes," Belkram replied as the warhammer swung, and they ducked and hastily sprang apart. "Scatter, men!" he added urgently over his shoulder to the dalesmen.

They needed no urging. Belkram heard the clatter of hasty booted feet receding, then the helm of their foe rang with hollow laughter. "Hah! See them run, largemouths! What say you now?"

The two old men threw down their swords, halted by the overturned table, panted for an instant, and then heaved it up to their shoulders and came back to the fray in a stumbling rush.

Itharr attacked, slashing repeatedly and jabbing at the helm's eye slits, forcing Srund to use his hammer to parry, and pulling it to one side. The table was driven in through the gap Itharr had created, crashing into the Wolf and sending him staggering back.

"Well met," Belkram replied mildly in answer to Gathen Srund's taunt, as he sprang forward to get the warhammer. He got a good grasp on it and was promptly dragged and battered about the floor as the awesomely strong Left Axe tried to wrench his weapon free.

"I wonder what the Right Axe is like?" Itharr asked him, stretching over the struggle to bury his blade in one of the eye slits of the Zhentilar's helm. Gathen stiffened, dropped the hammer, fumbled for it with failing fingers, and fell over on his side with a room-shaking crash.

The dalesmen rushed forward, but the room was emptying of Zhents as fast as they could flee. The warriors all ran down a passage to the right.

Belkram got up, breathing heavily, and watched them go. "I wager," he said slowly as he fought for breath, "that we'll . . . soon find out . . . once they get where they're going . . . and tell their tale."

Itharr nodded. "You're right," he said simply.

Then the two Harpers embraced each other and roared their delight. "What a fight this is!" Itharr shouted happily. "What a fight!"

The oldest dalesman looked at him, unsmiling, and shook his head. "They're still young, indeed," he said to another white-haired veteran, who only nodded.

Then they heard men begin to scream, down the passage.

* * * * *

Sharantyr came down the dark stairs like a vengeful wind. The lighted passage below was full of worried, running men with weapons. Armored men. Wolves. More to be slain.

In grim silence she leapt down among them, and started to slay. One fell, and then another. A third slipped, and she was past him to run her blade through a foolish one without armor. He clutched himself and collapsed with a horrible groan, and she was on to the next one. Was she killing with her eyes? Men fell wherever she looked, and the passage was warm with the smell of their blood and fear.

A fresh group of Wolves came running up the passage. She turned to them with a savage smile. The shortest warrior started the screaming as he tried to turn around and found his fellows in the way.

Then they were all screaming. Sharantyr had never thought she'd enjoy such a sound.

The men were fleeing from her. Behind them, bloody and bedraggled men were coming out into the passage, well-used weapons in their hands. Dalesmen!

She snatched a glance back over her shoulder. Wolves were fleeing in that direction too, falling back to join a guard of armored men in front of a set of closed double doors. In their midst was a dark-haired man in full armor who stood a head taller than the rest. "Hold fast," he said with cold authority. "They cannot pass us."

Sharantyr gave him a sneer and turned to join the dalesmen in their slaughter. She snuck a glance back, but the man had refused to be drawn out of the guard. He stood coldly waiting as they butchered the few milling Wolves in the passage.

The lady ranger embraced the two men in leathers she'd seen fight so well in the marketplace and said, "Sharantyr. Knight of Myth Drannor."

They bowed. "Itharr and Belkram of the Harpers, with true men of the dale."

They exchanged grins, and one of the old men lumbered forward. "Give us a hug, lass. Then, live or die, I'll do it happily."

Sharantyr shed a few tears as she put blood-spattered arms around him.

Then they all turned, in sudden silence, to face the Wolves at the door.

"Lay down your arms," the tall man said flatly, "or we'll kill you, as painfully as we know how." He looked at them with cold confidence and added, "Consider this: We are warriors of Zhentil Keep. We know much of killing."

"You certainly know much about dying, after this day," Itharr told him, "if this is all of you there are left."

"Save your brave words for pleading," the tall man told him contemptuously, "and we may let you live."

"My thanks to you," Sharantyr told him with biting sarcasm. "Your generous pacifism overwhelms me. 'Tis so sudden and heartfelt."

The tall man lifted his head, pointing his chin at her. "Bring me that one alive," he told the Wolves around him. "I have . . . plans for her."

"Aye, Right Axe," several voices murmured in reply.

Beside Belkram, Gedaern nodded suddenly. "Ah. This one's Heladar's Right Axe—his trusty, like, and probably their commander, now. A merchant told me, a few months back, that he's known for cruelty and butchering women and younglings when he gets a chance. Sunthrun

Blackshoulder's his name."

The tall man laughed shortly. "Your merchant friend was right."

Belkram saluted him with raised sword. "Then it will be a pleasure killing you, Sunthrun Blackshoulder."

The tall man sneered. "A pleasure you'll never live to see." He drew a blade as long as the shortest dalesman there was tall. Its blade was dull black and menacingly evil.

Belkram smiled tightly and looked around at Itharr, the dalesmen, and Sharantyr. He collected nods from them all and jerked his head forward. Calmly, unhurrying, they strode down the passage to where the Wolves waited.

Itharr struck first. His blade met that of one Wolf and thrust it sideways toward another. That man moved to avoid catching two battling blades in the face, and the Wolf on the other side of Itharr moved to take advantage of a chance to strike at the Harper's unprotected side. This opened a gap in the line, and Sharantyr leapt through it to lunge at the Right Axe himself.

The tall man smiled coldly, parrying with such force that her numbed fingers tingled. Somehow she held on to her sword, but now the men on either side of Blackshoulder were striking at her. She dodged, letting the blade of one man slip past her ear, and ran in under it to open his throat. Behind her, Belkram felled a man and came up against the Right Axe in his turn.

Sunthrun Blackshoulder attacked with dazzling speed, striking at Belkram's face and throat. Only frantic parries saved the Harper's life. Sharantyr turned, punched the back of a Wolf's neck she found within reach, and lashed out with her blade to cut the Right Axe on the elbow above his free hand.

Blackshoulder roared and turned on her. Sharantyr leapt to one side, got her arm around the neck of another Wolf, and swung him in front of her as a shield, just in time to take the Right Axe's vicious thrust. She fell back as the tip of his black blade came out of the Wolf's back, parting the plates of his armor as if it were rotten leather.

Sharantyr rolled on the floor and contrived as she came up to trip another Wolf's feet out from under him. Itharr killed that one, tossing her a smile as he attacked the next. One of the dalesmen gurgled horribly and went down as a blade found his throat.

They were still killing old men, these Wolves. Angrily Sharantyr ran at the Right Axe again as he shook the corpse from his blade. Belkram hacked down a Wolf to reach Blacksshoulder from one side just as the Right Axe's blade came free, and the lady Knight came at him from the other.

Blacksshoulder tried to duck and parry, to force them into each other. It would have been a good move against the inexperienced warriors he obviously thought them to be.

Both the Harper and the Knight followed the Right Axe's move. As Belkram's blade bound and lifted the Zhentilar's weapon, Sharantyr's sword found the armpit of his raised sword arm. She moved with him, driving it in deep. After a moment's resistance, her blade slid in easily. Right Axe Sunthrun stiffened, spat blood, and collapsed silently to the floor. Gedaern of the dale, intent on a battle of his own, stepped on the Axe's head a moment later and almost apologized before he saw whom he'd trampled.

"Are there more?" Itharr asked as the Wolf he'd been fighting fell heavily against the wall and slid down it, gauntleted fingers clawing feebly for a hold.

They looked around. Not a Wolf was left, but Gedaern and the oldest graybeard were the only dalesmen still standing. The two Harpers looked at Sharantyr, and she looked back at them.

"Shall I?" Itharr asked, waving at the door. Sharantyr smiled.

Belkram sighed. "Itharr, one always opens doors for a lady," he said in mock despair.

Itharr bowed and opened the door silently. They went in.

19
How High Dale
Changed Hands

The great hall seemed full of councillors, all of them frightened and trying not to show it. They fumbled nervously for swords as the guard of Wolves seated just inside the door stopped looking bored and leapt up to bar the way with bared blades.

Sharantyr did not slow down. With a set, grim face she struck aside the blade of the first Wolf and leaned past him to put her blade into the face of the Wolf behind, who was still rising. His gurgle as he slumped down again died away unheard amid the sudden babble of fearful voices.

"Gods! They've reached us—here!"

"A woman! Who—?"

"Zarduil's down! She's killed Zarduil! Wasn't he Heladar's best?"

"The men—those two! They're the ones who slew Longspear!"

"Steady! The guards can handle them!" Stormcloak snapped. He turned eyes of cold iron on Sharantyr, who looked icy death back at him, then deliberately turned his back on the intruders and waved the councillors back down into their seats.

"Ignore them," the wizard said coldly. "They will be dead in a moment."

Several of the councillors shot frightened looks past him, their expressions telling all who had eyes to see that they were not so confident. Another looked on with silent interest.

The leather worker, Blakkal Mord, had once been a fighting man. The scars on his face and arms betrayed his past to all. None in the High Dale, he was sure, knew that he was still a warrior, in the service of the Cult of the Dragon. If they had known, he would not be here still. This Stormcloak, or one of the lesser Zhentarim magelings, would have seen to that.

His place here was not to act openly, which was no doubt the reason he'd not been probed beyond the shielding strength of the little ring that he never took off, the one that masked his thoughts. He would save himself, and otherwise be as loudly ineffectual as these other councillors.

Nonetheless, he was a man of the sword. He knew battle skill, and he agreed with what the excitable Moonviper had said. Zarduil had been one of Heladar's best.

Zarduil should not have fallen. Blakkal leaned forward to see better. The door guard that Stormcloak had set for this meeting was more than the usual three thickheads, and their relief man had been added to make up a foursome of competent bladesmen. Heladar's former bodyguards had orders—Zhentil Keep's orders, Blakkal had no doubt—to diligently protect and serve the lord of the dale, whoever that lord was. Wherefore they, too, had been at the doors: Zarduil, Mashann, and Raeve.

None of those three were men Blakkal cared to face, even in an unfair fight. They were Zhentilar veterans—men of steel nerves, steel wrists, and the swiftness of serpents.

And they were being beaten. Blakkal watched one of the two men—Harpers? Thief-adventurers from Cormyr?—dart through Mashann's guard and run his sword tip in under the shoulder plate of the big man's armor. Something even more surprising happened next. The man in leathers ducked and wrenched and got his blade back out again to parry before Mashann's own fast sword touched him.

Blakkal did not even try to look like he was listening to Stormcloak. The self-styled Lord of the High Dale was blathering something about treachery from neighboring realms, as if only Zhentarim were allowed to usurp the thrones of strategically located farming dales.

Other councillors watched the fight just as intently. There were no other guards in the room. The rest had been outside the doors. The rebels should never have reached this hall.

On at least two of the watching faces, naked hope and glee were written. The tailor, Rundeth—what was his last name? Hobble? Hobyltar!—normally laconic and stone faced, had eyes as bright as new coins and was struggling not to smile. Down the table, stout Gulkin was grinning openly.

Stormcloak shot them a look that had a cutting edge to it. Blakkal smiled; the lord was beginning to learn how Heladar had felt, sitting in that chair with a table of men who were openly trying to bring about his fall. Boots may fit just as well on other feet, as the Sembians put it.

There was a crash as a Wolf and one of the men in leathers went through some of the chairs together, ending up on the floor wriggling like eels as they tried to get their blades into each other.

Then Mashann staggered back on his heels, raised a failing hand to his throat, and crashed backward to the floor. The man who leapt over him was only six running steps from the table where they sat. Timid Jatham scrabbled for his dagger. Stormcloak scowled but couldn't help but to break off and watch.

The last Zhentilar veteran reached sideways with his blade, and the charging man in leathers had to hastily dance back to ward off seeking steel. Raeve held the man for a moment, but the only other Wolf still standing was dropping his blade and sagging slowly to the floor after it, that wild-haired woman standing grim over him.

Raeve cast one look back at them all, shook his head, and as the tattered intruders advanced, suddenly ducked and bolted through them, making for the door. Steel rang on his warding blade, and then he was through.

Stormcloak roared at him. "Raeve! As you are loyal to Zhentil Keep, hold! Stand and fight for your lord, or by all the dark gods, I'll turn you into a dung worm!"

Raeve turned his head as he reached the doorway, sword rising to guard his exit. He looked at Sharantyr. Silent and blood-spattered, she glided toward him.

Raeve turned his eyes to meet Stormcloak's hot gaze

shook his head silently, and was gone.

The lord wizard's furious magic missile twisted in the air to become a beam of shining glass shards, but they shivered and crashed against unyielding stone beside the door. A head too far to the left, and a breath too late to impress Raeve.

Sharantyr turned smoothly to join the silent advance across the great hall. Councillors screamed, cursed, and toppled chairs in their haste to flee, as the High Dale they had ruled so cruelly and casually reached bloody weapons for them.

Lord Angruin Stormcloak trembled with rage and dawning fear. Where had these . . . these vagabonds come from? These three in leather, they were no dalefolk! They were Harpers, or worse, sent to bring him down.

Sharantyr had come for him that day, through guard after guard. Her sword arm was so weary that she could barely hold her blade, and stinging sweat and blood were running into her eyes. Only a few steps more and she would have this wizard.

Only a few steps more, but she suddenly could not find the strength to run.

The snarling wizard drew back his hand and pointed directly at her as he shouted words that echoed and hissed, and crushed something small in his other hand. Black blood ran out between his fingers, and he cast a wrinkled thing away—a leech.

Sharantyr could only go on, blade raised, face like stone. She was only three paces away . . . two, now—

The still-pointing finger erupted in writhing black light, boiling upward. A moment later, a rain of black daggers was falling toward her.

The lady ranger tried to struggle on, waving her blade to ward off the dark points. Her weapon swept through the daggers as though they were so much smoke, but when the blades struck an instant later, they were cold and very hard—and they went in deep.

Sharantyr screamed in pain and fell. Writhing on the cold, hard stone floor, clutching at her arms and gut in shuddering agony, she heard Stormcloak laugh.

The wizard put a foot on his chair and gained the top of the table, still laughing. He spun about to stand facing the attackers, as frantic councillors raised their weapons in a protective line in front of him, yelling for him to use his spells to slay. The two Harpers slashed at the waiting blades, but it was quickly apparent that some of the councillors were not the frightened tremble-wits they'd have others believe. Steel rang on steel, and the two Harpers were fighting for their lives, two weary dalesmen at their sides. One of the men threw a dagger at the wizard, trying to ruin whatever magic he was working, but as it left his fingers he knew he was too late.

Stormcloak's rolling laughter came again. Lightning leapt from his spread hands in crackling, spitting arcs, a bolt from each finger. He flicked his hands to lash all the rebels with the reaching lightning.

As the bolts leapt, however, they were changing, and Stormcloak's laughter faltered. One of his spells had twisted again. Where lightning had crackled with fury, feeble blue sparks were fading away around a cluster of ceramic vessels and earthenware pottery that had not been there an eye-blink earlier.

As Sharantyr gasped and groaned on the stones, crockery rained down out of thin air to shatter around her. A jagged shard laid open her cheek in one long gash as it spun past, and she ducked her head, hoping nothing would find her eyes or throat. Then the crashing sounds were gone and sudden silence fell upon the hall.

"Very impressive," a new, rather acerbic voice said into the thick of the hush, commenting calmly from the doorway. "But if ye hope to challenge Manshoon for control of the Zhentarim someday, ye'll have to do better than a few teacups."

An old man stood there, a gaunt but wiry old man in tattered robes, with long, flowing white hair and a longer beard. He stood taller than most men but was as thin as a sharp-tongued noblewoman. It hardly seemed possible that he had the strength to hold up the naked high constable, who dripped blood from many half-healed wounds and still trailed the long, heavy chains of his enslavement from arms that were gnarled and knotted with muscle.

Yet the old man not only held up the wounded giant, he half-carried him forward into the room and leaned him carefully against the wall. When he straightened up, his eyes were like two blue-white flames as they met those of Angruin Stormcloak.

"Ill met," he said, and every soft word cut like a leaping knife as it left his lips. His gaze bored deep into Stormcloak's eyes, and it was the Zhentarim who looked away first.

"Elminster of Shadowdale!" gasped Cheth Moonviper of the councillors, and ducked under the table.

Angruin Mvyrvult Stormcloak paled and snatched at the wand in his belt. He half expected the world to explode before he ever got it out, but exultantly he got it free, aimed, and hissed a word only he knew.

Lightning leapt and crackled across the suddenly darker great hall toward the old man in tattered robes who stood empty-handed, hair wild-tangled and blood running down his face from a cut on his forehead.

And Elminster stood there and waited for the lightning to come to him, watching calmly.

* * * * *

Ylyndaera Mulmar smiled a mirthless smile as a Wolf came out of a door ahead, saw them, and with a startled oath whipped out his sword. She advanced steadily, Ulraea trembling at her side.

They were both startled when Tanshlee suddenly burst past them, shrieking, "You! You're the one! You!"

She hurled herself on the Wolf, knocking his blade aside more by luck than skill, and took him to the floor, sobbing and raking with her nails.

The women broke into a run. In an instant the Wolf would find room and strength to get his blade out from under her, and then it would all be over.

It was Jharina who threw the mace she'd plucked up several rooms back, while they were still marveling at being inside the castle and unseen for so long. It wobbled through the air drunkenly and just touched the Wolf's shoulder as it went on its way past him.

He jerked, dropped his sword from numb, burning fingers, and snarled in startled pain. Tanshlee's hands found his throat.

She held on, white-faced, eyes blazing, as he gasped and struck at her and thrashed about, trying to break free of the deep-sunk fingers squeezing out his life. But he was too young to think of breaking those fingers, or gouging at the reproachful, staring eyes of his nemesis, or even breaking her hold by shattering her jaw with a punch—and so his face went dark and then gray, and he sagged back and died.

Daera and Ulraea stood over him, but the Wolf did not escape. They let Tanshlee have her revenge on the one who'd wronged her—months ago, now—and stood silently by as she sobbed atop the body of the unknown man who'd fathered the child within her.

Ulraea looked at Ylyndaera, standing there with her sword ready, and saw a much older woman than the girl who'd been hidden away in the mill. Daera raised eyes dark with fury to meet hers and said quietly, "Let's go kill us some Wolves."

They put a sword ready beside Tanshlee in case she needed it and wouldn't pick up the one the Wolf had wielded, left her in her own dark world of tears, and went on down the passage.

Ahead was the din of battle—the clash of sword upon sword, shouts, and cracklings—but muffled as if from behind a door. The three women exchanged glances. "The great hall," Ulraea said. "Of course."

Daera swept hair out of her eyes impatiently, swung her sword at nothing to loosen her arm, which was beginning to ache—how did men swing these things all day?—took a deep breath, and said, "Come on."

They'd rushed a dozen steps before four—no, six—Wolves came out of a side passage. The warriors halted, half-lowered their weapons, and smiled slow, cruel smiles as they began to advance slowly.

"Oh, gods," Ulraea said in her throat.

Daera laughed. "There are only six of them," she said loudly, "and Tanshlee showed us just how easily they die. Are you with me?"

Without waiting for an answer, she charged. Ulraea and Jharina exchanged despairing glances and followed.

Jharina's mace, lying unnoticed on the floor, tripped the first Wolf. He fell heavily, and Ylyndaera's blade slid into and out of his throat before he could even draw back the breath that the fall had driven out of him.

The Wolves saw a young maid rising to meet them, bloody blade in hand. One of them cursed, spun about, and ran. The others watched him go and then followed, breaking into frantic flight, as Ylyndaera's astonished laughter rang out down the passage.

"For the dale!" she called after them. "For the High Dale, free again!"

Beside her, Ulraea burst into tears.

*　*　*　*　*

Not far away, lightning reached the old man.

Sharantyr, struggling to her knees in pain, found the breath to scream, "No!" but as is the way with most despairing screams, the gods did not hear her.

Or perhaps they did. The blue-white bolt of death did not strike, but coiled in the air around Elminster's hand where a ring glowed suddenly blue-white in answer. The lightning coiled, gathering speed like an aroused serpent, then lashed back out, arrow-straight, across the great hall.

The wizard on the table stiffened as the lightning found a home.

The Lord of the High Dale shrieked, dancing involuntarily. Smoke curled out from his robes. Then the lightning was gone, leaving him staggering in the midst of a faint haze of smoke.

He turned a face of clenched hatred and pain to Elminster and gasped only one word as his hand darted into his robes, came out with something dark and round and metal, and hurled it.

"Die!"

The sphere flew through the air, expanding into an opening latticework of metal bands as it approached the Old Mage. In the instant before the sphere struck, Sharantyr recognized it as another set of iron bands of Bilarro.

The Old Mage stood quite still. The bands flared wide to go around him, pulsed with a brief flash of light, and then shrank with horrible speed, drawing down around the old man.

The two Harpers battled the councillors with frantic haste. One of the councillors fell with a ragged cry, but there were still many blades between them and the wizard atop the table.

Stormcloak crouched and drained a flask from his belt—a healing potion, Sharantyr had no doubt—and straightened, wiping his lips. As she struggled to find strength, biting her lip and whimpering against stabbing pain, the Zhentarim wizard calmly drew forth a glass bead from his robes, smiled a brittle smile down on her, and cast a spell that brought a shimmering sphere into being about him.

She'd seen one before: a globe of invulnerability or one of its variants. No ball of fire or bolt of lightning could touch Angruin now. The Lord of the High Dale drew himself up and sneered down at Elminster, who stood wrapped in tightening bands of iron.

"Toothless old men seem to have haunted me of late, hurling proud, empty memories of power against me— until I destroy them. If you had any wits left, graybeard, you'd stay at home, dreaming and grumbling by the fire, and leave mages of real power well alone."

Elminster whispered something, and the iron bands shuddered and fell away from him, clattering about his feet like so many hoops stripped from a barrel.

Stormcloak stared at him in astonishment. Elminster strolled forward, wand in hand, as if he were in a hurry to get to the other side of a peaceful garden, and observed mildly, "Talk grows no more expensive as the years pass, does it?"

The wand in his hand pulsed, and spat two magic missiles. Two councillors stiffened, and one hadn't even time to groan before Gedaern of the dale hewed him to the floor.

Councillor Xanther watched from the darkness under a table. So this was the Old Mage of Shadowdale, one old man who'd done nothing so far beyond the powers of the wand he held and a ring he wore. His magic must be gone, or failing. The Brotherhood could yet win this day.

How, though, with Stormcloak hurling death in all directions? Stormcloak must prevail, if Elminster was to be defeated at all. Could the Old Mage be compelled to surrender the knowledge of where some hoard lay hidden, how a particular spellbook was guarded, and what words governed a certain staff or rod or wand? That old man's head must be stuffed with a vast wealth of such thoughts, treasure beyond the grasping of most mages, but how could he be kept alive to reveal it?

From outside the great hall came the thunder of running, booted feet pounding on stone, followed by the sound of a young woman laughing, her voice high and gleeful. "For the dale!" she called. "For the High Dale, free again!" The door of the hall burst open, and a group of wild-eyed women burst in, blades flashing in their hands.

The councillors exchanged fearful glances. The castle was lost. They were doomed. The people would probably tear them apart bare-handed!

Elminster's unhurried walk took him to the woman in tattered leathers, still groaning on the floor. He took a ring from his finger—not the ring that had warded off the lightning, but one from his other hand—and slipped it onto her finger. Then he scuttled away from her, facing Stormcloak, a hand darting beneath his robes.

"Still so haughty, Zhentarim?" he asked, raising mocking eyebrows.

Angruin Stormcloak snarled at him and moved his hands angrily in the motions of a spell.

* * * * *

Irreph Mulmar tried not to gasp too loudly. Pain still throbbed deep inside with every move he made. He crawled slowly across the stone floor—one he'd strode across often enough in years before this one, covering the distance that now seemed so agonizingly long in a few swift strides. He watched the old wizard skillfully take the Zhent usurper's attention onto himself, and managed a smile. Gods, he hurt. He'd not worn that healing ring nearly long enough.

He crawled and crawled, the heavy layers of leather weighing on his shoulders. Elminster had found the hide in a room near the stables, and they'd wrapped his chains in it to silence them. The chains were heavier by far, now.

Trying to ignore their cold weight, he crawled past the still-writhing lady ranger. She wore the ring now, and needed it worse than he did by the look of her face. Gods, but she must have cut her way through most of the Wolves in the castle to get here! Irreph took a good look at her and managed a smile. The tearing agony of his movement turned it into a grimace as he went on. The high constable looked up at the table through a growing mist of red pain and wondered if he'd get there in time.

* * * * *

Stormcloak hurled lightning again. Councillors fled or cowered behind chairs all around the room as the white light flashed across to Elminster, was turned aside by his ring, and crackled back at the Zhentarim mage.

The shimmering globe around the mage absorbed the lightning. It was still sputtering and fading when the angry mage cast his next spell. Nothing happened.

* * * * *

Outside the castle walls, a tree tore up out of the earth with a noise like tearing canvas, shot up into the air past an astonished farmer, and headed west.

* * * * *

Stormcloak snarled his bafflement. His hands were already moving again. His only power lay in his magic, and nothing he'd seen yet could withstand it forever. This old man must fall.

Magic missiles streamed from Stormcloak's fingers in a glowing swarm that leapt and darted restlessly as they sped toward the Old Mage. Around and around him they swooped and ducked, only to turn back on Stormcloak and fade away as the ring on Elminster's hand glowed more brightly.

That glow was brighter and stronger than it had been. Stormcloak's eyes widened, then narrowed. Could the old fool be wearing a Myth Drannan ring?

Primitive things, made long ago, they had limits and could be overloaded by the sheer amount of Art hurled against them in a short time. Stormcloak grinned. Well, then . . .

Missiles streamed again from the Zhentarim's fingers, and the ring grew brighter as it hurled them back at him.

Angruin Myrvult Stormcloak laughed aloud. His hands moved again in the same smooth, rapid gestures as before.

The two Harpers hacked at those councillors who stood against them in the service of Zhentil Keep, or perhaps out of fear for the magic of the man who stood on the table behind them. The councillors knew how swiftly and harshly he would reward treachery, and so fought with the agility and recklessness of desperation. Their line held.

Magic missiles swooped and swarmed around the battling swordsmen and streaked at the old man with the white beard again.

Elminster stood watching them come. His face did not change, but the ring on his finger was fast becoming too bright to look upon. Glowing missiles circled it like sparks flying about a smith's grinding wheel and swept away again.

The Zhentarim smiled like a cat playing with cornered prey, and his hands moved again. Sharantyr stared up at him from the floor, sudden tears blurring her sight. Blazing missiles burst forth from his fingers again and flew over her.

Throat suddenly dry, Sharantyr turned to look. There was a sudden flash and a roar, and a puff of smoke hid the Old Mage from her.

As she choked for breath, frantically trying to scream, Sharantyr heard the Lord of the High Dale's low, coldly satisfied laughter.

20
Feast, Fire, and Fury

Even though Elminster was braced, waiting for the magic to strike, his body still shook—and it still hurt. The ring of spell-turning, old when this Stormcloak's great-great-grandsire was a babe, shattered under the onslaught of Art.

As Elminster had known it would. He closed his eyes against the flash and spread his fingers wide to keep them from being torn apart.

The ring burst, its shards leaping from him, and much of his nearby flesh went with it.

The Old Mage clutched the wrist of his torn, smoking hand and roared in pain. Well, he thought with surprising calm, staring at what was left of that appendage, those who spend centuries hurling spells must bear their share of spells coming back at them. But holy Mystra, it *hurt!*

Belkram laid open a councillor's face and literally ran up the man as he fell, leaping for the table. Too late. Too cursed often, he thought grimly, Harper blades came too late!

Stormcloak's triumphant laughter broke off long enough for him to hiss a word, and he abruptly vanished from in front of the astonished Harper.

Belkram slashed empty air in case the wizard had merely cloaked himself with invisibility, then looked wildly around, sword held high.

Sharantyr's raw-throated scream warned him. The Zhentarim mage stood beside Elminster, wearing a sneering smile. His hand was coming up from his robes quite slowly, and a long dagger gleamed in it.

A dagger with a tapering, up-curving blade, a blade of black glass that winked and sparkled with many tiny, moving lights.

"A death dagger!" Itharr gasped, turning from the councillor he'd been about to kill. "He *is* a Zhentarim!"

Stormcloak gave him that cruel smile and waved a hand. Magic missiles burst from his fingers and streaked across the hall.

Itharr stiffened as they struck him, light flaring for an instant. Then he collapsed with a groan.

The Zhentarim laughed again in triumph and raised the dagger above his head. He met Sharantyr's horrified eyes, and she cried weakly, "No! No!" as she crawled toward him. A sudden spasm of agony made her clench her teeth, swallowing her cry. She shook her head, helpless in pain.

Angruin Myrvult Stormcloak looked down at Elminster, dagger winking in his hand as he slowly raised it, and savored the moment.

And then the forgotten Irreph Mulmar rose up behind the Zhent wizard like a vengeful ghost.

The rattle of chains warned the Zhentarim. Stormcloak spun around, hands rising to ward off a heavy length of chain that swept into him like the mighty slap of a breaking wave. The first blow shattered the dagger and the arm that held it, and left Angruin gasping in pain. Tiny lightnings fizzed and crackled to the floor as the death dagger's magic fled.

"It's too late for you to learn, wizard," Irreph rumbled, pain making his words sharp and hissing, "to beware toothless old men." His shoulders rolled like the aroused leap of an angry old lion, and the chain swung again.

The second terrible blow split Angruin's skull like the shattering of a hurled egg striking a stone wall, and nearly tore his jaw off. The corpse clawed at the air convulsively and vainly—and fell.

Irreph stood looking down at the body for a long time, chain clenched in his hand for another blow, but the mage called Stormcloak did not move again.

Silence fell as dalefolk and councillors left off trying to kill each other. The high constable finally lifted his head and looked slowly around the room as if seeing it for the first time. His gaze fell on the Old Mage, who knelt clutching the wrist of a blackened, broken hand.

"My thanks, Elminster," Irreph said thickly, "for giving me my home back again. We must feast together, later." And with a rattle of chains, he collapsed atop the body of the wizard who had dared to usurp his post.

Elminster shook his head to clear the pain and started the long crawl to where Sharantyr lay. Her eyes had opened again, and the smile creeping onto her face was glorious to see.

"Hurry up and heal, lass," Elminster growled as he drew near. "I'm in fair need of that ring meself."

From atop the table Belkram said, "Drop your weapons, councillors, if you would live. All who fight on will be declaring themselves Zhentarim . . . and will know their fate soon, and painfully."

As he looked coldly down at the councillors, dalefolk encircled them with weapons ready, and Itharr struggled to his feet.

The trapped men looked around the room, and steel clattered to the stones as councillor after councillor held up empty hands.

Belkram waved his sword at the chairs around the table. "Sit," he suggested. "I'm sure the high constable will have some words for you before long."

Through the open doors there came the ring of steel on steel, running feet, and a short, cut-off scream.

Gedaern looked up at Belkram and said, "We can guard these—and Irreph, the gods bless him. Go hunting Wolves, Harper." He grinned and looked over many sprawled bodies. "The pair of you certainly seem to have the hang of it."

Belkram looked back at him and smiled rather sadly. "It seems that way, doesn't it?" he replied softly, and looked to his comrade-at-arms. "Itharr?"

"Here," Itharr said grimly, rubbing at parts of him that hurt. "I—I'll be with you, ready to end this slaughter . . . if you get down off that table slowly and give me time to catch my breath."

From somewhere nearby in the castle came a wild yell,

a clash of weapons, and another scream—this one long and lingering.

The two Harpers exchanged glances as Belkram's feet found the floor. "By the sounds of it," he replied, shouldering his way warily through the councillors, "there may be no Zhent Wolves left to see to."

Itharr only grunted. He limped as they started back across the great hall, but they were both trotting, blades in hand, as they went out into the passage.

Ulraea stared after them. "They seem more like things of iron and untiring magic than men."

"They're men," Gedaern told her with a light in his eyes. He hefted the weapon in his hands and stared at the doors the two had left by. "More than that—they're Harpers."

* * * * *

"Better, lass?"

"It's 'Shar,' remember?" Sharantyr reminded him with a mock severe look.

Elminster spread innocent hands. "I'm an old man, lass—Shar. I forget things, like all old men." He looked her slowly up and down as if seeing her for the first time. By the time his gaze rose again to meet her own, Sharantyr found herself blushing.

"Ye look whole now," he added. "What say ye?"

Sharantyr smiled ruefully and handed him the ring. "Well enough, Old Mage. Your turn."

Elminster put the ring on his finger and said briskly, "Good. I prefer to heal while I'm up and doing. Come." He plucked at her arm and set off for the doors at a steady stride.

Sharantyr followed. Behind them, Gedaern shouted, "Hey!"

Elminster did not pause. Sharantyr looked back.

"Both of you," Gedaern said. "You heard the Harper! Hold!"

Elminster turned at the door, and said, "Guard those councillors well, as he bid ye, young man. I've other busi-ess to see to yet." And he was gone.

"'Young man'?" Gedaern sputtered angrily. Sharantyr spread apologetic hands and followed the Old Mage.

One of the councillors watching them go frowned thoughtfully and reached inside his tunic.

Something shattered loudly on the stone floor. When Gedaern whirled around, darkness was already spreading smoky tendrils toward him.

* * * * *

Elminster moved slowly and kept his injured hand hidden in the sleeve of his robe. Sharantyr caught up to him and put a hand on his shoulder.

"Elminster," she said, earnestly, "I'm well enough to get about, and fight if need be, but you! Are you in any shape to be strolling around in the midst of a battle?"

The Old Mage gave her a tired look. "The answer to that one, lass, is the same one it's always been: I have to be."

He looked down a side passage and added, "So rest ye assured, I am. We go this way."

Sharantyr rolled her eyes and followed him. "Just answer me this, then. Where are we going, and why?"

"Ah, lass," the answer floated back to her down the dim passage. "Sages and drunkards alike have been arguing over answers to that double-bladed question for longer than I've been alive."

"Elminster!" Sharantyr wailed despairingly.

Behind them a councillor slipped out of the great hall in the concealing smoke born of the magical globe he'd shattered. He trotted to where he could watch the lady ranger and the old man in robes turn into the side passage.

Shouts echoed not far off, followed by the sound of running feet drawing nearer. The councillor frowned and looked hurriedly around. Selecting a certain door, he slipped into the room behind it, closed the door in silent haste, and in the darkness felt his way past the table he knew would be there to the floor beyond.

On his knees, he drew a slim, smooth wand out of concealed sheath on his forearm and muttered a word. The wand pulsed with a faint purplish-white radiance and from its tip a ghostly white glow spun away to form . . . an eyeball.

The orb stared back at him, looking very much like his own eye for a silent, floating instant, then faded slowly from view.

The councillor slid the wand back into its place, took hidden dagger out of its sheath inside his boot, and lay down on his face, hiding the hand that grasped the dagger under him, his other hand sprawled as if lifeless.

He blew dust away to ward off sneezing and lay still in the chill darkness. The invisible eye, driven by his will, slipped under the door and sped down the passage in pursuit of Elminster of Shadowdale.

* * * * *

Elminster rubbed his chin. "It's been many a winter," he said slowly, "and they've made some changes . . . but what I'm looking for should be about—here."

His slowing stride brought him to a halt between two closed doors. He retraced his steps to the first door and paced carefully along the passage from it. At a certain spot he took off one boot, leaving it as a marker, and padded unevenly on to the second door.

Pacing back carefully from that door, the Old Mage found himself at his boot again, nodded, and put it back on. He looked up at Sharantyr almost challengingly.

She merely shook her head. Elminster knelt down, touched with a questing finger the stone he'd marked, and nodded again emphatically.

Sharantyr cast a quick look behind her, sword in hand. The passage was dark and empty. Then she bent forward to watch as Elminster dug the fingers of his undamaged hand into a dark crack that looked no different from a hundred others in the flagstone floor, and heaved.

The stone shifted a little. Dust puffed up and swirled as it sank comfortably back into its place again.

Elminster grunted, dug his fingers in again, shifting
[f]or a better grip, and heaved. His shoulders shook.

Sharantyr leaned closer. "Want any help?"

The slab rose very slowly as Elminster looked at her
[s]ourly. Sharantyr shrugged.

Unseen above them, the floating eye drifted nearer.

The slab grated sideways. Sharantyr stared into the
[d]arkness of the hole that the Old Mage had uncovered.
[A]ir was moving upward. Foul air.

Sharantyr sniffed and wrinkled her nose. "A cesspool.
[Y]ou've found the castle's cesspool."

Elminster sat unconcernedly on the edge of the hole.
[A] lip ran all around its edge to hold the slab he'd
[d]ragged aside. He sat on the edge and felt around in the
[d]arkness with his feet for the footholds he knew would
[b]e there.

"Lass, we've no defense against magic anymore," he
[s]aid, holding up his blackened hand. "With the people
[r]oused, and the Harpers and Cormyrean agents I recog-
[n]ized among them, the Zhentarim cannot hope to hold
[t]his dale any longer and dare not try to openly seize con-
[t]rol of it, not with so many Zhentish coins owed to Sem-
[b]ian merchants right now."

One foot found what he was seeking. The Old Mage
[n]odded again and went on. "Our work here is done. I'd as
[s]oon be gone before some Zhent mageling or other finds
[u]s and decides to enhance his reputation by blasting El-
[m]inster of Shadowdale into little wisps of smoke."

Sharantyr raised her eyebrows. "Another gate?"

Elminster nodded. "Very old, spell-shielded—and just
[b]eside the cesspool, where no Zhent or other high-and-
[m]ighty mage would ever get dirty enough to look for it. If
[w]e find it now, Mulmar can feast as much as he likes, and
[w]e'll be long vanished in the night before anyone comes
[l]ooking for us."

He climbed down into the hole until only his head and
[s]houlders could be seen and beckoned her. "Ye're young,
[S]har," he said gently. "I know how it tugs at thy desires to
[l]eave this place before we've seen an end to it all. But
[l]earn a little wisdom and come now."

He waited until she moved forward, and added, "O[
aye. Bring the stone, lass, and pull it down above the[
Ye'll find lines scratched on its underside to mark how [
fits."

Sharantyr rolled her eyes in the gloom as she went t[
pick up the slab. With a sudden grunt of effort, she lifte[
it, staggered to the edge of the hole, and carefully set [
down. A strong whiff of air from below made her cough.

"You certainly know how to find troubles to land m[
in," the lady Knight complained as she started to follo[
him down the hole.

"Ah, that's adventure, lass. Adventure," Elminster sai[
cheerfully from somewhere in the darkness beneath he[
"Some folk would envy ye."

Sharantyr rolled her eyes again. They were beginnin[
to water. This gate had better be close by.

* * * * *

As the stone settled slowly back into place, the floatin[
eye dipped to inspect it carefully. After a moment [
soared into the darkness near the ceiling of the passag[
and sped away like an arrow fired from a strong forester[
bow.

* * * * *

"Lord Most High," Councillor Xanther Srildar said, i[
the safe confines of a tiny secret room deep under the ol[
est tower of the High Castle, "Brothers Angruin Myrvu[
and Heladar Longspear have both perished this day, an[
Harpers and agents of Cormyr lead the people of the da[
in armed rising. This dale is lost to us. Over my hea[
they're taking the castle as I speak. Almost all of ou[
sword brothers and mages are dead." Xanther's word[
shook only a little.

When it issued out of the floating, darkly glowing blac[
spindle in front of him, Manshoon's voice was silken in it[
easy softness. "Indeed. Have you an explanation for ho[
this came about?"

Xanther swallowed. His throat was suddenly dry again. The lord's tone was a sudden and cold reminder that his position as Manshoon's spy on the other Zhentarim here, a Brother above and secret from them, would not preserve his life if the lord was sufficiently displeased.

"Yes, Lord," Xanther said boldly. "Elminster of Shadowdale led the forces that attacked the dale, accompanied by at least one of the Knights of Myth Drannor. I saw Elminster myself and overheard him talking to this Knight, a woman in leathers. He called her 'Shar.' They're presently going down a shaft that leads to the castle cesspool, where there's a hidden gate Elminster hopes to escape by."

"Escape?" came that smooth voice out of the speaking stone, quick with interest, and Xanther began to breathe more easily. It might be that his news would please the Dread Lord of the Zhentarim enough to save his own life after all.

"Yes, Lord," Xanther confirmed. "I heard him tell the Knight that they had no defense against magic anymore. His hand was burned where Stormcloak's magic missiles destroyed a ring of spell-turning he was wearing—I didn't know such rings could be affected that way, but I saw it fly apart. He said it as if the ring had been his only defense against magic. Then he said their work was done and he'd prefer to be gone before some 'Zhent mageling or other finds us and decides to enhance his reputation by blasting Elminster of Shadowdale into little wisps of smoke.' Those were the words he used."

The speaking stone floated before him, silent for the space of two long breaths. Then the silken voice came again. Its words made Xanther glad that the stone's magic carried only voices, and that he could neither see nor be seen by the leader of the Zhentarim.

"Tell me, Xanther Srildar," Manshoon's voice asked him, "why—hearing that as you did—you did not attack them both at once?"

"I—was far away, Lord," Xanther said, swallowing, "using the wand you gave me. By one of its eyes I followed them across half the castle full of men fighting."

The spindle floating at the height of his head hun
silently.

Emboldened, Xanther added, "Had I been there, Lor
I doubt Elminster would have spoken so plainly."

"You've done well, Xanther," the smooth voice cam
again. "The Brotherhood is pleased with you, despite th
disaster in the High Dale. Hear now my orders. Do wha
ever you can, and enlist whomever you feel necessary, t
destroy Elminster of Shadowdale. Bring evidence of hi
death to me if you can—but whatever befalls and by an
means, you must bring about his death. Your reward wi
be very great."

* * * * *

The silently listening figure that neither Manshoo
nor Xanther knew was there decided it was time to with
draw before being discovered, with a chance to earn a re
ward instead of the cold, deadly weight of Manshoon
disfavor.

Hcarla Bellwind drew his robe more tightly about hin
self and hastened to a dark and winding stair he knew o
It descended directly to the part of the cellars where
certain noisome cavern held the cesspool.

* * * * *

Bellwind was in too much of a hurry to close the secre
door to Xanther's little room, once a private treasur
vault, no doubt, and discovered by the Brotherhood lon
ago. The councillor, hurrying along soon after, felt col
fingers of fear touch his spine as he stared at the ope
door. Who had found his secret place and listened?

Who knew Manshoon's orders and the truth about El
minster of Shadowdale; who was lurking somewher
near in the castle right now?

Xanther tried to look about in all directions and discov
ered, as others have before him, that it's not easy . . . an
that finding no immediate danger brings no comfort.

* * * * *

The hurrying Hcarla had no time for fear as his hastening feet descended stairs cold, dark, and worn smooth with age. Others might sneer, as Stormcloak had, at the Old Mage's feeble powers and strange behavior, but Elminster had caused Manshoon himself to flee a fight at least twice. No, Hcarla Bellwind would not begrudge the power he could gain from Elminster.

Not begrudge, but not fear either. If he could take the Old Mage unawares, he could cast his most precious magic: a stealspell. It would draw the most powerful spell out of the Old Mage's mind into his own, for Hcarla to wield. If that mind was empty of magic, the Old Mage's magic was truly gone and he could never hope to stand against the other spells Hcarla carried.

On the way through the cellars, a thought struck Hcarla. He paused in a room where glowing mold had been left to grow undisturbed to cast its eerie light over a workbench. He took down a hatchet from where it hung over the bench and caught up a moldering old sack from a pile nearby.

With the Old Mage's head in a sack, Hcarla could steal away to ask questions of it at leisure, using his own adaptation of the spell that Brotherhood priests used to speak with the dead. With Elminster's lore—directions to his spellbooks and hidden magical items would be enough—Hcarla Bellwind could forget about Manshoon's favor or disfavor and think instead about replacing him to command the Brotherhood himself. Aye, now there was a thought.

As he hurried on through the familiar darkness, Hcarla wondered briefly why Elminster had never tried to take control of the Brotherhood himself.

* * * * *

"Enough!" Itharr gasped. "I'm worn out . . . or at least my sword arm is. There can't be more than a hand's worth of Wolves left alive in all this castle."

Belkram came to a reluctant halt, nodding. "You mus‍ be right," he said. "Even the Zhentarim can't make me‍ out of nothing, and nothing is all we've found for six-‍ seven?—rooms now."

Itharr nodded. "That reminds me," he panted. "One o‍ the men . . . yelled after us. After Elminster . . . left th‍ hall, someone . . . created . . . magical darkness, and som‍ councillors . . . got away."

Belkram groaned. "Well, you've just proclaimed th‍ task left to us: rounding up a lot of scheming councillor‍ in their various hidey-holes all over this dale."

Itharr waved a hand. "Time for that on the morrow," h‍ said. "I'm more worried about archmages of Shadowdal‍ wandering about the place."

Belkram rolled his eyes as he opened his mouth t‍ reply, but another, familiar voice rang out instead.

"Hail, Harpers!"

They turned. The clangor of arms had faded away i‍ the bloodstained passages of the High Castle, and a ma‍ they knew was coming slowly toward them.

Gedaern was stumbling on a leg that was no longe‍ sound. Blood soaked his clothes and ran down his fac‍ from a cut where hair was tangled and caught fast i‍ gore. The blade in his hand was broken, its tip shattere‍ by the same fierce blows that had marked its length wit‍ deep notches. His breath was a wet, whistling sighin‍ that spoke of blood spilling inside him.

But Gedaern of the High Dale came on, eyes bright an‍ fierce, and through the blood he was smiling. A proud‍ dangerous smile. A smile that Belkram would never for‍ get, to the end of his days.

"Fair fighting, Harpers," Gedaern said. "I thank you fo‍ this chance to hit back, at last." And he smiled that terri‍ ble smile again.

* * * * *

"Gods, Old Mage," Sharantyr choked as they fel‍ around in the thick, foul air. "You sure know some roman‍ tic places to take a lady!"

Elminster made a harrumphing, throat-clearing noise from somewhere in the darkness nearby. "When ye've lived as many years as I have, Shar, ye know all the places!"

Sharantyr turned toward him. "So why come here instead?" A whiff of putrefaction set her to coughing again. "Can't we even go for a torch?"

"In this bad air, ye'd probably set off a blast that'd bring the stone above down atop us, after separating thy limbs from thy body and spreading ye all over the nearest wall."

The ranger Knight sniffed. "Without light, Old Mage, the alternative bids fair to be finding the cesspool before finding this gate, by the simple means of falling into it!"

Keep talking, idiots, Hcarla Bellwind thought with savage glee, coming cautiously nearer in the deep, velvety darkness. Their voices would lead him close enough. Cautiously he probed ahead of him with his foot, testing for firm footing before he committed his weight.

His foot came down on something yielding, something that squeaked and moved hastily out from under his toes. He felt the harmless pressure of teeth on his boot before whatever it was scurried away.

"Old Mage!" Sharantyr hissed, ahead. "Did you hear?"

"Aye," Elminster replied. "Someone stepped on a rat."

Silence fell, deep and waiting. Hcarla snarled a silent curse. Then he shrugged. No need to come within reach of the woman's sword while he had the stealspell.

Setting down the axe and sack with slow, stealthy care, he moved his hands in the gestures he'd learned from an old Myth Drannan tome, its ever-bright metal pages still clear in his mind's eye, and softly spoke the words that tied the magic together and hurled it on its way.

"No!" Elminster gasped roughly, a moment later. "Oh, no."

Like someone uncorking a wineskin and squeezing it, the power pent up within him started to flow, being drawn off into the darkness. "Lass," he snapped urgently, "close thy eyes!"

An instant later there was a blinding flash and a shattering roar that left their faces wet.

Hcarla Bellwind, with all his dreams, had been consumed in a white-hot fireball by the titanic power of Art surging into him.

* * * * *

In a chamber dark and warm, where soft limbs caressed his own in the flickering torchlight, Manshoon watched his favorite scrying crystal burst apart in the blue-white flame of Hcarla Bellwind's destruction. As the ladies in the wide bed around him shrieked and scrambled away, he sat up and hissed, "I'll have your head at last, Elminster!" His hand moved to the silken tassel of the bell cord to summon mages. Many mages.

"Dread Lord?" the best of his companions asked, standing uncertainly beside the bed. "Shall I summon the"— her voice faltered and dropped almost to a whisper— "beholders?"

Manshoon turned eyes that were very cold and dark on her. "You share my opinion of our current magelings, then? You expect them all to fail?"

Anaithe looked back at him with the eyes of a trapped animal, licked her lips, and managed to say, "Yes."

"Perhaps they'd do better," the High Lord of Zhentil Keep said in silken tones, "if you accompanied them in their search for Elminster. One who's seen so much she's not supposed to must have keen eyes indeed."

Anaithe trembled, bit her lip, and brought her hands deliberately down to her sides, recovering her poise with an effort. "I shall do whatever my lord desires . . . though I cannot see how I, without any magic, can be of any help in destroying an archmage."

Manshoon smiled suddenly. "As always, your spirit pleases me. You may live."

Anaithe's skin paled to the hue of old bone, all over. "My thanks, Great Lord," she said softly, and bowed. Manshoon heard the thread of sarcasm she couldn't quite keep from her voice, and his smile broadened. Perhaps he should teach this one magic—after she'd been humbled by a whipping.

* * * * *

Sharantyr spoke first, while their ears were still ringing. "What's this all over me?" she asked grimly.

"Droplets of ambitious Zhentarim mage, no doubt," Elminster replied wryly. "Are ye all right?"

"I—think so. I can't tell, in the dark." The lady ranger sounded angry. "Look . . . that was a blast, Old Mage, and the air around us didn't flame up to join it. So let us have light."

Elminster nodded, and an instant later remembered to speak. "Aye, lass, but one problem occurs to me."

"And it is—?"

"In this darkness, we'll be hard put to it to find a torch."

Sharantyr said something very rude and unladylike that made Elminster sigh and shake his head. And then, down the passage from which the attack had come, they saw the bobbing light of many torches.

"Say nothing of the gate," Elminster muttered hastily. "We'll seek it later."

The sputtering torches were coming fast. A few breaths later, the two men in leathers who'd slain Longspear in the marketplace burst into the room, blades drawn and trailing a handful of armed, bloody men. "Elminster?" one of them asked, holding his torch high.

"Aye, ye've found him." Elminster moved to stand beside Sharantyr's drawn, ready blade. "Who be ye?"

"Itharr," said Itharr simply.

"Belkram," Belkram added. "Storm sent us."

"So I need nursemaids now, do I?" Elminster grunted, and waved a hand. "Well met, and thanks for thy blade work outside the walls. Ye have my favor. Go and see if Mulmar needs ye for something."

Itharr and Belkram looked at each other, shrugged, and grinned. They were four strides back up the passage they'd come from when they heard Elminster chuckle.

They halted and turned. "We were asked to bring you with us," Itharr said rather hesitantly.

"By whom?" Elminster asked with an air of offended dignity.

"Irreph Mulmar, high constable of the High Dale."

"Oh." Elminster smoothed his beard with long fingers. "Well . . . let's go, then."

They went, climbing a long and winding way through empty passages, hearing excited voices echoing from here and there as they ascended through the castle, until they reached the great hall.

Irreph Mulmar sat on the high seat there, in fine clothes and with the chains struck off his limbs. Men and women of the dale stood around him with weapons in their hands. Elminster stepped through the door and nodded casually to him, and sudden silence fell across the chamber.

"Ah, Old Mage?" the high constable asked awkwardly. "We're grateful for your help an' all, but we've had a bellyful of wizards ruling things."

Folk of the dale stood watchfully by, weapons ready.

Elminster blinked at him. "By the good gods, man, what would I want to rule anyplace for?"

There was another moment of silence, until Gedaern started to laugh. His guffaws set others off. In a moment the hall rang with laughter, the first light and general merriment that had been heard there for many a day.

* * * * *

Another platter of steaming fowl banged down on the table between them, and Itharr plucked a drumstick from it without looking, his eyes on Belkram and Sharantyr.

The two leaned toward each other over the table, chins almost in their wine goblets, as they strained to hear each other over the general din in the hall. All around them, dalefolk who should have been too exhausted to do more than snore were laughing, dancing, devouring with the speed of starving wolves everything that was brought in from the kitchens . . . and drinking as if they sat in parched desert sands instead of a mountain pass.

"Baldur's Gate?" Shar said in pleased surprise. "Really? I was born there, too!" She grinned across the table at the tall Harper, then turned to Itharr. "So where do you hail from?"

Itharr rolled his eyes. "All the same places as him. We've walked together for some years now, in the service of the Harp. But as to my upbringing, well . . . I have the misfortune—in the eyes of Baldurians, at least—to have been born in Athkatla."

"We forgive you," Belkram and Sharantyr said in perfect, unplanned unison. They exchanged startled looks and started to laugh. When they had breath to talk again, Sharantyr refilled Itharr's goblet from her third wineskin of the evening and took a drumstick of her own. "So how do two men from such prosperous cities end up Harping across the backlands?"

Belkram shrugged. "My parents were crew on the *Dancing Dolphin,* a nao that sailed out of the Gate. They were slain by pirates during my twelfth summer. For a youngling, alone, the Gate's too pricey a place to fend for oneself, so I took to the roads."

"And I," Itharr said dryly, "grew up to hate cheating folk—"

"Commerce, my boy. 'Tis called commerce," Belkram put in, setting down a goblet that seemed to have rapidly emptied itself.

Itharr gave him a look. "Aye, commerce . . . what folk in Amn do. So I ran away, out of Amn, seeking something to do that was a mite more noble—and adventuresome too, if possible."

"We met at an inn . . . in Daggerford, wasn't it?" Belkram peered suspiciously at the barren depths of his goblet.

Itharr shrugged. "Wherever. Some house that had guests who worshiped the dead dragons."

Sharantyr raised an eyebrow. "The Cult of the Dragon?"

"Aye, and a witty old man with white hair and a wisp of a goatee slew them all, right there in the taproom, when they drew blades on him for being a Harper."

"And then," Belkram put in, "he sat down amid all the bodies and calmly played and sang for us. Osryk, his name was."

"A Master Harper who's been missing for a while now," Itharr said rather sadly.

Belkram nodded. "Aye, Osryk. Impressive, he was. We were both aflame with the idea of becoming Harpers, so he sent us to Berdusk."

"Where Obslin Minstrelwish didn't much like the look of us," Itharr added with a sigh of remembrance, waving a half-eaten drumstick, "and decided we needed some harsh adventuring experience before we'd be worthy of the Way of the Harp."

"It's the noise you made with his songhorn," Belkram explained patiently. "You shouldn't have claimed to be an expert horn player."

"How was I to know it was his favorite instrument?" Itharr protested, sliding his goblet over to Sharantyr for a refill. "After all, how many halfling horn players d'you know?"

"One is all you need," Belkram told him dryly. "And sometimes far more than you need."

Sharantyr watched Itharr answer him with a rude gesture, and looked briefly up at the rafters. "You two must be a riotous pair to travel with," she said, shaking her head.

"Is that an invitation?" Belkram asked eagerly, leaning even farther across the table. Shar rolled her eyes and decided she needed a refill of her own.

"I don't think so," she said firmly, only to start back as Itharr leaned across the table just as aggressively and asked, "So how does a beautiful lady come to swing such a deadly blade, and join the Knights of Myth Drannor, hey?"

"Ahhh," Shar began, taken aback.

Belkram grinned at her. "Aye, it's our turn," he told her happily, steering a goblet she'd never seen before into her hands. It was as large as a man's head, and it was brim full. Belkram winked at her over its lip.

After the moment it took her to sigh, she winked back.

* * * * *

The feast was long and loud, and went on through the night. Folk roared and cheered and sang old songs, and Sharantyr moved—accompanied by the two Harpers—to sit with Elminster. She was soon amazed by the rapidity with which his glass became empty, was refilled, and seemed to leak its contents yet again.

Sharantyr made the huge goblet Belkram had given her last the rest of the evening, and kept eyeing the merriment around her watchfully. If someone yet lived, particularly an archer or a wizard, who wanted the Old Mage dead, this joyful chaos would allow a very good chance to kill him.

About the time she loosened her blade in its sheath and pulled away from where she was pressed against Elminster to get steel out should she need it, she felt the pressing regard of a hostile gaze.

Looking up quickly, she saw the burning eyes of a councillor across the table dropping swiftly away from her. Hawklike, Sharantyr watched him, her blade a finger out of its sheath.

A long time later, amid the laughter and song and weary dancing, the man's eyes flicked up again, almost involuntarily. Xanther. Aye, that was his name. One of those who'd been spared, thus far. His eyes flicked away again to stare at something, roved about the table, and returned to stare at the same something again.

She followed his hungry gaze as he leaned just a finger or so forward to better study whatever it was he was so intent on.

He was eyeing the wand lying on the table by Elminster's hand.

Another wizard? Sharantyr drew a deep breath and pondered what best to do.

Feeling the sudden weight of the lady ranger's gaze upon him, Xanther carefully didn't look up.

He could not fail to notice, however, the sudden gleam of naked steel as the lady ranger drew her long sword and meaningfully laid it ready on the table, its shining tip resting over the wand.

21
Death Waits
Past the Lich-Gate

Black flames leapt up, casting angry red and amber shadows on the wall behind, but the man in black paid them no heed.

He'd seen them time upon time before, and had in fact chosen this spot for maximum effect. Blood-red dancing shadows outlined him as a tall and sinister figure of darkness—mighty, awesome, and dark. It pleased him to think of himself thus.

What use, after all, is great power if one cannot use it to indulge one's smallest conceits?

Wherefore Manshoon—Lord of the Zhentarim, Overmage of the Dark Ring, The Hand of Darkness, and the holder of many other titles he was pleased to give himself from time to time—stood tall in his high-horned cloak, thigh-high boots, and silken tunic and breeches. He looked down on a keen-eyed mageling of the Brotherhood, a young, hawk-eyed youth whose eager ambition burned so hot that one could almost smell it, and smiled.

"Avaerl of Sembresh," he asked softly and formally, "would you serve the Brotherhood in ways greater than you have so far?"

"Yes, Lord Most High," the wizard said quickly and proudly.

"Be not so swift to promise," Manshoon almost purred. "Others have tried and failed at the task I would set for you."

"I shall not fail," Avaerl said boldly.

Manshoon inclined his head and smiled. "Good," he said. "Go then, and bring me the head of Elminster of Shadowdale."

Avaerl's eager grin slipped, just for an instant, hung

lopsided on his face in a perfect match of the ghastly smile worn by many a corpse, and then returned in full. It did not waver as he bowed his head and looked back up at Manshoon. "Lord," he promised, "it shall be done. I will not fail."

Manshoon bowed his head in dismissal. "Your reward, then, will be very great. Go in power."

Avaerl turned on his heel, robes swirling, and strode away down the path between two waiting lines of motionless armored forms. They turned in unison to face him as he passed, impassive visors down, but made no sound or other movement.

Avaerl carefully did not look at any of them. Their silent vigilance unsettled braver magelings than he. It was whispered among the lesser wizards of the Brotherhood that the suits of armor were empty, or appeared to be. Fell spirits, or worse magic, moved them to Manshoon's will. Helmed Horrors they were called.

When Avaerl stepped onto the spell-guarded stair that led away from Manshoon's cave-lair, the last two Horrors stepped forward behind him to ceremoniously cross curved, naked blades, barring passage along the silent gantlet the ambitious mageling had just walked.

Ascending steps that glowed vivid blue under his feet, Avaerl heard that whisper of metal kissing metal, and shivered involuntarily. The very sight of the uncanny Horrors chilled him, probably because the cold, deadly watchfulness of Manshoon himself moved them. It was a reminder—deliberate, without a doubt—of the awesome power of the Lord Most High of the Zhentarim.

Not for the first time, Avaerl thought himself crazy to even contemplate challenging Manshoon, some day, for lordship over the Brotherhood. Yet . . . with the power of Elminster, the Old Mage of Shadowdale, under his belt, bards would tell a different tale. He grinned as he saw himself blasting Manshoon to screaming bones, the Overmage's mind pleading for mercy as it faded away, the bones softening, sagging, and collapsing into windwhirled dust before Avaerl's might.

Gulkuth, he reminded himself. Gulkuth. His key to

making this mere dream into reality. It was a mage's tru-ename, the key to mastery over the man, whoever it was. By where he'd found it, written in blood on a hidden altar, it belonged to a wizard alive today. A wizard who served Bane. A wizard of great power.

One of the Inner Ring of the Brotherhood, without doubt. But who? Or was it a trap laid by one or all of them against ambitious mages?

Avaerl dared not reveal that name until he had power enough to use it. That meant magic enough to overmatch Manshoon, for the name could very well be his.

If it was Manshoon's truename, and Avaerl held the knowledge and power of Elminster, the Lord Most High could not stand against him. The Zhentarim would know a new lord.

And then a small, cold voice deep inside him added, "For a little while." Avaerl shivered again as he reached the top of the stair.

* * * * *

As the blades came softly together at the far end of the gantlet, Manshoon beckoned with a long and lazy arm. One of the dark-robed and cruel-faced men who'd stood silent and motionless among the dark, fanglike stalagmites stepped smoothly forward.

"Zalarth, I have work for you."

"I await your orders, my lord."

Cold eyes met. Each stared into cold, falling depths in the soul of the other, and Manshoon said slowly, "Follow that puppy and do what he will undoubtedly fail to do."

"Me, my lord?" Zalarth asked, inclining his head at other, mightier mages who stood watching from the shadows.

Manshoon held his eyes. "I trust you the more," he said coldly, "and believe your thinking in battle to be clearer. You shall succeed where he fails, and bring me Elminster's head . . . if you would rise in our councils."

"May I use items, or the aid of others?"

"Use what you deem necessary."

* * * * *

As Zalarth climbed the glowing stairs in his turn, faces swam in his memory—faces of thieves and trained killers of the Brotherhood. From those faces, the Zhentarim wizard chose the members of the band he would lead. Elminster would die. Manshoon had commanded the death; it was as good as done. The sentence would befall.

After too many hundreds of years, Elminster of Shadowdale would perish. Zalarth would seize his might and his magic. Zalarth would use them to rule. When bards, tavern drunks, and wizards whispered of high and mighty deeds in years to come, it would be Zalarth's name they would remember as the one who brought down Elminster of Shadowdale, not Manshoon's. Zalarth would see to that.

* * * * *

It was late. Smoke hung thick in the air; wine had been spilled here, there, and everywhere else; and arms that had swung swords, axes, and clubs all day were stiffening to painful, iron-hard immobility.

All around the great hall of the High Castle, happy but utterly exhausted folk slumped in chairs or simply sprawled on the floor and gave themselves up to snoring slumber. Sharantyr stifled a yawn and glanced at the Old Mage.

Elminster winked at her and raised a drinking jack of shadowdark ale whose owner was too fast asleep to miss it. It was full.

"Had enough, Old Mage?" she asked, challenging him.

"There's no such thing as enough, lass," Elminster told her severely. "After ye've seen a few hundred winters, ye'll know that. There's no such thing as too much, either. Only too little time to enjoy it in." He winked again and added with apparent innocence, "That's true for drinks, too."

Sharantyr sighed. " 'Lass' again, is it?" she protested, then added in quieter tones, "Do you still plan to leave by the gate tonight?"

Elminster nodded. "I'd located the gate just about the time every daleman still able to stagger along with a blade hastened up to watch. They're still watching us now—no, lass, don't look around at them; they'll get excited. We'd best to bed, or we'll never be free of all these interested eyes."

"Bed?" Sharantyr crooked a forbidding eyebrow at him.

Elminster rolled his eyes. "Let them show you somewhere to sleep. I'll go out for a pipe, and . . ."

Sharantyr nodded, yawned theatrically, and got unsteadily to her feet.

Down the table, an old dalesman's face dipped forward gently onto the table. Over the now-bowed head, Gedaern, whose face had been wearing a fierce smile all evening, saw her.

He rose a little unsteadily. "All well, Lady Knight?"

"Aye, goodman Gedaern," Sharantyr told him truthfully, "but I am most weary after all that blade work. If there's any place in this castle I can sleep . . . ?"

"But of course!" Irreph Mulmar said heartily from behind Gedaern. He extended a massive hand to her. "I've never seen such fighting as yours, today. We and the dale owe you much. The best bedchamber in the High Castle would be honored by your presence. Let me take you to it, if—?" He turned his head.

"It is ready, Sir," Ireavyn assured him quickly, beaming. At her shoulder, Ulraea nodded happily. Shar could ask for the moon, this night, and they'd climb atop each other on the battlements to reach it down for her.

"No, no," Sharantyr said, "please. Nothing grand. Just somewhere quiet and out of the way, with a good bed." She glanced back at Elminster, who had arisen and was unconcernedly filling his pipe. "Ah—with room enough for two, or with two beds."

Elminster turned one twinkling eye to meet hers as he tamped and fumbled, but said nothing.

"I know such a room," Ulraea said. "Up high, in Guards' Tower. A guest chamber. I can take you there."

"Please," Sharantyr said. "Irreph . . . my thanks. Stay. You belong here, in this hall, with your people around you. Stay, please. Enjoy the castle being yours again. I don't want to take you away from this."

At Irreph's shoulder, his daughter Ylyndaera smiled and nodded at the lady ranger from within her father's encircling arm.

Irreph looked down at his daughter and then at Sharantyr, and said roughly, "My thanks, Lady Sharantyr. You see as keenly as your blade cuts. Until the morrow, then."

"Until next," Sharantyr answered with a smile. Behind her, Elminster bowed silently.

"Goodnight, Lady Sharantyr," Ylyndaera said, eyes shining, and Gedaern echoed her words.

Farther down the table, Itharr and Belkram had their arms around two dark-eyed dale maids. They waved, and Belkram called, "Keep an eye on him, Lady, will you?"

"This night more than ever," Itharr added.

"Oh, I will," Sharantyr replied in a voice that brought guffaws from all around, and she went out, Ulraea at her side.

Elminster came back from the fire puffing his pipe to life, gave the two Harpers a severe look, and followed.

Gedaern looked after him and said thoughtfully, "Now there goes a man that kings and wizards and dragons an' all have found hard to kill, for more years than I and my old one and grandsire together have seen."

Irreph watched the Old Mage walk out of sight and replied, "They don't stop trying, though."

* * * * *

It was a clear night. Above the dark, reaching shoulders of the peaks, stars glittered like tireless torches.

Elminster looked up at them as he had done on countless nights, from battlements on as many worlds as he had fingers, down too many years to remember, and puffed at his pipe. He'd told the earnest young dalemen on guard that he'd just have a pipe before he retired, and to go and get drunk while there was something left. They'd laughed kindly but sensed he wanted silence and solitude, thank Mystra, and had left him.

As the feast went on below, he'd heard them drift away, one by one, from watching a closed door. He only hoped Sharantyr wouldn't really fall asleep. After all she'd done today, waking her would be as cruel as it would be difficult.

Elminster blew silvery-green winking sparks around himself in a friendly, dancing cloud and sighed. He'd seen so many beautiful, capable, bright women die, down the long years. He hoped Sharantyr would not perish soon, and that he'd not be the cause of her death when it came.

He turned back to the doorway that let him watch over the guest chamber's closed door. He was regarding it fondly—gods, but this lass, one of the quieter and younger Knights, apt to be overlooked in all the bustle of their deeds back in Shadowdale, was a sparkling blade, to be sure!—when it opened softly and a cautious face peered out.

A long puff later, Sharantyr stole barefoot out of the dark room, carrying a bundle in front of her from which her scabbarded sword protruded. Starlight shone briefly on shapely bare legs, and the lady ranger brushed damp hair back over her shoulders, then frowned as she deftly caught a boot on its way toward the flagstones underfoot.

"Disrobed again, are we?" Elminster's tone was amused as he took the pipe from his mouth. "I thought so. Young lasses have such predictable notions of adventure."

"Hush, Old Mage," Sharantyr hissed severely, holding her breeches aloft with one hand while the other struggled with a large number of extremely heavy, awkward, and active items that seemed to be continually trying to slip out of her grasp. "You may not mind if you stink like a pig in a wallow, but being sticky and filthy bothers *me*. I availed myself of Ulraea's kindness and had a very nice hot bath, if the word 'bath' means anything to a certain old, hard-headed, and rather strong-smelling wizard. I think the High Dale owes me that much, at least. Here—

hold my sword, will you?"

Elminster bowed, took the scabbarded blade in skillful silence, reached in to help hold her shirt up at the throat while she struggled with the lacings, turned his back with courteous haste, and then turned around again to hold Sharantyr's gloves while she did up her belt.

Then he reached up and took hold of the pipe that had been patiently floating in the air waiting for him all this time, and puffed on it again.

Sharantyr stared at it, and at him, and sighed and smiled. In answer to his curious look she said, "Never mind, El. The pipe—it's a close personal friend and a thousand years older than I am, right?"

Elminster took the pipe out of his mouth and winked at it.

The pipe opened a rather world-weary eye and winked solemnly back at him before swiveling to do the same to Sharantyr.

Elminster was chuckling as he tapped the pipe—which instantly went out, leaving no smoke or odor behind— and put it in a hidden pocket inside his robes. The lady ranger never was sure if the pipe was alive or if she'd just been the victim of one of his pranksome little illusions.

* * * * *

Xanther sneered silently at the two dale youths who stood guard. They were barely old enough to hold their spears properly and did not see him where he stood in the dimness of the passage. The Zhentarim slipped behind the concealment of a shadow cast by a bulge in the rough stone wall, and did something.

The two young guards heard the slight noise that the secret door made as it swung open and then instantly shut again, but by the time they reached the shadow, there was nothing to be seen but an empty stone passage. They hunted around for a bit—there *had* been a noise, both agreed—and looked warily upward. When they thankfully saw nothing waiting to fall on them, they shrugged and went away.

By then, Xanther had slain Stormcloak's old, stupid watchspider with the heavy stone block he'd thoughtfully procured earlier, and taken the scrolls he knew it guarded. Their capped tubes rattled, and he shook a large gem out of one with great satisfaction. The other yielded a fine chain linking three plain brass finger rings, and a dagger whose quillons were a pair of batlike, furry folded wings, dusty gray and looking very much alive. He was careful not to touch it bare-handed and so activate it.

Xanther packed all this revealed magical treasure back into the tubes that had held it. Then he hurried on, descending through dark, secret passages scarcely wider than his own hips, heading for the cellars. Heading toward the dark, waiting cesspool where he knew Elminster of Shadowdale and the wench Sharantyr would come . . . to meet their deaths.

For the greater glory of the Brotherhood. Xanther smiled a smile that held no humor and slipped on through the darkness.

* * * * *

"The gate lies just here," Elminster said, pointing in the fetid darkness.

"Without light, I can't see a thing," Sharantyr said crossly, "but from the smell, I can tell that we're very near the edge of the pool. Watch where you step."

Elminster felt for her hand, seized it in his own, and squeezed reassuringly. "That's the beauty of it, d'ye see? Kneel down here, beside me, and feel."

His hand led hers to trace cold stone. The stink around them was indescribable. Elminster continued an unconcerned lecture. "One enters the gate by stepping out over the pool, off the edge as if one were stepping right into it. One has to start here, though, just between these two raised stones, or the step forward is into empty air and ends as a fast plunge into the muck."

Sharantyr let him guide her hand to two stony knobs. "Do you mean we're kneeling right on the edge of it now?"

"Aye. An exposed position, indeed," Elminster replied. "Let us up and proceed, without further delay. Hold tight to my hand."

"Old Mage," Sharantyr said calmly, "I'm doing so. I've got a very good grip on you, in fact, and I'll yank you beard-over-ankles into this cesspool right now if you don't tell me just where this gate you're so eager to use will take us, before we step so boldly through it!"

Elminster sighed. "Ye want all the Zhentarim in this place—and those who serve Sembia, Cormyr, the Red Wizards of Thay, and the Cult of the Dragon, besides—to find us here, don't ye? I may know a few tricks and carry a few magic trinkets, but if ye'd see my skin stay whole and my thousand-odd years stretch to a few more, ye'd not force me to fight off every eager hedge-wizard and sharpknife in this dale!" He turned and glared at her as he spoke. The lady ranger felt the burning weight of his unseen eyes on her in the darkness.

"Old Mage," Sharantyr said firmly, "just tell and we can be on our way, provided it's not to a certain plane of fire and evil, or the center of the Grand Hall in Darkhold, or another such lunatic destination. I'd like to know what I'll have to fight before I get wherever we're going."

Elminster tried to pull away. Her grip shook with weariness but held him like iron as she added, "And since you threatened me with all those names, suppose you also tell me just who, in this mountain dale so crammed with Zhentarim wizards, serves Thay, the Cult, Sembia, and Cormyr."

The Old Mage sighed. "The councillors, Shar. Among them are men still loyal to the dale, a handful who bow to Manshoon—all the newer members, no doubt—and those who were there before Longspear's takeover, seeing to the interests of those others in secret. Trust me. When my Art served me, I spied on many a secret meeting and took note of many, many faces. Most of the High Dale's councillors are more than they seem to be."

"And we're slipping away and leaving Irreph to that?" Sharantyr blazed at him. "All of them tired and hurt—Ylyndaera, Ulraea, Gedaern, and all the rest? Is your heart a stone, Old Mage? A gravestone for them all, perhaps?"

"Easy, lass, easy," Elminster rumbled. "Didn't we rid them of enough Zhent mages to rule a small dale, between us? While ye were so busy glaring at Xanther—the weak-willed one who wanted my wand; unless my nose has lost all smell, he's a Zhent sneak—at the table this even, I gave both Gedaern and Irreph identical lists of what cause each councillor serves, at least so far as I knew. Gedaern read it then and there, I know. I saw him go out, and later he came back and told me a name."

Sharantyr frowned. "I remember that. 'Blakkal' or something, he said to you, just when the Zhent councillor got up to leave. I didn't know what he meant."

"Aye," Elminster said to her in the darkness. "The leather worker. He served the Cult of the Dragon until Gedaern saw to him." He sighed again. "I doubt Gedaern will let Xanther live to see another sunrise, even if Mulmar leaves reading my note until then."

"Why wouldn't he read it?"

Elminster gave her a look that she could not see, but felt. "Everyone of the dale wanting to talk to him, his daughter clinging to him and in tears every second breath, and the first proper meal he's had for a long time —with too much to drink, I don't doubt. It would also come as no surprise to me to learn he's abed with Ireavyn right now."

It was Sharantyr's time to sigh. "True enough. I don't suppose the Zhent councillors will amount to much. With all the wizards Manshoon already had strutting around the dale to back up their usurper, he wouldn't have needed great warriors or mages, only good spies. And I can't think agents of Cormyr and Sembia are much to be feared, given that each country will counter any moves to gain control that the other makes. But you spoke of Thay. You're going to leave a Red Wizard running loose here?"

"Hardly that," Elminster told her. "He's a wizard, aye, but rather a decent sort and much too careful to reveal himself. When they come for him, of course, it'll be too late for him to do more than run. He's the local weaver, a fat, kindly little man by the name of Jatham Villore. I feel somewhat in his debt. Someone cloaked the Zhents' searching spells as we and the two Harper lads were gallivanting around the dale, and I rather think it was him."

"Why?"

"Will ye never run out of questions, girl? To shake the rule of the Zhentarim here, of course." Elminster cleared his throat. "We looked into each other's eyes, in the great hall just now, and if hundreds of years of measuring folk with my eyes has taught me anything, he's not quick to slay with his Art, that one."

Sharantyr reached out in the darkness, found his beard—it felt like the soft bristles at the base of a horse's tail—and patted his cheek. "Well enough," she said. "You've done what you could for the dale. So tell me, where are we going?"

She heard the grin in Elminster's voice. "By Mystra, lass, but ye're a keen, feisty blade! Well, then, this gate should take us to another castle—much grander than this one, but in ruins—in the Fallen Lands."

"Clear across Anauroch? How will we get back?"

"One disaster at a time, lass. Come." The Old Mage tugged at her hand, and Sharantyr allowed him to pull her to her feet. The stinking darkness swirled around them like soiled velvet, disturbed by their movement. Sharantyr nearly choked.

"What castle?" she managed to ask, feeling for the hilt of her sword.

"Spellgard they call it now. Long ago, when it belonged to a friend of mine, it had another name."

"What happened?" Sharantyr asked, but Elminster towed her forward with surprising strength, and the words that began above the cesspool of the High Castle ended in a cold, shadowed hall lit by glowing mosses.

Dark archways gaped in the walls around them, and more moss hung from stone balconies above. The floor was an uneven tumble of disturbed marble, its smooth paving broken upward as if a giant had punched it repeatedly from beneath.

Cold breezes blew around their ankles, coming from

somewhere unseen, and there was no sign of life. Dust hung thick in the air, and there were no furnishings to be seen except stone seats carved into the walls in little curl-ornamented niches.

Elminster was nodding in recognition. "Spellgard?" Sharantyr asked, to hear more about it rather than to confirm where they were.

"Aye," Elminster said, striding forward. "As to what happened, well . . . it's a very long story and happened a long, long time ago. Let's just say that the realm of Netheril fell, and the friend I spoke of—the sorceress Saharel—lived on here. But mages had very few ways of stretching their years, then." He fell silent, looking around at the moss and the tumbled stone.

"Except being chosen by Mystra," Sharantyr said softly beside him.

Elminster nodded slowly. "Save for the grace of Mystra," he echoed. He stood looking at nothing for a long, sad moment, then lifted his head and said almost defiantly, "Best we look about. Ye never know . . . some Zhent wizard might find the gate behind us."

Sharantyr's sword slid out as she spun around to see only dust and empty air. "Not yet," she said, turning back. "Lead, El. You know this place."

Elminster strode toward an archway. "Saharelgard it was called, when I knew it. I've been here once since, but I was too busy running then to look around."

"Too busy running?"

"Running from, and fighting, a family of mages who'd learned how to turn themselves into dragons."

"Oh."

Elminster waited, and her expected question came: "What happened?"

"I'm with ye today, eh, lass? What else would ye know?"

* * * * *

In a room that was deep and dark and spherical, a figure stirred on a round bed. Dark robes rustled, tatters falling away into dust, as the thing on the bed sat up and leaned forward as if sniffing the air.

It had been awakened by an intrusion, the sudden presence of more magic than it had ever felt in one being before. Awesome magic. What befell in the Realms above now? The figure rose in a sudden, smooth movement and spread its hands.

A door that had been closed and sealed for centuries suddenly ceased to be, exploding into dust. The figure strode forward in uncanny silence.

22
Magemoot at Spellgard

One instant saw a high-ceilinged hall empty of all but glowing moss and tumbled stone. In the next breath, a young man in robes stood in its midst, crouching as if facing a foe—but his hand held a wand, not a sword. He darted hurriedly four steps to one side and looked all around. No sign of anyone. Where was he?

Silence hung heavy in Spellgard. Avaerl of Sembresh peered around in the weird, dim light of the glowing mosses and muttered a quick spell.

Abruptly he disappeared. Invisibility cloaked him as he stepped carefully to another spot and murmured his next spell.

Unseen, he rose slowly and silently to the uppermost balcony, glancing into archways and along passages as he passed them. In some, cold radiances pulsed and flickered, but Avaerl had seen the mushrooms called glowcaps before and knew them for what they were.

He'd learned of Elminster's woman companion from his informant in the High Castle, but of those two or the route they had taken, he saw no sign. Avaerl breathed out a soundless sigh, then shrugged and set foot on the stones of the highest balcony. Let the hunt begin.

* * * * *

"Itharr," said a voice from the darkness at the foot of the bed, "I hate to do this, really I do, but we've got a problem."

"The Zhentarim have sent an army? Well, defeat them, and tell me about it in the morning," Itharr said sleepily.

"Not as simple as that," Belkram said kindly. "Get up, and bring your sword. Elminster's gone."

"Oh, *dung,*" Itharr said, coming all the way awake, little chilly feet of foreboding racing down his spine. "When?" As he asked the useless question, he gently slipped a warm but very heavy head from his shoulder. Its owner murmured something, slid a caressing hand along his thigh, settled into a new position, and began to snore.

"Mine did that, too," Belkram said in amused tones, handing Itharr his scabbarded sword. The buckle hit the younger Harper in the face.

Itharr spat it away and snarled, "Clothes first, you dolt. I don't consider them optional."

"Here. Hurry."

Itharr hurried, grumbling all the while in low, muttered whispers. "He's probably just gone to relieve himself, or look at the stars, or find a wench who'll have him."

Belkram tried to hand him his sword again. This time, Itharr was ready.

"Remember what Storm told us," Belkram said. "Even if he is just out on the nearest battlement, his safety is too important to risk. Besides, Sharantyr's gone too, *and* their clothes and weapons."

"Tymora aid us," Itharr groaned, leaping up. Together they ran to the door. Itharr winced as a lonely and bewildered voice called his name softly and sleepily from the bed behind him, but he did not answer or slow down.

Belkram clapped him on the shoulder as they hurried down the passage. "Gedaern woke me up, and he did it by running into the room bellowing at the top of his lungs. He smashed straight into the bed and fell on top of us. I thought you'd appreciate a gentler awakening."

"My thanks," Itharr said dryly. "Has he left it just to us, or have we a band of willing idiots to help us scour the dale in the dark?"

"We have such a band, and now they have two willing idiots to lead them," Belkram replied brightly.

Itharr grunted something that his companion didn't quite catch.

* * * * *

Zalarth Bloodbrow smiled grimly at the startled shout and the splash. A fitting reward for disobedience, he thought, watching the thief thrashing and spluttering in the cesspool. There were only two others left. The rest of his men had walked exactly as he'd directed, and the gate had taken them elsewhere already. He motioned those two forward as if to aid the one in the pool. The moment they were in front of him, he moved his fingers in the quick movements of a spell.

The limbs of the thrashing man abruptly froze, and he stared at the wizard in wide-eyed, openmouthed, silent horror as he sank slowly into the thick brown ooze. The soundless mouth slid from view, then the unmoving, staring eyes. The hair coiled momentarily amid bubbles . . . and then there was nothing.

The two Brotherhood thieves turned to look at Zalarth, their throwing knives leaping into their hands as if they commanded their own magic.

The cruel-faced Zhentarim shook his head and sighed. "His heart? A seizure, perhaps? Better it happened here, I suppose, than in the midst of whatever we'll find through there." He nodded at the empty air where the gate must be.

"Mind you step off the edge there, between the two bumps, and not try to jump in from one side as Lesker did." He shook his head again, frowning, thin-lipped. "He didn't have seizures, did he? Or anything of the sort?"

The two men shook their heads silently. The knives did not leave their hands.

Zalarth frowned down at the now-placid surface of the cesspool. "Unless," he said slowly, "there's something alive in there, feeding on Lesker now."

He looked up and said briskly, "We'd best be gone from here before it sends up tentacles or the like."

He'd scared them sufficiently. Without further demur the thieves stepped forward into the gate—and were gone. Zalarth hastily advanced to position himself between the two stone knobs before the torch went with them.

In the sudden darkness, he conjured up an invisible

protective shield of force around himself, just in case one of his men had second thoughts and decided to greet him with a thrown knife.

Then Zalarth of the Zhentarim stepped forward in the darkness and went to war.

* * * * *

"I think I know where he might be, or might have gone, at least," Itharr said suddenly as they stared wildly around at empty battlements.

"Well?" one of the dalemen demanded. "Speak!"

"Where we caught up to him earlier," Itharr said, turning to Belkram, "and he called us nursemaids. Remember?"

Belkram nodded. "You think he's down there? At the cesspool?"

Itharr shrugged. "He was after something there, amid the stink, and we interrupted him. He'll have gone back to it when he thought everyone was too drunk or to asleep to see him."

"Treasure?" Belkram asked, raising a puzzled eyebrow.

"No," Itharr said very quietly. "Another gate, if I'm not mistaken."

Belkram stared at him and swallowed. Then they were both sprinting through dark, empty passages, seeking stairs that led down and taking turns cursing and panting for breath.

The men of the dale thundered after them. "The only folk crazier than these Harpers," one grunted, rounding a stair post at breakneck speed in the darkness, "is wizards."

"Thank the gods for that," said the man behind him. "If they weren't, we'd still be kissing Longspear's feet—and another part of that Stormcloak's body, too."

They'd bounded down another flight of stairs before the first daleman replied dryly, "I'd wondered what you were about, those long evenings."

He was answered in turn by a ruder suggestion. Then they were nearing the cellars, and Gedaern hissed them to silence.

* * * * *

Xanther waited and waited, but there came no further sound. He'd heard the wizard—one of Manshoon's killers, if his memory held right—muttering, and then the faint scrape of a boot on stone. Then, only silence.

Xanther carefully emptied one scroll tube into his lap and felt about until his fingers closed on the cold hardness of the gem. He knew what it must be, given the three words written on the inside of the scroll tube's cap that he'd read earlier, and closed his eyes as he spoke the first of those words.

The prism-shaped gem gave forth a cone of pale light. Good; he'd chosen the right word. By its light, he saw that the cesspool and its surroundings were empty of all people.

Hmm. "Between the two bumps," the wizard had said, and intimated that passage between them was critical to avoid falling into the cesspool. Xanther put away the tube's contents again, except for the handy gem, and got up. Two bumps, on the edge of the cesspool . . .

There was a sudden sound behind him. A muffled thud—no, a flurry of such sounds. The thudding of booted feet coming quickly down stone steps and along the echoing passage. Dalefolk!

Xanther hurried toward the stinking pool, eyes searching frantically. Ah—there! Two bumps!

He eyed the reeking pool and sighed. He'd have preferred time to make sure of the route before stepping out over that.

The sounds grew louder, and he heard the unmistakable voice of one of the men in leathers who'd fought Stormcloak in the great hall.

Xanther sighed again, and stepped out from the edge. The light in the cavern abruptly went out.

* * * * *

"A light!"
"Where?"

"Gone now, sir, but there was light here a moment ago, tell thee!"

"Throw your torch forward," Belkram ordered. "Those with bows to the fore, but no one advances until I give word."

He and Itharr looked each other over quickly. "Got a dagger or two, besides your blade?"

Itharr nodded. "As usual." He grinned as he added, "I think it's your turn to go first."

"My thanks," Belkram told him in dry tones and darted forward, keeping low. He crouched near the guttering torch, peering around intently, then beckoned them with a wave.

What could be seen of the dark, foul-smelling cavern was empty. In the center of the cracked, uneven stone floor was the cesspool, its surface still. Itharr waved the men with torches toward the far reaches of the place, to light up every niche and corner.

He and Belkram exchanged glances and nodded. "A gate, without doubt. We have to enter it in exactly the right way, or we'll never find it."

"That could take days," Belkram sighed.

"It could," came a voice from behind them. "But if you'll allow me to show you the way, it can take you but a moment."

They all turned. In the passage behind them, the fat weaver, Jatham, stood in his night robe, holding a hand lamp and regarding them calmly.

Gedaern's eyes narrowed. "You—"

"Serve Thay? Aye. I thought Elminster might tell you." The weaver watched the frowning daleman come toward him and added, "I'd like to make a deal with you, Gedaern."

"Oh, aye? And what sort of deal could you and I come to?"

"You let me live, to leave the dale peacefully with my possessions on the morrow. In return, I tell you all I know of the other councillors' loyalties and doings, and show these two Harpers the gate they seek."

"Just let you go, after all you've done? Why—"

"Or you could thank me. Most of what I've done, thi
last year or so, is work against the spells and schemes o
the Zhentarim as much as I could. My efforts have kep
many in the dale alive, even some here in this cella
now."

"How could you save lives and trick wizards? Aye? Te
me that!"

Jatham spread his hands. In the gesture, his left han
let go of the oil lamp, and it hung motionless in the air i
front of him, its flame flickering slightly. "With my ow
magic, of course," he said mildly. "It's not much, but it'
enough to make any thoughts of slaying me or drivin
me out of the dale very, very foolish indeed."

Gedaern eyed the weaver suspiciously. He darted
glance to the two Harpers. They looked back at him ex
pressionlessly and spread their hands to signal their in
decision.

Gedaern frowned. "What's to keep you from blasting u
all with your magic the moment we go to bed, then?"

"I am," said another voice from behind the weaver.

Jatham turned quickly. "You should not have com
down, love. This is not safe."

"It was necessary," Ulraea told him crisply. Her eye
were lined with sleep, and her unbound hair hung in wil
tangles about her, but she drew herself up in her tattere
nightdress proudly and regarded Gedaern with wha
seemed almost like a challenge in her eyes. "Jatham i
mine, Ged. I know him as no other in this dale, and I te
you he has not worked against us of the dale while Long
spear lorded it over us, and will not do so this night. I
you must, set a guard in our room tonight."

Gedaern stared at her, openmouthed. It was severa
long breaths later that he visibly remembered to swallov
"Ulla?" he said at last, voice cracking. "Y-you . . . lov
him? You'll go with him?"

Ulraea nodded, eyes on his. "If you'll let me." Sh
looked around at them all. "If you're so fearful of wha
my Jath will do with his magic, guard me—and take m
life if he works ill."

Jatham reached for her involuntarily. "No!" he cried, i

n anguished voice.

"No," Gedaern's voice overrode his, loud and flat. "It von't be necessary. Go back to your beds, both of you, fter you show us this gate and tell us where it leads. If ou'll do that, we have a deal."

He sheathed the notched, scarred sword he bore and valked slowly to where the weaver stood. He raised his and, palm out, standing nose to nose with the Thayan gent.

Jatham did the same, and slowly they both brought heir hands down to touch each other's chest in the old ale custom. A bargain was made. Both men nodded olemnly.

Then Jatham said briskly, "The gate can only be en-ered by stepping out over the cesspool from a certain lace, the spot between the two little humps of stone, on his side—see, here? It will take you across half Faerûn o the far edge of Anauroch, the Great Desert. Those who o through reach a central hall in an old, ruined castle, a lace they call Spellgard today. It's a one-way journey, nd the castle has a fell reputation. I recommend that hose who love the High Dale not take the gate. The way etween there and here is long, and not safe."

"That's our road, then," Itharr said quietly.

Belkram nodded and said, "Our thanks, Jatham . . . nd Gedaern, and all of you, for risking your necks again his night. May the High Dale know peace for a good long ime now. We must leave you in haste, for we're charged o follow Elminster and keep him safe."

Jatham raised an eyebrow. "May I ask why?"

The two Harpers exchanged a look. Belkram shrugged. The one who set us this duty told us it was the most im-ortant task in the Realms. Elminster of Shadowdale nust live—or, I fear, even gods will fall."

In the shocked silence that followed, the two young nen saluted their fellows-in-arms with raised blades, odded a special farewell to Gedaern, and without hesi-ation marched out over the cesspool.

In midstep above the mire, with all eyes on them, they anished. Itharr and Belkram were tired, hurt, and walking into unknown danger. But they strode ahead without pause, for they were Harpers.

* * * * *

Spellgard was tall and dark and gloomy. Mushrooms and luminescent mosses grew here and there about its empty stone chambers. There was no sign of life. Even the torn, dusty cobwebs seemed to have been spun long ago by spiders now vanished. Yet there was a curious presence about the place, a silent, waiting feel as if something unseen were watching. They went on in silence.

Room after room was empty save for little heaps of collapsed wood, gilt, and stone where furniture had fallen before relentless passing years. Here and there, the archmage without magic and the lady Knight found the scars of battle: scorched, blackened areas on the walls and floor, shattered stone panels, and buckled flagstones. This strife had happened long ago. Mold, moss, dust, and rot overlaid all. Elminster shook his head from time to time as they went on through the silent, waiting castle. Silence reigned.

* * * * *

The Zhentarim thieves were trained, experienced men. Gloomy ruins did not begin to test their nerves. They spread out, slim black-bladed swords ready in their hands, and moved slowly forward, watching and listening intently, making no more noise than a faint breeze. Behind them, Zalarth tried not to make too much noise as he followed.

The brightest archway opening out of the high-ceilinged hall led into a smaller chamber. It was thickly grown with gray-green glowing moss, and dark stalks of mushrooms half the height of a man reared up in the corners. The men peered all around the room carefully, paying special attention to the ceiling, before they proceeded through it, avoiding all the growing things, to the archway beyond.

It led into another chamber, smaller still. A large, smooth-carved, unadorned stone table leaned in the center of this room, one leg crumbling. Beyond the table were two arches—and someone standing facing them!

Or some*thing*. It was tall and very thin, clad in dark and dusty robes. Its face was skull-like and white, its eyes dark sockets.

A lich! Or perhaps just an illusion, a trap laid by Elminster—or even by Avaerl. The men cast glances back at Zalarth. In calm silence he gestured, making the Brotherhood's hand signs for "advance" and "beware." In cautious unison they approached.

The figure moved. Something tinkled to the stone floor, falling and rolling. An unmistakable sound: coins. Another trap-lure, or just a pocket collapsing in the rotting garment of something that should be in a grave, not on its feet?

They were close enough now to see the figure was—or had been—female. Long gray-white hair framed a withered, dead face. As Zalarth watched, a chill spread icy fingers along his spine. Two points of glittering light, deep in the dark eye sockets, were expanding rapidly.

As the Zhentarim wizard tensed to lash out with a spell, the skeletal figure spoke. "Well met and welcome, adventurers. Put aside your weapons and speak with me in peace, if you would. I mean no harm. I've waited so very long for someone to find me."

More looks. Zalarth gave the "weapons out and ready" sign and asked calmly, "Who—or what—are you, and what place is this?"

"I am Saharel, and this is my home. The years have been no kinder to me than to Netheril itself, but I still abide here. Who are you?" The voice was feminine and dry, as loud as Zalarth's own, and held a trace of pride.

Once-beautiful long hair, now a mold-covered, wild mane of gray and white, clung to the shriveled, half-skeletal travesty of a face as the figure bent forward.

In answer, Zalarth began the ugly syllables of a spell to control undead.

The figure scowled and said sharply, "Now is that

friendly? What do you here? Are you come merely to plunder?"

She waved a skeletal hand, and a thief more frightened than the rest hurled his knife.

The figure watched the blade whirl through the air at her, and raised a hand with sudden speed to protect her face. The knife tore through the wasted flesh to lodge between two bones in the forearm. The figure raised her arm to study it.

"So you would bring death to me, where the gods failed? Die, fools, and despoil my home no longer!"

The figure gestured. Purple and black bolts of magic spat from each bony finger, streaking unerringly across the chamber to smite the thieves.

His spell done, Zalarth watched aghast as his men shrieked, stiffened, and died. The lich—if it was a lich—was ignoring his magic, and he could feel no ties of Art to give him power over it.

"What are you, that you defy my Art?" he asked, one hand darting to the other.

The undead lights of her eyes regarded him coldly. "An archlich. Apologize, if you would live."

"I'm sorry indeed to have met with you," Zalarth said from the depths of his heart, and turned the ring he wore.

Abruptly he was elsewhere, back in the great hall he'd first entered when coming through the gate. He ran then, ran as he had not done for years, feet pounding on the stones. Headlong down a dark passage, up a stair, through a weirdly lit, moss-choked gallery, and up another stair.

It opened onto a landing that led to another ascending stair on one hand and an archway on the other—an archway that opened onto a balcony overlooking another large hall. What ruin was this? It was huge, and— He glanced over the edge of the balcony, stopped, and stood very still.

In the room below stood Elminster of Shadowdale, the ranger Knight at his side. Her sword was drawn, and he held a wand. Both were facing that young fool Avaerl.

"Die, old fool," Avaerl taunted the bearded, battered old man, a wand glowing in the young mage's hand. "Die by the order of Manshoon, Lord Most High of the Zhentarim! Die at the hand of Avaerl of Sembresh!"

Sharantyr drew and hurled a dagger in one smooth, lashing movement and charged after it, leaping over small piles of rubble. "I think he's trying to talk us to death, Old Mage!" she cried, raising her blade.

Avaerl howled and clutched at his slashed fingers, the wand falling as the dagger spun away into the gloom. Sharantyr raced toward him, hair streaming behind her.

Lightning flashed and cracked from a balcony above, outlining her in blue-white dancing death. She staggered, groaned loudly, and fell to her knees.

Zalarth stared across at the balcony whence the bolt had come, then swiftly ducked low and moved far aside from where he had been standing.

Cold laughter came from the dimness that had spawned the lightning. "Not so threatening now, are you, Sharantyr?"

The speaker moved to the low, broad stone balcony rail and stared down triumphantly. "And so it is by the hand of Xanther that the famous Elminster shall perish!"

The old man had moved forward involuntarily as the lady ranger was struck. He stopped now, amid the rubble, and sighed. "If ye knew just how many times I've heard that line down the years—and mind, mageling, Manshoon himself has said it, twice, and I'm still standing for all his empty boasting!"

Xanther snarled and aimed his wand. Elminster calmly took out his pipe and sucked on it.

Lighting flashed, but Elminster was suddenly elsewhere. He appeared out of empty air on the balcony just behind Xanther, pipe glowing in his hand, and calmly tipped the councillor forward over the rail.

Xanther had time for the raw beginnings of a scream as he plunged—just before he struck the raised edge of a shattered stone table that rose out of the rubble like the edge of a giant's shield.

It was old and gray and very, very hard. The sharp

sounds of Xanther's bones shattering echoed loudly in the hall. His body bounced limply and then hung motionless atop the table. Rivers of dark blood ran swiftly down the stone.

"Shar! Shar, do ye live?" Elminster called, his voice trembling.

The lady ranger lay still in the dust, but the Zhentarim she'd not managed to reach snarled a word and pointed an angry hand at Elminster.

Magic missiles flashed through the air. The Old Mage sighed, cursed, and sat down on the balcony floor to await them. Their strike shook his body, and he grunted in pain.

Zalarth Bloodbrow smiled savagely and cast a fireball grandly but carefully, onto that balcony.

Its flash and roar shook the hall, and Zalarth reached for the teleport ring he wore. The she-lich could hardly fail to hear that. He had to snatch some proof of Elminster's demise—whatever was left, he supposed—and hie himself back to Manshoon before she came.

Under his boots, the stones were still hot. Roiling dust and smoke curled in the air. Zalarth searched all about, coughing and waving smoke away, but look as he might, he could find no sign of Elminster.

He heard a thud below and struggled to the rail to see Elminster standing over the fallen Avaerl, pipe in one hand and a bloodied chunk of stone in the other. "That's for what ye did to the lass," the old man told the slumped mageling severely before he scurried to the fallen ranger, did something, and was gone again.

Zalarth frowned and reached for his own ring. Two could play this game.

He chose another balcony, stared at it until he'd seen it clearly, and turned the ring on his finger.

From this height, the broken body of the councillor looked like a sprawled toy. Zalarth looked around hastily. Except for some mushrooms, he was alone. Behind him dark archways led off to unknown chambers. The wizard crouched, drawing a wand from its sheath on his thigh, and peered over the balcony rail.

There! On another balcony, below and across the hall, stood Elminster. The Old Mage of Shadowdale was puffing his pipe into life and looking down into the hall.

He'd manage no last-breath escape this time. Zalarth held the wand up and ready as he turned the ring again.

Abruptly his view of the hall changed to include Elminster, two steps away, raising sardonic eyebrows above his pipe. An instant later, the old man was gone, and Zalarth's wand spat death at empty air.

Zalarth choked off his snarl of anger as he saw the she-bitch through an archway, striding up a broad stair toward him. His wand spoke again, but she only smiled and shook her head as the wand's magic was turned away by an unseen shield in front of her. She raised a clawlike hand, and Zalarth desperately twisted his ring as he looked over the balcony rail.

The ring took him there, to the floor of the hall, in the shifting rubble. In a breath or two she'd be hurling spells down at him, to say nothing of what Elminster might do. He had only an instant to choose a new destination.

Unfortunately, the mageling was rising up in front of him like an awakened zombie, face streaming blood. Wild eyes met Zalarth's, and bloody lips parted in surprise.

"Master Zalarth! How come you h—?"

Zalarth snarled in frustration. The wand crackled, and Avaerl of Sembresh stiffened, sobbed, and buckled at the knees.

"Gulkuth," he whispered hoarsely, with his last breath, raising a faltering hand. "Gulkuth!" And then he crashed on his face and lay still. Dust curled up around him.

Zalarth shrugged. Gulkuth? A spell? He looked through the nearest archway, reaching for his ring. At any moment rending magic could rain down on him from above.

Something stirred under his feet, and the Zhentarim staggered and almost fell. He looked back.

Sharantyr was struggling to her knees, feeling for her sword. Dust caked her wild-tangled hair and the side of her face, and her eyes were bright with pain—but a ring

gleamed brightly on her finger, and she was rising, stee
in hand.

She meant his death. Zalarth's wand came up and he
said coldly, "It is always a pleasure to destroy a Knight o:
Myth Drannor. Die, bitch!"

"Excuse me," said a calm new voice from very close by
and Zalarth felt his elbow struck sharply. His aim was
driven wide; the wand's power smote a stone wall harm
lessly.

"Met are we, mage of the Zhentarim," another voice
said formally, "and the pleasure, I assure you, is all ours."

"Aye. Farewell, tyrant mage," the first voice said, and
Zalarth Bloodbrow scarce had time to look from one
grimly smiling speaker to another before two long swords
passed each other in his chest, sliding in with silken ease
and leaving a sudden rising burning in their wake, a
burning worse than anything he'd ever felt.

Zalarth felt himself falling, falling with mouth open
but no breath left to speak, hands open but with nothing
to grab. He stared hard into the rising white mists that
had not been there an instant ago, and sank forever into
the nothingness beyond them.

"Best chop off that finger, there. There's no telling
what Zhent rings will do, and I'd hate to have to kill this
one four or five times," Belkram said briskly. Itharr nod
ded, looking all around.

"Where's Elminster gotten t—ah, there!" He pointed.

Belkram looked up to the balcony where the Old Mage
was unconcernedly puffing on his pipe. Elminster wave
to them lazily.

The two Harpers shouted in horror. Behind Elminster
a bone-white face had appeared, a gleam in its dark eye
sockets and a widening grin stretching its ghastly jaw
Long, skeletal arms reached for the Old Mage, and there
was nothing—utterly nothing—that Itharr or Belkram
or Sharantyr coming unsteadily to her feet beside them
could do.

Sharantyr threw back her head in despair, and
screamed. "Mystra, aid us all!"

23
Until Magic Do Us Part

"And so it ends," Manshoon said in disgust, turning away from the glowing scrying bowl. "As always . . . mages of the Brotherhood cut down by sword-swinging louts because they're too foolish, or arrogant, or set on their course with no wits to spare for looking around them. This bodes ill for us all. Time and time again we suffer these embarrassments. If the Brotherhood does not triumph in such little things, we will surely fail and be swept away and forgotten."

Silent faces looked back at him, Anaithe's among them. Fear was written plainly on all—in dark eyes, sweat upon temples, and lips that trembled in their hard set. The Lord Most High looked around at them all in long, sour silence. In sudden rage he turned, robes swirling, to snatch down a staff from where it floated in the air above.

"This is too important to ignore," he snapped. "Elminster's carrying greater power in him now than I've ever felt in any being. Left alone, he is a great danger to us, and if we can seize what he holds, none will be able to stand against us. Guard this place well in my absence, Belaghar, or you will pay the price."

"But, my lord," the wizard called Belaghar protested, waving a hand toward the bowl. "Is this wise? The Brotherhood needs your leadership now more than . . . ever . . . and, if . . . you . . . sh . . ." His words slowed and finally died to silence under the cold weight of Manshoon's venomous gaze.

"Think you I am a fool?" the lord of the Brotherhood asked coldly. "Do I seem likely to be thrown down by any of those"—he stretched a long finger toward the glowing waters of the bowl—"as two minor magelings were? If it so seems to you, then it is you, Belaghar, who are the fool."

He strode to a certain archway in the shadowed gloom, then slowed, turned, and added with dark humor, "Gain wisdom, Brother, while I am gone, if you would hold your place among us."

He looked around slowly at the other mages in the room and added softly, "All of you know, I think, what sort of torment will befall you if any treachery or misjudgments occur in my absence. It would be prudent to see that no such unfortunate supervenities greet me upon my return." He stared at them for two long, silent breaths and added, almost in a whisper, "And I *shall* return."

The lord of the Brotherhood made a certain sign in the air before him, and a beholder that had hung invisible over the bowl until now faded slowly into view, its dark eyestalks coiling and writhing menacingly.

Manshoon made a slight bow in its direction and said, "Watch well, Quysszt, as you always do. You have my permission to act freely to keep things here as we have agreed." He smiled slowly, turned away, then looked back and added, "Guard yourself, my love." It was unclear if he addressed the silent, white-faced Anaithe or the beholder looming low above her head. The High Lord of Zhentil Keep favored the wizards with a calm, deadly look and went out.

The sigh of men letting out long-held breaths was audible all over the room. A moment later, it was underlaid by the deep, dry humming few men hear and live long enough, thereafter, to tell of: the sound of a beholder chuckling.

As the sound grew, the gathered Zhentarim suddenly recalled various urgent tasks and concerns that required their immediate presence elsewhere. The room emptied in almost undignified haste.

The eye tyrant's mottled body descended slowly into the glowing water of the bowl, and the sound it made deepened into the gentle, steady humming of contentment.

A rat scuttling across a far corner of the room stopped,

amazed, at the sound. An eyestalk turned its way almost lazily, and the dark rodent was plucked into the air. It soared helplessly into the gigantic, crooked, many-toothed maw of the monster, which opened to receive it. With a grunt of satisfaction, the beholder settled into the water and rolled.

When it rose up, dripping, it began to indulge itself in one of its favorite amusements: spitting the bones of prey at nearby targets.

Nearby stood a lifelike statue of a nude woman holding an oil bowl over her head. Whispers among the Brotherhood that this brazier was a captured slave turned to stone were supported by the expression of terror on the openmouthed stone face. Quyssztellan turned slightly in the air above the bowl, and the rat's freshly bared skull struck that mouth with such force that the bone shattered into dust and fragments.

The beholder chuckled again and chose another target.

* * * * *

"Where will it all end?" Nouméa's voice was anguished. "And why was I ever chosen as Magister? I am too weak for this. Mystra needs a war leader among archmages now, not my feeble powers and doubting."

The tall, slim, conical column of silvery gray light beside her emitted what could only be called a mind-sigh. Its mental voice echoed in her head.

Ye were chosen, and the Lady is seldom mistaken. Thy kindness and care will be much needed in time soon to come. After the destroyers lash out, the harder task must follow: rebuilding, so that the next destroyer will have something to work upon. The silvery cone flickered, and tiny motes of light drifted about within it. *Be of stout heart, Lady Magister. We shall all have need of thee.*

Nouméa brushed long hair back out of her face for perhaps the six thousandth time since the Lady had fallen silent. "But how can I fight Manshoon? I have not his power, nor his—ruthlessness. I was not made to slay or lay cruel Art upon anyone."

Ye will do what ye must, as we all do. And soon ye must curb Manshoon. He grows ever more powerful, and there are no gods to gainsay him. Azuth's mind-voice sounded grim, resolute. *Have ye not understood what we have seen of his doings?*

The Magister swallowed and nodded. "That spell he devised, it urges on wildness in Art. When he casts it on mages or their spells, their Art is more likely to go awry and destroy them, or bring harm to them through the anger and fear of others."

And so, daughter of Art: what must ye do?

Nouméa brushed hair back from her face again and drew herself erect. Her skin had turned the color of fresh-fallen snow, but her face was set in determined lines. "I must fight Manshoon." She stared into the darkness around them for a moment, looking regal and serene in her power. Then she turned to the silver-hued cone and seemed to crumple.

Trembling, she whispered, "Lord Azuth, I am afraid."

Afraid? Of Art?

"No," Nouméa gasped into the silvery light, "I'm afraid that when I strike with Art, I'll find . . . I enjoy it."

If ye do, does that give thee the license to do nothing, Lady Magister?

The slim maiden shook her head. "Against gods, I cannot act. Against runaway mages, I *must* act."

The silvery cone that was all that was left of the Lord of Mages sent her a warm, comforting mind-touch of agreement and satisfaction. Nouméa embraced it suddenly, weeping. Where her tears fell on the warm, electric softness of the glowing cone, tiny winking lights were born.

* * * * *

Laeral watched the delicately fluted wineglass float silently and smoothly toward her. When it paused before her, she thanked it gravely. Lathlamber sparkled and glowed within. She smiled, and her slender fingers closed gently around the warm crystal.

"Lord?" she called softly, knowing he who sent it must be near. In answer, the table grew a fluid, shifting wooden hand, reached out to her leg, and scratched her . . . just on the itch where her boot tops always chafed. Laeral purred contentedly and sighed, "Oh, Khel—I do love you."

"I know it," came a quiet reply from her feet. The grave face of the Lord Mage of Waterdeep rose out of the floor and ascended steadily as his body floated up through the solid, polished obsidian slabs.

Laeral's dark, beautiful eyes widened for an instant over the wineglass. Then they crinkled into a smile of pure pleasure. "You never cease to amaze me," she said lightly, set down the glass, and threw her arms about him.

They embraced, there in an upper room of Blackstaff Tower, kissing in fondness and then in passion. After fiercely embracing one another for a time, they loosed and studied each other, and sighed as one.

"More bad news, Lord?" Laeral asked, knowing her lord and love well, and reading in his face more than he ever thought it showed.

Khelben nodded, unsmiling. "Chaos grows across the Realms. Beasts not seen in an age swarm over the land, roaming even into the streets of large cities like Iriaebor and Crimmor. Brigands and all manner of orcs, drow, and goblinkin are on the move, raiding, and from everywhere come reports of religious fanatics burning, slaying, and inciting others to open war. The gods themselves are walking Faerûn, destroying this and ordering that—and always, Art grows wilder, less reliable, more savage and apt to have unforeseeable effects."

Laeral nodded. "So much has been apparent for some days, Lord. Yet I sense a darker shadow. Unburden yourself, please. We work better together than when one of us broods alone."

Khelben smiled. "I apologize . . . I can see myself when you speak so. Well, then, my dark thoughts are bent on Manshoon of the Zhentarim. He has set to work in all this fright and wild worry to develop a spell that augments the wild effects of other spells. He's been using this dark magic to turn the Art of foes back on them, or to bring harm through the wild effects of twisted spells."

Laeral nodded, her eyes large and dark. "So I have heard from two sources, now. You have seen him work this?"

Khelben nodded grimly. "It is high time, and past time, that we dealt with the Black Master of the Zhentarim, whatever the cost to us. I think I shall begin preparations."

Laeral reached for him. "The danger! Especially now, when our Art is needed to protect and defend, and this wildness of magic aids his dark spells."

Khelben nodded again. "I know all this, and yet it is a responsibility I cannot evade longer. If Nouméa were more . . . warlike, the task is rightfully hers. But time passes, and his power grows, and she acts not. So . . ."

Laeral managed a smile. "If you go up against the Dread Lord," she said quietly, "do not deny me room to stand at your side."

Khelben came toward her then, opening his arms to her embrace. "No," he said quietly, "that one thing at least I have learned in our years together. I will not try to keep you from the fray, or tell you what is wisest and safest, or try to shield you. I love you too much, Lady, to so insult you anymore."

A thought then came to him, one he'd had several times before. Nothing in all Faerûn tasted so sweet as one of his Lady Laeral's kisses.

*　*　*　*　*

Long, skeletal arms went around the Old Mage. He took his pipe out of his mouth as he saw them come into view, turned smoothly within their tightening embrace, and said, "Ah, it *is* you. Well met, my lady."

Then, without a trace of repugnance, he leaned forward and kissed the tattered skin and bared bone and teeth of the undead thing's grinning mouth.

"Oh, Elminster," came a loud, dry voice in reply. "The

years have dealt with you far more kindly than they have with me."

"Not by my Art," Elminster said gently, and his tone was sad. "I am as you see me now by the grace of Lady Mystra—and it is not, I must tell you, entirely a blessing."

"Live by your charm, Old Spellhurler," came the wry response, "and die by it."

Elminster chuckled, then seemed to remember the shocked audience below. "Excuse me," he asked, "but do you mind if I introduce you to my companions?"

"Not at all, El. They are welcome in my home."

Elminster bowed to her as if he faced a queenly lady and not a mold-covered, half-skeletal horror clad in rotten rags. Then he turned and looked down over the balcony rail.

Three silent, openmouthed, wide-eyed folk stood with blades wavering in their hands, looking up and obviously not knowing what else to do.

"Will ye come up?" Elminster asked. "I'd like ye to meet the Lady Saharel, queen in this, her castle of Saharelgard."

The undead lady came to stand at his shoulder and beckoned them with a smile. It looked ghastly, but its warmth was evident in her tone. "You may as well call it Spellgard, El. I've heard that name often down the years and become used to it. I think I'm even starting to like the name. Terribly pretentious, if I'd laid it upon this crumbling pile of mine, but rather impressive when bestowed out of fear by someone else."

She leaned over the rail, her wild, gray-white hair trailing forward. "Come up, yes. Please come up, and excuse the mess and general . . . decay. I've not the skill at Art or practical knowledge to keep my home in good repair. Moreover, I sleep much of the time, and when I wake I half expect to find that the whole thing has come down on top of me and I'm buried under my own folly . . . not an unusual fate for wizards, I'm told."

Elminster winced. "Ye haven't changed," he complained.

"Oh, no? Tell that to my mirror, the only one I haven't

broken in rage over the years. I was beautiful once."

As Belkram, Itharr, and Sharantyr came hesitantly up the stairs, weapons sheathed, they saw Elminster draw the gaunt, long-haired lady to him. Her bared bones clung to his old arms.

"Ye still are, Saharel," he said, "when I look at you, and not merely what's left of your skin." After a moment he grinned and added, "Didn't I tell thee, once? Ye have beautiful bones."

The undead lady in his arms sighed loudly and swung her skull-like face toward Sharantyr. "He hasn't changed much, has he?"

Despite herself, Sharantyr came to a halt, but she managed a smile and said, "If you mean he was prone to shameless flattery and leering ways, when first you knew him, Lady—no, he has not."

Then she forced herself to step forward and sketched a court salute, that archaic bob of one lady to another.

Saharel shuddered. "*That* didn't catch on, did it?" Then she put bony fingers to her mouth. "Forgive me, Lady," she said, quickly. "I did not mean to offend . . . I have had few visitors of thy gentle nature, and am somewhat out of practice at common courtesies. Pray accept my apology."

"Lady," Sharantyr said haltingly, "none is needed."

The undead sorceress turned to Elminster and poked him sharply in the ribs. "Well, Spellhurler? I've never known your tongue to be so laggard before! You said you'd introduce us, and here I am speaking to a charming young lady and know not her name. What manner of gallant are you?"

"No gallant, Lady," Elminster said in an affected mock-courtier's voice, "but, I fear, a rogue."

"Words more true were never uttered," Belkram said to Itharr in a whisper loud enough to be heard all over the vast hall.

Elminster's glare was lost in the mingled, tinkling laughter of Sharantyr and Saharel. The Old Mage sighed loudly, looked up at the ceiling (which offered him no visible support or even agreement), and said, "May I present the Lady Saharel, Sorceress of Saharelgard, of the

High Mages of Netheril?" He knelt, and lifted his hand to indicate the undead sorceress. "The Lady Saharel!" he declaimed grandly.

The two Harpers bowed solemnly and Sharantyr repeated her salute. Elminster rose between them and said to Saharel, "Good lady, I present to you three distinguished adventurers of the sword. Firstly, the Lady Sharantyr of Shadowdale, Knight of Myth Drannor."

Saharel stepped forward to lay a hand over Sharantyr's. The bones were cold, smooth, and hard but patted her fingers reassuringly. "Try not to mind my looks," came the dry voice. "I would be your friend." Then she added, "I am glad to hear that Myth Drannor flourishes."

"Well, actually," Elminster said rather sheepishly, "it does not. It lies in ruin, but the Fair Folk have recently withdrawn from the elven court, and this brave lady is one of a band who have dedicated themselves to guarding the city from those who would pillage it, and to rebuilding its glory someday."

"So how come you here?" Saharel asked, gazing at Sharantyr.

The ranger sighed and said, "I came to guard *him*." She pointed at Elminster.

"Guard?" The undead lady, obviously astonished, turned to look at Elminster. "From me?"

"Ah, no—no," Elminster said. "It's a delicate matter. Oh, gods blast, ye may as well know it, too." He straightened up. "The gods walk Faerûn, Saharel, even as we speak. They are thrown down among us by a greater power, and much of their might stripped from them. By Mystra's will I hold much of her power, and the carrying of it has stripped from me the use of my own Art. I can't conjure up even a hand-glow . . . and I must survive, to pass on what I hold to Mystra or to some mysterious successor she spoke of."

He sighed and then grinned. "It's all rather a mess, I suppose."

"And *I* suppose," Saharel said archly, "you're going to try to pretend to me that you had no part in causing all this?"

"Ah, indeed," Elminster replied. "For once."

Two twinkling lights rolled in the skull's empty eye sockets, a sight that made Sharantyr and the Harpers burst into helpless laughter. The glowing eyes came down to fix themselves on the two young men, whose laughter rapidly died away under the eerie scrutiny.

"And who are these two loud, handsome young men?"

"These are Itharr and Belkram," Elminster said with a grand gesture, "of the Harpers."

"Oh, so *that* caught on, did it? Welcome, gentle sirs, welcome."

"That?" Itharr asked, guessing what she meant.

At the same time Belkram said, "Lady, we have come here from the High Dale by means of a magical gate, to defend Elminster. We have been given to understand that his survival, and that of the Realms entire, are one and the same."

"Well, ye don't have to be so melodramatic about it, lad," Elminster said testily. "It's not the first time around for me at this, ye know."

"What?" the ranger and the two Harpers erupted, more or less together.

"Oh, no," Saharel said, obviously enjoying this. "But come. Let us find a place where there's furniture left to sit on in some comfort—the Fountain Hall, perhaps, so you can drink your fill. This one, at least"—she poked the Old Mage again—"is apt to flap his jaw so much he gets thirsty."

"Besides," the undead mistress of Spellgard added as she led the way from the balcony along a narrow, dark hall, waving aside cobwebs, and down a crumbling stair, "there are things I must tell you before I grow tired of your fearful looks, you young three. I'm an archlich, not one of your evil lichnee. I don't eat people, or chill the life from them, or steal their spells or souls, or suchlike. It's quite safe to touch me."

"Aye," Elminster agreed absently. Saharel favored him with a look. Elminster's companions all saw it, in the darkness, by the light the archlich had begun to shed. Her hair and white flesh seemed to glow with a faint silvery radiance.

They noticed another curious thing. As Saharel walked along, her arm now linked with Elminster's, she seemed to grow more substantial with each passing breath. Her silvery skin seemed to expand into the smooth curves of a tall, beautiful woman. Her face now seemed almost whole, and her eyes more the orbs of a living maiden than two weird, twinkling lights in the empty eye sockets of a skull.

"If I may ask," Sharantyr ventured as they turned into a rubble-strewn gallery and walked on over the fallen, dusty ruins of arched double doors into a darker chamber, "what did that look mean, Lady? Or is it something private between you?"

The archlich, who swept along like a silvery beacon in the gloom before her, looked back. "It was, once. This old rogue of yours had the temerity to break my defensive spells and walk in upon me one night. In time, we . . . came to be lovers."

One silvery hand, not quite all flesh yet, stroked Elminster's cheek. Itharr shivered despite himself as they strode on in the darkness, and his hand crept to the hilt of his sword.

"It seemed the best way to end our rivalry," Elminster murmured.

Saharel laughed. "So calculating, Old Spellhurler? You seemed rather . . . warmer, at the time."

Elminster came to a sudden halt. Three swords grated out of their scabbards in response, but Saharel scarce had time to look her reproach their way before Elminster swept her into a tight embrace and kissed her. The tensely watching Sharantyr reflected, with sudden rueful amazement, that this is what bards meant when they sang "kissed deep, and with passion." Their lips met and clung, and Saharel began to moan and murmur in Elminster's embrace, and move against him, her tall body swaying.

Itharr coughed loudly and said to Belkram, "Did you notice, back in the dale, that the price of potatoes was a full two coppers above what the merchants were selling them for in Shadowdale?"

"Aye," Belkram agreed brightly. "That I did, and commented on the fact to one shopkeeper. A bad harvest, he told me, and higher transportation costs. They ship entire wagonloads of manure up from Sembia, you know, to dress their fallow fields."

"Wagonloads? Sembia has that to spare?"

"Well, all those people, crowded together in the coastal cities. It can't all flow out to sea, you know. When the gratings and sewers and all back right up, they set to work with shovels, and start thinking of the High Dale. Then, of c—"

"Do you gentle sirs mind?" Elminster asked testily. "You're worse than Azoun's jesters! I'd like to kiss my old friend a time or two in dignified silence . . . *if* it's not too much trouble."

Three mouths opened to reply, but their chance was forever swept away from them in the tumult that abruptly followed.

The floor ahead of them erupted into a rising pillar of red, swirling flames—flames that wailed with the tortured voices of unseen men. The room shook, and dust and small stones fell from the unseen ceiling above.

Three swords flashed back reflected firelight before blue-white, blinding lightning spat out of the pillar and snaked three long, frighteningly fast fingers out to kiss the drawn steel.

Three swords blazed with cold fire, and three throats screamed in agony. Dazed and burned, scarcely clinging to life, Sharantyr and the two Harpers dropped their smoking weapons, staggered, and fell.

Deep laughter roared and echoed from the flames, and a voice that boomed around the chamber bellowed, "Ah, but it feels good indeed to fell those dear to you, Elminster of Shadowdale! I'll make you suffer before I steal the very wits from you!"

"Manshoon!" Elminster said in disgust to the archlich in his arms. "He'll never grow up, I fear. All this grand voice and needless cruelty . . . like a small child playing at being a wizard."

"A small child, Elminster, is what you'll be," the booming voice continued, an edge of anger in it now, "after I send a mindworm into your mouth to eat its way up into your brain and steal all your thoughts, to make them mine!"

Elminster made a rude sound and waggled his fingers in a certain old gesture much used by small children everywhere. Gently he disengaged himself from Saharel and took out his pipe.

A bolt of lightning snatched it away from him.

"Oh, no, you don't, 'Old Mage.' I watched you earlier. Think yourself clever, don't you, with your rings and your spheres and your little pipe? Stumbling along from droll little joke to impressive little phrase, hiding your lost Art behind cryptic words and wands that are almost drained now, aren't they? What a feeble fool you've become! Scarce worth my taking on the spells to defeat you." As the great voice rolled across the room, the faint cries in the flames died away. Manshoon's cruel magic had drained the last life energy from certain unwitting Zhentarim mages—those he deemed his most powerful rivals —all over Faerûn. Their energies had brought him here to triumph. The flames drifted nearer and grew brighter. "You can't trick me, Elminster. And you can't hope to stand against my magic. This is the end of you, finally. The defeat and utter destruction of the much-vaunted Elminster at the hands of the Zhentarim he hates so much. At the hands of Manshoon."

There followed much laughter. Sharantyr, lying in darkness with the healing ring Elminster had put there earlier glinting on her finger and the stench of her burned hair heavy in her nostrils, heard it faintly as she struggled back to consciousness.

"You won't trick me as you did Bellwind. I'll take your power and your knowledge both, through the worm, and not link our minds. You cannot escape, Elminster. You are doomed."

"Oh, no," came a soft reply. "Doom will come here, indeed, but I believe you have mistaken the being who will fall."

Not far from the shaken, smoldering Old Mage stood the archlich, tall and erect, a silvery glow around her wasted, bony form. She stood proud and fearless, and from her outstretched hands streams of silver radiance erupted, arcing toward the pillar of flame.

"That is not your only mistake, Manshoon," the soft voice continued. "Your first was coming uninvited into my home. Here, my power is supreme."

The silvery radiance was expanding into a gigantic shield of light, englobing the flames. Bolts of lightning and great blades of shimmering white force sprang out of the fiery pillar, but the silver glow absorbed them, growing ever larger and stronger. The very air crackled with power.

"Your second and greatest mistake, Manshoon," Saharel continued calmly, "was in daring to attack my beloved, a man who is also my guest and thus under my protection. And your third, if you must speak of fools at Art, was to so dismiss his magic—and mine."

Silver radiance shrouded the flames now and hid them from view. The light grew and grew until it seemed like the moon itself shone in the chamber. Saharel stood like a small, silvery flame, flickering at the base of it all. Her voice wavered with her light and came more faintly.

"It is given to every archlich to choose his or her passing, and to spend all the force of life and love and Art in a task. Mine is thy death, Manshoon."

The silvery shroud grew suddenly blinding in its brightness. On the floor, Belkram cried out and covered his eyes.

"Remember me, El! Remember me!" came the archlich's wavering voice.

"Aye," Elminster said, through sudden tears. "I shall never forget thee, Saharel.

There was a sudden sigh, perhaps of satisfaction, and the light winked out.

Somewhere across the room, amid faint, fading silvery motes, the bare bones of Manshoon fell to the floor with a clatter.

Elminster watched them shatter and crumble, and

stared at the last silvery motes until darkness came again.

Then he said roughly, "I can never forget thee, Saharel. So I will remember thee . . . with honor."

His voice caught, and when it returned, it was bleak. "Along with the others. All the others."

He stood in lonely silence among his fallen companions for a long time.

Of Saharel of Spellgard, no trace was left. Sharantyr could see clearly again long before she was able to move, and she saw the glistening spot on the stones in front of the Old Mage, the spot that grew and grew with each tear that fell.

Then there was a sudden burst of light behind her—warm, golden light, like sunlight.

Elminster turned a face wet with tears toward the light before Sharantyr could. Upon his face she saw a look of recognition, then of pleasure, then of faint exasperation. His voice, when it came, was calm and gentle, as though he'd just looked up from a soothing book while at ease beside his beloved pool.

"Nouméa," he said, "why must ye always be just a little too late?"

* * * * *

Elsewhere, deep and dark, something stirred in musty gloom. A hand slid out from under a shroud thick with dust, pushing the fabric aside, and took up the rod it knew would be there. The rod of rulership. Just in case.

The hidden crypt was dark, its air stale and bad, but only a few steps were needed to cross to its door, pull down the ornate handle, and shove hard.

Thick wax broke and fell away in crumbled ruin, and light flooded in. A startled man in black armor turned with a curse, hands darting for a scabbarded sword.

The hand that did not hold the rod shot out of the darkness and closed around the man's throat before that blade could be drawn. A slow, cold voice said, "You know my orders. You are never to be without a weapon in your hand. Seal up this place again and await the doom I shall pronounce on you. After dinner."

The speaker released the man, heard him fall to his knees with a strangled cough, and strode on. The cobbles ahead rose up in a long ramp toward the sun and the streets of the city above. He was halfway up the ramp when the guard far behind him managed to call hoarsely, "Yes, Dread Lord. Your will be done."

He did not look back.

The streets of Zhentil Keep were crowded. The weather was fair and trade brisk. Startled looks were many, but even the thickest crowds parted or melted away, as if by magic, at his approach.

Manshoon strode steadily across the city toward the Tower High. This long walk in dusty garments meant that his enemies—accursed Elminster doubtless among them—had won. Again.

The black-robed, dark-eyed Lord Archmage of Zhentil Keep checked then, half turning to look back. Had there been other bodies—more waiting Manshoons—lying in the crypt beside him? How many times had he made this walk?

How many more times would he make it, in seasons and years and ages to come? And would it ever seem less lonely?

24
The Void, Love, and Doom

Gentle hands touched her shoulder. Sharantyr stopped her agonized struggle to sit up and sagged back thankfully into the comfort of those hands. Looking up, she saw Elminster's old, bearded face looking down at her, lined with compassion.

She moved her lips, found them very dry, and managed to ask, "Do I look that bad, Old Mage?"

Elminster smiled then. It came slowly but stretched his face with pleasure for a long time before he said, "Well, ye are certainly better than I'd feared, lass—Shar. Lie ye back awhile and rest. I need the ring that is healing ye now, to use on these two impetuous Harpers, or we may lose them."

Sharantyr managed a nod and smile, though pain still raged within her at every movement, and she felt weak and sick. Itharr and Belkram must feel far worse.

Elminster's slow, careful hands turned her on her side, pillowing her head on her arm, before he drew off the ring. Its loss left a cold tingling in that hand. Then slow waves of pain came from her other arm, her sword arm, where the wizard's bolt had burned.

"Lie easy, Shar. We've given Manshoon a death this day. Not his final one by any means, but he'll be a weak wizard for a time, and that is something."

Past the kneeling archmage, Sharantyr saw what was left of her sword—a half-melted, misshapen sliver of twisted metal. Her eyes went to Elminster's hand, where Manshoon's lightning had struck. She swallowed and looked away. The fingers handling her so gently were only ashy stumps.

Sudden tears blurred her sight, and she stared at the sword until she could see again. Beyond it stood Nouméa.

The Magister's face was happy as Elminster rose and turned toward her. "It's all right, Old Mage," she said. "I've used my magic on the two Harpers. They sleep, but they'll be fi—" She broke off, eyes widening in horror. She was staring at Elminster's burned hand.

Sharantyr felt fresh tears welling up in her eyes. The image of Nouméa's shocked, wounded face would be with her forever.

Nothing should ever happen, to make folk look like that.

A burning rage began to build in her, bringing a lump to her throat. "Manshoon," she snarled through her teeth, "one day you'll pay for Saharel and all the other pain you've caused, if I have to cut my way through an army of your lackeys to get to you. This I swear."

Elminster turned to look at her. His face wore surprise and anxiousness, and just a hint of pity.

Sharantyr lay there in rising pain and gasped, "Don't look at me like that, El. I can . . . protect myself. I—I can stay on my feet long enough to cut down Manshoon, when my chance comes."

Elminster just shook his head and knelt to put the ring of regeneration back on her finger. "Oh, Sharantyr," he said softly. "There are such better things to do with thy life than to waste it in ending his." He stroked her hair, as Nouméa came hesitantly closer. "I've lost Saharel—and others, before her—to him. Don't add thyself to his take. I need ye, lass."

He knelt then to kiss her cheek, and Sharantyr felt a wetness on her forehead as he straightened up again. A tear had fallen on her.

The Magister came to stand over them both. A blue-white glow was growing around her slim hands, and her eyes were very dark.

"Elminster," she said quietly, "I would heal thee, if I you would allow."

The Sage of Shadowdale peered up at her, beard bristling. He looked very old just then. "Do ye dare, Nouméa?" he asked. "The power I hold can be deadly to those who touch me with magic. One Zhent wizard died when he tried a stealspell on me."

He waved his charred hand at her. "Ye hold much of Our Lady's power. What if ye touch me with it and release what I hold? We could both be slain, and the Realms laid waste around us."

The Magister wavered, seeming a very frail and unsure young girl for a long breath.

Then she said, as quietly as before, "If that is the price, then let it be so. I would not want to live on as a mage if Mystra's power will let me topple towers, deal death, and blast apart peaks but not let me heal one I am honored to count as a friend, who has rendered this world such service as few understand and none I know can equal."

She faced him while Sharantyr clenched her hand around the familiar tingling of the ring and held her breath. Silence stretched.

Then Elminster thrust his charred hand toward her and said simply, "Thank you. Do it."

Nouméa stepped forward, extending her own hand. The blue-white glow around it grew stronger. She reached out slowly.

They touched, and the radiance was suddenly blinding. Sharantyr closed her eyes, shaking her head against the searing white light in her head.

She heard Nouméa gasp raggedly, then hiss in pain.

"Easy," Elminster rumbled, and Sharantyr heard the Magister moan in reply. She opened her eyes again but could see nothing.

She heard Nouméa stagger backward, and heard the panting breaths that followed.

"By Our Lady," the Magister said unsteadily, "but that was close, as close to disaster as I ever want to be. I never knew . . . Art could . . . hurt so much."

"I did," Elminster said, and Sharantyr heard pride in his voice as he added, "I am pleased, indeed, Lady, that ye stood so much pain and stuck to thy task."

He chuckled. "I also find it hard to be displeased that thy task was to make me whole."

The Magister laughed then, a little unsteadily, and said, "I don't know if I'm strong enough, after this, to go chasing Manshoon."

Elminster shook his head. "Don't waste thy Art. Ye are so much better at healing and aiding, Nouméa. Healers and helpers of power are so much rarer, in this and other worlds, than those who can rage and slay and lay waste with little effort. Manshoon will spend time now fending off rivals in his own Brotherhood who'll see his weakness as a chance to destroy or supplant him. Yet if ye go into Zhentil Keep after him, they'll all strike at thee for the glory and the power they'd hope to win. The Realms have only one of thee, but they seems to have an endless supply of evil, power-hungry magelings. Don't throw all away fighting them, for ye'd surely go down in the end."

Nouméa bowed her head. "You're right, I suppose. I have little love for war, and less skill at it." Sharantyr saw the movement; sight was coming slowly back to her.

"So I've noticed, a time or two," Elminster said dryly.

Nouméa looked up at him quickly through wildly disarranged hair, anguish in her eyes. "Have I made many mistakes, Old Mage? Should I know better how to deal with this wild magic? Am I worthy to serve Our Lady at all?"

"Ye have done well—better than almost all of thy predecessors I have known. The Art needs thy caring, not brilliance of invention at spellcraft, or a lot of cold-hearted scheming and vain, spectacular spellcasting," Elminster replied gravely. "Ye continue to surprise and please us, Lady Magister. Ye cannot help who ye are, and ye have dealt well with what ye now are. Don't try to change thyself. It never works, and will make thee as unhappy as those ye mistreat in the trying."

Nouméa beamed at him, damp-eyed but radiant. Then she sighed and said, "I must go, Elminster. There is so much to do. Art everywhere is awry. Without Mystra, all is in chaos. Hurry and give her power back to her, Old Mage."

"There is still a Mystra? Ye have spoken with her, then? Why has she not taken it, if she wants it?" Elminster asked sharply.

The Magister looked at him, her gentle face suddenly

terrible in its fear. "I fear she cannot. She dare not speak to thee, for fear something will reach through her to snatch at the power you hold." She walked across the chamber, searching for something, and seemed to find it.

Stopping, she looked up at him through her long hair and said urgently, "Be very careful, Old Mage. Our Lady depends on you, and I cannot stay to guard you."

Elminster chuckled. "So ladies always seem to say to me, just when I'm hoping they'll stay for a time. Go with my good wishes, Lady Magister."

Nouméa gave him an unsteady smile, stepped onto a stone that held a deep-graven rune, and vanished.

Elminster stared at where she'd been for a long time. Then he turned, looking old again, and walked across the floor to where Saharel had stood. He bent down in the darkness, and when he straightened again there was a pitiful, crumbling, charred skull in his hand.

The Old Mage looked at it, shook his head slightly, kissed it, and tucked it into his robe. Then he came back to Sharantyr. As he extended a hand to help her up, he managed a smile, but it faded quickly, leaving a face haunted by old memories and weariness.

"Old Mage?" she asked. "What now?"

"I know not," Elminster told her. "Where to run that other mages cannot follow? And who knows where the fallen gods may lurk in the Realms? If I meet with one, I cannot hope to survive any disagreement that may befall, and risk losing Mystra's power to the grasp of another. That, in turn, must not occur if the Realms as we know them are to weather this great storm."

He spread weary, empty hands, then suddenly brightened and hurried over to the rune Nouméa had found.

"Hah!" he said happily, and Sharantyr's heart leapt. He was confident again, and she felt safe once more.

"We can use this," Elminster said in satisfaction. "Rouse the two snoring beauties, will ye?"

Sharantyr chuckled, shook her head, and went over to the still forms of the Harpers.

* * * * *

Storm drew in a deep breath, let it out slowly, and smiled.

"Well?" Jhessail and Lhaeo asked together, across the table. "What happened?"

The bard closed her eyes, still smiling, and said, "Manshoon died. Elminster lives."

"Manshoon destroyed? Elminster's work?"

Storm shook her head. "He died, but he has worked at dark Art hidden since Netheril fell, and has other bodies to flee to. The Old Mage was there, but the magic that slew Manshoon was not his."

The bard trembled with weariness, and Jhessail laid a warning hand on Lhaeo's shoulder. They exchanged glances, saw Storm hide a yawn, and fell silent.

In the kitchen of that farmhouse in Shadowdale, time passed in slow silence. Storm's eyes fluttered and then closed, and her head sank lower. Careful, quiet hands moved her mug out of harm's way. The bard did not notice.

Jhessail and Lhaeo put their arms around each other and sat in companionable silence. Slowly, before their eyes, it happened. Still smiling, Storm Silverhand laid her head on her hands and slept.

* * * * *

"Draw thy daggers," Elminster said gruffly. "Ye seem to feel better when ye have some piece of sharp steel in hand. And my first thoughts, as always," he added, irony heavy in his tone, "are for thy comfort, ye three."

The Old Mage watched steel flash out in answer, then nodded, turned, and said, "Follow."

He stepped onto the rune and was gone.

Sharantyr sighed, hefted the knife—what good would this little fang do?—in her hand, and followed.

Abruptly she was elsewhere. Behind her, she heard Itharr exclaim in surprise.

All around them was darkness—a deep, chiming void of blackness lit only by faintly glowing purple mists and by drifting, winking lights. The mist curled lazily about, and there was no horizon or boundary or anything solid to be seen, only endless darkness. They stood on nothing, hanging in emptiness.

"Old Mage," Sharantyr asked fearfully, "what is this place?"

A little way distant stood Elminster. He had grown somehow taller and stood outlined with a blue-white aura.

He turned and smiled at them reassuringly. "This is called by some the Flame Void. It is a strange place, not quite out of the Realms yet not in Faerûn—at least, not in the Faerûn that most folk can see and reach. Take a good look about at all this nothing. 'Tis probably the only time ye'll ever see it." He looked past her at the two Harpers, nodded reassurance to them, and said to them all, "Come."

Then he turned and walked confidently away, treading on nothing.

"Where are we going?" the lady ranger said, hurrying to catch up with the Old Mage. Though she still felt nothing under her boots, and a sharp, falling feeling seemed alive in her stomach, she could move merely by thinking of moving in a direction.

"To a place I know," Elminster said, "where Lady Mystra often leaves messages, or things, for me. It is my hope that she can feel my arrival and respond."

"Oh," Sharantyr replied, not much enlightened and showing it in her tone. Elminster said no more, and she fell into step beside him. The two Harpers caught up to flank them, and all four went on together.

They walked for a long time, and Sharantyr began to notice things around them that had escaped her before. Flitting shadows swirled half-seen in the mists, like living things—they probably *were* alive, she realized with a faint, crawling fear—and weird lights danced and glimmered in the distance.

She exchanged glances with the two young men who strode with them, and saw in their eyes the same fear and wonder that she knew shone in her own.

"Elminster," Belkram asked after a while, "is your

magic back?"

The Old Mage simply looked at him in reply.

Belkram frowned. "Then how is it you brought us all here?"

Elminster shrugged. "The rune held the power; it is a gate. I merely selected its destination by bending my will to the choice." He looked around at them all. "An exercise all of ye would benefit greatly from: thinking hard about what ye're doing, from time to time. A novel idea, I'll admit."

The Harpers sighed almost as loudly as Sharantyr did.

Then Itharr asked, "How does one find anything here? You seem to know where you're going, but I can't see any trace of our passage, or landmarks to guide you."

Elminster nodded and grinned. "No, ye can't, can ye?" was all he said.

They walked on until a glowing yellow light could be seen in the distance ahead. It seemed brighter than the other lights and gradually grew larger.

They approached it at a steady pace until they could see that it was a translucent sphere of soft, golden light with something inside it. The mists seemed to avoid it; the light hung alone in a clear space of velvet darkness.

The two Harpers peered ahead, frowns on their faces.

"Is that—a tower?" Belkram asked hesitantly, moving his head from side to side to get a better look at whatever it was.

Elminster nodded. "A simple stone tower, a hollow cylinder with a spiral stair climbing around its inside to the top. If there's no creature hiding there, leave your daggers—and anything else metal ye may be carrying, no matter how small; don't forget buckles and hairpins and any other jewelry ye may have—at the bottom and get to the top, all of ye."

"Why?" Itharr asked.

Elminster sighed. "Ye have no idea just how tired of that particular word one can get, after even a few hundred years. Just do it. After all ye've gone through to keep me alive, I'd like to see ye survive this. It's thy turn."

* * * * *

There was no lurking monster; the tower was empty. The three left all their metal at the base of the tower, as Elminster had ordered—and, necessarily, most of their clothing with it.

Feeling more vulnerable than ever, they hurried up old, worn stairs of some smooth black stone none of them had ever seen before and soon came out on a bare circular battlement.

"What is this place?" Belkram asked, looking down.

Below them, Elminster had also discarded all the metal about his person—dagger after dagger, hidden item after hidden item, from various pockets of his robes —and now stood quite alone in the middle of golden nothingness.

He faced away from them and spoke a Name.

He whispered it, so that they never heard what it was, but its echoes burst back at them with a sound like thunder, shaking the tower and causing the golden light to pulse with sudden brightness.

There came a burst of blue-white radiance beside Elminster. It was so bright that they had to look away, but it faded quickly.

When they could see again, a young girl stood beside the old wizard. They faced each other, and a shimmering blue-white light pulsed about the girl's bare back.

She seemed nude, and yet light played about her so one could not be sure. She spoke with Elminster for a few breaths, then they stepped forward into an almost fierce embrace.

"Ye gods," Itharr muttered. "I've seen this old man kiss more maids, since first I laid eyes on him."

"It's a wonder he has any lips left, after six or seven hundred years, or whatever his count really is," Belkram replied.

"Hush," Sharantyr hissed. "Look!"

Below them, vivid light pulsed, more blue than white and coming from the joined lips of the wizard and the girl. Blue-white flames suddenly burst from that joining of their faces and enshrouded them both.

Itharr stirred. "What if that's killing him, after all w—"

Belkram laid an iron hand on his arm. "Stay. I think not. And even if it does, I fear there's not a gods-blessed thing we can do."

The flames died, and the two figures below parted, patting each other like fond old friends saying farewell. The flames seemed to have harmed neither.

Then the girl was rising toward where they stood watching atop the tower. Sharantyr swallowed.

"You know who she is, don't you?" she said. Two slow, fearful nods were the only reply.

The girl—no, the lady—had risen smoothly up to meet them. She floated in over the battlements, and they drew back to make room for her.

She was thin, and clad only in shifting motes of blue-white light. Her beauty was awesome, matchless. Sharantyr felt suddenly coarse and clumsy in her presence.

She did look like a young, thin maiden, but taller than any human girl would be. Long, dark hair moved about her shoulders as if with a life of its own. She was sleekly graceful, and as she moved, her body shimmered with those tiny winks and sparkles of ever-shifting light, motes that seemed to curl out of her skin. Her eyes glowed with the same eerie blue-white light. She made no sound as she came, and her feet did not touch the stone but floated just above it.

She smiled, and her eyes glowed bright blue.

"You have my thanks," she said in a voice that held soft thunder, "and that is no small thing. You have guarded my champion and have my deep gratitude. While I hold any power in the Realms, you cannot be harmed by magic."

And then Mystra reached out a hand that glowed with power and touched each of them fleetingly.

The touch was like a leaping spark that left a tingling and an exhilarating feeling of lightness, strength, and alertness. Wonderingly, the three looked at each other and saw that their eyes glowed faintly, blue-white.

A head came up out of the hole by their feet—a familiar, bearded head. It was followed by the rest of the Old Mage's body, as the wizard climbed the last steps of the stair to join them.

Mystra smiled fondly at him, reached out a slim hand to caress his cheek, and whispered, "As usual, my thanks, Elminster. We'll meet again . . . soon. Beware wild magic. I go now, to face Bane."

In a flare of blue-white flames, she was gone.

The silence that followed was broken by Sharantyr, who drew a shuddering breath and said faintly, "What now, El?"

Elminster threw his arms around her and hugged her tightly. "Ah, Shar, ever that question, eh? I cannot see. Mystra remains a prisoner of another god—Manshoon's god, Bane—and is not free to use the power I returned to her. There's another who must free her . . . I cannot safely act, for if I fall to Bane and he learns, through the power and knowledge that are still mine, who and where the rest of the Chosen are, he could still wrest Mystra's power from her and have governance over all Art—or lose such order, for all of us, in his destruction of Mystra."

The Old Mage looked at the two Harpers and asked almost challengingly, "Excitement enough for ye, lads? Adventure enough?"

Itharr and Belkram shook their heads and chuckled rather faintly.

Elminster stood still, his face buried in Sharantyr's hair, and said roughly, "Ah, Shar—I have grown to care for thee very much in these few days since ye took out thy sword to guard me. Whatever befalls now, when we find our way back to the Realms ye know—stay with me, will ye?"

Sharantyr kissed him and said softly, "Of course. I can't guard you if I don't, now can I?"

Belkram tapped her shoulder. "Ah, if you're in a kissing mood . . ."

Sharantyr wrinkled her nose and thrust a strong arm around Elminster, straight into the Harper's midriff.

He doubled over with a comical roll of his still-glowing blue eyes and staggered back, colliding with the low battlement. He overbalanced with a startled cry and fell backward off the tower.

Sharantyr screamed.

Elminster turned in her grasp and made a lazy gesture.

In the air below them, a huge phantom hand appeared beneath the falling Harper.

He fell into it as softly as a feather kisses the ground it falls onto and was borne gently upward, cradled in the giant hand, to rejoin them. Belkram stood up on the palm of the hand as it came, tottering about uncertainly like a man on stilts hopping about in a cesspool and likely at any moment to come to a far closer acquaintance with it. His efforts and expression made Itharr bellow with laughter.

Sharantyr turned to embrace Elminster again. She was ecstatic. "Your Art—it's back! You can work magic again!"

"Aye," the Old Mage said with a sigh that could not quite conceal his grin. "That, d'ye see, is old Elminster's doom."